BOOKS BY JAMES BRADY

Superchic
Paris One
Nielsen's Children
The Press Lord
Holy Wars

HOLY WARS

A Novel By

James Brady

SIMON AND SCHUSTER

NEW YORK

Brady

3 7834 00042915 8

v\

This novel is a work of fiction. Names, characters, places and incidents are either the product of the author's imagination or are used fictitiously. Any resemblance to actual events or locales or persons, living or dead, is entirely coincidental.

Copyright © 1983 by James Brady
All rights reserved
including the right of reproduction
in whole or in part in any form
Published by Simon and Schuster
A Division of Gulf & Western Corporation
Simon & Schuster Building
Rockefeller Center
1230 Avenue of the Americas
New York, New York 10020
SIMON AND SCHUSTER and colophon are registered trademarks of Simon & Schuster
Designed by Eve Kirch
Manufactured in the United States of America

10 9 8 7 6 5 4 3 2 1

Library of Congress Cataloging in Publication Data
Brady, James, date.
  Holy wars.
  I. Title.
PS3552.R243H6 1983   813'.54   83—4669
ISBN 0-671-42589-7

For Fiona, for Susan, and for my brother Tom,
a good priest, a good man.

BOOK I

CAMBRIDGE

1

"Reality is a crutch."

They were tearing up Harvard Square for a subway extension and as Peter Cobb deftly picked his way through the raw wood barricades and hoardings of the construction site he was abruptly confronted by these words on the printed T-shirt of a young man hurrying toward Dunster Street. Nothing in the young man's pale, empty face seemed to qualify him to make such sweeping philosophical statements but Cobb, an optimist not yet soured by age, was always willing to suspend critical judgment about the young. He made a mental note to use the line. If reality really were a crutch, then why weren't more of us cripples? A construction gang's whistle blew, interrupting this promising speculative premise.

At the Harvard Book Store, Cobb stepped aside to permit two young women to pass in the awkwardly narrow passage between storefront and guard rail, and there in the shop's window, as it had in such places for months now, his own face stared out at him—ridiculously solemn, multiplied over and over again on the dust covers of the pyramid of books that bore his name. His book dominated the window, with more famous authors pushed disrespectfully into piles in the window's dusty corners.

It was morning, late August, a slim and quiet season. In a few days the new freshmen would arrive, eager, nervous, passionate. Orientation week would blunt all that. He remembered his own first year, his father's typical insistence on accompanying him to an interview with the dean of his college, the Rolls Royce whispering to a halt in front of the ivied building, the chauffeur in livery opening doors for them as if they could not do it for themselves. Deans of Harvard colleges do not customarily come down to the curb to greet incoming freshmen. But then it was not every term that Charles Cobb's son entered. Cobb remarked on this to his father, and the older man had laughed humorlessly.

"They sniff an endowment."

Gaudy chance of that, Cobb reminisced now, twenty years after the fact, not the way those four years at Harvard had changed him, driving that first and lasting wedge of bitterness between father and only son. Any thought of endowments had gone a-glimmering then. Cobb smiled at the memory. But a passerby might have thought it was because the sun was now coming through the morning haze and Cobb was dressed for the river.

He was an oarsman, not one of the large, bulky sort you find in heavyweight eights and rowing for schools like Wisconsin and Syracuse and Washington State. Even now he was a lean, trim man, who had been for three years the stroke for Harvard's lightweight crew. All three of those years his boat had beaten Yale, which used to mean something—and, Cobb supposed, still did if you were twenty. He was a slender man except for the hands and wrists, oarsman's wrists, a pleasant-enough-looking man in his thirties dressed now in nondescript sweat pants and a crew shirt with an old Harvard sweater. His tropical tan had faded. He was no darker now than most Bostonians of a late August.

He picked up a copy of *The Boston Globe* and shoved it under one arm to be read later. Now, halted by a red light before crossing Memorial Drive to the Charles, he shook the paper open to glance at the front page. A three-column headline below the fold shouted at him:

US Blames Mirador Massacre on Reds,
Will Send Arms to Bolster Regime

Jesus! The damned book a best seller and no one had *read* it! No one in Washington was listening. Not one! Hadn't they learned a goddamned thing since Vietnam?

He balled the newspaper and fired it into a trash barrel.

The boat house smelled of laundry and old socks and airplane glue. Larsen, the boat builder, was patching the eggshell-thin hull of a racing eight.

"Mr. Larsen?"

"Aye?"

"I'm Peter Cobb. I stroked the lightweights back in the sixties."

Larsen put down his sandpaper.

"By God, you are. You were in the boat all those years they beat Yale. Went to Henley too, didn't you?"

"I'm on the faculty here now. Would it be possible to borrow a single? I'd like to get out on the river, get a little work on a regular basis."

Larsen had been building and patching boats since before the war. Cobb had been one of his hundreds and hundreds of undergraduate oarsmen. Both men maintained the niceties of that relationship, Cobb addressing Larsen as "Mister," the builder using Cobb's Christian name. Larsen wiped his hands on the seat of his trousers and walked with him through the long, dim shed to where the small, single shells were stacked. Cobb reached up into one of the cradles and swung a shell out easily, holding it over his head. He set it down gently on the dock and went back inside to pick out a pair of oars.

Carefully, competently, Cobb set up the boat, his oars flat on the water steadying the narrow shell like outriggers. Beneath him the wheeled seat moved smoothly along its oiled track, a few inches forward, a few inches back. He had not been in a shell for a long time but already there was the feel of familiar haunts revisited, of muscle-memory stirred. Locking his thick wrists, he was ready. Then, as he swiftly unlocked them, the blade of each oar dug cleanly into the Charles, his legs slowly straightened, and the boat sprang forward into motion. It felt wonderful to be back on the water.

To an oarsman as experienced as Peter Cobb sculling was an instinctive process, demanding no thought. Rowing freed a man from the necessity of thought, enabling him to think. Much of *Speculations* had been written in a boat, though nothing like this one—a native canoe on a great tropical river dark with menace. Now, in the center of Boston, on this small, smelly tidal stream, he sensed that same comforting isolation, with only the faint hum of auto traffic along the expressway underpinning the click of the oarlocks.

He had not wanted to come back to Harvard. His book had brought him an entirely unexpected celebrity, but that was not the reason he had written it. He had been happy where he was—not so much happy as . . . fulfilled. He was doing good work. Until the end. That was not pride talking, although he was a proud man, but a lean, objective self-honesty. His new fame, he suspected, was not totally deserved. There were those who read his book, and raved about it, who had entirely missed the point. Even his sister Jane, cabling from Milan, had confessed: "Loved your book. Didn't understand a word of it but am very proud of you. Love."

Not a bad trade-off, Cobb thought: critical sense for instinctive love.

There were those who understood but did not love. The cover story in *Time* magazine had put a shrewd finger on Cobb's predicament:

> His message is as appealing as it is dangerous, and the more dangerous because of its attractiveness. Peter Cobb is a reticent, almost diffident, young man until he begins to talk about his book, the extraordinary characters who people it, and their

turbulent, tragic land. Then another Cobb emerges, no longer shy, but suffused with a hot passion that is very near zealotry. Many of his colleagues mistrust Cobb's passion. They also mistrust Cobb. They see him as a rabble-rouser, a rallying point around whom other young men, restive under the authoritarian yoke of their calling, are starting to gather. Cobb's book is a big success. It is bringing him fame, money, adherents, celebrity. It could also bring him big trouble. There are those in his great organization who think Peter Cobb has gone too far. Those who want him silenced.

If the photo on the dust jacket and the painting on the cover of *Time* hadn't made Cobb recognizable overnight, Johnny Carson certainly had. In the plane back East the stewardess had been the first fan, fetching him cup after cup of coffee and asking for his autograph. At Kennedy the cab driver informed Cobb he didn't read many books, "but I'll read this one, I can tell ya." In the weeks and months since, as the newspaper articles and the magazine covers and the television talk show appearances pyramided, a cult began to build around Cobb's book. And around Cobb.

And that was the trouble.

Peter Cobb was a priest, a Jesuit, a member of the most traditionally disciplined of Catholic religious Orders, a Society that even in the turbulent 1980s, when it found itself embroiled in near-rebellion against Rome, did not believe its own priests should become, as one aging provincial sniffed of Cobb, "movie stars."

Speculations was a freak. Like a *Love Story* or a *Jonathan Livingston Seagull* it had surfaced in a quiet season and without fanfare to explode on the public consciousness, a literary nova between hard covers for $10.95, a slim price, a slim book. Dorset House, the publishers, had taken it reluctantly and only because Cobb's editor, Epstein, a Jew and a poet *manqué*, had insisted. Non-fiction works about missionaries and the slum poor of Latin America's civil wars do not sell, but in the end Epstein had his way and 2,500 copies were printed up, a nominal check was dispatched to a mysterious box number in Mirador, and review copies sent out with the most modest of expectations to the handful of minor literary critics who specialized in "this sort of thing." The book would have died there, drifting drearily, inevitably, to the remainder counters, had it not been for Judson Riis.

No one at Dorset House could later quite explain how a copy had gone to Riis in his *sanctum sanctorum* down a bosky lane in Sag Harbor. Riis, the grumbling, shambling, crippled giant, lurching about on his sticks, cursing his legs and the decline of letters, thundering in a dozen different "small" publications and several that were very large, was hardly the breed of critic to whom you sent slender volumes of poetic sociology in hopes of a favorable review. But it got to him somehow, and in a now famous essay on the front cover of *The New York Times Book Review* Riis had hailed the still unknown Cobb as "a voice for our time." "This man Cobb," he wrote, "is a major dissenting voice for this year and for years yet to come, a social commentator whose poetic shuttle weaves hope out of bleak despair, who discerns entire spectrums of brilliant light in the primeval night of oppression, poverty, savagery. Even his anger is not righteous but loving. Cobb is clearly a great writer. I suspect he is also a great man."

Judson Riis's adulation stirred enthusiasms in lesser men, dragged reluctant encomiums from cold, unforgiving stylists, and when Dorset House, with calculated understatement, issued a brief biography of the author, revealing almost as an afterthought who and what Cobb was, they all took him up then. It was *Time* magazine that discovered he was the only son of the monstrous Charles Cobb. And by then it was only time before *Speculations* would be the best selling non-fiction hardcover book in America.

Like most impressive works it was simple. In his response to Dorset House Cobb had written:

> I am 39, American, have been a Jesuit priest and missionary for six years, the last three of which I have spent working in the missions of Mirador. The people I have written about all exist. I have changed their names to avoid embarrassing them and to protect them from possible danger. Their stories are true.

So was the book. Elevated by his intelligence and his art out of the ruck of journalistic sociology, it evoked in a few pages the lush, sybaritic prosperity of the Miradoran aristocracy and the contrasting squalid, angry despair of the tin-shedded slums; it delineated the sullen, unfeeling corruption of the entrenched bureaucracy and the schizoid agony of an embattled Church torn between social concern and paranoid fear of Marxism and violent men, the atrocities and heroisms of a civil war. It was a book without heroes, a book that wondered, speculatively and aloud, without pretending to provide the comfortable simplistics of slick solutions, if there were no middle ground between wealth and poverty, long-suffering patience and

13

urban warfare. He "speculated," in this slim volume, on the role his Church might effectively take in places like Mirador and Brazil and Chile and Argentina and San Salvador—places where too often the elders of the Church sought prudent accommodation with repressive regimes out of fear of the Communists, where just as often young priests joined the guerrillas as chaplains, frequently abandoned their priesthood entirely, and took up arms and the women of the forest bands with equal fervor.

But it was not the intellectual paradoxes or Cobb's speculative inquiries that had stirred old Judson Riis to eloquence out in Sag Harbor, or that was now selling *Speculations* at the rate of several thousand copies a week, that had drawn the professional notice of the jurors at Columbia who would vote on the Pulitzer Prize. It was Cobb's people, his people and their lives. They had become, the missionary nuns and Cobb's Miradoran friends, the stuff of his book.

When Cobb's book had become a literary sensation, a shaken Jesuit Missions director had ordered Peter Cobb to leave Mirador and come home.

So now Peter Cobb was a priest in trouble. Ironically, because the book had sold on the basis of Judson Riis's review and Cobb had reluctantly, unexpectedly, become famous, the Church did not know precisely what to do with him. Churches, it seemed, were as sensitive to their image as auto manufacturers confronted with the forced recall of a million cars.

It was an angry, impulsive book, as harrowing as the annual reports of Amnesty International, as honestly wrought as an honorable man could make it. In Mirador, the government was embarrassed, and governments headed by colonels do not enjoy being embarrassed. A promising truce between state and Church was abruptly broken off. A new and more brutal minister of the interior was named. A dozen political prisoners were hanged and a score more, including two rural priests accused of ministering to guerrillas, simply disappeared. The Cardinal found his access to high officialdom severely circumscribed. And a forty-million-dollar tax credit to parochial schools was mysteriously canceled. It could not be said that Peter Cobb's little book was entirely to blame. But it was a symptom, and a dramatic one, of an exacerbating conflict between Church and *junta*. And if the *junta* was not pleased, neither was the Church.

This was, at bottom, the point of *Speculations:* that the interests of a Church that had for two thousand years considered itself to be one, holy, Catholic and apostolic were not necessarily identical with the interests of a phalanx of colonels.

Peter Cobb rested on his oars and wondered, as he had so often, about this basic argument he had with his own Church, to which he had solemnly vowed eternal obedience. Had he disobeyed? Neither in *Speculations* nor a hundred times since in private examinations of conscience was he sure. Were his self-doubts the product of a genuinely priestly humility? Or of intellectual pride? Was he crying out for the righting of terrible wrongs or setting himself up as an authority larger than the Church to which he had sworn fealty?

Now, staring at Boston and its river, and seeing not them but the swift, dark currents of the Rio Negro, he thought wistfully of Mirador and a simpler time when he was neither famous nor controversial but only a priest hard at God's work. The nuns, the destroyed Figueroa, his brigade of rebels, and the colonels angered by his book made it impossible to turn back calendars, except in the mind.

Cobb drove his oars savagely into the Charles and headed for the Cambridge shore. *Speculations* had irritated the Church, had driven him into this comfortable, boring academic exile, but it had also made him famous. He had more to say about Mirador, more to say about his Church, more to say about the nature of the priesthood, more to say about man's relationship to man. And to God.

Maybe they *would* silence him, as *Time* magazine had warned and as fellow priests whispered. But they hadn't done it yet.

At the apartment he stripped off his sweat clothes and lighted a cigarette. The usual stack of fan mail awaited him. An odd correspondence for a priest. He riffled through it now, slicing open the envelopes with a serrated steak knife from his Pullman kitchen. The letters from young women, the ones that enclosed photographs, he threw away. There were other, serious letters, from Catholics and non-Catholics, from aging nuns and young priests, from seminarians and from boys and girls considering the religious life, to all of whom Cobb and Cobb's book had become a sort of beacon.

He sat down at the kitchen table to finish the cigarette and to read again one of the letters. It was from a priest about his own age, no longer a boy, sweating out a miserable existence as a curate in a black parish in inner Cleveland:

> . . . a vicious circle, Cobb. A hopeless, despairing place and I drink to blunt hopelessness. Next day, at morning mass, hung-over and guilty, I realize once again the bottle simply exacerbates despair. I am no longer of any use to these people. They have no use for me nor I for them. To the diocese I am

15

an embarrassment. To myself a failure. Then, the other night, I read your book. I read it a second time, sober, next morning. It would be simplistic to tell you gushingly of how it has already changed my life. Obviously, it hasn't. But I haven't been drunk for two nights. Can I make it three? Pray for me, Father Cobb . . .

When Peter Cobb came out of the shower a few moments later and went into the kitchen to light the burner under the coffee and to knock another cigarette loose from a new pack, the letter was still there, propped against his typewriter. Next to it was a box of writing paper, crisp and white and unused.

"Well, why not?" he said aloud.

He was still free to write, he had something to say, the paper was there and the typewriter. And he had something else. Fame, a fame he had never sought or expected, a fame that had given him as grand a pulpit as any priest ever had.

2

Peter Cobb had been a rich boy. He realized this even when he was quite young. The Cobb estate on the north shore of Long Island was a small, comfortable universe bounded by privet and boxwood, curling with gravel driveways white as milk that wandered across green lawns past tennis courts and water-lilied pools, startled pheasants and formal gardens where gnomed Portuguese staked and watered and pruned. Beyond shimmered the blue Sound, and beyond that, still more distant, hung the low, gray hills of the Connecticut shore. Above the lawns and the flowers towered the battlements and crenelated walls of turn-of-century architecture, the moated dwelling place of the rich. The house in which Peter grew up was a monstrosity, but warm, comforting. When he was eight a sister was born. Jane. A severe disappointment. He had expected a younger brother complete in all respects, understandably smaller, but a ready-made playmate, equipped to toss a ball, ride a bike, share a cool, shaded and very secret hiding place painstakingly gouged out under one of the vast, squared hedges. Jane had blue eyes and pink cheeks and golden hair.

"I love Jane," he assured his mother. Nan Cobb smiled her gentle smile and said she was sure that he did.

"No, really," the boy said, "I'm not fibbing."

And he was not. He had thought it through very carefully, these reservations he had about Jane, and concluded that, yes, he did love his sister. He was very grave about it.

"And I'm sure she loves you, Peter."

"Oh, no," he said, his eyes wide, "she's much too young. She doesn't even really know my name."

His mother was fair and beautiful. He loved her without having to think it through, as he had had to do with Jane. His father was dark and preoccupied. There were servants in the house, other servants for the grounds.

17

Sometimes there were parties, on the lawns in summer, in the formal rooms at other times. Even when there were no parties men came to the house to see his father, carrying briefcases and often going away more somber than they had arrived. His father traveled. And even when he was working in New York he would leave early and return late. In bright weather he took a sea-plane. There was a limousine and, occasionally, the Long Island Railroad. He loved his father, too, but he had to think about it.

He was sent away to boarding school. Then Harvard. He had a brilliant Harvard. Until that last, apocalyptic year when he became a Catholic.

"I'll be damned if I understand him!" his father raged. "Always such a normal boy. Until this!"

And he had been normal. Prep school was rowing and the school news-paper and the Latin prize. It was also masturbation and dirty pictures and the ritual spring drunk of junior year and the aching, convulsive agony of a first, nauseous hangover. He was a popular boy who played a wonderfully talented piano and who made friends easily, with other boys and with the faculty. There was no hint anywhere during the prep school years of the slightest bent toward spirituality.

The Cobbs were very rich and had been for a long time. Charles Cobb, C.C., as he was known on the Street, had made them richer. An easterner, he had gone into oil when oil men were looked down upon as *arrivistes*, cow-boys, drunken, shambling loafers who had happened to turn a spadeful of dirt in the right square mile of prairie. The Cobbs had been old money for a long time and now they were also new money. Nan Raden's people were— comfortable. To most Americans the Radens would be wealthy people; to the Cobbs, merely comfortable. In neither family had religion been an ob-session. The Radens were Scots-Irish, which meant Presbyterianism. The Cobbs, longer here and distantly New England, were Episcopalian. As far as Nan and C.C. were concerned, the terms were interchangeable.

Harvard changed all that, for Peter. More precisely, a second-year survey of philosophy, taught by a man called Diskin, changed it. Diskin was a lapsed Catholic, a small, neat man with crow's wing hair, a pitted face, the vaguely disheveled wardrobe of a minor poet, a cultivated Oxbridge stutter, a gentle irony. He had taught at a small Catholic college before coming to Cambridge.

"Catholics are much easier to confuse," he would remark epigrammati-cally; "they know what they believe. Protestants are so distressingly vague, one simply doesn't know where to begin to challenge their faith."

One soft day in April, Diskin dropped his books on the platformed desk, stared through sun-smeared windows at the verdant Yard, and stammered:

18

"It is spring. The smell of manure is in the fields and young girls are in heat. I shall not lecture today."

On most days he did. Halfway through the second semester Peter Cobb went to him after class.

"I'm mixed up."

"Good," Diskin said, smiling broadly. "That's the notion behind survey courses. A smattering of shallow knowledge. If you weren't mixed up I'd be disappointed. It's the men who claim they understand who bother me."

"Well, I *don't* understand."

Diskin regarded him closely.

"Are you a . . . Catholic?"

"No, I'm not much of anything, I guess."

"Excellent," said Diskin, rubbing his hands together. "You're not carrying any excess baggage."

"Baggage?"

"You don't believe in anything. Which makes learning simpler." Diskin paused. "Which one are you?" he asked ingenuously.

"Cobb, Peter Cobb."

"Oh, yes, Mr. Cobb. You write an intelligent paper. Now what is it you don't understand?"

Cobb exhaled.

"When we read Plato I thought, well, this man is convincing. His definition of reality makes sense. Then we read Aristotle and suddenly Plato seemed all wrong. Then Plotinus and Spinoza and Descartes. Each of them was convincing as the very devil when I read them. Then along you'd come with the next philosopher down the line and you'd punch holes in the theory that went before. I just don't know. There seem to be questions but no answers. Nothing definitive."

Diskin pursed thin lips.

"Am I making sense, Mr. Diskin?"

"Mr. Cobb, I've been teaching philosophy for twenty years. There are always going to be more questions than answers."

Peter grinned.

"Then it's hopeless."

Diskin shook his head. "No, every hundred years or so a new man is going to come along and take philosophy a few paces further than the man before. The fashionable theory right now is that nuclear physics and philosophy are the same thing. That philosophy and the higher realms of math are identical. Who knows? Continue to ask questions. Maybe you'll be the one with an answer."

"Mr. Diskin, I'm a sophomore. With one term of philosophy behind me."

Diskin nodded.

"Good. Then you're aware of how much you don't know. Here," he said, taking out a pen, "I'll give you a few books to read during the summer. Come see me in September. We'll talk again."

It was 1961, the first summer of Jack Kennedy's presidency. Charles and Nan Cobb would again spend a month in Europe, once more in France. Jane Cobb, eleven years old, coltish, still golden haired, would accompany her parents. Her brother Peter, nineteen, and with two Harvard years behind him, would not. His roommate, Tom Hathaway, was the reason. Hathaway was a political-science major who planned to enter the law, or politics, or the foreign service. Or something. Like apparently half the men his age he was caught up in the whirling glamour of that brightly promising young administration. Camelot! Not even the Bay of Pigs could mar its sheen. Tom Hathaway had a friend who was a friend of Bobby Kennedy's. And for ambitious young men with even the most tenuous of links to the Kennedys the only place to be that summer was Cape Cod.

"Girls, sun, sailing, Hyannisport, beer!" Tom gushed.

"And girls," Peter repeated, aware of Hathaway's weaknesses.

"Girls," said Hathaway gleefully, lust in his heart and in his voice.

So they went to the Cape. Sensitive to his father's politics, Cobb omitted mention of Hyannisport or the Kennedys. Cobb senior grumbled and shepherded wife and daughter aboard the _Queen Elizabeth_.

He had a good deal of reading to do, Peter had said. Crew had cut into academic time, especially in the spring semester. He had Diskin's foot-long shelf of books.

Also, and this was equally tangible, and even more appealing, he would have Kiki Loomis. She was a junior at Radcliffe with a brother who rowed for Yale and she and Peter had met at one of those roistering, beery evenings following the annual four-mile grind of the Yales and the Harvards. That year the race was in New London, on the Thames, and Cobb's lightweights had won. Kiki, it seemed, was the trophy. On a soft day in early June, exams behind them and the marks blessedly not yet posted, she and Peter and Tom Hathaway squeezed into Peter's MG-TC and drove out of Boston and through the endless Irish suburbs to open country and the Cape.

"Tom?"

"Yeah?"

"Do you think Peter is in love?"

Kiki and Hathaway sat on the low dune in front of their cottage watching a red sun drop into the bay, watching Peter casting an optimistic line into vacant water. It was July, the summer already half over. Hathaway was smoking an impressive cigar. Kennedy men smoked cigars and he had loyally given up Lucky Strikes.

"I dunno. You ought to be the one to tell me. Is he?"

She had pulled on a faded sweatshirt over one of those new European bikinis she wore all day long, delighting the beach; and Hathaway, who was half in love with her himself, reached out to stroke her long, brown leg.

"Damned if I know," she confessed. "I mean, if someone told me last winter I'd be sharing a cottage for six weeks with a man and not be sure we were in love, I'd have said she was nuts."

Hathaway's face soured.

"You're sharing the cottage with *two* men, you know."

"Oh, you know what I mean," Kiki said impatiently. "You've always got some languorous creature you've just picked up at the bar, or one of your exalted connections from Hyannis. Peter's just got me. And still I don't know."

She and Peter were sleeping together, had been almost from the first week. Kiki had her own bedroom but was rarely in it. Mornings there were usually strange girls with sleepy eyes and sheepish grins introducing themselves over breakfast. Those were Tom's girls. Neither Peter nor Kiki played his promiscuous game. They had each other.

Tom Hathaway was very quick. Not deep, but with a swift and nimble surface intelligence, he was not yet twenty and already had a shrewd appreciation of his own strengths and weaknesses. "I'm a sprinter," he told himself, "and young Cobb very much the long distance runner, the marathon man." So now, because he knew it would please her, and because it was the cordial, tactful thing to do, Tom said that *of course* Peter was in love. "In love with *you*, my passion flower, as what man wouldn't be."

Kiki leaned over to kiss him and hoped it was true.

Cobb, uncomfortably, was silent on the subject of love.

He sailed, he drank beer, he pounded out the season's songs on a battered upright, he shared the cooking with Kiki as she shared his bed, he applauded when Hathaway at last gained entrée into the vestibule of the pantheon, a Kennedy touch football game, and laughed at Tom's Spartan delight when a broken ankle brought him brief Clan immortality. And he read. All of Diskin's books. He was still only a nineteen-year-old college sophomore and he did not understand all that he read, he brought no new fresh insights to the writings of Aquinas or Sartre or the Sophists. But his reading ignited a burning intellectual curiosity that crackled fierce as brush fire. Kiki watched him as he read, on the beach, in the sundown dunes, on the worn couch with disillusioned springs facing the old fireplace in the cottage's living room. She watched him and sent out pulses of love. Sometimes, she thought, especially in the tossing, tumbling, moist wonder of bed, he returned them. Sometimes, ruefully, he did not.

Sometimes he told her what he was reading. His reading was rumpled and eclectic, like an undergraduate's clothes. Teilhard de Chardin and Locke might share a weekend, the Hellenists and the *Summa Theologica*. Kiki understood less of it than he did. Her favorite was Plato, the cave myth. It touched the romantic, despairing chord of young people in love. She did not care that most of what he told her whistled by like Cape seagulls. It was sufficient that he cared enough to involve her in what was obviously important to him. That, vicariously, made her important. For Kiki, that was enough.

Labor Day came. Kiki flew to San Francisco to see her parents, Hathaway went off to Washington hinting of summonses from the White House, Cobb drove to New York for ten days with his family. That autumn he decided to major in philosophy. Diskin was no longer teaching him but the two men would meet to talk, tutorially, over port.

"I left the Church," the older man said one night in response to an impertinently direct, and typically Cobb, question, "because it was too strong for me. It demanded too much. It made no concessions. Too rigid, too unbending, too doctrinaire. I'd done a lot of reading, higgledy piggledy, as you've been doing. Half-baked ideas, of course. I was older than you but still quite young and full of myself, a Sophist one week, an Aristotelian the next, God knows what I was, if anything. That's why I gave you those books to read last summer. You reminded me of *me*. The same thirsting curiosity, the same eagerness, but with me there was the Church leaning inward, crushing me. You're a fortunate man to be free. You've no shackles to break."

He drained off his glass.

"I hope to hell, young Cobb, you find what you're looking for. I haven't."

Peter was going through one of those post-adolescent passages Maugham described so well in *The Razor's Edge*. Asceticism, the parched need for knowledge, a flirtation with higher, spiritual realms. To her despair he was not seeing much of Kiki Loomis and when they were together it was for a film or a spaghetti dinner in one of the Italian joints of the North End. He had not slept with her since the Cape. She wept on Hathaway's convenient shoulder.

"I dunno, Kiki," Tom said. "I know he isn't seeing anyone else. He's as jolly as ever sometimes and then he'll just go off. You know, he's in the same room with you and then he isn't. I've seen the symptoms before. In lovesick boys."

She laughed mirthlessly.

"I wish he *was* lovesick. Over me."

In his blundering analysis, Hathaway was right. Peter was in love. Lovesick, if you will. Not with a girl but with ideas, concepts, schools of thought. Except for a predictable C in freshman math, a required course soon forgotten, Cobb had scored straight A's in every one of his classes for three years. He had never been bookish about it; grades just came naturally. He had good study habits, was alert in class, his papers bore a decidedly non-undergraduate panache, but he had never become a grind. Philosophy was changing that. Hathaway would reel into their room at two in the morning following the usually successful pursuit of some Radcliffe siren or salesgirl from Southie and Cobb would be at his desk, or in the library's stacks, scribbling notes, annotating texts, or simply reading.

A man in love with ideas. And, as disturbing to him as it would have been to his friends if they had known, a man falling into love with God.

It was difficult to say precisely where or when or indeed why belief began. Perhaps the spark was all the reading he had done that awakened a latent curiosity. Perhaps, surrounded by wealth and privilege and physical love, he had asked himself, as the song later went: "Is that all there is?" Perhaps, without knowing it, he had been piling one upon the other, haphazardly, messily, the fragments and pebbles, the rocks and bits and pieces, that would become a personal philosophy, a foundation for life, a stability amid the restless, shifting sands, a place to stand.

Certainly, his mother's awful, wasting death had been a catalyst, had demanded response, as it had demanded of his father.

Nan Cobb's illness reached the cold, distant Charles Cobb as nothing else had ever done. She had been the loveliest woman, soft and funny and incurably romantic and the best doubles partner at tennis a man or a husband could ever want. His friend, his wife, his lover, the mother of his children, the necessary and balancing antithesis of everything he was. And when she died she weighed 57 pounds and had gone bald and did not even cry anymore or give out those terrible little grunts of pain because by then she lacked even the strength to groan. Her hair had been so beautiful, thin and fine and the color of ears of corn. It had fallen out from the chemotherapy.

Charles Cobb had never before cheated on his wife. It was part of the discipline of class, of his own personal style. But now, with Helen Gatewood, he did. He had to. He could not day after agonizing day simply sit by Nan's side and then, exhausted, stagger off to his bedroom to lie, stiff and angry,

23

remorseful and alone in an empty bed. He needed somebody. And Helen Gatewood had come along. In those last months she saved his sanity.

When Peter learned about Helen Gatewood there was the initial resentment, the sense that his father had betrayed a woman who deserved better. Bitterly, he referred to her as "the Duchess." Then, sitting with his father at the bedside during the weekends of Nan's last, dying winter, seeing his lean, tired face, a startling maturity took hold of the boy, an understanding of why his father did what he did, and he forced himself to erase anger.

"I need her, Peter," his father said one night, and knowing what he meant, and who, Peter had laid a hand on his father's arm and said, "Yes, I know you do." She was still "the Duchess," but he was always polite, no longer accusatory, and his father, to whom he had never been close, appreciated him for that.

On a sleeting day in January of Peter's senior year, Nan Cobb died. Her husband, raging at a world and an unjust, merciless God who had first destroyed her and then killed her, retreated into a shell not even his son could penetrate. Jane, who had seen Nan die, had lost a mother. With a child's shrewdness she had no intention of losing a brother and she clung to him, weeping at the funeral, telling him he must break through to his father, must not let grief drive them apart. But always Jane and Peter must stick together, *always*, whatever happened, whatever they did, wherever they went.

"Swear it, Peter, swear that you'll always be there if I need you."

And looking down into her lovely, tear-streaked, unformed face, he swore it. Despite the bedside truce he and his father had negotiated, he sensed C.C. would now try to reconstruct another life, a life from which he and Jane might be shut out as painful reminders of the mother who bore them, the woman who had for so long been his wife and lover and best friend.

Sometime that same month, none of his friends knew quite when, Peter called on the priest. It may have been Diskin, out of his love-hate relationship with Catholicism, who gave him the name. Father Bergé was a spare, desiccated French-Canadian, a Jesuit at Boston College, a few verdant miles outside the city on Chestnut Hill, the setting and the man tailored to the questing boy.

"What are you looking for, Mr. Cobb?"

"I thought you might be able to tell me."

"I am a theologian, Mr. Cobb, not a soothsayer."

Bergé believed in letting the other fellow work for it. If it was there, it came. He was not going to push or pull. He liked the cut of this young man from Harvard, questioning, skeptical, crisply intelligent, none of the breathless passion of the zealot about him, a rational approach to things that puzzled him. Bergé knew how few thunderbolts struck men from their horses on the Damascus road.

"I'm not sure I can accept that," Cobb would say.

Father Bergé smiled thinly.

"That is what you are here to find out."

Cobb liked the old man, he liked the serene calm of his bookish study, he liked the bucolic loveliness of the Chestnut Hill campus, a few miles but so far from teeming Harvard Yard. Their studies continued. Bergé, like Diskin, gave him lists of books to read.

That February Cobb and Tom Hathaway and Kiki drove up to Stowe for a week's skiing. Toward the end of the week Peter told Kiki over dinner that he was becoming a Catholic, that Bergé had agreed to baptize him. Kiki cried and said she would become one too.

"It isn't that easy, Keek, it's something you've got to feel strongly about, a conviction that you have that's so powerful you really don't have a choice."

She looked miserable.

"That's how I feel about you," she said, "that I have no choices."

They were no longer sleeping together and she feared he was slipping away from her.

At Easter Cobb flew to Palm Beach to tell his family. Jane thought the idea was very exciting. Precociously, she was reading Stendhal, *The Red and the Black*, and she identified her brother with Julien Sorel. Charles Cobb called the notion sophomoric and reminded his son of the Inquisition, to say nothing of the contemporary Church's uncomfortable intimacy with the Kennedys and with big-city Democratic politics generally. Peter said Yes, Father, and was baptized in a private ceremony that May in a small chapel at Chestnut Hill.

His senior thesis was an ethical analysis of Saint Augustine's *Confessions*. He was still earning straight A's and the head of the philosophy department urged him to do graduate work, to expand the thesis and polish it up a bit and publish. Peter said he would think about it. Charles Cobb wanted him to come into the business. He said he would think about that as well. Hathaway had taken the exam for the foreign service. Why didn't Peter come along? Kiki had recovered from the shock of his conversion, optimistically had put his coolness down to religious aberration, and had embarked on a renewed campaign to lure him into marriage.

So many alternatives, so many pressures. How many of us know at twenty-one precisely what it is we really want to do?

But he was a Cobb. And Cobbs prided themselves on crisp thinking, on decisiveness, on moving ahead where others hesitated. Peter would hesitate

25

no longer. He would become a priest. And not *any* priest.

A Jesuit. A member of the Society of Jesus, largest in point of membership of all the male orders of the Catholic Church, those "monsters of efficiency," as Merton had it, founded in 1534 by a Spanish soldier of fortune named Loyola and a handful of rootless friends. The Jesuits considered themselves, and were considered by others, to be the elite of the Church, the shock troops, the Marine Corps. High standards were set, high performance demanded. Sometimes, as during the Counter-Reformation, the standards were exceeded and performances overplayed. One Pope, Clement, had actually disbanded the Order. Obedience has never been one of the Jesuits' cardinal virtues and his command was quietly disregarded. Nothing the Jesuits ever did lacked drama. Proud men, they gloried in their humility. Impoverished by vow, they amassed great wealth. Four hundred years earlier they traveled as casually as men did today. Francis Xavier was in India before the Raj, in Japan three centuries before Perry. In upstate New York the Iroquois pried out the ribs of one of their number, Isaac Jogues, and hanged him from a tree by a belt of his own skin while he was still alive. Marquette first navigated the Mississippi. The sort of company that would attract a Peter Cobb, who, having decided first to become a Catholic would not be satisfied until he was a priest, and having decided to be a priest he must, logically, become a Jesuit.

It was what he would do with the rest of his life. He had flown to Boston to speak again with Father Bergé, who had written certain letters for him. There was a storm at home with a raging father and a sobbing Jane and interviews and then a week-long meditation in a creaky old retreat house on Staten Island in New York. In July he took Kiki to dinner at the Copley. She had taken her degree a year earlier and was working as an editorial assistant at Little, Brown on Beacon Street. He told her he had applied to the Jesuits, that he would enter the seminary that fall, that he had decided to become a priest. He had also told Hathaway, swearing him to secrecy. Tom had cursed and raged and then, uncharacteristically, had thrown both arms around him and told him, "Fuck them, Peter, if that's what you want, then do it!"

As such things happen, word got around their old set at Harvard. There were snickers, raised eyebrows. Men who had been chummy with Cobb assumed airs:

"*Men* don't go into religion. Younger sons and queers, that's what the Church is for."

Hathaway defended him.

"Peter Cobb's no queer," he said. Privately, having heard hints of Charles

Cobb's parental rage, he considered what Peter was doing to be quixotic, even absurd. But he knew his friend was no queer, remembering the glowing, placid look on Kiki Loomis's face those contented, satisfied mornings at Cape Cod after she had risen from Peter's bed.

In September Kiki married a Yalie. Catty people said she barely knew him.

Cobb had crossed his Rubicon. Then, shockingly and anticlimactically, came the summons from Father Bergé. The Society of Jesus had decided Cobb's conversion, his application to the seminary, the brutal wrench in direction his entire life had taken, were simply too abrupt.

"They fear this may be an impulse," Bergé told him. "They are concerned you are getting into something for which you are not ready. They want you to wait another year, and if you still feel the same way, to reapply."

"But how can they know?" Cobb demanded. "How can they ascribe motivation?"

Bergé shrugged.

"They can. And they do, Peter. They've been doing it for four centuries."

Distraught, and with a painfully keen suspicion he was doing nothing more than proving the Jesuits had been right to reject him, Cobb got drunk that night in Boston for the first time since prep school.

A week later he enlisted in another sort of Praetorian Guard. Ten thousand miles away politicians and soldiers, diplomats and revolutionaries, brown men and white, had combined, though this was not their intention, to provide a shaken and confused young man the breathing space he desperately needed before making up his mind as to just how he was meant to invest the next thirty or forty years of his life.

3

A war had begun.

It would drag on for a decade, a bleeding wound that would drain and divide a nation, destroy a presidency, kill 50,000 Americans and God knows how many Asians, and raise ethical and political sores still suppurating today. In the early sixties it was a skirmish, as the sophisticated would have it. As Cobb's platoon sergeant would later apologetically remark, "It ain't much but it's the only war we got."

Peter Cobb went to it. Not reluctantly, as men would do increasingly in the next few years, but with a cheerful fatalism and a muddled sense of rejection, a religiosity blended from equal parts of the duty to serve and the need to expiate, the whole adolescent stew spiced by a still-boyish delight in spiting his father, who understandably opposed both the war and his only son's participation in it.

"The wrong war in the wrong place at the wrong time." Charles Cobb growled the aphorism. He was a premature dove, not out of pacifism but out of conviction this stupid Asian intervention was unnecessary, unwinnable and, harshest judgment of all, bad for business. It was less than ten years since the French had finally extricated themselves from the damned place.

Peter Cobb's enlistment was not entirely without its logic, not completely the impulsive decision Charles Cobb considered it. There was a draft on and it would have been unthinkable to evade it, within the law or without. As a college graduate and an athlete it would have been a simple matter to arrange an appointment to one of the various officer candidate schools. He chose not to. The fires of his religious conversion had not yet been damped by routine or familiarity and a new humility he saw quite clearly as Christlike pointed to the role of an ordinary enlisted man as more suitable. Paradoxically, he chose the elitist Marine Corps on grounds that it,

28

like Harvard, like the Jesuits who had refused him, seemed to do better than anyone else what it was supposed to do.

Charles Cobb raged.

"A man with your education, your advantages, serving in the ranks. What a ridiculous waste, self-abnegation. First this priest business. Now, a private soldier!"

"Father, it's for two years, not a career. I'm not precisely becoming a thirty-year man, you know. I'll do my two years and get out."

His father regarded him sourly.

"You do these things to torment me, Peter. I know you do."

In part, Peter knew, the old man was right. He had taken his son's conversion badly. Now this curious display of patriotism. Peter endeavored to make it up by doing what he had rarely done at Harvard, writing him long letters, of the routine, the personalities, the incidents of military life. As such the letters were a gracious tribute to C.C., although he did not see them as such, and they would become the precursor of the sort of essays he would later write in *Speculations*.

He passed first out of his platoon at Parris Island. The drill instructors, hard, unimpressed men, had their bit of sport with him in the early weeks. He was, after all, their only Harvard man. Other recruits got hometown newspapers and scrawled love letters from their girls at mail call. Cobb received mail from brokerage houses and Brooks Brothers' catalogues. Gradually his endurance, his quick intelligence, his physical coordination, his cheerful acceptance of the hazing and rote stupidities of boot camp won their grudging admiration. Cobb had decided to treat Parris Island as a sort of rambunctious romantic adventure. His fellow boots, farm boys and big-city delinquents, unlettered blacks and scared eighteen-year-olds just out of the high schools, did not know quite what to make of him.

Camp Pendleton, the staging ground for Vietnam, was different. During their two weeks on the firing range a sulking, raw-boned southern boy with straw hair took exception to what he considered Cobb's "Yankee" ways and challenged him to a fight after supper one night behind the old, faded, two-story barracks. The newly awakened Christian in Cobb tried to avoid the confrontation. The proud Cobb lineage and the competitive oarsman in him broke the boy's jaw. An impressed platoon sergeant promptly promoted Cobb from rifleman to fire team leader. Dawn Monday to noon Saturday Cobb and three thousand other lean young men trotted up and down low, dusty California hills, running field problems night and day under full packs. Weekends he drove a rented car up to Laguna Beach to snorkle for abalone out on the mossy, submerged rocks of the Pacific littoral, to eat huge, cool salads and big, underdone steaks, to reread *War and Peace*, and to wonder, as young men have always done, how he would react to combat.

The *General Meigs*, an old President Lines cruise ship converted to troopship, took nineteen days to cross the Pacific with the 3,000 marines of what would be the first big replacement draft of the still small but decidedly promising war. Cobb, who had crossed to Europe in first-class staterooms on Blue Riband liners, took an ironic pleasure in the cramped, sweating accommodations assigned the lesser ranks in the bowels of the *General Meigs*, the chipped beef on toast, the boredom, the relentless drills and chivvying of the non-coms. Vietnam, steamy, exotic, alien, dangerous, would be a relief.

Cobb's rifle battalion was trucked swiftly through Saigon and up into the hill country beyond Khe Sanh to interdict Charley, as the Viet Cong were familiarly known, when they came down over the border from the north, rampaging through the countryside, burning villages, cutting up army units. Everything was relative in Vietnam. The hills were marginally less damp than the valleys, the days less hot, the nights somewhat cooler. But the bugs and the snakes and the leeches and the wild, savage cries in the night were the same and there is really very little to choose between a humidity of eighty percent and one of ninety. The battalion was stretched out over three miles of ridgeline, a skirmish line really, and dug into trenches and bunkers more reminiscent of World War I and the Western Front than of warfare in the nuclear age.

"Not proper marine duty at all," sniffed a gunnery sergeant with a waxed mustache and a firm sense of military propriety.

Nor was it.

"The tradition is," he wrote his father, "that we splash gallantly ashore through the surf on some hostile beach, shoot up the place, plant our flags, and retire in good order to rest and recreate and prepare for yet another dazzling rapier thrust. The reality, I'm afraid, is that we sit here week after week on the slopes of a soggy rain forest trying to keep our weapons dry and ourselves immune to green mold and heat exhaustion. The goonies are rarely seen by day but crawl about energetically at night, rolling grenades into our foxholes and firing off burp guns at anyone careless enough to silhouette himself against the sky. I have had a touch of diarrhea, nothing serious, but awkward. Otherwise fine if occasionally scared and when not scared, bored. Love to you and Jane."

Cobb's squad leader, a sour, brooding man from Montana, an ex-rodeo rider named Bright, was invalided home. Three of the men in his squad, restive under Bright's whining harassment, had laid for him in the trees one morning and had beaten him to a pulp, breaking his nose, damaging an eye, knocking out several teeth. True to his own peculiar sense of honor Bright claimed to have sustained his hurts in a fall. The platoon leader, a plump young lieutenant from Baltimore, suspected the truth but, like Bright, preferred not to exacerbate the situation. He arranged the sergeant's evacuation and, recommending him for corporal, named Cobb his successor.

"You'll have to watch that second fire team," he warned, "they're the ones gave poor Bright most of his trouble."

"Yes, sir," Cobb said, understanding the lieutenant was suggesting more than he was saying.

"Just run your squad, Cobb. The platoon sergeant and I will back you."

"Aye aye, sir."

He ran his squad, as he had run his crew at college, with, as he now put it to himself with wry amusement, a "muscular Christianity," rewarding the virtuous and punishing the wicked. The wicked, leader of the three men who had ganged up on Sergeant Bright, he took out into the boondocks one evening just before dusk. The chastisement there delivered was so effective all three would become model soldiers, one of them eventually being promoted himself to corporal.

It was after becoming squad leader that Cobb saw his first dead men. By February, he was a sergeant. By then he had seen too many of them.

Peter Cobb lay face down on a flinty hillside. Charley had been too smart for them. Cobb's patrol had started up the hill before dawn. Making too damn much noise. The point man, Brandt, had snagged on a trip wire and set off a couple of grenades. He was somewhere below them now, dead probably. The sun was up and the marines clung with fingernails to the slope and waited for someone to tell them what to do. If they turned now, in daylight, and went back, the VC would take them one by one. They had to go up, to the crest of the hill. They knew that, but nobody moved. Cobb's back under the flak jacket was slick with sweat. Only an hour before, in the darkness, he'd been cold. Now the dungarees stuck to his body like wet laundry.

His corporal was from Philadelphia. Nice, quiet sort with lank black hair. He crawfished across the slope now to where Cobb lay.

"We gotta go up there. How many of them you think there are?"

"I dunno," Cobb said, "could be just two or three. Could be a dozen."

"Yeah."

They were working blind. When Brandt tripped the wire and went down, another half-dozen grenades were tossed down the slope toward them, there were four or five bursts of automatic fire. It was hard to figure how many Charley had up there. The corporal and Cobb both knew if there were a dozen VC or more, they had no chance. Fewer than that, they just might pull it off.

"We gotta call in artillery," the corporal said abruptly.

Cobb lifted his head and stared up the slope toward the ridge of the hill.

"Fifty yards," he said, "that's not much clearance."

"I know," the corporal said gloomily. "Not a hell of a lot at all."

Lying face down with his fingers literally digging into the shale and sand Peter remembered the lieutenant's cheery voice in the pre-dawn darkness as they jumped off. "Jesus, today's the Army game. Wish to hell I was there."

And one of the enlisted marines, less enthusiastic, had murmured in the blackness, "You and me both, ace."

Now the lieutenant, whose name was Kretchmer, crawled to Cobb's side. He wasn't talking about Army-Navy anymore. The enthusiasm had leaked out of him. Cobb guessed that Brandt was Kretchmer's first dead man.

"Sergeant, you think we can get up there?"

Cobb turned his head sideways so his cheek lay hot against the hillside.

"Got no choice, Lieutenant. Start back in daylight like this they can just pick us off."

"Yeah, you're right." Kretchmer did not sound happy about it.

Cobb and his corporal and the lieutenant crawled to the other men in the patrol, telling them what they were going to do. In whispers. The ridgeline and the VC were too close.

None of it mattered. The plan. Their whispers. None of it. Charley just murdered them.

"Let's go," Kretchmer had yelled, and then they were all on their feet, twenty men trying to sprint uphill, bent low, seeking invisibility, yelling and firing as they went. Cobb was in the wire when the first grenades started to come over.

"Oh, shit!" someone shouted.

"Look out below!"

The grenades started to explode among them. Some of the grenades were just rolling down the slope toward them. As if in slow motion, coming on, getting bigger and bigger. Some of them were wrapped in socks, with gunpowder to intensify the bang. An old VC trick. Cobb was through the wire now, leaving half of one trouser leg and a gouge of calf behind on the barbs. He had the M-16 A-1 at hip level. There were no targets yet, Charley was too well dug in, but he was firing off short bursts.

"Keep their goddamned heads down," he yelled.

To his right a man fell.

"Jesus!"

Kretchmer was a few steps ahead of him. The grenades kept coming and then Kretchmer caught one and threw it back.

"Good man," Cobb shouted, "score one for Navy!"

At least he thought he shouted that. Maybe it was only in his head.

Then Kretchmer caught another grenade. It went off in his hands. Cobb sprinted past him. The lieutenant was rolling over in the dust, blood spurting from his wrists, from where his hands used to be. He was saying something but Cobb didn't understand the words. Maybe they were only sounds.

Then Cobb was at the ridgeline itself. Two marines were there before him, firing their weapons into a shallow trench. Without really aiming he lowered the muzzle and ripped off a longer burst.

"Shit, only three of them."

One of the marines had turned to Cobb, his face reflecting disgust.

"Three lousy gooks and they fuck up half a platoon."

It was true. There'd been only three VC on the hill. It was the slope and the grenades rolling down that had killed the marines. Not numbers, not firepower, just three smart gooks with sense enough to keep their heads down and toss grenades. Well, they didn't have sense enough to stay alive.

"Search them," Cobb said. Then he turned to see what was left of the patrol and to get them started back.

Brandt was dead. He lay on his back, his head downhill, his eyes staring at the blue morning sky. Kretchmer was alive. The corpsman was working on him. He had no hands and one eye was gone. He kept talking but it was nothing Cobb wanted to hear. He kept going downhill. In the wire a man twisted and turned. He was caught on the barbs. Cobb tried to pull him free.

"Corpsman!" he shouted.

Perhaps a dozen men lay on the slope, dead and wounded both. Eight or nine marines were still on their feet. The two he'd left on the ridgeline were back now, their dungaree pockets bulging with whatever they'd taken off the bodies. One of them stood by Cobb's side as he wrestled the wounded marine off the wire.

"Shit, Sergeant, that's a waste of time."

Cobb knew he was right. The man's ribs were sticking out under his flak jacket. A grenade must have hit him flush. The man's eyes stared at him. The blood pumped out of his chest.

"Get that damned corpsman," Cobb said. "Give this guy some morphine, anyway."

That was all they could do. Cobb knew it. He tugged again and finally the marine came loose, his trousers tearing free. He lay the man flat and sat down in the dirt, waiting for the corpsman.

There was the Army-Navy game. And there was this.

"Shit."

He felt a touch on his hand. Instinctively he recoiled. It was the wounded man.

"Father . . ."

"What?"

"Father, please . . ."

"Just take it easy. You're okay," Cobb said. Where was that damned corpsman?

"No, Father, I've had it. I want . . ."

"Yes?"

"I want to confess. Please hear me."

"But I'm not . . ."

The dying marine wasn't listening. He was talking now, a litany of sins, of failures, of regret. Cobb slumped there next to him, holding his hand, exhausted and drained, praying with the boy under his breath.

The marine was wandering now, not making sense.

"Don't," Peter told him. "Just say you're sorry."

The boy's eyes rolled white. A pink froth bubbled at his lips.

"Yes, Father," he said. And died.

"C'mon, Cobb, we're going back."

"Yes," he said. They picked up their dead and their wounded and Cobb led them home. He had wanted to respond to the dying marine, to say something, to do something. All he could do was to mourn over the body bag.

Four months later he was back in the States. He wrote to Father Bergé from San Diego. And while he waited for a reply, he took a last leave before discharge, passing the days visiting the old Spanish missions along the coast, praying for his mother and for the men who had died, men he had killed, men who had died alongside him, remembering courage and cruelty, dead men's faces, and a boy praying to him for a forgiveness he could not grant.

His Christianity was no longer as muscular. But it had matured.

In September of that year Peter Cobb, carrying a single suitcase, entered the Jesuit seminary of St. Andrew in western Massachusetts, a hundred miles from the city of Boston.

BOOK II

MIRADOR

4

Ten years can seem a lifetime—be a lifetime.

Yet in the Society of Jesus those first ten years of seminary study, broken by a year or two teaching as a scholastic in schools like Regis and Loyola and Fordham Prep, are but a beginning. Once a year Cobb, lean and with a rangy elegance even in the stiff black stuff of a cheap clerical suit, was let out to visit his family. Cobb senior, grown no more tolerant with age, would receive him, chat meaninglessly of the commonplaces of their lives, and hurry away to more congenial company, which Peter assumed, correctly, meant Helen Gatewood. The Duchess. Jane Cobb, grown beautiful and wild, would break the hearts of her various young men by insisting that during the two weeks of his visit she belonged to none but her brother, and would sit curled at his feet or lie stylishly prone on a convenient couch, asking him awkward questions about the sex lives of priests and nuns.

For the other fifty weeks of the year Cobb worked hard at becoming a good priest. As he had done in the Marine Corps, he prospered. The quick mind, the intensity of fires banked within, the maturity that conversion and abnegation and war had brought, combined in Cobb to create at least the potential for an extraordinary priesthood. It was not Peter who thought this of himself but those around him. His own self-judgments were more harsh. Only he and his confessor were aware of the passions and rebellion still smoldering inside him, forces so strong that Cobb could not honestly say a single day (or, more to the point, night) of those ten years had been without its fierce struggle for control.

He had expected an academic assignment, teaching, writing, a contemplative sort of life at one of the many Jesuit colleges, perhaps at the seminary itself, lecturing in theology and philosophy. These were his fields; Harvard had given him the intellectual underpinning. But he took his unexpected exile to the South American missions in reasonably good grace.

39

He had, after all, signed away his right of choice, and he was undeniably fluent in both Spanish and Portuguese, Nan Cobb having early been convinced of the advantages of Iberian domestics. Peter and his sister Jane had grown up jabbering foreign languages to a series of cooks, maids and gardeners who, for much of the time on the great Long Island estate, passed for playmates and companions.

Assignment to a mission church and school in Bolivia, while disappointing, had not seemed irrational. Bolivia had led to the Indians of Uruguay, Uruguay to Central America and Mirador.

But it was not an admirable bilingualism that had fetched Cobb south but the malice of a superior, a man who harbored certain amorphous, and a few specific, resentments: Cobb was too rich, too Harvard, too intellectually assertive; his father too rich, too famous, too influential. Ten or fifteen years in the horse latitudes, as his superior would have it, might knock a bit off the gloss, might bring him down to humbler, more seemly rungs of the social ladder.

And so, by the accident of language and the envy of an older, less gifted man, Peter Cobb was gotten out of the way, shipped off to a Jesuit St. Helena, the least likely of men to make a revolution, to stir a continent, to shake a Church.

It was in Mirador that everything began to change.

There was a small Jesuit mission with two other priests, both of them Germans in their seventies. They were not so much inhospitable or resentful of Cobb's youth or his Americanism as simply uninterested. When they were not at prayer or visiting the sick or burying the dead the two old men muttered Teutonic pleasantries to each other and exchanged heated commentaries on their passion, which was soccer. Except for their priesthood, Cobb had little in common with the Germans and treated them with a distant deference they accepted as their due. Neither of them read the newspapers except for the sports pages, neither seemed touched by or even curious about the turbulent near-revolution and the violent counter-revolution launched by the colonels of the regime, now shaking Mirador and its people as terriers shook rats. When Cobb naively attempted to discuss such matters with the Germans, they stared blankly and wondered if he had taken a malarial fever.

Then, miraculously, from the archbishop of the country, came the request for a priest to establish a chapel and possibly a school in the rancid slum of the capital city. When Cobb volunteered, the German Jesuits shook their heads and wondered aloud about the emotional stability of young men. It was in the slum that he met Figueroa, and through him

Joaquin, and the other Miradorans who would become the stuff of the book he was to write, the life he was to live.

Figueroa was a young physician, dark-eyed, intelligent, placid, and coincidentally sharing his name, Pedro. Pedro Figueroa and Peter Cobb worked side by side in the fetid slum day after day, sat together evening after evening on their shared veranda or in the coffee shops, wearing the same short-sleeved shirts and cool trousers of the ordinary Miradoran working man, agreeing on the absolute necessity not to give in to despair, not to permit justifiable anger to slop over into *plastique* bombings and bank raids and the shooting down from ambush of policemen.

"Joaquin and I are at odds on this, of course," Pedro had said, his pleasant, good-looking face twisted into a half-smile, half-grimace.

"He's young," Peter Cobb had responded. "Young men are impatient. They want everything to have happened yesterday."

Pedro had given a short laugh.

"Do you blame them, Peter? You've been here long enough. You've seen the two-tiered society in operation. I marvel that all of our young people have not followed Joaquin. I marvel not at their impulsiveness but at their patience. You really don't expect Latins to conduct themselves with such admirable restraint. We are an emotional people. We tend to feel things out loud. Very loud."

Pedro had spent time in the States. He could be more objective about Mirador and the Miradorans than most of his countrymen. Hard to credit, they still considered themselves to be Catholic. Neither revolution nor violence nor the horrors of repression had extinguished that last, clinging vestige of religion. Nor, even more incredibly, had the seeming uninterest of the Church itself.

All around them was the lively stir and hum and chatter of the place, the waiters hurrying, patrons shouting orders, even the lovers conversing not in the furtive whispers of Anglo-Saxons but seemingly at the top of their lungs, the jukebox screwed up to maddening volume, outside and beyond the horns and screeching brakes of the motorbikes and the Mercedeses and the hurtling buses. One million people, the largest city in the country, and it seemed to Cobb, in whom a faint and disapproving New England puritanism still resided, that none of them ever went to bed, drew breath, or stilled the incessant gesticulation of articulate hands and dramatically rolled eyes. He had noticed this even with Joaquin and his collaborators, deep in seditious conspiracy. In Mirador, it seemed, one even plotted *coups d'etat* with shouts instead of murmurs.

"Another coffee?" Pedro asked. Cobb nodded. Coffee was the fuel on which they ran. A young girl with Indian blood fetched it, her black eyes dartingly alive.

It was then that he noticed, beyond the girl, lounging at a table securely backed against a corner of the crowded room, the two men in sunglasses. He had never seen them before but he knew them. Knew just who they were. Policemen. After a few years in Latin America—it doesn't matter which country or how nobly democratic its constitution sounds—a foreigner, especially an American, gets to be able to recognize policemen. It was not that the policemen *did* anything. They just sat there. Watching. That was what was menacing about them. It sent shivers up his spine. Seeing the policemen in their dark glasses evoked in him the feeling of those early mornings when, dull with sleep, he would shake out his shoes and a scorpion would come tumbling out to scuttle across the earthen floor.

"Friends of yours?" Peter said.

Figueroa followed his eyes.

"Ha," he said disdainfully. "More likely your CIA."

Cobb shook his head. No, he thought, dear, decent Dr. Figueroa, no policeman in the world, not the CIA, not even, he imagined, the KGB, conveyed the quality of menace of a Latin American plainclothesman watching you through his dark glasses.

In Europe he was a foreigner. But he could handle Europe. An American passport in your pocket, comfortably stamped by drowsy functionaries at airports and in the echoing sheds of dockside—there was a sense of bureaucratic order, a traveler's security blanket. Here, in the millions of square miles south of the Rio Grande, no such womb-like consolation existed. Here, all men were strangers. Aliens. Potential enemies. Through the dark glasses of the police, all visitors were suspect. It didn't matter if you were a Yank, a Brit, anything. No consul could save you. No embassy. No legate. No emissary plenipotentiary.

Well, Peter thought, despite all that the people were fine. And people were what made wonderful countries. Then he saw himself again reflected in the lenses of the plainclothesmen's black glasses. A wonderful country but too long run by colonels. He had steered clear of the local politics, had retained his few friends, had done his job, had declared a sort of personal, benign neutrality. He was a *Yanqui*, an outsider. Let Mirador solve Miradoran problems.

Because he held himself above politics and because he was an American, Cobb had so far avoided the lethal curiosity of the police and of their more casual and even more murderous rightist militias. How fortunate he was to have been thrown in with Pedro Figueroa, a decent, civilized man,

42

clinging to reason in the cruel mindless maelstrom of war. They had been together in the slum for nearly two years now. Figueroa's friends had become his friends. Through Figueroa he had met the terrorist Joaquin, Joaquin had brought him to Flor. And through them he had come to understand Mirador, to understand himself as he had only partially done before, and in the knowing and the understanding an immature priesthood was deepening, growing, broadening.

And it was through Figueroa's friends that word eventually reached Cobb about the nuns, the atrocity that would, for a brief season, tug at the sleeve of world opinion. And alter forever the placid boulevard of his own priestly life.

Joaquin, slim, intelligent, violent, passionate, the son of middle-class *commerçants*, had been recruited to urban terrorism at the university. By the time he took his degree he had already killed a policeman, participated in several bank robberies and the bungled assassination of a minor ministerial bureaucrat, and had begun a serious flirtation with Marxism. By the age of twenty-five Joaquin was the acknowledged leader of one of the most violent cells of urban guerrilla terrorism in the capital, a man with a price on his head and a murderous fury in his heart, a heart still softened by love for Flor.

She was the daughter of privilege, who in one of those unfathomable quirks had left behind her the young men and the music and the sports cars and the string bikinis of the chic Pacific beaches to go into nursing, working out of a clinic in the Manaos quarter of the city where venereal disease, malnutrition, rat bites and even leprosy tormented, ate away at and killed the young and the aged of a country which, it seemed, simply did not care.

Joaquin and Flor were now hundreds of miles up the Rio Negro, in the feverish backcountry, Joaquin training guerrillas in the use of automatic weapons and in a basic Marxism, Flor tending the sick, the wounded, the aged, in a crude aid station open to the deluges and blistering heat of the tropical rain forest. Cobb knew all about the place. He had gone there with them, secretly, ministering, tending to the Catholicism they still desperately claimed, and in a canoe on the Negro had fashioned the first, hesitant thoughts that would become *Speculations*.

He was tempted to stay there, on the Rio Negro. They needed a chaplain. They needed . . . well, they needed *everything*.

But he had come back, a holidayer home from the country after a diverting fortnight. They needed him in the slum. Figueroa needed him.

43

There were children to be baptized, last rites to be given, the dead prayed over and buried, kids taught to read and to wash their hands and to boil water before they drank it. There was malaria and syphilis and cancer and bitterness and despair and poverty. *This* was his war. As deadly as that on the Negro. He had enlisted here. Here he would fight. Not with guns. With love, with faith, with an intelligence the Jesuits had honed and a humanity Figueroa had taught.

What would happen to the nuns changed all that.

5

For three years now in the mountains and in the bush, in the isolated fishing villages of the Pacific littoral, in the provincial market towns of the rich farming deltas, even occasionally in the capital city itself, the war had raged. It was a bloody little affair, a series of raids and counterraids, shots fired from ambush, roads mined, patrols lured into *cul de sacs*, hostages taken, buses strafed, grenades lobbed through the doors of cafés and police stations. The guerrillas called themselves "freedom fighters" and the regime called them "Communists."

The upcountry religious missions were, if you credited the regime, notorious nests of sedition and revolution. It was difficult to get troops to penetrate that deeply into a hostile countryside. Too many of their comrades had simply vanished on such missions. The Catholic missions were simply too remote, too insulated from retribution. In the capital and in the provincial fortress towns, the regime waited, frustrated, angry, wanting to lash out with effective and devastating counterstrokes at something or somebody. If only the rebels would come down out of the country and fight a fixed-piece battle.

But they did not. And the colonels, sullen and confounded, bribed their informers and dispatched their spies, and raged at the injustice of not being capable of smashing the mission sanctuaries, once and for all.

The old DC-3 banked once over the low coastal hills and descended toward the pleasant little airport gouged out of the red clay that gave the buildings of the capital their burnt-sienna, vaguely Italian look, and bounced three times on the tarmac before shuddering to a halt. The plane had long ago been gutted of seats and it offered approximately the interior creature comforts of a tractor trailer truck, fitted out with a sort of hardboard bench along each flank of the cabin. Among those who braced themselves on the bench as the DC-3 descended were three nuns.

The nuns had been able to glimpse an arm of the Pacific, a hint of golden beach, and the rooftops of the capital as the aircraft banked. Mirador City was only eight miles away and this close to the capital the roads were secure. Only the flight was perilous. Noisy, pushing, stifled by the heat of the cabin, the passengers disembarked, relieved to be on the ground, blinking in the brilliant sunlight of tropic noon, heavy with the sweet smell of wild orchid and liana of the forest just beyond the field. The oldest of the three nuns brushed dust from her ample cotton drill trousers, glared about her as if about to discipline a mischievous kindergarten class, and nodded briskly to the two younger women with her.

"All right, Sisters," she said in the piously chiding tone only a convent lifetime could perfect, "come along now. No lollygagging."

The passengers straggled toward an old school bus parked at the verge of the tarmac, only the three American women purposeful in their stride. They did not often have the treat of a day in the capital, an overnight stay at a sister convent, a different table, a few hours in the bazaar, and the pleasant, diverting haggling that invariably went with the purchase of even such basic goods as medical supplies and school materials and bolts of finished cloth that were needed by the mission. But it was Christmas week and permission had been given.

In the control tower of the airport a militiaman watched as the three women walked toward the waiting bus, and then picked up the microphone of an army radio.

"They came in on the plane," he said into the radio, "three of them."

The soldiers were waiting for the bus. A corporal beckoned and four men moved out into the road, languidly waving their hands. The driver was accustomed to being stopped along this stretch of road. Sometimes it was the rebels, but this close to the city it was usually troops or one of the armed right-wing gangs roaming the country and playing soldier. He only hoped there would be no long delay.

"What passes?"

"Nothing," one of the troops said, "just identification control."

The bus driver nodded and lighted a cigarette. Behind him the peasants and salesmen and children and the other passengers began rooting in pockets and bags for their papers. It was all routine. Even the nuns understood. In a country at war with itself you carried papers. It was only sensible.

The four soldiers climbed heavily into the bus, carrying their automatic weapons, their khaki shirts wet with sweat and the cartridge belts hanging heavy on their stocky Indian bodies. Mary Zumsteg, the oldest nun, stared through the dirt-streaked window toward the bush while she waited for the soldiers to reach her. She could see the others lounging by the side of the road, squatting on their heels or sitting with their backs against the trees. Only one soldier was walking around. He must be the officer. A few yards beyond was the bush. On the seat behind her the two young nuns sat waiting for the soldiers, not as relaxed. Mary Zumsteg had come this way more often. She understood the drill. In front of her an Indian woman pushed her whimpering baby against her chest and began to breast-feed it. In the back the salesmen lit cigarettes and joked. It was very hot in the bus without the moving breeze from the windows.

"No good."

"What?" Mary's instincts were dulled by the heat. She looked up into the black eyes of the soldier who held her identity card.

"No good," the soldier repeated, dangling the sodden identity card between stubby fingers.

Behind her Mary could hear one of the other soldiers talking to the younger nuns. They seemed to be having the same difficulty. It was aggravating to have a document issued by the government questioned by the government's own soldiers. Mary shook herself into wakefulness. When the bus reached the capital they would clear up the confusion; there'd be someone to deal with more intelligent than this boy who probably couldn't even read. She smiled up at him, shaking her head in a motherly fashion. The soldier pushed her identification back into her hand and motioned for her to follow him. Mary turned. Behind her the younger women were also getting to their feet.

"We'll soon settle this," Mary Zumsteg said firmly. She hoped the officer would be able to read.

They climbed down off the bus. Only the three nuns and the soldiers. Behind them there was a relieved silence. Odd, Mary Zumsteg thought, the check of papers had not been completed. Those in the back of the bus had not even had to show their cards. The driver watched them through the windshield. His cigarette had burned down. He flipped it through the open door. One of the soldiers turned and waved to him.

"Please?"

"You can go," the soldier said.

The driver shrugged and pulled on the bar that closed the door. Mary Zumsteg heard the bus shift into gear.

"Sister Mary?" One of the younger nuns, Alicia, reached out to take her arm.

"It'll be all right, child. I'll have a talk with their officer."

They were herded off the road now and onto the narrow verge between road and bush to where the other soldiers lazed. Mary walked ahead, the two girls behind her, the soldiers following. Mary was relieved to see two of them had slung their arms. If they meant any harm they wouldn't have done that.

"Come here." It was the standing soldier, the one she assumed was the officer. He was slim with a small mustache and a lighter skin than the others. He stood waiting.

"My captain," Mary Zumsteg began, with a confidence she did not feel, and with the rattle of the bus receding down the road behind them, "may I ask just why these other sisters and I have been . . ."

It was then that the officer gestured with a slender hand and one of his men raised his automatic rifle to shoulder level and slammed its butt into the small of Mary Zumsteg's back.

Jean Luzinski was the youngest of the three nuns, a chunky, blond-haired woman from Chicago, a girl who had grown up in a tough Polish neighborhood bordering the black ghettos of Division Street. The youngest at twenty-four, but perhaps the most streetwise. Now she and Alicia Moran supported Mary Zumsteg between them in a staggering, seemingly haphazard march into the bush, soldiers in front and behind them, the flanks of the march limited by the jungle itself. At the very head of the column, out of Jean's sight, was the officer who had ordered Mary Zumsteg silenced.

"Why did they hit me?"

The question was more a groan of pain and of bewilderment than a protest of righteous anger.

"It was a mistake, Sister. The soldier was nervous. They didn't mean to hurt you."

Jean did not believe this. But with Alicia whimpering and the older nun hurt and dazed, she did not know what else to say.

Across Sister Mary's sagging, just barely erect body, Alicia looked at her, her eyes wide and frightened.

"Jean," she said, "they're going to kill us. I know it. They . . ."

"Shut up, Alicia," Jean snapped. "Just shut up."

In front of her a soldier wheeled, wanting to know what the women were saying.

Jean tried to avoid his eyes.

"Hail Mary, full of grace, blessed art thou . . ." she began praying silently, wishing Mary Zumsteg had not been hurt, wishing Mary were shepherding them through this as she often had when things were bad, in the epidemic and the drought.

"Hurry," snarled the soldiers, and the three women staggered ahead, past orchids they did not see and no longer smelled, deeper into a forest that closed behind them.

The commander of the militia that had taken the nuns from the bus was named Montoya. He was not a very good officer and his soldiers would not have been considered first-class troops by any professional army in the world. But when the regime learned through its spies at the upcountry air strip that Mary Zumsteg and the other nuns would be flying to the capital, Montoya's detachment was routinely patrolling that stretch of highway between the city and the airfield and the orders were radioed to him. A more seasoned officer might have done a neater job of it. Not, of course, that it would have mattered to the three nuns.

Montoya stood now in the center of a small forest glade, one hand nervously slapping the stiff leather of a holster that hung from his slim right hip. Of the thirty men in his platoon, about half had already flopped down on the ground, their rifles simply dropped into the grass and weeds. A few men stood with their back to the little clearing, urinating against trees or into the bushes. The nuns remained standing, the old woman sagging between the younger, not knowing if they were to continue the march. Montoya had not meant for the old woman to be hurt. When he had raised his hand it was simply to silence her, to threaten. The boy who had smashed his rifle into her back, rupturing a kidney, had mistaken Montoya's gesture for an order.

Well, thought Montoya now, what did it matter. The old woman would soon be out of her misery. He slapped his holster once again, liking the weight and heft of it against his slender leg.

"*Muchachos*," he said, trying to make his words crisp and authoritative, "bring the shovels."

Several of the soldiers slung off their packs and unhooked entrenching tools. Montoya pointed to a bare patch of ground roughly in the middle of the clearing.

"There," he said, "that's the place."

One of the militiamen bent stolidly to the task and began to dig.

"Stupid," Montoya shouted, "to do a woman's work. Let them dig the holes themselves."

He shook his head. Most of his troops were Indians from the back country. Montoya had been born in the capital, had attended the university, and had the sophisticate's contempt for these rustics.

The soldiers handed their shovels to Jean and Alicia. But before they took them they lowered Mary Zumsteg gently to the ground.

Jean picked up her tool first.

"My captain," she said in midwestern but fluent Spanish, "we'll dig as many holes as you want but Sister Mary is badly hurt. Can't your men carry her over into the shade and give her some of your water?"

"Badly hurt?" Montoya asked.

"Yes, can't you see that?"

He nodded.

"But first you dig," he said.

Jean Luzinski shook her head but began to dig. Their situation was bad enough without irritating this strutting little man any more. "Alicia," she hissed, "snap out of it and start digging."

"Yes, Sister," Alicia said dully.

All the troops were off their feet now, a few squatting Indian style, the others sitting on the ground. A few lay full length and one or two seemed already to have fallen asleep. Montoya alone remained standing, slapping at his holster and smoking a cigarillo, turning his head this way and that, striking poses. The men expected an officer to affect a certain style. Montoya liked giving orders, liked it when, as occasionally happened, even in *this* army, they were obeyed. A few yards from where he stood the two young American women, bent nearly double over the stubby entrenching tools, dug into the clayey loam. He watched the movement of their arms, their braced legs, their strong backs, the way the sweat of their exertion molded their cotton shirts to their upper bodies. Some of his men were watching now as well.

Jean Luzinski drove the spade deeper into the earth. She was no longer praying. She was thinking. A few yards away Alicia Moran sniffled as she worked, and just beyond her Mary Zumsteg lay unconscious, her face, once rosy as apples, now pale and strangely old. For more than a year Mary had done Jean's thinking for her, had led her and the other younger sisters of the mission at their work, their teaching, their devotions. That was finished now. Jean drove her spade deeper. She was beginning to hope the whole thing, being pulled off the bus, this stupid forced labor, even Mary's injury, was all merely part of a sophomoric harassment, that no more sinister intent was involved. At first she feared she and Alicia were being told to dig their own graves. She had begun to hope this was just a form of debasement, an amusement for the troops, sitting back smoking their cigarettes and watching the *gringas* sweat. She dug the shovel in once more, and at her side Alicia continued to work despite her blubbering.

And Montoya continued to watch them work, watch them sweat under the hot sun of a Central American false winter's day.

Later on, when his superiors hypocritically asked Montoya how the affair had gone so wrong, he lied, saying it had been the fault of the men, half-trained, undisciplined troops, inexperienced non-coms who had lost control. The truth was that Montoya himself was to blame.

"*Muy bien, señoras,*" he shouted, his voice pleasingly crisp and echoing against the trees encircling the glade. "You can stop for a moment."

Jean Luzinski looked up, brushing the sweat from her eyes with the back of a hand. Beside her, Alicia Moran's spade hacked away at the earth.

"Alicia, you can stop digging. They're going to let us rest."

Both women let shovels slip from their hands and sank to earth, breathing deeply in the heavy, humid air, their faces brick red from exertion, cotton trousers and shirts sodden with sweat.

Montoya strutted over to the two women and looked down, hand reflexively slapping at his holster. Jean Luzinski stared at his boots.

"*Hay mucho calor,*" Montoya remarked, "too hot for such work."

Jean said nothing. She was concentrating on breathing and on not wanting to irritate this pompous little man.

Montoya continued to talk, almost conversationally. And as he did so, he leaned down over the sagging figure of Alicia Moran.

"A shame to work so hard dressed like this," he said. Jean looked up now, sensing something had changed in his voice, as if his tongue had thickened, making it difficult for him to form the words. She watched as Montoya reached down and took Alicia's shirt in his hand, pulling it open, at first gently and then harder, until a button popped away and then another.

He half turned and saw Jean's eyes on his face.

"You too," he said, his voice hoarse, "take off your shirt."

Jean knew then what was going to happen.

The three nuns, one of them semi-conscious and groaning on the scuffed earth of the little clearing, the other, younger women standing, their shirts and bras tossed on the ground, their hands held chastely across their breasts, were now the focus of attention on the part of all thirty of the militiamen. Even those who had been asleep were alert now, staring at them. Montoya, pleased at having aroused his men from their lethargy, nodded at the discarded spades.

"Now you dig again," he said.

Alicia did not move.

"Alicia," Jean Luzinski said softly, "it's time to work."

She picked up her own shovel; then, an instant later, Alicia reached for hers.

The soldiers formed a rough circle, staring at the women's breasts as they resumed digging, watching the sheen of skin slick with sweat. Jean tried to ignore them. She was praying again now, not so much the measured cadences of formal worship, more a repetitive wish that something would happen, some miracle that would save Alicia and herself, that would get Mary Zumsteg to a hospital. Her prayer echoed empty and without hope, but it was better to pray, to blunt imagination, than to think about what the soldiers would do next, what this man forcing them to labor half-naked would want.

The trenches they had been digging for what seemed hours were now more than knee-deep, the red clay piled in little hills, the two women standing inside the holes, hacking at the earth, loosening it, then tossing it up and to the side. Montoya, like a windup soldier, marched up and down, smoking and slapping his pistol. He'd cut a switch from the bush, a sort of swagger stick, green and pliant, and he amused himself and drew guffaws from his men by slapping it lightly across the backsides of the women as they bent over their shovels. He was enjoying himself immensely now. For the first time he really felt like an officer.

"Well, *muchachos*, not bad, eh? Good to see *gringas* doing a little honest labor for a change."

"Yes, sir," the men said. But they were not watching Montoya strut. They were watching the two girls. Watching them work, watching their bodies gleaming in the sunlight.

Alicia Moran was the first to give up.

"I can't," she said, half to herself, and fell forward on her face, her upper body out of the trench, her knees buckled.

Jean dropped her spade, not even noticing the bloody patches in her blistered palms, and dropped to her knees beside the other young nun.

"Alicia, Alicia, it's all right. They'll let us rest now."

She looked up to see Montoya's boots again looming above her.

"Poor little rabbit," he said, "the heat is too much for her. Perhaps," and now he looked around at his men, "perhaps if she took off those heavy trousers she would be cooler. It would be more pleasant. No?"

The men began to shout then and three or four of them rushed to the trench, brushing Jean aside, and pulling Alicia bodily across the ground, tearing at her pants, not stopping until she was stripped, her lower body strangely white against the sunburned and clay streaked torso.

Montoya stared at Jean.

"You too, my dear," he said, his voice shaking with excitement.

She did not answer but spoke to Alicia, crawling to her and sliding an arm around her shoulders, murmuring consolation.

Behind him, Montoya could sense his men's impatience. He must not lose control of them now. He had them, he must keep them.

He raised his hand and brought the switch down hard across Jean Luzinski's back, raising a thin red welt, causing her body to jerk with pain. The soldiers, as excited as he was, growled their approval. And when he nodded a half dozen of them grabbed Jean by the arms and legs and dragged her from where Alicia lay deathly still.

Montoya had been given three orders. The first, the abduction of the mission sisters, he had accomplished. Now, asserting control of his own growing excitement, and having broken the women to a point where they were unlikely to resist, he must wring from them the names of the collaborators in treason.

"Hold her like that," he said.

Sister Jean was spread-eagled across the mound of red clay she and Alicia had formed, her back arched as she lay looking up at Lieutenant Montoya.

"Now," he said, looking down at her, enjoying the posture of total authority, sensing the excitement in his men, "now you will give me the names of those at your mission who are working with the Communists. All the names. Sisters, renegade priests, *gringos* and Miradorans. I want all the names."

A corporal, one of the few of his soldiers who could write, showily pulled out a dogeared notebook and licked the stub of a pencil.

Jean said nothing.

"I am waiting," Montoya told her, "but I am not a patient man."

One of the soldiers holding her laughed.

"None of us is patient," he murmured, reaching out with one hand to squeeze a nipple.

Jean shook her head.

"I am a Catholic nun," she said, dully and without hope, "I work with the children. I know nothing of the rebellion."

"The names," Montoya repeated.

She shook her head again, this time unable to form the words of denial.

It was then he brought the switch down hard across her white belly, again drawing the reflexive spasmodic jerk of pain, again leaving a startling streak of red in the flesh.

"Hold her tight, *muchachos*," he said, the excitement rising in his loins.

The four soldiers tugged harder at her limbs, stretching her body taut.

And Montoya began to whip her.

Methodically the pliant switch moved from plump thighs to mound to belly and finally to her solid young breasts, where with a fury he had not previously felt, Montoya lashed over and over again at her nipples until they squirted blood.

She was babbling now, giving him names, not of "collaborators" but of everyone she could remember at the mission. At Montoya's side the corporal stolidly composed his list.

Then Montoya threw down the switch, red with her blood, frayed from its task.

He turned toward his men.

"Now," he said, "you can have them."

The soldiers hurried forward. Alicia was dragged a few yards away and the men formed rough queues before her unconscious form and Jean's red-streaked body.

"Wake them up," someone shouted, and a half dozen canteens were emptied over the faces of the two women. Jean groaned but Alicia sat up, startled. And when she saw the men and looked down at her own nakedness, she screamed.

Then they began the raping.

There was only one brief distraction. Mary Zumsteg awoke. The pain in her lower back had become but a dull throb, and, getting both hands pressed against the earth behind her, she rose to a sitting position. Her eyeglasses had vanished and she blinked in the afternoon sunlight, trying to imagine where she was and who all those men were, why they were shouting, what they seemed to be doing in little groups. Then she saw Montoya and remembered.

"My captain," she began, the formal address habitual, and when he turned toward her, she realized for the first time what the men were doing, whose naked bodies were crucified across the little mounds of red clay.

"May God forgive you," she said, and raised her right hand to make the sign of the cross.

It was then Montoya motioned and a young soldier, the front of his uniform still wet with Jean Luzinski's blood, fired a burst from the automatic rifle into Sister Mary's stomach.

The impact of the bullets seemed to lift her and then she fell back, while behind and slightly to her left, a soldier fell heavily to earth, a ricocheting slug through his head.

"*Madre de Dios,*" Montoya groaned, as several of his troops rushed to the fallen man.

The others, impatiently waiting a second turn at the two girls, shrugged and blessed themselves or muttered a low curse.

When the militiamen had finished, only Jean Luzinski was still alive, and that just barely, her tough Polish body unconsciously, fractionally, only marginally alive. Until Lieutenant Montoya pulled his .38 from the stiff leather of his new holster, and fired a single shot through her left eye and out the back of her blond head.

Then he ordered the men to bury all three women in the shallow trench they had dug, but before the first spadeful of red clay had fallen on the bare, bloody bodies, he held up a slender hand.

"Wait," he said, "they must be dressed in their clothes."

The soldiers shrugged at this strange notion but then, their passions spent, they reassembled the torn and filthy cotton rags that had once been trousers and shirts and underwear and tugged them on over rapidly stiffening limbs.

Then the three women were tossed casually into their graves and covered by a few inches of Miradoran soil. In these latitudes, in this heat, the ants and worms and the animals of the forest night would soon be at them. In a month grass and vines and wild orchids would have grown across the graves. In a year not even the bones would remain.

The dead militiaman was slung between poles to be carried out to the highway where a vehicle would surely come by.

Montoya had already fabricated a story. There had been a fire fight with a rebel band. The man had died a hero's death. He smiled to himself. Not for nothing had he attended the university.

And Lieutenant Montoya had carried out the third order. He had killed the nuns.

It was a month before the first soldier talked. It had been his brother who had been killed by the shots fired at Sister Mary Zumsteg. He had mourned his brother, lighting candles in the church where he was garrisoned, dully resentful of Montoya, as a Catholic vaguely guilty for what all of them had done to the nuns, as a soldier fearful of what might happen if he complained or requested an inquiry. Then, on his saint's day, just as time had begun to blunt guilt and loss, he got drunk and in his drunkenness told the story of what had happened in the forest to another Indian from his village who served in another regiment.

"Ah," the man said, only marginally more sober, "it is this filthy war."

And the soldier, because it was his saint's day, shook his head.

"No, what was done was wrong. A sin."

His friend looked around the *cantina* where they were drinking, fearful that a sergeant might be listening, or a spy for the regime.

"*Cuidado*," he said, "be careful what you say."

"No," the soldier said stubbornly, "I have been careful too long. Someone must be told of this affair. Someone must know why my brother died. It is my saint's day and I know this must be done."

In the end the man from his village told him of medical missionaries who worked in the slum above the capital among the poor, one a *gringo* and not to be trusted, but the other a doctor who treated people who could not pay and who had the reputation of a wise man. If the people of the slum trusted him, perhaps the doctor would know what could be done, who could be told.

"Perhaps," the grieving soldier agreed. He was out of his depth and needed counsel. And that night, before they left the *cantina* to reel drunkenly through the dusty streets, he had gotten the name of the doctor and of the mission where he worked. Figueroa, Pedro Figueroa.

There was also the American at the mission. Dr. Figueroa's friend. He too was a good man, they said. But who could trust a *gringo*?

The American's name was Cobb.

6

On a soft, tropical February evening Peter Cobb lazed in a big rattan chair on the veranda of the small house he shared with Dr. Figueroa, seeking the late breeze off the Pacific, gazing up the starry southern sky, smoking one of those brown cigarettes to which he was addicted, the house and its porch dark but for the cigarette's glow against the insects of the summer night. Far below, sensually curled around blue bays, was the capital city of Mirador, still ablaze with moving light. Oddly, the best views of the city were to be had from its poorest quarters. The shantytowns, pasted to the city's sun-baked hills like papier mâché to a theater scrim, hung shamefully above the magnificence of the city the way vultures cling to branches above a kill, dun and dull and ugly. Cobb and Pedro Figueroa lived in one such shantytown.

Always lean, Cobb was leaner now from his annual siege of malaria, a suntanned man of above medium height, dark-haired, good-shouldered. The yellow ravage of fever marginally clouded eyes that were otherwise green and bright, despite long days teaching, and, although he was not qualified, helping Figueroa nurse the slum poor.

Cobb lighted another cigarette and leaned back in the rattan chair that one of the shanty dwellers, eager to earn a few pesos, had fashioned for their house, and wondered where Pedro Figueroa had gone off to and when he was coming back to tend to his patients. He puffed at his cigarette and thought about Pedro and listened to the roar of cars speeding along the superhighway, intent on their destination in the splendors below, prudently bypassing the slum in a series of discrete ess curves before plunging toward the capital and the sea.

Occasionally Cobb had visitors. Usually during the northern winter. Men Cobb had known at Harvard passed through, men who traveled now for great corporations or for governments or for pleasure. A marine with whom he had served came through on an estuarine survey. His sister Jane came several times, once when her husband was driving in a race in Panama. Cobb's father never came but of course it was not expected that he would. When these Americans came to Mirador at first they rhapsodized over the beauty of the place, the Mayan ruins, the magnificent coastline, the richness of the soil, the spectacular mountains. By the time they left a week or a fortnight later, his American friends were informing Cobb quietly, almost with embarrassment, that Mirador was not a democracy.

Cobb had long been aware of this. He had eyes, he was not stupid. In the night he had heard the sound of the *plastique* bombs in the capital. He saw the planes heading east toward the hills and the upcountry, the tanks clanking along the brief stretch of superhighway that after a few kilometers simply came to an end in the bush beyond the airport. He heard the same rumors that had sent Figueroa off on his mysterious quest for information about some Maryknoll sisters who'd simply vanished.

None of these things diminished his attachment to the country or affection for its people. Cobb had declared an admirable neutrality. Let the Miradorans run Mirador. That had been his philosophy for the three years he had been here, as it had been for the other Latin years. It was a philosophy rooted in his personality and in his vocation. It would not change until Pedro Figueroa came home to their house.

The more romantic of Cobb's friends, as well as his sister, liked to think of him as a character out of Conrad, a latter-day remittance man sweating out a life that had once glistened with promise here in the backwaters of a drowsy, postage stamp of a country. This did not upset Cobb. He knew himself and he knew he had been sent here for a reason, even when that reason seemed blurred and indistinct. As it did on this soft night on the veranda of his house in the slum.

"Where the devil *is* Figueroa?" he wondered aloud, startling a dozing parrot into whirring flight.

Along the highway where it curved closest to the shantytown the motor of a heavy car slowed and died as the car rolled casually up on the dirt shoulder to a halt. Beyond the ditch of an open sewer that served the scatter of lean-tos, the dim light of lanterns and candles shone through the hacked-out glassless windows of the corrugated metal and waste plywood of their walls. Sounds of the tropic night, soft and subtle, hummed beneath the clashing music of portable radios, the occasional laugh, a child's cry, a drunkard's impotent bellow of blunted despair. No one emerged from any of the shacks to investigate the parked car. Visitors who came in automobiles were rarely there for benign purposes. Here no questions were asked of men in heavy cars.

Inside the parked car was the subdued glow of cigarettes, and the murmured voices of men between tasks, punctuated by a low whimper such as might come from an injured animal. Along the highway, dipping toward the brightly lighted city and the sea, fast cars and the occasional lumbering truck whirred past. Somewhere, a dog howled. Peter Cobb, dragging on the fag end of a final cigarette, heard that same howl on the veranda of his house and shivered. Probably a last vestige of fever, he thought, and got up and went inside.

Midnight.

Both front doors of the automobile swung open. The man on the passenger's side then turned and opened the rear door and through it a naked man, crouched and trembling, was pushed sprawling onto the bare scrabble of the shoulder. His hands were tied behind him and after a moment of hesitation, he began to squirm, rather than crawl, toward the drainage ditch and the lights of the shacks beyond. The two men stood there, watching. And then they moved briskly to him, one on each side, and lifted him bodily to his feet, turned him toward the nearest of the shacks, and shoved him into motion.

The naked man sprinted away from the highway toward the scatter of huts on the slope of the tropical hillside, running recklessly, desperately, as if pursued, or frightened, or in pain, into low fences and poles, bouncing off the corners of sheds and stumbling across little truck gardens and tearing down clotheslines as he ran. Behind him the car was again idling powerfully at the edge of the highway, the men poised so they could watch his mad run and be amused. Inside the car, a fine Buick immaculately kept, a third man had taken a packet of Wash n' Dri from the glove compartment and, quite methodically, was scrubbing the blood from the back seats and the upholstery of the Buick so that the car, and their uniforms, would not be stained.

The wounded man lurched ahead, falling, scrambling again to his feet, uttering small sounds that trembled between a groan and a whimpered sob, his legs still strong, but his face bloodied and his eyes closed. He was only vaguely aware of what he was doing. He ran because he was in pain, as people do who have been set afire, knowing that the rational thing is to fall to earth and roll over and over to extinguish the searing flames, yet not doing so because pain and panic have stripped them of reason and in their agony the only course is mindless flight. As if man could outrun suffering.

Crouched in their huts or lying abed, the poor of the slum could hear him coming. The few who screwed up their courage to peer through cracks in the doors or out the windows saw a naked man running berserk among them, colliding with dogs and scrub bushes, slipping and falling amid offal only to rise again and resume his mad dash. A man who wept and cried out to God, alternately between hope and despair: "Oh, God, save me . . . oh, God, let me die."

Finally he fell and did not rise, a lean, stringy figure, angular and tormented. High above, a patch of cloud skirted across the moon, turning the shacks and the sobbing, exhausted man into a ghastly chiaroscuro of light and darkness, groans and silence.

At last, by twos and threes, the slum dwellers, frightened and reluctant, emerged from their shanties to poke at him with cautious sticks. And finally, to carry his torn body to the little house where he had lived with Peter Cobb.

Cobb, ready for bed, wearing only the undershorts that passed for pajamas in the heat of Miradoran nights, heard them coming, as they did sometimes when a child was ill or a woman in labor or a man cut in a drunken brawl. He hoped it was something else this time, no one sick, no one hurt. Figueroa had taught him the fundamentals of crude, emergency medicine; he knew first aid from the Marine Corps; but for more exotic wounds, more subtle illness, Cobb was always uneasy if treatment was needed when Figueroa was off circuit-riding through the slum or deeper in the bush.

"Where are you now that I need you?" Cobb said half aloud, half kiddingly, as he tugged on a pair of khaki pants and padded barefoot to the door and out onto the veranda.

And then he saw Pedro Figueroa hanging limp between two of the poor who stared up at Cobb with frightened eyes. Cobb hesitated for an instant in the shock of recognition. Behind him, tacked over the doorway of their home, a small, hand-carved figure of the Christ seemed to look down on both of them from His cross of banyan wood.

Cobb knelt over the still figure of his friend. They had slashed the ropes that bound his arms and in the half light of the now-high moon, Cobb could see at a glance the mutilated fingertips and the bruised and punished body. He stared at Figueroa's face, bloody, swollen, the cheekbones purpling and blackening from hemorrhage under the skin. The ugly cross-stitching of heavy black thread puzzled him at first and then turned him, dry-retching, to his knees on the hard-packed earth. He was drawn back again to Figueroa's face by an animal's squeal of pain and the spasmodic jerking of bloody hands toward that devastated face, pawing helplessly at those swollen, grotesquely closed eyes.

"Bring him inside," Cobb shouted, and ran into the house where he grabbed a flashlight and began to root among a tray of medical tools for the surgical scissors. He knew then what was wrong with Figueroa's face. He had heard such stories. And he prayed frantically that he would not vomit when he did what he knew he would have to do, prayed he could save his friend.

They carried Dr. Pedro Figueroa to the dining room table so familiar to most of them as an operating table on which he had mended them. Scissors in one sweating hand, Cobb bent over Figueroa and began to cut.

They had put live cockroaches into his eyes and sewn the lids shut.

Figueroa was a strong young man and he did not die. They even saved the sight of his left eye. The right had been eaten away. But he did not recover. He lay, half blind and mad, in the provincial asylum of Manaos, where the doctors let him play with string and fed him on gruel and fruit. Cobb visited him once. Only once. Memory was too painful, the subtle, clever, gentle Figueroa turned crippled child. Even for Cobb, whose adult life had largely been distinguished by control and the reticence of will, there were emotional prices too costly to pay.

The police shrugged and suggested the guerrillas might have done this terrible thing. "They're animals, you know," an official informed Cobb soothingly. "There are no atrocities they will not commit." The American Embassy was of no help. "Miradorans are killing Miradorans every day," Cobb was told. "If the doctor had been an American citizen . . ." Letters asking an appointment at the Ministry of Justice went unanswered. The government's bureaucracy, always lethargic, grew positively stony. Figueroa's fate became for Cobb a sacred cause; for Mirador it had become but a statistic.

Perhaps, except for corrosive regret, that might have been where it would have needed eventually to end for Cobb as well. No man can retain forever the cutting anger Cobb felt as he knelt over Figueroa and first saw the bloody ruins of his eyes. But then, during Easter week, Joaquin slipped into the shantytown with the frightened peasant who told Cobb of his brother, a militiaman, and of his drunken confession about the three nuns, a story he had related only once before: to Pedro Figueroa, on the night before the national police abducted him and, unable to get the doctor to respond to their questions, sewed the voracious little vermin into his living eyes.

It was then, with a sly caution he had practiced only once before in his thirty-seven years, and that in war, that Peter Cobb began to steal into the hills and up the backwaters of black streams into the deep bush and the craggy mountains where Joaquin's people bivouacked and made their conspiracies and plotted the ambushes and assassinations and bombings they hoped one day would topple the regime of the colonels.

And it was then that Peter Cobb began writing his book.

7

The woman's voice was urgent and familiar.

"Hurry," it said, "you must go with us. Now!"

Cobb was instantly awake. In the gloom of the bungalow Flor Duarte was leaning over his bed, shaking him by the shoulder. Cobb spun and quickly his bare feet were on the floor and he was reaching for a shirt and a pair of trousers.

Flor had moved to the door, where she stood peering out across the flattened earth of the slum toward the highway beyond. Three months had passed since Figueroa's mutilation. Easter week was a month ago. With the instinct of the hunted, Cobb did not stop to pose questions, to consider options. Someone he trusted had told him to hurry.

He and Flor left the bungalow traveling light. He had grabbed a rucksack and stuffed it with a clean shirt, a breviary, a cheap utilitarian chalice, a faded poncho against the rain, the small medicine chest Figueroa had carried, and one of Figueroa's medical books that seemed to deal most practically with common ailments. Cobb had a hunch it might be useful. The girl, slender and quick, led him to the truck. Joaquin was waiting.

"Hurry," he said, "they are coming for you."

The truck was already rolling off the shoulder and back onto the highway, heading inland, away from the city, as Joaquin clambered over the tailgate and tumbled in next to Cobb. The night was warm but Cobb, roused from sleep, shivered in the drafts that swirled through the antique body of the old truck. Around him in the dark slumped Joaquin's people.

The Catholic Church, he suspected, would take no note of his departure. Cobb had crossed a Rubicon and there was none to mark his passage. In Rome yet another elderly Pope dithered toward the end of his days, surrounded by solicitous men who feared he was dying but feared even more the senile mischief he might do if he lived. In Mirador itself the archbishop, Perez, alternately negotiated with the regime for money for the schools and stormed against it in pastoral letters no one read. What was Cobb, anyway? Just another priest vanished into the back country, a drinker, a womanizer, a rebel, or simply lost, dead, perhaps of fever or the wilderness. In a civil war there were always people disappearing. One more, and a *Yanqui*, a *gringo*, would hardly roil the surface of consciousness.

The truck rolled east. Now a hand reached over and patted his knee. Cobb could see the white teeth and the bright eyes penetrating the darkness.

They drove all night. Crossing the coastal range it was cold and Cobb tugged the poncho from the rucksack and wrapped it around himself. The rebels seemed to have only the clothes they wore, cotton shirts and trousers, bare feet in sandals. One of the women had a threadbare Indian blanket. Peter felt guilty about the poncho. Then he pulled it tighter around him. He dozed until toward dawn the shifting of gears woke him. The truck was descending now, he could feel it. And it was warmer, sticky, once again tropic.

The rebel camp wasn't much. It straggled for a hundred yards along a branch of the Rio Negro on the only dry ground for miles, a six-to-ten-foot height of land dividing the river from the swamp behind and beyond. There were lean-tos and a few tents. Perhaps a dozen canoes and skiffs lined the bank, tethered close to shore, concealed under the overhang of the big trees that shaded the camp and the river, turning it the black that gave the river its name.

Flor was there, scrambling down from the cab where she had sat all night.

"Padre Pedro," she said, smiling and coming right up to him, extending a lean, brown hand.

"Hello, Flor," he said, grinning back.

She was Joaquin's girl. And more than that. Peter liked her very much.

"You're okay?"

"Good, Peter, really fine."

He nodded, hoping it was so, but dubious.

"But this is splendid, Peter," Joaquin exclaimed. "Now we will have our own chaplain. Just like a regular army!" He looked very pleased with himself, as if he had rather cleverly put something over on Cobb.

The sun came up through the river mists. There was the usual racket of birds at dawn. Women had begun to stir ashes into smoky breakfast fires. Here and there children, barefoot, barelegged, wearing only shirts, came out of the tents and the huts, rubbing sleep from their eyes.

Cobb stooped and entered the tent Joaquin had assigned him and began to stow his few possessions.

That afternoon, toward four, a government plane came over, saw nothing, and droned off. The next morning at dawn Joaquin led out a squad of men on some ambitious venture. They returned late that night, tired, sweating, plastered with swamp mud. Whatever their prey, they had not killed it. But then, neither had they been killed. That night there was some drunkenness and angry shouts. Flor, usually cool, looked alarmed, glancing toward Joaquin. Cobb stayed out of it, whatever the dispute was, and scribbled at his notebook.

There were other ambitious ventures. Cobb shouldered his rucksack with its cargo of medicinals and went along on one of them. It ended badly. Three men were hit, one of them died and Cobb labored over the others. He wished Figueroa were here. Removing a splinter from a child's hand or treating fever was one thing. Setting a leg broken by fire from an automatic rifle was something else.

The truth was, Cobb soon realized, that Joaquin's "brigade" of rebels, as it self-consciously termed itself, was but a rabble in arms. Joaquin was dialectically pure, petulant, personally courageous, militarily ambitious. He also had no notion at all of small unit tactics, terrain, fire control, logistics or the principles of leadership. Cobb assumed many of the insurgent bands must be as badly led, as poorly organized.

"The men resent me," Joaquin said one evening as he and Peter sat by the campfire. River mud had been tossed into the flames to create a smudge. That and Cobb's cigarettes, chain-smoked, helped keep the insects down. "I don't blame them, but it makes things difficult."

"Class resentment?" Cobb asked.

"Naturally. They are peasants from the cane fields and the coffee plantations. I'm an intellectual from the city. From the university. We barely speak the same language." There was contempt in his voice.

"You fight the same enemy."

"Well, yes. We have that." It was a grudging concession.

Cobb said, "And you're all Miradorans. I'm the only outsider. The only alien."

"Some of the brigades have Cuban advisers," Joaquin said morosely. "I said No. This was to be a national revolution. Probably I was wrong. The brigades with the Cubans somehow do much better."

Somewhere a night bird screeched. Cobb lighted a fresh cigarette from the butt of one that was dying. He knew what Joaquin wanted, what he was going to ask.

"Peter?"

"Yes?"

Joaquin seemed to take a long breath. Then, "Will you help me? Tell me what to do? Work with the men on their weapons?"

"Joaquin, you know I can't."

"But why not? You're one of us. We have a common enemy. The same men who killed my brother and seized my property did that obscene thing to Figueroa. They were the same bunch that came for you. If you hadn't joined up with us you'd be dead now or in prison. Or worse."

"I realize that and I'm grateful."

"I'm not asking you to fight, just to advise me, tell me when I'm wrong, show us how to keep the weapons functioning. These men know machetes and shotguns. A machine gun, a bazooka, these are beyond their capacity. Beyond mine, dammit."

"You know why, Joaquin. Don't make it harder for both of us. Jesuit priests don't fight guerrilla wars."

Neither man spoke for a time after that and finally Cobb said good night and took his poncho a few yards closer to the river, rolled into it and went to sleep.

Then there came the incident of the burned village and somehow rules of conduct that had seemed so crisply delineated, so firm and immutable, blurred and began to fade.

It was one of those route marches Joaquin insisted they make, more out of a sense of maintaining discipline than of actually accomplishing anything. They had moved out at dawn, perhaps forty men, Cobb with them, swinging away from the river and toward the higher ground of the marginal farms and hamlets that eked out an existence along a dirt road that optimistic maps called a provincial secondary highway. They hit the road ten kilometers from the Rio Negro, crossed it quickly to avoid the reconnaissance planes, and struck off into the cane fields. To their left lay the village of Coptacl.

"A useless sort," Joaquin had said on an earlier trek. "Indians. Nothing on their minds but cane and the price of sugar. Trying to radicalize those people is a waste of time. We steer clear of them. The government leaves them alone. You'd think it was Switzerland."

Now, in the late morning, they saw the smoke rising and they knew Coptacl was no longer Switzerland, no longer an island above the storm.

"Adelante," Joaquin ordered, "maybe we can catch their patrol."

Even while they were still hurrying through the cane fields, hundreds of meters from the nearest house on the edge of the town, Cobb knew something really bad had happened. The first body was that of an old man. He had reached the fields, running from the town, when the bullet caught him in the back. Cobb knelt and touched him. The body was still warm. But there were flies in the wound and working at his ears. He muttered a swift prayer for the dead and rose to follow Joaquin and his men as they trotted toward the village, rifles and shotguns unslung and ready.

Now there were more bodies. Some of them women. A boy who could not have been more than six lay curled with his legs pulled up to his belly as if with a cramp. Blood had dried on his little hands where they covered the gut shot that had killed him. The sickening sweet smell of burning sugar hung over the place, bringing the flies.

The town was laid out around a small plaza, the sand smooth as a bull-ring's, with the church and the sugar warehouse facing from either of two sides, shops on a third, and the low sprawl of a stucco school on the fourth. Only the warehouse was still burning. The church, blackened and pitted with bullet scars, was where they found the priest.

"But why?" Peter Cobb asked himself as he stared at the dead priest. "Why?" This wasn't a rebel town, certainly this priest wasn't one of the militants stirring up the peasants and supporting the guerrillas . . .

There was a stone cross in the small graveyard off to the left of the church and the priest was tied to it, Christlike, with lengths of barbed wire around his wrists and his ankles, and another length of wire affixed roughly around his temples like the crown of thorns. Except for his clerical collar, carefully still in place as if to make a point, the body was naked and torn by a dozen machete and bayonet wounds. His flat, dark Indian face looked down from the cross at Cobb, unseeing. Peter knelt on one knee to say a prayer for the dead. Somewhere an infant cried. A dog howled.

The men were all dead, their white peasant shirts and trousers stained with blood that was already turning rust brown in the sunlight. It was in the school that they had herded the women and raped them. Fourteen were still alive. Several of them were functioning, going from house to house, looking for their men or their children. Others wept, or sat cross-legged on the floor, shocked and dazed. Most of the children had disappeared.

"The soldiers took them in the trucks," one of the women told Joaquin, her voice dull and metronomic.

"But why?" Cobb demanded.

Joaquin shook his head in rage. "So they can't grow up to join us. To be raised by the government and sent out to kill us. How do I know? Who can explain the motives of men who do such things?"

One of the women began to wail. It was a sound beyond description, more animal than human.

Joaquin's men, with more energy than purpose, ran this way and that through Coptacl, searching for the government troops who had destroyed

66

the town. They were long gone. The guerrillas knew that, but it was better to run around and to shout at one another than simply to stand here looking at the dead, or to do nothing under the accusing eyes of the raped women of Coptacl.

Cobb picked up his bag and wandered through the town. He had seen towns like this before.

Eventually he found himself again in the plaza before the church. Someone should cut down the priest, he thought. Lay him out properly, say a few words. The dead, brown Indian eyes stared out at him. The priest's mouth had fallen open and flies were nesting in it, laying their eggs.

Finally Joaquin called his men together. They stacked their arms on the neatly swept sand of the plaza and began to drag the dead into long rows, pulling them by the feet when they were heavy, carrying them over their backs when they were lighter. Sentries ought to be sent out, Cobb thought. It did not seem to occur to Joaquin. Or perhaps he knew that when government troops did something like this they hurried away to their barracks and their beer, to obscene laughter and, later, perhaps, to the nightmares of guilt. Men who commit atrocities do not hang around at the scene. They do what they come to do and are off. Still, Cobb knew, there should be scouts.

When they had finished three of the women came to Joaquin.

"Will you take us with you?" they asked.

"Yes," he said, knowing it was stupid.

"And will you find our children?"

"Yes," he said again, knowing it was a lie.

They cut down the crucified priest and laid his body alongside the others. Cobb blessed the bodies and said the words of extreme unction. The guerrillas removed their battered hats and stood silently. They blessed themselves and shuffled back to regain their weapons.

"All right," Joaquin shouted, "let's go."

They turned then, not in the direction of the road and the government's trucks and the missing children, but back toward the Rio Negro. The women, who marched with them, continued to look back for a long time at the burned village.

Miles away Cobb imagined he could still smell burning sugar, still hear the drone of flies.

That night, as they sat and smoked by the river bank, Joaquin asked him again.

It was a lovely ambush.

Peter Cobb lay flat on the low knoll in long grass that rustled sufficiently in the humid wind of early morning to mask involuntary movement or carelessness. The night's dew had not yet burned off and the insects that would come later in the morning, crawling, slithering, biting, hung wet and motionless on the blades of grass or crouched numb on the black earth. Cobb's khaki trousers and shirt and the worn tennis shoes were soaked from the night march and the wet grass. But there was no chill. It was just after six o'clock and the temperature was already in the eighties.

To his right he could see for several hundred yards along the recently oiled blacktop of the road to San Jacinto and the sea. It was along this road that the trucks would come. It was here that Joaquin's little band of guerrillas would hit them, the platoon of soldiers in two trucks and perhaps a jeep or two, heading up the San Jacinto road from the port to the coastal hills to relieve the platoon that had gone up this same road just twenty-four hours before. They're getting careless, Cobb thought, with their unvarying schedules. Contempt for the rebels, he supposed.

Joaquin's men, twenty of them, were sited along the littoral of the road for a hundred yards. Cobb could see only three or four of them. But he knew where the others were. The machine gun, an old .30-caliber American heavy gun with a water jacket, was set up under a big tree whose low branches made the gunner and the assistant gunner feeding the belt almost invisible in the deep shadow of the tree. The muzzle of the gun was pointed toward the highway. A small stake, visible to the gunners but virtually lost from the vantage of the road, had been driven into the rich soil near the shoulder of the road. The gunners would use the stake to start their traverse. It was a very competently laid gun with an excellent field of fire. Peter Cobb had laid it.

It was a very heavy gun with its tripod, and the small, lean men who had carried it through the swamp and uphill toward the road had done well not to fall behind in the line of march. Cobb insisted they hand off every thirty minutes to two other men, so as to keep them fresh. When he first saw the gun in the encampment by the Rio Negro it was rusted, its barrel fouled. Fortunately the ammunition cans containing the belts were sealed against the damp. Peter used boiling water and a rifle ramrod to clean the gun and he lubricated it with Three-in-One oil one of the women had unaccountably brought along for a Singer sewing machine she no longer possessed. Crude, but the gun would work.

Several hundred meters down the road toward San Jacinto, Joaquin, under Cobb's direction, had placed two men, one with grenades, another with an automatic rifle. Cobb could see one of them from where he lay in the tall grass. The man would be invisible from the road. That was essential.

Now they need only wait. Lie still and wait. Cobb had waited like this before and he knew how. He hoped the guerrillas would demonstrate equal patience. It was their country, after all, their damned war, and they should be able to wait, unmoving and quiet. But you never knew with irregulars . . .

They heard the convoy before they saw it. Gears grinding as it came toward them up the hill from the coast, the growl of the heavy trucks, the different sound of a jeep as the driver shifted into four-wheel drive. Cobb looked around. Joaquin waved to him from a hundred meters away where he waited under a tree. Good, Cobb thought.

Then the jeep, familiar olive drab with some white numbers painted on its hood, came into view, approaching the man with the grenades and the automatic-rifle man. There were two soldiers in front, one of them an officer or an NCO, and one in back, riding high with a submachine gun on his lap. Good, Cobb thought again, knowing you could hit nobody with those damned things at any range, knowing how they tended to jam. Now came the trucks, two of them, the canvas furled, perhaps twenty men in each truck, the men dozing in the morning heat. Then the jeep reached and passed the spot where he had placed the grenadier. Good, he told himself a third time, no one's panicked, no one's blown the ambush. The first truck had passed now. Then the second was abreast with Cobb's men with the grenades and the automatic rifle.

"Now!" he said, hoarsely, almost silently. "Now! Do it now!"

From the tall weeds just off the shoulder of the road something small and black, the size of a tennis ball, arched lazily through the air toward the last of the three vehicles, hit one of the uprights of the flatbed, bounced, and exploded. In that same instant another grenade was in the air, tumbling in a lovely arc toward the truck. Now he could hear the sound of the first explosion, could feel the shock wave.

"Now!" he said again, this time a shout. "*Ahora! Ahora!*"

A long way off, at the tail of the convoy, the automatic rifle began to chatter, and the jeep and the first truck shot forward, wanting to put distance between themselves and whatever it was that was happening behind them. They sped toward where Cobb crouched. Then the heavy gun began to fire and the jeep, twisting and then tilting crazily, spun off the road and turned onto its side, sliding a dozen meters into the bush with its momentum. All around him men were firing now and soldiers were jumping from the first truck, hitting the ground and thudding to a halt in the dust, hurt by their falls at speed, shocked by the firing that seemed to come suddenly and from everywhere.

"Ahora!" Cobb shouted again, and near him men took it up.

"Ahora!" they shouted, their voices punctuated by the chatter of the heavy gun and the sharp crack of the grenades.

It was all over in a few minutes.

Joaquin slapped Cobb on the back.

"Peter, you did it. Marvelous. Forty of them and three vehicles. And not a man lost."

Cobb stood up. He could see Joaquin's men coming out of the bush and onto the road, turning over bodies, firing the occasional round at men who were still alive.

"Peter," Joaquin said, "it's just as you said it would be. Perfect! Simply perfect!"

He was very excited.

Cobb nodded. He reached down to pick up his rucksack. The guerrillas were all excited now, dancing around in the dust of the road, picking up revolvers and binoculars, and lifting a light machine gun and a mortar and automatic rifles from the trucks. The dead troops lay scattered across the road or hung limply from the flatbeds of the two trucks, one of which was burning from the grenades.

"My God, Peter . . ." Joaquin said, his handsome face split by a smile.

Cobb nodded.

Yes, he thought, 'my God.' And he said a brief prayer for the men lying on the road.

8

That was the beginning.

By autumn, when the rains came, Joaquin's brigade had grown to six hundred men, with a platoon of mortars, a dozen machine guns, and all the automatic weapons they could want. The road between San Jacinto and the Rio Negro had been closed and three regiments of regular troops were assigned full time to the region, trying unsuccessfully to bring Joaquin to ground. In the barracks and in the capital there was talk of American mercenaries fighting side by side with the rebels, there was said to be an entire company of Cuban regulars fighting with them. Joaquin took on airs, swaggered through the encampment wearing two automatics and a pair of good field glasses, the class distinctions between himself and his men more evident than ever, but no longer an impediment to efficient operations.

Peter Cobb, who planned the battles but would not carry a gun, filled his notebooks and tended the wounded and prayed over the dead and wondered if he would ever again function as a priest of God.

Occasionally in their criss-crossing of the province they would run across some rural priest and Cobb would be able to confess himself. He did not tax these simple men with the complexity of his doubts but in his Act of Contrition recited silently he asked forgiveness for whatever he had done or said or thought which might conceivably be sinful. Then, of course, he was speaking directly to his God and with God Cobb had no reservations about whether his dilemma was too subtle to be appreciated.

He was a pragmatic man and he understood that Joaquin and the *brigadistas* valued his military craft more highly than his chrisms and his murmured prayers. But he continued to pray.

He said mass, administered the sacraments, baptized infants and buried the dead, and prayed for wisdom. It was, he had no doubts, a *just* war the rebels were fighting, perhaps even a holy war. Only his role in it raised ques-

71

tions. How could he have let these amateurs continue to blunder, to suffer, to die when it was in his hands and his head to teach Joaquin what to do, to show him how to do it? He had not wanted this. The regime had created the situation that had now sucked him up in its maw. The murder of the nuns, the torments of Pedro Figueroa, the burning of Coptacl, and a thousand other atrocities had brought him to where he now was, wrestling with guilt on the banks of a fever river called the Negro.

How far he had come, how twisted the road.

The war was becoming conventional. In the countryside bands like Joaquin's now rode into the dusty towns in trucks and jeeps with machine guns mounted, and the crowds formed to greet them with flowers or with sullen lowering of eyes, depending on the town's political leanings. Behind them were the dank swamps of the Rio Negro and the camps where the rebels had for so long sheltered under the trees, shivering face down against the wet earth when a government plane swooped low, striking their tents, burning their huts, and slipping deeper into the swamps or further upriver when informants alarmed them with news of a punitive expedition headed in their direction.

Now, instead of running, they turned and fought, breaking off only when tanks lumbered up to bolster the government troops or when the obsolete American jets, the most sophisticated weapons the regime had, swooped low over the fields with their rockets racing angrily ahead of them. But such retreats under pressure by now were rare.

At least in the provinces, the rebels seemed to be winning.

Occasionally Cobb would pick up an American newspaper, weeks old, in one of the towns they had liberated or a car they had ambushed, and he would riffle quickly through its pages seeking news of the war. Only occasionally was there a story, usually from one of the wire services, and the thrust was invariably the same. "Communist rebels," usually "Cuban-led," had won or lost this or that encounter with the forces of the regime. The stories were always datelined from the capital of Mirador, and were, understandably, more favorable to the regime that held the city than to the guerrillas who were attempting to isolate and encircle it.

"It isn't fair, Peter," Joaquin said one evening after dinner in a village they had liberated that afternoon in a brief fire fight distinguished only by the speed with which the government garrison had fled into the surrounding tobacco fields. "*The New York Times* ought to know better than this. Of course there are Cubans here. Of course some of us are Communist. But to portray the revolution this simplistically . . ."

72

"He's right, you know, Peter," Flor said.

"Yes, I know."

"We need a minister of propaganda to tell the world of our glories. What d'you think, Peter, shall we nominate Señorita Duarte to the post?"

"Why not?"

Flor scowled.

"I'm not amused. You, especially, Peter. Surely the American newspapers would react to a letter from you stating our position and telling the truth about what the regime is trying to do. You have a senator. You could contact him, have questions raised in the Congress. Your father is an important man. Isn't it possible that he could bring pressure to bear? At least to force people to adopt an open mind about Mirador."

Joaquin leaned forward, elbows on the table, his handsome face now clouded, eyes eager.

"Yes, Peter. She's right. You are the one who must carry our message."

They stayed that night in the liberated town. A passably pleasant inn had been commandeered as the brigade's headquarters. The innkeeper, a plump, equivocal sort who might well the night before have been entertaining the officers of the government garrison, had showily led Joaquin and Flor to what must have been his best room. Cobb, being a *Yanqui*, was given next best.

So I'm to carry the message, he thought.

The bed was clean—which was itself a miracle. There was a pillow Cobb now stuffed behind his back, and a decent lamp on a battered night table. Cobb sat in his shorts with a week-old Miradoran newspaper propped against his legs. His face, his forearms, his neck were burnt brown by the Miradoran sun, and his long legs seemed almost bleached by comparison. Bleached and skinny. He was skinny all over, he realized as he stared into an unfamiliar full-length mirror in the common bathroom on the floor. Blessedly, the walls of the old inn were thick stucco, keeping out the heat of the day, providing now a refreshing dry coolness in the tropic night.

On one of the inside pages of the old newspaper there was a grainy photo of a newly delivered shipment of American tanks on the wharf of Mirador City. A smirking captain posed proudly in front of them, his soldiers standing in a line more or less at attention, while a monsignor of the Catholic diocese blessed the tanks and the crews who would man them.

Cobb groaned. How could his Church be so blind?

And he threw the paper aside and reached into his rucksack for a notebook.

73

Someone had to carry the message. Someone had to tell the truth of what was happening here.

He picked up his notebook and resumed writing.

In January the rains ended and the government, excited by the arrival of a small fleet of helicopter gunships to hone the cutting edge of their forces, resumed the offensive. And Peter Cobb came down with dysentery.

"Poor Peter."

Flor Duarte looked down at him on his cot. Even his suntan seemed to have faded under the ravage of disease. Cobb felt drained, his anus was rubbed raw, he lacked even the strength to prop himself up on one elbow to look at her. But he tried to grin.

"Next time," he said, "just let me die. It's cruel and unusual punishment to keep a man alive who feels this bad."

"I know," she said, "even Joaquin feels terrible about it."

"Even Joaquin." Not just a casual remark. Not anymore. Joaquin was changing.

"I don't like it," Joaquin had said to her. "I'm the brigade commander. It isn't right that the men look to Peter for instructions. In the beginning, yes, when I was myself still learning. But now . . . it demeans me to have a *gringo* giving orders, plotting our strategy, planning the battles."

"Joaquin!" she said sharply. "Peter isn't a *gringo*. He's your friend. *Our* friend. Everything you know about leading the brigade you learned from him. He doesn't ask a thing from you. Only your friendship."

He had gone off sulking. And it had gotten worse. Now, with Cobb ill, Joaquin was planning a battle, the first he would fight without Cobb since that day, so long ago, when Peter had laid the machine guns and planned the ambush that destroyed the government convoy. The prospect turned Joaquin once again into the smiling, charming boy Flor and Peter both remembered.

Now he came into the tent to stand over Cobb.

"My dear fellow," he said, cheered immeasurably by the sense of unshared authority.

"Hullo, Joaquin, *qué pasa?*"

Joaquin threw himself down on an old ammo box and rubbed his hands.

"Tanks, Peter, a platoon of four tanks. And I know how we can make them ours."

Peter started to move, felt the burning pain of his backside, and groaned.

"What? What? You don't think I can do it?"

Joaquin jumped up and began pacing the tent.

74

"Not that, Joaquin," Cobb said, even the strain of conversation exhausting him, "not that at all. But if you get the tanks, what do you do with them? Where do you get gasoline, spare parts, ammo for the guns? You don't have any mechanics who can repair tanks. Even I don't know a damn thing about it."

"Even *you?*" Joaquin said, the enthusiasm gone from his voice to be replaced by sarcasm. "Well, now that is something. And I thought you knew everything about the art of war. The marines didn't teach you about tanks? And I thought you were a regular General Patton."

"Joaquin," Flor snapped, "Peter's sick. He feels awful. This is no time to fight with him."

He wheeled on her.

"So you're both against me. You don't think I can run the brigade without his help either, do you?"

Cobb again tried to sit up but he fell back.

"Joaquin," he said, his voice a croak, "if you take these tanks you're restricted to the roads and the cleared ground of the *haciendas*. This brigade survives because whenever the regime exerts too much pressure, we fade away into the bush. Add tanks to the brigade and you limit your ability to maneuver. They'll send in gunships and jets and murder you. It's what they want, a set-piece battle. Those they can win. You know that. They can't beat you in the bush but if they get you out in the open . . ."

Joaquin said nothing, his handsome face clouded, sullen.

The brigade was bivouacked in the grassy uplands north of a market town called San Pablo. It was here the government had stationed a company of riflemen and the four obsolete, but still impressive, American surplus tanks. Cobb, weak and dehydrated, lying on his stomach, heard the troops move out shortly after midnight.

"Good," he told himself, "they'll hit them at dawn." Joaquin had learned that much. Would he lay the bazookas to catch the tanks from the side, where the armor was lighter? Would the machine guns be properly placed? Where would he enter the town? Would scouts move in first? What was the fallback position if the attack failed? Who was his number two if he were hit? Had Joaquin arranged signals?

Cobb wished Joaquin had come by to say *adios*, to be told *buena suerte*, as Flor had done.

"So you're going with him?" Peter said.

"Yes. He doesn't have you. I can't let him go alone."

At six in the morning Cobb woke to hear the distant firing. It was over within an hour. By ten o'clock the first members of the brigade were streaming into the camp.

Cobb painfully slid off the cot and got slowly to his feet. He stood unsteady and blinking in the hot sun just outside the sleeve of the tent. Men were running, shouting. The brigade's handful of trucks were being backed up and loaded. Tents were being struck. Now the wounded were coming in, carried piggyback or on stretchers.

"*Malo*," a soldier said as he passed Cobb, "*muy malo*."

Another came by. An older man. He shook his head at Cobb. "The tanks kept shooting us down and Joaquin kept shouting, *Adelante! Adelante! Para la causa!*"

Peter nodded. Dialectical purity. It was fine stuff. Until you were outgunned.

9

It was after that that the men came to Cobb and asked him to lead them. And with them was Flor. They came to his ponchoed lean-to in a camp set up in the bush the night after they fled.

"And what does Joaquin say about it?" Peter asked her.

She shrugged.

"What can he say? He knows now it is either you or call in the Cubans. After yesterday the men will no longer follow him."

"And you?"

"I am with the men. Forty men dead. The brigade cannot sustain such losses. If you don't take over it will melt away into the brush. The fight will be over. Everything we've done for three, for four years will have been for nothing."

"Flor, I'm a priest."

She shook her head angrily.

"Priests have fought before. The Crusades. The French Resistance. There are a thousand precedents. Just wars. Holy wars. There is nothing sinful about fighting against evil."

A half dozen of the most senior of the *brigadistas* nodded. Their faces were solemn, determined. When she had finished talking each of them had his own say. Peter listened, saying nothing. In the end he told them he would consider their request.

They moved again at dawn the next day, fearful the army was closing in. And they moved twice again, including a half day's march through swamp. They lost two men there, one from wounds suffered in the disastrous fire fight Joaquin had ordered, the other drowned in a sinkhole. They're getting weaker, Cobb thought, weaker and frightened. It was as if all the progress of the past months had never happened. The next night, three men slipped away. Deserters. Finally, nearly a week after their defeat, they stopped and tried to reorganize. They were six thousand feet up in the hills, above the rain forest, far from any road better than a dirt track. Here, at last, they would be safe, they could rest, they could mend their wounds.

Joaquin and Flor had erected their tent at the edge of a clearing in the pines on the bank of a small, cool brook that would supply the camp with its drinking water. It was typical of the recent Joaquin, choosing the best site for himself. A year ago, Cobb thought, he would have chosen his own campsite after all the men had been taken care of. Flor was seated cross-legged outside the tent darning a khaki shirt.

"Joaquin," she called, "Peter is here."

The guerrilla leader came out of the tent, bent double to get through the low entryway. The sulky expression that had been there since the battle crouched on his handsome face.

"Oh, yes," he said sarcastically, "our newly elected commandant. *Nuestro jefe.*"

Joaquin crouched down on his heels like one of his peasant soldiers and toyed with a few twigs on the ground before him. Flor got up.

"I'll let you two talk," she said, and strode off briskly toward the center of the camp. Neither man spoke. The sun had just gone down behind the shoulder of a hill and the sudden tropical dusk descended on the camp. There were insects and the start of the night sounds and when Cobb lighted a cigarette he remembered that night in the shantytown. The night Figueroa had come back.

He held out a crumpled pack of cigarettes to Joaquin. "Want one?"

"Sure."

The two men smoked in silence for a while. The sounds of mess stirred in the camp. A child cried. Two small boys raced across a clearing.

"Just like on the Rio Negro in the beginning," Joaquin said.

"Yeah. I guess so."

Small talk. But at least, thought Cobb, we're talking.

"Peter?"

"Yes."

"I blundered back there. I got those men killed." Joaquin took a last drag on the butt and then flipped it arcing into the night.

"They don't want me as their leader anymore. None of them. Not even Flor."

"I know."

"They want you. A *gringo*. An American. The marine."

"Well, then?"

"They want you, Peter."

78

"A priest. An American priest." Cobb shook his head. "Some way to run an army."

Joaquin got to his feet.

"Well, it wasn't my idea. I hate the idea of *anyone* taking over for me. I built this brigade, I've commanded it for four years. Suppose you and I meet with the men together. Tell them we agreed on a reorganization of command. That I will continue to give the orders but that you'll be my executive officer. Or commissar. Any damn title you want. That we'll work in tandem. That . . ."

Cobb got up too.

"Joaquin, get realistic, man. You screwed up. You threw everything you learned in four years right out the window and you got a lot of guys killed. You used to give those lectures yourself, right out of Chairman Mao's little book. 'When the enemy advances, we retreat. When he retreats, we follow. When he camps, we harass. When he consolidates, we scatter . . .' I remember it all by heart. How could you have forgotten?"

Joaquin turned sulky again.

"You really want to command, don't you? You really want the job."

"No, I *don't.* I told Flor and the men I'd *consider* it. I'm telling you that."

"All right, then," Joaquin said angrily, "I'll contact the Cubans. They'll fly people here in a day. They'd love to have this brigade."

Cobb stared at him.

"You'd bring them in? After all your talk about a national revolution? About Mirador being for the Miradorans?"

"Peter, in hell you make pacts with the devil."

Cobb nodded grimly. "Me before the Cubans."

The next morning Cobb took command of the brigade.

He gave no explanation to the men. He said simply he was acceding to their wishes. Joaquin, he said, would continue to be addressed with all due respect and would, in his absence or incapacitation, resume command. Joaquin listened, as solemn as the others, and said nothing.

For the next three weeks Cobb worked the brigade hard. And himself harder. At night he scribbled incessantly in his notebooks. He knew now, he thought, what he wanted to say about this war, about Mirador, about its people. The harder he worked, the more tired he was, the better the writing seemed to flow, as if all of his frustrations and fears and guilts were being expiated through the tip of a stubby pencil in a sweat-stained series of children's copybooks.

For three weeks he refused to let the brigade, or even a single man, go into action. Confidence had to be rebuilt. It had been shattered by Joaquin's vanity. Cobb was intent it would not be tested again until he was sure. Then, on the last day of the month, a scout came in to report a government platoon had been sent to garrison San Ysidro, but a day's march away. One platoon. A detachment large enough to cow the villagers, small enough to provide a tempting target for the brigade.

"We're in luck boys," he told the men. "We were patient, we waited, and now the damn fools have come to us."

San Ysidro tended to prove that however stupid the rebels might be, they had no monopoly on stupidity. The regime was becoming careless again.

"They think they have us beaten," Cobb said as the brigade prepared to march, "they think we're licked and scared and that we're running away. We're going to take San Ysidro back. And it'll be a long day before they send one lousy platoon that far out into the country again after we do."

San Ysidro, even the pouting Joaquin had to admit, was beautiful. They came in just before dawn in a long skirmish line across cultivated fields without even a preliminary mortar barrage. Cobb didn't want to wreck the village, didn't want to kill civilians. Thanks to two of his men who'd played at being drunks in the local *cantina* the night before, he knew exactly how the garrison was placed, and where. The fire fight was over in ten minutes. Twelve soldiers dead, the rest captured. The brigade lost two men. They took four machine guns and five trucks and a jeep. And perhaps 5,000 rounds of ammunition.

There was even a piano.

"Hell, yes," Peter Cobb said joyously, "get it on one of those trucks. We'll take it along."

And from then on, unless they were fighting or an enemy patrol was in the neighborhood, he played every night at sundown, medleys of old show tunes he remembered from Broadway musicals, as Flor and the rest of them and even Joaquin, sometimes, sang along.

These were the good times. And after the singing, after he had draped an old tarp over the tinny piano and the brigade had prepared for sleep, Cobb would again take up his pencil to write. Then, in one of those inexplicable coincidences, an American came to the camp. A minor Red Cross official, he'd been dispatched more as a gesture than anything else to investigate stories of atrocities in the undeclared war, and had stumbled onto the brigade when he was really looking for someone else three valleys away and had gotten lost. He turned out to be a man who was at Harvard two years behind Cobb.

A week later when he left, with a guide and pledge never to reveal what he had seen and where he had seen it, the man carried with him a stack of grimy notebooks which he promised to send off to a New York publisher once he was beyond the restraints of Miradoran censorship. Flor and Joaquin had wanted somebody to tell their story to the world. They wanted Peter Cobb to do it. And now, without much hope it would ever get back to America, or if it did, ever see print, Cobb agreed to let it go, a long note in a small bottle tossed into a vast sea.

Nine months later, Cobb himself left Mirador. He left under orders from a Jesuit provincial. But by then, he was ready to go. By then, the civil war had gotten to him.

It happened in Coptacl.

More than a year and a half had passed since the regime's troops had sacked Coptacl, raped its women, killed its men, kidnapped its children and crucified its priest. The brigade was the strongest it had ever been, nearly a thousand men, with more joining every day. The disaster of Joaquin and the tanks was forgotten. The brigade had become a large and mobile and very dangerous force. On a bright winter morning, following a series of successful skirmishes that had sent several companies of government regulars fleeing toward the coast, the brigade rested on the crossroads of two provincial highways. Five miles away, just beyond the horizon, was Coptacl. There were rumors a small garrison still hung on there stubbornly. Cobb ordered two hundred men under Joaquin to take the town, leave a detachment behind, and rejoin him for a continuation of the drive without fretting about trouble on the Coptacl flank. Joaquin gave a mock salute and he and his men piled into their trucks.

Through the morning there was desultory firing but when noon came and Joaquin was still not back, an annoyed Cobb climbed into a jeep with Flor and two riflemen and drove over there. Even before he got to the town he knew something was wrong.

The jeep skidded into the square and stopped; Cobb's feet hit the ground even before the jeep had halted. Along the far wall, what was once the sugar warehouse, a straggly line of bodies lay in the dust. Uniformed bodies. Joaquin came out of one of the houses and saw Cobb.

"Mission accomplished. Thirty-four enemy dead. No prisoners. Our casualties, three wounded. Not bad for a morning's work, eh?"

Cobb strode toward him.

"What the hell is this, Joaquin? These men weren't killed in a fight."

"No, you're right. They were executed. You remember this town, don't you, Peter? Where they raped the women and stole the children?"

"Of course I remember it. How could any of us forget?"

Joaquin gestured with a slender hand toward the dead troops. "Poetic justice. When they surrendered, the women in the town wanted me to turn them over to them. I didn't think it proper. Instead, I had them shot."

"We don't shoot prisoners, Joaquin," Cobb said coldly, "we never have."

"This is Coptacl, Peter." His eyes were cold.

Cobb shook his head. Jesus, he thought, it doesn't get any better, does it? Only worse.

Then he heard Flor's voice calling.

He trotted toward the church. She was standing just outside the churchyard. When he got to her she said, "Peter, there."

On the same stone cross where the government troops had crucified the village priest nearly two years before hung the body of a young man in uniform. The bars of a lieutenant were on his shoulders. His hands and feet were fastened to the cross by barbed wire. A length of wire encircled his head at the temples.

Cobb looked around behind him in a helpless fury.

Joaquin was smiling.

The title of the book Cobb had written about Mirador, its war and its people was *Speculations*.

BOOK III

BOSTON

10

The Jesuit provincial of New England, the Very Reverend Malachy Hanlon, had only once been accused of a dangerous tendency toward social liberalism and he had long since repented and been forgiven. His one aberration, and even his critics saw it as such, occurred earlier in the seventies when he had rashly composed a pastoral letter tepidly in favor of the busing of black children into the schools of Irish South Boston and the Italian neighborhoods of the North End. The resulting violence, those vacant pews at Sunday mass, and a drastic falling-off of collections, basket donations, endowments, and other revenues, had shaken Hanlon badly, convincing him of the wisdom of pious silence in any future controversy. Yet Father Hanlon was neither cruel nor callous. Simply prudent. He had, in fact, only recently if unknowingly manifested his humanity by saving the life of Peter Cobb.

One of Hanlon's bright young men, a Jesuit with intellectual pretensions, had months before called his superior's attention to rumors that some local "wild man," as Cobb was called, was about to publish a subversive little tract that sailed perilously close to the Marxist wind. Although he was now assigned to the Jesuit missions and no longer directly a concern of the New England Province, the man had studied and been ordained under Father Hanlon and there remained a certain, though vague, residual sense of responsibility for the fellow.

"My sources at *America* tell me this Cobb ought to be pulled up short. Things are just too chancey in Latin America right now to have some young firebrand issuing his own encyclicals and stirring up the politicians against the Church," the younger priest declared, pursing his thin lips in distaste and anticipating avidly the notable rage of his superior.

Hanlon never read *America*, the Jesuit monthly. Spiritual reading, *The Boston Globe*, and *Time* magazine were quite sufficient. But if they were already gossiping at *America* about Cobb's book the rumors would soon be common coin.

85

"Had the book been cleared?" he asked.

"Apparently not."

The era when clerical writers begged the *permissu superiorum,* the imprimatur, the "nothing objectionable" of the *nihil obstat* from higher authority was, unhappily, long in the past. So many men had abandoned Orders following Paul VI's disastrous policy of leniency that even a Jesuit provincial was forced to turn the occasional blind eye to all but the most blatant irregularity.

"What's the damned thing about?" Hanlon demanded.

His aide provided an enthusiastically inaccurate summation. He had once served briefly with Cobb and disliked his manner.

"Cobb apparently got in with a bad crowd down there. The worst sort: revolutionaries; prostitutes; terrorists; the professional poor. Swallowed the anti-government line entirely. The book's a mishmash of high-flown poetry and half-baked pinko politics. A wonder the local generalissimo hasn't kicked him out of the country by now."

Better if he had, Hanlon told himself.

"Is this a book that's likely to sell? Cause a stir?"

The younger priest permitted himself a discreet chuckle.

"Hardly."

Hanlon had not achieved his current eminence by swallowing whole the conclusions of younger men. Probably this Cobb and his book would sink without a trace. Still, if they were chatting about it over port at *America* . . .

That evening Father Hanlon phoned a very senior colleague at the headquarters of the Jesuit missions in New York to alert him to the potentially embarrassing activities in Mirador of one of his young priests. Within a month a startled and reluctant Peter Cobb had been hustled into a tourist seat in a Pan American jet heading for New York via Miami and, in a series of retreat houses and Jesuit seminaries, handed on from one grave and disapproving superior to another, none of whom seemed quite clear just what it was he had done.

Later, when Judson Riis had turned his "little" book into a national best seller and put his face on the cover of *Time,* Father Hanlon wondered righteously whether he wouldn't have been wiser to leave the fellow squatting down there in the jungle, covered with green mold and ten thousand miles away from the nearest television talk show. In irritation Hanlon had conjured up this ultimate exile, the innocuous job of ministering as chaplain to a bunch of college boys.

Neither Hanlon nor the disgruntled "chaplain" knew that Cobb had been ticketed for "chastisement" by the same goon squad that had dealt with his friend Figueroa and in the very same imaginative fashion: the introduction of roaches into his eyes.

Father Hanlon, to his own surprise, had thanked young Cobb more profusely than was called for when he agreed to take the Harvard job. They had only a brief interview. And Hanlon, who held all the cards, who spoke from a position of inarguable and righteous authority, was the nervous partner in the dialogue, rather than Cobb, the man in trouble. There was something about Cobb he didn't like, something that, silly even to think it, frightened Malachy Hanlon.

Harvard, rather than the Society of Jesus, would provide quarters. A reflection, perhaps, of relative liquidity. A Jesuit school, Boston College, slumbered just outside the city on Chestnut Hill. It was there Peter had met and been inspired by old Bergé, now dead, where he had first wrestled with the magnificent, challenging paradoxes of faith. Boston College had generously offered hospitality, but Boston College was the past, a chapter closed. Surely his superiors considered Harvard and the chaplaincy a conveniently isolated beach on which a troublemaker could safely be stranded. The choice was his, to sulk his way through the unwanted assignment, in which he clearly read punishment, or to do what he had always done, throw himself enthusiastically into the task.

If they insisted he tend to whatever spirituality still resided among the young at Harvard then he would live his life at Harvard, giving his work a full measure of energy and resource. Who knew whether, out there in the teeming Yard, there might not be another Peter Cobb, young, savage, confused and questioning, looking for another guide like Diskin, another mentor like Bergé, another blurred and twisting road map toward wisdom? If such a boy existed, Cobb owed it to him to be on call, his door open.

It was the fan letter from the whiskey priest in Cleveland that spurred Peter to start writing a second book. And it had been a thousand such letters, ten thousand, that had alarmed Father Malachy Hanlon. Hanlon had his spies. He knew what was going on, what had happened since Cobb's book soared to the top of the best seller list. How many times had he seen Cobb's face on television, read about him in magazines, been handed sheafs of review clippings from newspapers. Now something else was happening, something more ominous than the publicity being generated by this arrogant, subversive young priest.

Young men applying to the seminaries had begun to use Cobb's name, Cobb's book, as the basis for vocations. Finally, they eagerly informed their interviewers, the Church seemed relevant once more. Cobb was proving that a young priest *could* make a difference. That there was more to being a priest than mumbling prayers and hearing confessions and consecrating wafers. There was now a more significant role for young men of the Church, active, exciting, meaningful. Hanlon shuddered. Mass hysteria, that's what it was, frighteningly akin to the "worker priest" movement that had swept France and Belgium a generation before and that had led not to sanctity but to sacrilege. Now it seemed to be happening all over again. Hanlon shuddered. That was all they needed, a whole generation of glamorous pinkos like Peter Cobb taking Holy Orders!

And now, worst of all, whispers that this troublesome, aggravating Cobb was writing another book. It was time, *past* time, Hanlon concluded, for another little chat with Peter Cobb.

They met in Hanlon's lavish, wood-paneled office. The provincial had decided against bluster. He would try to reach Cobb by reminding him of just what he *was*. Not a writer of pamphlets, but a priest of God.

Malachy Hanlon knew that he was a dull man. He had none of Cobb's background, his style. But Hanlon was not stupid.

"Look, there's any variety of Jesuits," he said now, his natural rancor subordinated to wheedling. "They do their jobs. They enjoy their little avocations. Nothing wrong about it. Nothing at all. There's this Italian feller down in Brooklyn. Runs the damned aquarium. Brilliant feller. Goes deep-sea diving, knows more than I care to know about whales copulating and skin cancer on lobster. The emperor of Japan writes him letters. They correspond about jellyfish or some such. Feller has all the charm in the world. Like that froggie Cousteau on the television. You get me?"

"Yes," Cobb said, not sure that he did.

Hanlon leaned forward.

"Well, then that's the point. This feller in Brooklyn writes his learned theses about codfish and goes about wearing flippers and goggles and no one raises a stink about it. Because, y'see, Cobb, at bottom he's still the one thing he was born to be . . . a priest! The rest of it's dressing on the old salad, boy. The rest of it doesn't mean a thing . . ."

Cobb nodded. He decided against defending himself at this point. Let Hanlon weave his net first.

"Take Teilhard de Chardin. Closer to your line of country. A writer. A thinker. Mind, he's not my cup of tea. But there are those who think him the biggest thing since Aquinas. I met him once. Right here in Boston. Skinny feller, all bones and sinew."

"Yes?" Cobb said, seeing now where Hanlon was heading.

"Well, that's the point. Even Teilhard, with all his fancy friends and

88

grand airs, all his academic honors and gaudy doctorates, he remained what you and I and he are at bottom and always will be: a priest. You see that, don't you?"

"Father," Cobb asked coldly, "are you suggesting I'm no longer functioning as a priest? I am, you know."

Hanlon had to make a nearly physical effort to control his anger.

"I'm sure you are, Cobb. Sure you are."

"Well?"

"But you're writing again."

"Yes."

"Same sort of thing?"

"It's early days. Barely taken shape as yet." Peter knew he was being evasive. So did Hanlon.

"But the same message? Activism? Revolution? Discord?"

Cobb smiled. "Right now I'm researching the Crusades, Father. Hardly a controversial theme."

Hanlon grunted. He was getting nowhere. He decided to drop the *politesse*.

"And will you submit it for approval?"

Cobb shook his head. "I don't think so. Not unless I'm ordered."

When Cobb left the handshake was perfunctory, chilly. Peter realized he was skating on exceedingly thin ice. Hanlon knew he had been defied. This new book, if it really were another *Speculations*, could fan flames that were still under control, but barely. The provincial had visions of young Jesuits around the world picking up M-16s and going into battle. Damn! Why had Cobb been imposed on *him*? Why was Cobb *his* problem?

That night Malachy Hanlon wrote a personal letter to Rome. That same night Peter Cobb dined with friends. The Salomons.

Peter Cobb liked Jews. Kurt Salomon, the Talmudic man at the theology school, was perhaps his closest friend at Harvard. Epstein, his editor at Dorset House, patient, wise, pragmatic, was a Jew. Cobb sat now in Salomon's book-lined study, sipping beer from a can, watching Kurt watch the Red Sox on television, enjoying the smells wafting from the kitchen where Rosa Salomon was preparing what he knew would be another epic meal.

"The Red Sox," Salomon said hopelessly, as a promising rally pinched out with his team still two runs behind, "are the true wandering tribe. The Yankees and the Orioles hold the cities and the forts. The Red Sox are leaderless in the desert. Moses has lost his way, Aaron is nowhere to be found, and they lack right-handed power."

Salomon was huge, bearded, jolly—except when suffering through another losing season with the local baseball team. He worried about the Red Sox and his wife worried about Peter Cobb.

"So skinny, Peter. They don't feed you. The Pope should realize even a priest needs a wife. To cook if nothing else."

Cobb laughed. "If you live in a rectory there's always a cook. She doesn't actually have to know anything about cooking, just be the canonical age."

"And what's that, the canonical age?"

Her husband answered.

"Too old to do anything but cook."

Salomon regarded his guest. "And is this the uniform of the day for Jesuits this season? Sneakers and a track suit?"

"I was rowing. Even Jesuits take off their vestments when they row."

Salomon shook his head.

"To row on the Charles when you could be sitting comfortably in right field in Fenway Park, or right here in front of the tube. 'Tis a puzzlement. All that sweating, those blisters, that silly little boat."

"To work off Rosa's cooking," Cobb said, "the only reason."

Rosa Salomon beamed, leaned over to kiss his cheek, and returned happily to her kingdom in the kitchen.

Kurt turned serious. "How goes the writing?"

Cobb shrugged. "You know. A second book. Always difficult to get it started."

"But more of the same. Not some new tack?"

Cobb shook his head.

"Even the working title is the same, *More Speculations*. There's so much I didn't say the first time around, so much Dorset House cut out. The subject promised to be sufficiently arid even at a hundred and eighty pages."

"But it wasn't arid at all. A delightful book. An important book. I envy you that book, Peter. Really I do."

"Thanks. Coming from you that means a lot. But this incredible sale, it bothers me. I have a sense of people plunking down their money and asking for it and then never reading it. Or reading it and not having the foggiest of what I was trying to say."

"Nonsense! You write beautifully. With great clarity. Of course it's a difficult thesis, but certainly you never left the literate layman straggling along behind in the dust."

Salomon had proved a tower of sustenance when Hanlon, the Jesuit provincial, had turned so sour. Kurt Salomon knew that Cobb was permanently in the bad graces of senior clerics who considered him an intellectual upstart whose book evoked dangerous deviations from the mainstreams of serious Catholic thought. He knew they had done what they could: barred him from further public appearances.

"No more damned talk shows, no more newspaper interviews, no more magazine profiles," Hanlon had thundered, in a glacial sequel to their conversation.

Kurt Salomon knew all this. And now Kurt, at Peter Cobb's request, would be asked to read this latest manuscript of his, softening a line here, suggesting a deletion there, a crisply hard line of resistance somewhere else. He was a Jew who had loved Cobb's first, slim book and the young man who wrote it and he did not want him to go so far he would be destroyed by an institution to which Cobb owed eternal allegiance.

Still, but for different reasons and lacking specific knowledge, Salomon sensed trouble coming. He got up heavily from his recliner and went to the wall of books, taking down a well-thumbed volume.

"Peter," he said, searching for a passage, "in the fifteenth century Savonarola made himself a pain in the ass going about the country preaching goodness, decency, justice, faithfulness to vows. He attacked immorality and injustice and mendacious men, in the Church and without. Today he is rather a hero to most people. But not then. Listen to what Pastor says about him:

"'In his burning zeal for the reformation of morals he allowed himself to be carried away into violent attacks on men of all classes, including his superiors, and he completely forgot that, according to the teaching of the Church, an evil life cannot deprive the Pope or any other ecclesiastical authority of his lawful jurisdiction.'

"Note well what he says, that even when a Pope or 'other ecclesiastical authority' is proved to be inarguably evil, not just naughty or frivolous or addicted to the Red Sox, those wicked men still possess legitimate authority and cannot be attacked. Listen to this even from Cardinal Newman about poor Savonarola: 'He thought too much of himself, and rose up against a power which no one can attack without injuring himself. No good can come of disobedience; that was not the way to become the apostle of either Florence or Rome.'"

Cobb threw back his head and laughed. "So now you have me running for apostle of Florence."

"And Rome," Salomon said, "don't overlook Rome."

"Well, I'm not. And I'm not running for Father Coughlin, either."

"I should hope not." Then, closing the book, and more seriously, Salomon said, "But remember what happened to Savonarola, this good man who was trying to get everyone to be good again."

Cobb nodded. "They burned him."

"Yes," said Kurt Salomon, "that they did."

Back in his apartment, Cobb picked up the letter again and reread it:

Dearest Peter:

I am sending this brief and breathless letter of admiration along to your publishers since I haven't the foggiest how to reach you otherwise. *Speculations* is a lovely and touching book, even for a Godless illiterate like myself. It so clearly focuses for me, and I'm sure from the Best Seller lists for thousands of others, the tremendous dilemma you and men like you, if such exist, face in trying to hammer out a decent middle ground between your religious duties and your responsibilities as a man. I am awed by your surehandedness. What in the world would Tom Hathaway think of you now? Where, I wonder, has Tom fled? I think of you often and with great fondness. If you have not forgiven me long ago for my bitterness and abrupt goodbyes, I ask you to do so now. God bless you, Peter. As always.

It was signed Kiki Loomis Oldham.

Who, he wondered, was Mister Oldham? Did they have children? Was Kiki happy? Through the half-opened door a warm breeze stirred the single page of blue stationery on which she had written him.

Whether heterosexual or homosexual, a priest is as aware of the intense pull of his sexuality as other men of his age. If he has entered a seminary or a pre-seminary prior to having experienced a sexual relationship, it is normal for him to wonder more or less frequently what, if anything, he has been missing. Peter Cobb *knew*.

He lay now on the lone twin bed of his Harvard bedroom, wearing a pair of cotton boxer shorts, uncovered even by a sheet against the oppressive summer heat, smoking a cigarette and remembering Kiki Loomis and those days, and nights, when she was so terribly sure they were in love and he sometimes suspected she was right. Perhaps the fault had been his, that inability to give himself with the same enthusiastic abandon Kiki found not only easy but instinctive. He admired her reckless openness then; her generosity now. Kiki was not only forgiving him but praising his work and apologizing for faults she never had. Compared to Kiki, how selfish he had been, how self-oriented, how coldly intent on what he wanted to the exclusion of her needs, her desires, her love.

He thought of her as she must be now, a forty-year-old woman, quite possibly battling weight and gray hair and varicose veins and all the other marks of age's cruel, inexorable erosion. But on this hot night in his narrow bed it was not the forty-year-old he saw or remembered, not the writer of this silly, generous, exuberant fan letter, but the Kiki of twenty years before, every curve and plane and loving orifice of her familiar, impulsive, responsive body, the unfinished loveliness of her face, the smell of her hair, sweet and distinctive as mown grass, the taste of her mouth, the darting pleasure of an avid, searching tongue.

Kiki, twenty in memory, faded into a tumbling, disturbing erotic imagery of other women, other bodies, other faces. Good Lord, but he had been tempted! A healthy young man in the subtropics—the extraordinary attraction of young girls conjured up in the cuisinart of mixed blood that was Montevideo, Mirador. Cobb was neither stone nor saint.

Joaquin, taking pity on him in the January heat, before the fighting began, had lured him into a few days' holiday in a friend's condominium on the beach at Mirador. The girls, as in the song, tall and tanned and young and lovely. Brown legs and backs and arms and breasts glistening wet from the sea, oiled and slick against the sun, languorous from the heat.

Lighting the lamp on his night table Peter sat up, trying to break the mood.

All that had been his, or available to him, as it was to most men. He had turned from it. No one had twisted his arm, no psalm-singing evangelist had lured him, no authoritarian family had pointed him toward Holy Orders and pushed. He had understood the terms of the bargain from the very first. One variety of love, physical and transient, bartered for another, spiritual, deep, eternal. A fair trade-off, he told himself, an honorable contract.

To every thinking man, even the most convinced, the firmest, the most dedicated, occurs the occasional doubt. If we never doubted, how could we ever be sure? Yet such doubts were no less disturbing for their rarity. Cobb was not immune. Suppose, he sometimes wondered, just suppose there is no God, no heaven or hell, no life but this, suppose all of the rubrics and the rituals and the praying and the sacrifices—and they damned well *were* sacrifices!—were all meaningless. Wouldn't the cynic's laugh be on him, on those like him. Suppose when we die we don't know that we're dead because beyond this, there is . . . nothing?

It was at such despairing moments that Cobb and other Cobbs through the centuries had cried aloud their faith, their passionate belief that went beyond reason, damping down desire and burying doubt in the consoling knowledge that another, an extraordinary man, two thousand years before, had given testimony to this faith of theirs, nailed to a convict's cross.

Cobb thought for a few moments of that cross. And of a stone cross in Mirador. And slept.

11

Popes and kings and heads of state and men like Charles Cobb maintain a certain standard when they travel. Telexes chatter their intentions, subordinates smooth their paths, computers determine their itineraries, airports clear runways and hotel managers empty entire floors. C.C.'s company ran a small fleet of planes, with their own markings. One of them had flown into Logan that afternoon and the limo was there to take Mr. Cobb and his lady to the Ritz-Carlton, which is the best hotel in town and where they would occupy, for less than a day, the best suite. He was in Boston on business. He would use the occasion to see his only son, his major disappointment. It was not fair, Cobb thought, not fair at all to be deprived this way of a son. It was one of several reasons why he hated the Roman Catholic Church.

"Don't worry about it," the woman said from the door of her bedroom when Cobb told her he would be dining with his son, "I've always liked Boston. If there's a new play trying out in town I'll go to that. Then you and Peter can have your talk and I'll meet you back here after. We can have a drink downstairs later if you're not tired."

"Good," Charles Cobb said. She was a sensible woman. She had been his mistress for many years and she had never been trouble, which was more than you could say for most wives, for most women. Even his son liked her. But it was always awkward to have them meet and there were things he wanted to say to Peter that were best said alone. Helen Gatewood had been an actress. She was in her forties now, a big, handsome woman with wonderful legs and the smoothest skin and dark hair that curled naturally and owed nothing to pomades and fixatives or to those awful pink and blue plastic things women wore in their hair. Helen had been with Charles since before his wife died. When Nan was dying he had needed somebody, had needed Helen.

Charles Cobb and his son were not close. In late October Cobb senior

95

had telephoned Peter from Chicago. Dinner was to be at eight. In the hotel. The dining room of the Ritz is up a broad flight of stairs from the mahogany and the heavy carpets of the lobby. The best tables are at the long windows that give on Boston Common. Charles Cobb's table was one of these. His son was waiting for him there. He had been there for several minutes, amusing himself by watching the other tables, the splendid, stately old Boston ladies, perhaps among the last women in the world who wore hats indoors, the plump, monied movie people there to premiere a film, the smooth, talcked and tweedy bankers and publishers and lawyers of old Boston. Peter Cobb was the only man in the room in clerical black.

His father saw him right away and came toward him, a captain and an under-captain scurrying in his wake on polished shoes. Charles Cobb extended a dry, lean hand, his narrow, intelligent face tightening as he noticed his son's collar, then unexpectedly brightening, expanding to see his face.

"Father, you look well. And the Duchess?"

"Thank you, well. Helen is at the theater. Sends her regrets."

"Of course," his son said, the amiable fiction observed.

Waiters hovered. Charles Cobb explained to one of them how his martini was to be prepared. A methodical man, accustomed to issuing instructions, accustomed to having them carried out. His son, easier, ordered vodka on the rocks.

"So you're in costume," Charles Cobb said. "I thought there was more license about such matters currently."

"Oh, there is. Some of us have gone all tweedy. I thought I owed it to you to show up in uniform."

His father responded with a dry, mirthless grin.

"You've always been considerate, Peter."

It was the standard jousting of their intermittent meetings. For several years they had not met at all, had neither spoken nor corresponded. Religion had come between father and son. Men like Charles Cobb tended to live their sons' lives for them, seeing in their sons younger facsimiles of themselves, full of rich promise, offering the potential for extending their own years, for denying their own mortality. To have sons was to possess the future. To lose a son like Peter to the superstitious medievalism of an alien sect truncated his own life, set limits, narrowed options. Ah, he thought once again as their drinks arrived, what a shameful, stupid waste.

He did not say this. He had said it too many times. There was now between the two men an unspoken pact, there were areas around which they trod cautiously. Superficially C.C. accepted Peter's priesthood as his son accepted the Duchess, a nettle to be grasped lightly.

"Your book's still selling, I see. The *Times* has it on the list for what, twenty weeks now?"

Peter nodded.

"Exactly twenty weeks. Authors tend to be rather precise about such things."

"As do their fathers."

Speculations had been published six months before. The Cobbs had not seen one another in that half year, not face to face. Each had seen the other on television, in the press, had heard the other's voice over the radio. Charles Cobb had been a famous man for more than thirty years. His son's celebrity was decidedly more recent.

"You haven't read it, I assume."

His father hesitated, then lied that he had not. "It was good of you to send it to me. Thoughtful of you to have dedicated it to your mother."

Peter knew the question had been answered. "Jane read it," he said, "she sent me a cable praising its virtues and assuring me she didn't understand a word of it."

Old Cobb grunted.

"Your sister is constitutionally incapable of reading anything that doesn't fit between the covers of V*ogue* or *Town & Country*."

Peter laughed.

"Does she write you?"

"Oh yes, the duty note, every month without fail. Except for those months when she doesn't."

Jane Cobb Orsini lived in Milan, occasionally with her husband, an Italian industrialist who built fast automobiles and drove them the same way. She had been in Italy for six years now, she was thirty-two, and had become a reliable staple for the slick gossip magazines of Europe and America. One of the latter, in tribute both to her physique and to her colorful exploits, had christened her "Crazylegs" Cobb. The nickname had stuck. Charles Cobb found it demeaning and raged when it was uttered in his presence. She had two children and, if one could believe the reports, at least as many lovers. Orsini was hardly in a position to complain. His own extramarital adventures were neither rare nor covert.

What had he done to deserve two such children, old Cobb often wondered. How brilliantly they had both begun, how well had Nan raised them. And now . . .

The captain had brought the menus, heavy and leather-bound. Charles Cobb waved his away.

"I know precisely what I want," he said.

"Don't you always?" Peter asked innocently.

Cobb took no offense. It was true. Great companies like Cobb Industries were not built by men unsure of what they wanted. Single-mindedness was their strength. The sort of quality you found in corporate chairmen. And in men who founded and led great religions. Cobb, of course, did not draw this particular parallel. A foreign religion had taken his son, a foreign spiv had taken his daughter. The Cobbs had been Americans since the French and Indian Wars, with all the chauvinism and xenophobia such a weight of generations entailed. Cobb personified bias. Institutionally in the bone, and now, because of his son and daughter, personally and fiercely. He did not like Italy, he did not like Italians. They had produced Gigi Orsini, they had exported their faith. There had been no way of keeping Jane Cobb insulated against the Latin charm of an Orsini. But one would have thought an American WASP secure at Harvard from the predations of foreigners.

Dinner came. Scrod for Charles Cobb.

His son laughed. The old man assumed an attitude of mock indignation. "In Boston one eats scrod."

"When in Rome . . ."

"Don't spoil my meal, Peter. I prefer to ignore the existence of Rome."

"But it won't go away, Father. Eternal City, all that."

His father pushed at the fish. Then, a marginally different note in his voice, he said:

"This new man of yours. This new Pope. What do you make of him?"

Peter Cobb resisted the easy evasion with which a priest would normally turn away the question. His father was not the sort of man to make small talk, to exchange pleasantries. His father was not the man to pose polite questions about new Popes out of idle curiosity. His father, customarily, did not, he knew, give a damn about Popes, new or old.

"I'm as intrigued, and impressed, as everyone else. We really don't know yet. The experts are all issuing hourly bulletins, of course. I don't think they really know any more than the rest of us. I've read whatever he's written that's available in English and Latin. Not too much. I've tried to stay in touch with his pronouncements since the election. When he was here last month I heard his mass on Boston Common. An impressive figure. Charismatic. I can believe all that, easily. I was as moved as anyone else. But do I know him, understand him, can I tell you which way he'll take the Church? No."

Cobb nodded. His son had an analytic mind, crisp, disciplined. Whatever their differences Charles Cobb had never underestimated his son's brain. Only his inclinations.

"Why, Father?"

"This book of yours. This . . . best seller . . ."

"Forgive me that, Father. Not my fault. Social commentary is supposed to sell a few hundred copies to libraries and colleges. Had I known . . ."

"It's caused trouble."

Peter Cobb smiled. "Well, some of my more traditional colleagues have been politely critical. Some, not so polite. When you attempt to mine new ground you always . . ."

"I don't mean criticism in learned journals."

"Oh?"

Charles Cobb was an extraordinary man. In many ways. He was nearly seventy and except for sunglasses and shooting glasses and ski goggles, he did not have to wear spectacles. This advantage, however, involved complementary handicaps. He could not now whip off nonexistent glasses, polish them on his breast pocket handkerchief, stall for that ripe moment during which clever responses to difficult questions are phrased.

He pushed his plate aside impatiently. His son noted that the scrod had been eaten. Whatever was disturbing his father had not taken away his appetite.

"I have sources in Italy," he began.

"You hate Italy," Peter said.

Cobb shrugged.

"Our government trades with Communist China, with fascist banana republics, with South Africa and Zimbabwe, with Israel and Syria. We sell missiles to the Arabs and anti-missile devices to the Jews. I do not believe it irrational that Cobb Industries, despite my parochial reservations, do occasional business with wops."

Peter Cobb looked pained.

"Father, most people have given up even Polish jokes."

"What? What?" Clearly he was confused by this irrelevant reference to the Poles.

"I mean, Italians aren't wops. Not anymore."

"Nonsense, wops are wops, spics are spics, niggers are—"

"Father!"

Cobb waved an attenuated hand. "Peter, this isn't a discussion of linguistic distinctions."

He sobered. "No."

It was futile to argue such matters with the old man. Cobb was a regular department store of prejudice. He hated something about nearly everyone. He was an educated man, a university graduate, in many ways a subtle, cultivated man, which made his bias more difficult to accept. But it was a losing fight. Perhaps, Peter often thought, perhaps one day he will understand, one day, in that repugnantly trendy phrase, his consciousness will be raised. Until then, his son did not intend to batter hopelessly against that wall of prejudice.

His father resumed.

"I have information that your . . . organization . . ."

"The Jesuits?"

"No," said his father, distaste palpable in his voice. "The Church in Rome, the Vatican, is . . . displeased with you."

Peter Cobb laughed.

"Father, you amaze me. How could you *possibly* have such information?"

The question delighted Cobb. He gloried in his own shrewdness, the canny, instinctive sense that had made him such a respected, such a feared adversary in business.

"I hear things," he said, purposely vague, "people tell me things."

His son shook his head.

"But why should you care? You've never before taken an interest in what I do, except critically."

Charles Cobb snapped his fingers for the captain. He wanted a cigar. That negotiation completed, the dramatic pause suitably drawn out, he said:

"I just don't want the bastards ganging up on you."

Helen Gatewood, in a long robe, had mixed the ritual drinks and now she came into Charles Cobb's bedroom, kissed him lightly on the forehead, handed him one of the glasses, and asked, "Did you tell him?"

"Oh, yes."

"And?"

"He is dubious about my sources. He does not think there is anything to it."

She sat down in one of the deep easy chairs. Cobb was still dressed, still thinking about dinner with his son. He turned now, his face brightening at the sight of her.

"The play. Any good?"

She laughed. "Ah, well, it probably won't run. But for an evening in Boston, quite nice."

He lifted his glass in tribute. "You're a wonderful girl, Helen. I drag you to Boston and then leave you to make your own way through the evening. Will you forgive me?"

"You were forgiven the moment you said I was wonderful."

His face darkened.

"Peter is a very proud boy. I don't think he quite realizes how powerful, how remorseless this church of his can be."

"Oh, Charles, how do you know anything about the Catholic Church? You've never taken the slightest interest . . ."

He looked at her steadily.

"I am interested in power, my dear. And for all my strictures, Rome is power. My son was a fool to enlist but now that he has, I worry. Rome's mills grind slowly but exceedingly fine. I would not like to see Peter milled into grist."

"Charles, he's a very intelligent man. He's forty. He wrote a wonderful book. Peter knows what he's doing."

"Does he?" Cobb asked. "Does he?"

She reached out a slender hand to touch his.

"But of course. He's your son, isn't he?"

Helen Gatewood, the "Duchess," sincerely hoped so. Her lover's doubt unsettled her.

12

As he had told his father, Peter Cobb had seen this new Pope just once, and then at considerable distance, far across a crowded field as he said mass before a million people on Boston Common.

A new Pope and a strange one. In the dank cells of Cistercian monasteries, in the devout Catholic homes south of Eboli, in the hushed chanceries of great cities, and in the hearts and heads of 600 million of the faithful, Gregory was pondered, measured, considered and weighed. Dry-loined nursing nuns and randy young Dublin undergraduates inquired as to his background, his philosophy, his plans for the Church to which they all paid allegiance.

And it was not only Catholics who wondered. In the White House, in the Kremlin, in Downing Street and in the Palais d'Elysée, in Peking and in any number of grandiose Latin palaces more or less permanently occupied by colonels, Gregory was being assessed.

Now Peter Cobb, a mere priest, had had his opportunity to see the man and to draw conclusions.

The arguments about Gregory had begun the instant of his surprise election. He was a foreigner, not an Italian, therefore he was suspect. A liberal, not only a liberal, a radical! Implicit in his papacy was the promise of legalized abortion, married priests, women taking orders, an armistice with Kung, an opening to the Left, *rapprochement* with the Jews, the Protestants, the Eastern Church. All things were possible! No, insisted others. The man was a provincial, superstitious and, despite his relative youth, old-fashioned. He'd crack down on the liberals, bring back Latin, smash the abortionists and the women, straighten out the convents and tell the Jews and the Archbishop of Canterbury that if they wanted better relations, it would damn well be on Rome's terms.

No one really knew, of course. Perhaps not even Gregory, still stunned by his own election, knew in which direction the compass needle of his brand new papacy would eventually point.

Cobb, beset by his own problems, had no theories. Only curiosity.

Gregory had come to America as Popes seemed to do routinely these days, preaching and blessing and shaking hands, consulting and listening, advising and orating, calming down and stirring up, a regular Cook's Tour of personal appearances that had everything but a gig on the *Tonight* show or a televised little heart-to-heart with Mike Wallace. Cobb had his reservations about such caravans. In the old days Popes stayed at home behind the Vatican's walls, emerging occasionally to visit the poor and the orphans of Rome, to sojourn at their summer place, to wash the feet of beggars on Holy Thursday. Except when the French sent in an army and hustled the Pope over into protective custody at Avignon for a decade or two, Popes did not leave Italy, rarely strayed out of Rome. Cobb suspected that was how it should be. Distance lent enchantment, retained the mystery, cloaked the papacy in a decent, awesome dignity that it seemed to lose when these white-robed, supposedly austere and saintly men were forever tripping in and out of Boeings, putting up at hotels, working the crowds and shaking hands in the Rose Garden like any other politician with delegates at stake in the primaries. Old-fashioned of him, he realized, but it was how he felt. Up close what was a Pope but just another old man with an old man's shuffle, with brown spots on his hands, with a nose that turned red in the cold and a forehead that glistened with sweat in July. Sure, Saint Peter had traveled, but he was a fisherman, a recruiter, a pioneer. And look what happened to Peter when his travels took him round the bend of the Mediterranean and landed him in Rome. They killed him.

Cobb's titular superior, the Jesuit provincial of New England, had his ration of tickets to the various ceremonies on Gregory's itinerary. By some oversight, no invitations were issued to Peter Cobb. Had the tickets and the invitations arrived, Cobb would have sent them back, thrown them away, handed them out to faculty acquaintances curious to witness the spectacle. He had no wish to be there.

They had built a plywood altar on the Common, carpeted in scarlet underfoot, canopied in gold above against the rain, floodlighted against the dusk. The mayor had to go on television to explain that private offerings from Boston's faithful had financed the thing and that no tax monies were involved. The chief of police, a devout Catholic, muttered imprecations and set out in despair to map routes and reverse one-way streets to avoid the massive, historic traffic jams for which he, inevitably, would be blamed. And the clergy of Boston collectively polished its black shoes, starched its collars, aired out its vestments, and surreptitiously pocketed Instamatic cameras with which to immortalize the great occasion and their intimate role in its glory.

Cobb left them to it. He went rowing on the Charles.

Gregory, he knew, was an impressive man. He intended no discourtesy. This was no doddering old Italian who had made his way to the throne of Peter through the convoluted politics of the Vatican's inner circle. This was no Paul VI, so tired and beaten down and enfeebled toward the end that when they confronted him with yet another awful decision, another spiritual dilemma, another carping objection to his latest dictum on birth control, celibacy, or the use of Latin in the mass, he had, or so it was said, burst into helpless tears. This was no John XXIII, jolly, cunning, and perhaps just a bit reckless, unleashing on a Church not quite ready to digest it a recipe for change that would telescope the centuries and impose twentieth-century rationales on an institution still functioning at a seventeenth-century mentality. This no Pius XII, wringing his hands over the Jews while negotiating cynical concordats with Ribbentrop and Ciano, performing balancing acts of statesmanship and moral astigmatism that would have drawn from Cardinal Richelieu a gasp of admiration. This no John Paul I, smiling, waving, winning an immediate, emotional response to his humble assertion that 'twere better they had left him running the archdiocese of Venice, where he knew everyone, where he felt at home, where he had such doubts about his competence as he now expressed on his translation to Rome.

This was Gregory, a different man in a different time, cut from a different cloth.

As he had told his father, Peter Cobb had read, not deeply as yet, but broadly, in the small literature that had sprung up about Gregory since his startling and dramatic elevation to the papacy just six months earlier; had read, where they were available in languages he could grasp, Gregory's own writings. He was impressed by what he read, impressed by what he heard, impressed by what little he had seen of the new Pope on television.

For one thing, as Popes went, he was young, still in his fifties. Churches, like nations, are not enthusiastic about the election of young men. Young men are impatient, impulsive, subject to whim and to passion, they have illusions not yet battered out of them by defeat and disappointment, they lack the grand, the long view, which only age can clearly focus. Young men are rash, impetuous, impractical. Dangerous. Besides, chosen young and spared by providence, they tend to reign too long, to have too great an impact on institutions which, traditionally, are better served by older men with a briefer authority. Old men revere evolutionary change; young men ignite revolution.

Then there was the question of his nationality. It was all very well for a church that called itself "universal" to venture beyond the narrow national boundaries of Italy in its selection of cardinals. The Pope, however, was another thing entirely. Premier among his titles, his roles, his responsibilities, was that of "Bishop of Rome." How did one justify the election of a man who was not Roman, not even Italian, but an outlander from some obscure eastern corner of Europe, some polyglot bazaar where not even the natives were quite sure just what they were: Slav, Serb, Croat, emigré German, exiled Russian, Pole? Gregory was not one of "us" but one of "them."

Further, the question of his career, his life style, if you will. Extraordinary, even the skeptics had to admit, so extraordinary, some said, as to cast doubt on his fitness to serve and, more significantly, to lead. For one thing, and this frightened his critics, he had lived too long in the world. Blame that, said his advocates, on Hitler and on Stalin. When Gregory was still a boy, in that obscure "bazaar" they sniffed at, the Nazis had marched in, jack-booted and gray, clamping down on his small, feisty, vulnerable country a bleak terror that would prevail for six years, bridging his maturation from child to young man. What, precisely, demanded the cynical, had young Gregory been up to in those years? Runner for the underground, guerrilla fighter, saboteur, smuggler to safety of Jews, troublemaker? There were unseemly tales of a youthful romance with a young girl in the Resistance, whispers, even, of a teen-aged marriage, and of the girl's death under the torturer's ropes and boots and blades, a tragedy that had sent the young man careening headlong, thoughtlessly, into a premature application for Holy Orders. Such stories were silently ignored by Gregory, clucked at by the sensible, clutched at enthusiastically by the less charitable, the more malign. And what of his rise to churchly power in a country subsequently occupied and administered by Stalin's men? When a nation goes Communist, slaughters its priests and intellectuals and liberals by the tens of thousands, promulgates socialism, organizes state schools parroting the party line, permits a few churches to remain open by fiat and by sufferance as a sop to a restive people, how much backing and filling, how much trimming and compromising, must a man do to rise to monsignor, then to bishop, then to archbishop, finally to red-hatted cardinal, under that godless system? Just how cozy had Gregory been with the Communists after all? Gregory, clearly, had lived a strange life, had enjoyed a most curious career.

Cobb knew all these things, heard all these stories. And more. That the man had once thought of the stage as a career, that he wrote poetry and composed folk music, that he played the guitar and sang, around campfires to his own priests, at fairs and festivals. That he smoked cigarettes and enjoyed the wine of the country, that he climbed mountains and skied, that he swam in the rivers in mixed company, that several of his intimates were Party members, that he associated with intellectuals and read novels, that on a platform or over television he was a bit of a ham. That the Russians let him be because he was malleable. Better to indulge this jolly extrovert than to have him replaced by more sullen, less manageable men.

As he sat on the river in one of Larsen's borrowed shells, in that late summer in Boston, Cobb found himself thinking about Gregory, a man who seemed to be even more misunderstood by the Church than was Cobb himself. Past him, on the riparian freeways, most of Boston seemed to be flowing toward the Common, to a rendezvous of curiosity, of piety, of communion with Gregory, the new Pope who had come among them.

Suddenly, quite unexpectedly, Peter Cobb realized that he had been acting petulantly, like a child deprived of candy and made to stand in the corner. He grinned, thinking how accurate his father would find the portrait, how apt Peter's wry, honest, self-description. On both banks of the river Boston was hurrying to see the Pope. Cobb dipped one oar crisply into the river and spun his shell, heading it swiftly back to the old boat house.

Gregory had landed in America at a familiar port of entry, Logan Airport, a few miles, a few centuries, from Plymouth Rock. Once more, the Old World was visiting the New, another pilgrim had come among the savages.

This time, not in a 400-ton brigantine with sprung seams, but in a 747.

There was rain on Boston Common, not drenching but falling straight and windless, the sort of day the Irish call "soft," the worn brown grass of late summer turning oozy underfoot, the full-leaved trees dripping, pit-pat, pit-pat, a damp, murmured litany falling on umbrellas, heads, shoulders, on the disregarded swan boats in the pond. It had been a dry summer but Gregory seemed to have brought the rain; it would follow him to New York, to Washington, to Chicago.

Seeing the rain coming, Cobb did not bother to change out of his rowing gear, track-suit pants, blue with a gaudy stripe, T-shirt, the old crimson letter sweater retrieved from a locker and pulled on, sweat socks and sneakers. There was no money in his pockets and he borrowed a few dollars from Larsen, the boatman.

"Goin' to see the Pope?" Larsen sniffed, unimpressed.

"Well, I thought I would, yes."

Larsen shrugged. To his knowledge no Pope had ever rowed at Henley or even in the Dad Vail. To hell with Popes. But he gave over the money cheerfully.

Cobb took the "T" into town. It was like the day of a big football game, people excited, flushed, enthusiastic, hurrying lest they miss the kickoff, carrying cameras, picnic baskets, ponchos and blankets for the grass. At the Common station hawkers sold balloons and programs and dollar plastic buttons with the Pope's picture and brave scraps of bright ribbon.

Cobb was swept up in the crowd. No need to ask directions, they flowed instinctively, forcefully toward the plywood altar, already floodlit against the rain and the gloom of late afternoon. There was no need to be self-conscious about his clothes. There were people in shorts, in plastic garbage bags presumably rainproof, in suits, in tennis gear, in mini-skirts and the antiqued ivory dresses of proper tea parties, in raincoats and jeans. Some boys were bare-chested in the soft rain. Girls' breasts glided smoothly under damp T-shirts, their buttocks quivered under denim cut-offs. They were all going to see the Pope and there was no uniform of the day.

Still, Cobb was here as a spectator, just another of the million Bostonians drawn, as they might be to a parade, and not as a participant, duly robed and somber. He permitted the crowd to carry him along to within a few hundred yards of the altar and then, having to make an effort to do so, he broke away and grabbed the spindly trunk of a white birch and halted. Close enough. He was not dressed for the occasion, he was not functioning as a priest, he was a sightseer, one of the curious, one of the mob. He got his back comfortably against the tree and waited.

Then, above the rain, chat and hum and shouts, above the casual conversation of the thousands, there came a sound like rising wind, louder and louder, more and more powerful and insistent, and then no longer a wind but a roar that now became a chant: Gregory! Gregory! Gregory! The motorcade, red lights flashing, had turned into the Common from Commonwealth Avenue. Old ladies taking tea at the Ritz put down their spoons to listen. The flashing lights were closer now, the sound rising, submerging all. Gregory! Gregory! Gregory!

Bishops and cardinals and monsignors scurried about, busy as tugboats berthing a great liner. The TV crews had their lights on now and the rain fell harder, the Common all in gloom but the centerpiece of that makeshift altar, brilliant, glistening, klieged, a scene, it occurred to Cobb, as professionally—as dramatically—staged as any *son et lumière* at Versailles.

After what seemed inordinate delays, the figure of the Pope, white-robed and appearing tiny at this distance, mounted the carpeted steps to a sort of throne, turned, still standing, and waved. Gregory! Gregory! Gregory! came the responding chant, even louder, more powerful, more insistent. Cobb did not chant. Around him they were chanting, applauding, yelling, waving damp handkerchiefs. It went on for perhaps ten minutes, nervous clerics consulting wrist watches and pursing discreet lips. Gregory paid them no heed, but continued to wave. Finally, and very suddenly, the mob fell mute. The Pope spoke.

When he read the speech next day in the *Globe*, Cobb remembered having heard it all. On that afternoon on the Common in the rain, he remembered but a single line:

"I propose to you the option of love."

At last the mass began.

Around Cobb many of the people were kneeling in the mud, on the wet grass, on folded raincoats and damp newspapers. He continued to stand, his back against the birch, looking out over the thousands and thousands of heads and shoulders and backs at the elevated, floodlit platform on which Gregory re-enacted the tremendous, mysterious, loving sacrifice of his God. A chorus sang, flashbulbs exploded, the huge crowd roared its responses, Gregory's voice, accented but clear, reverberated across the lawns to echo against trees and traffic and tall buildings beyond.

Then, the mystical moment of transubstantiation, when the bread and wine were altered, literally, it was believed, into the body and blood of the Christ. A silence fell, muffling and palpable. Only Gregory's voice:

"This . . . is . . . My . . . Body."

Peter Cobb dropped to his knees in the slop of Boston Common to pray for Gregory, for Pedro and Flor and Joaquin, for his father and for Jane, for his mother's soul.

For himself.

And the voice of that tiny, inexpressibly distant white figure, echoed:

"I propose to you the option of love."

13

Churches, like governments and great armies, have their tables of organization, their ladders of priority, their old maids' ways of doing things. Thus it was that the letter from Rome came not straightaway to Peter Cobb in his post office box at Harvard, but through channels, a half dozen pairs of sanctified hands, until at last it reached the Very Reverend Malachy Hanlon, S.J.

Morning mass, *The Boston Globe* over breakfast, and his first Havana cigar illicitly, pleasurably behind him, Father Hanlon had barricaded himself for the morning's work behind his great mahogany desk. His secretary, an efficient young woman, had stacked the mail, this one letter conspicuously atop the pile, and now, having read it twice, Father Hanlon continued to stare at it as a man might regard a particularly loathsome insect on the tile of his bathroom.

As a prudent bureaucrat, Hanlon's first instinct was to review his own performance in the case, to determine whether he might himself have done something wrong. He thought back to the letter he had written the night after his confrontation with Cobb. Had the letter been a mistake? Had he said too much? Or too little? Should he have cracked down mercilessly on Cobb without reference to Rome, as senior churchmen were supposed to do? Should he have ignored Cobb as unworthy of his time? And Rome's patience?

Malachy Hanlon worried a cuticle and cursed Peter Cobb.

Such concerns, Hanlon told himself, were sufficient to irritate the most equable of men. His morning egg lay leaden and gassy on his stomach. The letter from Rome was exasperatingly vague, no hint of its actual import, only this slender, rather curt request. Hanlon was accustomed to second levels of meaning, to thirds. Subtle men are always suspicious of simple explanations. He picked up the letter a third time to read between the lines, search out double meanings, gauge the writer's true intent. In the end, bilious and out of patience, he rang for a senior aide.

"This man Cobb, the fellow we have at Harvard. They want to see him in Rome. A monsignor called Lonsdale, secretary to Cardinal Grassi."

"*Curia* Grassi?" the aide asked, clearly impressed.

Hanlon nodded ponderously, pretending greater knowledge than he had. It always did to keep subordinates guessing.

"And are we to scout up a replacement for Cobb at Harvard?"

Father Hanlon withered the man with a look.

"Cobb's there on ice," he said. "Since when was Harvard worth a priest?"

Winter came early to Boston. The first snow fell in November, the week one of Hanlon's people had handed Cobb his traveling orders. That same morning he had been out on the river, slushy with scum ice.

"That's it, Peter," Larsen the boatman had told him. "Don't want you holing one of these shells. Another week of this and it'll be fruz solid."

Cobb was still "Peter" to the boatman, not a priest or a celebrity but simply an old Harvard oarsman back on the Charles. There was no point of explaining what he had become. Larsen would have shrugged and gone back to talking about a new aluminum outrigger he was working on. Cobb hated to hang up his oars. It made spring seem so far off. Still, this early freeze might not be all that bad a thing. The second book was going better now, the false starts behind him, the writing moving ahead, the long hours in the stacks of Widener Library paying their dividends. Kurt Salomon was reading typescript as he went along.

"It's wonderful stuff, Peter. I wish I had your felicity with words. Lovely, just lovely."

"But . . . ?" Cobb said.

"Ah, well, of course there's a 'but.' Isn't there always when one writes seriously?"

The two men were sitting in the living room of Salomon's faculty house. The Game had been played that afternoon in sleet and driving rain and they had stayed through to the bitter, Yale-triumphant end, while Rosa Salomon remained rationally at home simmering the soup and the meaty stews she hoped would stave off pneumonia.

"What is it that bothers you?" Cobb asked. "The specifics or the whole tone of the thing?"

Salomon made eloquent gestures with his large hands. "Peter, you're taking on a large, unruly beast here, you know. Rather like tackling a grizzly bear with an air rifle and a jaunty optimism. Even your new title sends chills along my spine: *Holy Wars: Further Speculations on the Modern Church.* That word 'modern.' Your Church is two thousand years old. That's not so old as we Jews measure things, *arriviste*, in fact. But I suspect many of your more conservative colleagues break out in shingles and a cold sweat at this categorization of the Church as 'modern' or 'not modern.' Am I correct?"

Cobb nodded.

Salomon grunted. He tossed the typescript and his notes on the coffee table and stretched. His wife could be heard in the kitchen. Salomon had mixed hot buttered rums and he drained his now.

"Now then," Salomon said, "what about this Rome business? What more do you know?"

"Damned if I know what to think. If they were upset about *Speculations* or all the publicity they would have told Hanlon to give me a slap on the wrist or ship me off to Rome on the first plane. This is pretty leisurely, having me check in after the holidays, what, six weeks from now?"

"Torquemada wouldn't have waited six weeks, I'll grant you that."

"So you think it's the Iron Maiden, hot pincers, and the rack?"

"I'm a Jew. I'm paranoid, Peter. What else should I think?"

Rosa Salomon summoned them to the table and the talk turned to football and the depredations wrought upon fair Harvard by Yale that day.

And when, in mid-December, the Lonsdale response arrived to Peter's letter, it was bluntly unhelpful. No, there was no special preparation or reading Father Cobb should be doing. His travel arrangements sounded satisfactory. He should report to Lonsdale when he got to Rome.

So much, Peter Cobb thought, for composing "clever" letters to Vatican *monsignori*, even those with Anglo-Saxon surnames.

On Christmas Eve he said a midnight mass in the Catholic chapel. His "three and a half" devoted followers were there, fleshed out by a boozy, marginally unruly crowd of partygoers. Everyone else seemed to have gone home for the holidays, even his "curious" atheist. Cobb got through the mass quickly. One of the pretty, polo-coated young girls up front looked pale and he did not want her Christmas spoiled by being ill in church.

He spent a part of Christmas week with his father in Manhattan, an awkward passage. He understood his father would rather be with Helen Gatewood at her apartment. In deference to Peter, Charles stayed at home or the two men, father and son, dined at restaurants. Jane was in Italy.

"Says she's spending the holiday skiing. With the children. Apparently Nuvolari is driving fast cars in South Africa or somewhere."

"Nuvolari" was, of course, Gigi Orsini. Cobb could not recall ever hearing his father refer to Orsini by his own name.

"I assume we'll be brought up to date on both Jane and husband in the next issue of *People* magazine or one of those other dreadful sheets. They have an absolute affinity for having their pictures taken in exotic settings."

Peter was aware of his father's sacrifice of the Duchess for these few days and he had resolved not to bicker. Neither would he permit his sister to be pilloried in absentia.

"Jane's a good girl and he gives her a rotten time. You know that. She tries to make a life of what's left after Gigi has his sport."

"Don't sermonize at me, Peter. I'm too old for conversion."

Old Cobb hated his Italian son-in-law as he hated many things, including the Church that had taken his only son as surely as in the time before penicillin scarlet fever could take a child.

He and his son were dining, alone, in one of those exclusive men's clubs his father favored. Outside, on Park Avenue, snow fell. Not the fluffy snow of Boston, but the soggy snow of New York. Peter moved his feet uneasily under the table. Somewhere in the dining room an old man coughed, a glass tinkled, there was the murmur of ponderous, important men, stranded in the city and resentful of it, when they should be in St. Moritz, in Hobe Sound, at Lyford Cay. Men like his father.

"You brought the correspondence?"

Peter reached into his pocket and handed over the several letters ordering him to Rome. His father scanned them carefully.

"Lonsdale," he said, "odd name for a dago."

"He's English, I believe."

"Who works for the wops."

"He's Cardinal Grassi's secretary."

Charles Cobb's eyes brightened maliciously.

"Your inquisitor. He's the one who'll strike the match when you're at the stake. I can picture it now, all those little wops dancing about, rubbing their hands, holding up rosary beads, calling on you to repent your wickedness, to confess your sins. A scene right out of Salem. Witch hunts and hysterical little girls writhing about. Steam issuing from the earth, ominous clouds and thunder crashing."

"You sketch a delightful picture, Father. Goya couldn't have done it better."

Charles Cobb sipped at his claret.

"Peter, I told you months ago this was coming. If I seem amused by your predicament, believe me, I'm not. The damned dagos are on your case. Just as I said, as my sources informed me—"

"I survived in Mirador, Father," Peter said quietly, in a rare interruption.

"And damned fortunate at that, lining yourself up with the worst criminal element and writing tracts against the government. Wonder those spic colonels didn't just put you up against a wall."

"They did, to some of my friends. That 'criminal element' of mine."

Cobb stopped hectoring his son. His face grew solemn.

"I know that, Peter. Someone who read your book told me."

"Oh?"

Cobb went on now, scorn and pride mingled in his voice and the gaze with which he fixed his son.

"Whenever you've had an option in life, Peter, it seems to me you've taken the wrong road. Your conversion to Catholicism, your decision to take Orders, your behavior in Central America. Inevitably you've chosen the less attractive alternative, enlisted on the losing side. My point of view, of course. You obviously see it differently. When I learned what you were up to down there in Mirador, and I had hints of it even before your book came out, I knew you'd done it again. That's a stable government down there, not your cup of tea, perhaps, or even mine, but they run the country with a marginal efficiency, they keep the Reds in their place, they haven't kissed Castro on both cheeks or leased the navy yard to Russian subs. I'll grant much of what you say about them is true, that they're brutal, despotic, crooked. So are half the governments in the world with whom Washington has good relations."

"Which doesn't make them, or Washington, right."

"Granted. I have no love for our own government when it comes to that. My point is not political, Peter, it's personal. I don't want to see my only boy chewed up by Rome or by spics. I don't want the colonels pulling out your fingernails or the damned Dominicans threatening you with fire and brimstone."

"We agree on that," Peter said wryly.

They went on to the club brandy after that until their conversation grew arid and died, the brief, spontaneous instant of Cobb's solicitude for his son having passed.

BOOK IV

ROME

14

. . . down the nights and down the days
. . . down the labyrinthine ways

The poetry of Francis Thompson, a relic of early schooling long thought forgotten, drummed inexplicably in Peter Cobb's consciousness almost from the moment of wakening. Thompson's God, the mystical "Hound of Heaven," pursues the sinner, patient, inexorable, stealthy as a bloodhound, sniffing out the fugitive's track, not to bring him back to punishment but to his destiny, an eternity in paradise. A hound pursued Cobb now—a hound called Lonsdale.

He said mass for he last time in the tiny Harvard chapel. Cobb had packed the night before. Two suitcases, one of books, a portable typewriter. Gray Boston hinted rain or snow but his battered umbrella hung abandoned on its hook. One last brisk walk along the Charles, skim ice and muscle memory. A grave black man tipped his hat to the collar. A civil city, Boston. Cobb hoped Rome would be as gentle.

A late afternoon shuttle to New York, the surly cab to Kennedy, the evening Pan Am to Rome, a 747 blessedly half-empty. There was a film, a meal, a book, a rough blanket and a few hours of awkward sleep and then, at what should have been midnight, the daily miracle of the dawn, somewhere out in that dark void between Iceland and the Hook of Kinsale. At nine they crossed the Channel, at ten the Alps, at eleven they were in Rome, in the vast echoing glass and steel of Leonardo da Vinci airport with the submachine-gun-toting soldiers sneaking cigarettes and watching girls.

He had a room at the Hassler. The province had offered to arrange accommodations and Cobb had refused. He knew what it would be, some slim and pious *pensione*, reeking of tomato paste and sanctity, a crowded hostel for impoverished, transient clerics. Cobb had told Father Hanlon he would handle his own arrangements. He was in Rome, presumably, on serious business. He wanted privacy and quiet, not the false cheer and unwonted confidences of other unknown men of God. The Hassler was where the Cobbs always stayed. Feeling slightly guilty, Peter had asked his father's secretary to make the reservation. It would be expensive but it would be worth it. If Rome drew him to her bosom for more than a week or two, he would look for a flat.

The management was Swiss, a guarantee the Hassler would be efficient and dull. The chambermaid was mustachioed and impressed. Mere priests did not book rooms in the Hassler. Cobb must be, despite his youth, at least an archbishop. She hung his suits in the veneered armoire, laid out his shaving gear and Yankee toilet paper, and fell to her knees showing him her scapular and begging a blessing.

His room was in the front, on the Piazza Trinità dei Monti, looking down on a small square and, to the right, the Spanish Steps. It was always startling to see palm trees in January but they were there, partially masking the leafy ceramic terrace of someone's private apartment. Cobb threw open the French doors to the thin winter sun and to the noise of Rome. He wanted the street noise, fondly remembered, the cacophony of talk and shout, horn and brake, the controlled explosions of motorbikes, the commerce and conflict of the hawkers and hippies lounging on the Spanish Steps. They were comforting sounds, reassuring and familiar. This was the Rome he had known as a child, a college boy, a young and still uncomplicated seminarian on holiday. No hostile menace in such sounds.

He napped until four. Monsignor Lonsdale's instructions were to report on arrival. With a clear conscience Cobb disregarded them. Lonsdale knew only that Cobb would be here this week. What did the day matter? Better to appear fresh and rested in the morning rather than at the frayed end of a jet-lagged day. Besides, there was an errand, a place he wanted to go.

Peter showered away sleep, dressed in gray slacks, an antique blazer, and a new Burberry raincoat, and walked down the carpeted stairs and through the tranquil, ornate lobby. The plaza was thronged with rush-hour pedestrians. Cobb ventured out into half-remembered Rome, blundering into cul de sacs and obscure wrong turnings. He was unsure of his course, certain of his destination. By six he was there.

Rome, lighted against the winter night, pulsating, bustling, confused, noisy; the Fiats and the taxis and the Alfas performed their honking, careening ritual dance through the narrow streets, across the old bridges, around the crazy quilt traffic circles.

Then, suddenly, awesomely, the crashing, rasping throaty roar of sound was stilled. Cobb had passed through the arches that opened into the Piazza San Pietro.

It was not so much that the great square of St. Peter was empty or totally stilled. Around its rim the souvenir shops still flourished, doing their brisk trade in post cards and prayer books; platoons of pilgrims and tourists shuffled across its expanse, the occasional robed and hurrying priest passed, back bent, flat hat curling in the wind. It was more that the sound and the movements and the vast, cobblestoned enclosure itself possessed a different, muted quality from the sounds and motion of the outside. Within the plaza words, footsteps, even a hawker's cry, a tour guide's avuncular sibilance, rose unfettered toward the sky, rising like smoke, instead of, as in the rest of Rome, banging and cracking and crashing against buildings and across narrow streets, echoing and strident.

Around him the circumference of the place seemed welcoming and warm, like arms embracing. Cobb muttered a brief and simple prayer for himself, and stepped into the great space, absolutely certain he was entering an undefined but undeniably new chapter of his life, a new life itself, perhaps.

Around here somewhere, he forgot details of the legend, they had crucified Peter. Upside down, it was said, at his request, signifying his unworthiness to re-enact the tableau of the Christ. Cobb tried to imagine how it would feel, the nails through the hands and feet, the dead weight of a mature body tearing at the wounds, the rush of blood sickening to the head, the jeers and taunts of a half-savage Roman mob whetted on circuses and the arena. He could not. Then, unaccountably, the face of Pedro Figueroa was before him, gentle, joyous, patient, quizzical. He tried to imagine vermin feasting on his living eyes and could not.

They had closed the basilica at six. Cobb was too late. Three nuns fluttered out, habits like crows' wings, tiny feet tapping down the worn steps, their faces carefully averted from the watching Cobb. He stood there, on the cold stones, the doors closed before him, no Roman collar or black suit as passport. St. Peter's and the Vatican rose before him, dark and predatory. Cobb, who had expected to find Rome warm in contrast to New England, shivered, staring up at the immense facade, wondering where it was that Lonsdale lurked, where they would meet tomorrow, what would be said, implied, suggested, threatened. Behind him the huge void of the piazza loomed black and silent. Above, the few feeble stars of cities, blinking through the smog, competed with the neon. Again he shivered.

The shabby doorkeeper had left, the nuns fluttered away, behind him the lights of the shops winked off, the tour guides melted through the arches, the hawkers and the peddlers shut their cardboard suitcases and shuffled off to *tavernas*, to warm, lighted places. A winter's night and Cobb stood alone in St. Peter's square.

"*Signore.*"

A hand, tentative and uncertain, had touched his arm. Startled, he wheeled. A face, old, small and wizened, stared up at him.

"*Signore,*" the face said again, "*sigaretta?*"

Cobb reached through the slit pocket of the raincoat to his blazer pocket and pulled out the pack of Gitanes.

"Here," he said in Italian, wondering about the accent.

"*Grazie,*" the beggar said, taking two cigarettes and diving into pockets.

"*Prego.*"

The pack out, Cobb lighted one now, then, seeing how the old man watched him, seeing the need in his face, he lighted another and handed it to him, butt end first.

"*Grazie,*" the man said again, sucking greedily on the cigarette, inhaling deeply.

"*Rien,*" Cobb said, immediately regretting the slip into French.

The old man nodded. He understood. He may not have known the word, but he understood.

"*Americano?*" he asked.

"*Sì, americano.*"

"*Buono.*"

Cobb turned back again to the Vatican wall, high and dark and impenetrable. Here and there a lighted window accentuated the darkness of the mass. Beside him the beggar stood quietly, puffing at the cigarette, docile and satisfied.

I'll give him a few lire, Cobb thought, for keeping the vigil with me. Giddily he thought of Christ, that night he had gone off to pray on the hillside, and of the three apostles left behind to watch, who had not watched, but who had slept. This old man was awake. The moist, sucking sound he made puffing at the cigarette said so.

"Could ye not watch with me one hour?" Cobb said aloud, in English, quoting the gospel of that night.

"*Signore?*" the old man asked, confused.

"*Niente,*" Cobb said. Was that the word for "nothing"?

He had hotel Italian, taxi Italian, restaurant Italian. Ever since they landed at da Vinci he had been slipping into French, into Latin, into Portuguese and Spanish. Thank God his inquisitor (unconsciously he took his father's word) was to be English. Monsignor Lonsdale, for whom we are duly grateful. He laughed now, a small laugh, but enough to raise an answering cackle in the old beggar, to arouse him to a quaint, shuffling dance on the worn stone.

"*Americano*," he said again, delighted. Cobb understood. Americans were all mad, standing in the wintry dark of the piazza, giving away cigarettes and laughing at jokes untold.

Then the beggar grabbed his arm. His bony, clawlike grip had a surprising strength.

"*Signore*," he said, his voice falling, secretive as a tout's.

"*Sì?*"

The old man half turned Cobb toward the facade of one of the larger of the Vatican buildings. His eyes turned upwards and Cobb's followed. There, high on the building, a lighted room.

"*Il papa*," the beggar said in his now hushed croak. "The Pope."

Cobb stared at the lighted window. Large but undistinguished, it was shut against the January night, flimsily curtained. If there were drapes, they were not drawn. Nothing to indicate it was anything but a window.

"*Il papa*," the man said again, reverential and certain.

The usual tourist come-on, Cobb thought, the sort of thing tour guides and panhandlers knew sent thrills of excitement through the out-of-towner and the innocent. Of course the Pope had a bedroom, logically it would give out onto the piazza, the most spectacular view, presumably, at this hour, the room would be well lighted, probably, since the Italians ate late, the Pope would be in his room. Still, how would this old man know, how could he be sure, was he not simply gulling Cobb out of another cigarette, a lira or two?

"*Il papa?*" Cobb said, repeating the man's certainty as a question.

"*Sì*," the beggar said, his hand gripping more fiercely, "*il papa*."

15

Lonsdale was a wasted man of medium height with thinning hair and the look of one who had lived well—small, broken veins in his nose and cheeks, grainy eyes, a mouth that suggested it knew its way around vintages, small, manicured hands suggesting a lifetime of shuffling papers and nothing heavier.

"My dear Father," he had begun, "how good of you to come all this way. How thoughtful. How . . ."

Further courteous adjectives seemed beyond him. Patently, his smile said, Peter Cobb had done him a great service for which Lonsdale would be ever grateful.

"Now what, if anything, can I do to make your arduous journey worth the while, make your stay here as pleasant as it can be?"

"Nothing at all, Monsignor. I've always loved Rome. My hotel is fine." Lonsdale fluttered his hands.

"You know Rome? But, of course you do. A village, surely, not London or Paris or New York, but with its compensations. You must dine with me. Some of these little out-of-the-way *tavernas* can be charming."

As Englishmen do, he spoke of the weather, apologizing for it. The tension began to ease out of Cobb. Lonsdale might be ridiculous, he was clearly no threat. Cobb relaxed. How fortunate they shared a language. No matter how gracious, how effusive, how hospitable, Cobb would have found this sort of preliminary fencing more difficult in Italian.

Even locating Lonsdale had been surprisingly easy.

Walking through the square in the Roman morning, he had wondered how it could have been the night before a frightening, traumatic place. This morning it was just another Italian piazza, a bit larger perhaps, and without the neon and the sidewalk cafés, without the motorbikes and the pushcarts. But a piazza. Nothing more, nothing menacing.

A civilian waved him past, his letter from Lonsdale a passport no one even cared to examine, to stamp. He had expected Swiss Guards, *monsignori*, dark little men with suspicious eyes. Surely it could not be the black suit, the collar. Ten thousand men in Rome wore such clothes. Could any of them simply wander into the *sanctum sanctorum* this easily? Was the Pope at hazard to any misanthrope with a grudge, a fancied injury.

At the end of a narrow corridor of small, banal offices in which nuns typed and men in mufti yawned and paged through computer printouts, he found Lonsdale behind a bare desk, flanked by filing cabinets and fronted by an IBM Selectric typewriter at which he was staring blankly.

Lonsdale looked up at his visitor.

"I'm Peter Cobb, Monsignor. From Boston."

"Oh, yes, splendid. Cobb, Cobb, not Irish, is it?" His voice, his eyes, were bored.

Cobb shook his head.

"English, I think, a long way back." He tugged out his letter from Lonsdale and handed it over.

"English, yes, well, have to see what we can do for a fellow countryman."

Lonsdale looked at his own letter. Oh, yes, he thought, *that* Cobb, the Jesuit from the missions.

"My dear fellow . . ." began his greeting now that he realized Cobb had been sent for, was not just another wandering nun's priest seeking a boon. Then had come the fencing, the list of highly recommended *tavernas*, a discussion of the filthy January weather; and, cleverly programmed by Lonsdale's harmless banter, Cobb had relaxed.

"I read your book," Lonsdale said, his voice indefinably less fruity, more reinforced concrete.

"Oh." Cobb had not been an author long enough to know precisely *what* to say in response.

"Yes."

"And?" Cobb asked, unable to resist.

"There are those who find it . . . naive," Lonsdale said.

"Oh?" Cobb said once again, feeling self-conscious and stupid, very much the bad boy on the headmaster's carpet.

Lonsdale unaccountably turned jolly and unfocused once more.

"Not I, of course. I found it charming, touching, much of the writing quite a cut above so much of the clerical work that regrettably reaches print."

"And its thesis?"

123

Lonsdale made a little, helpless gesture with his hands.

"I'm not sure I'm really all that competent to say, you know. Not my line of country, the Latinos."

Cobb had lived long enough among Latins to know that the American conversational style of getting straight to the point simply did not work. He assumed Italy demanded a similar indirection, that even an Englishman like Lonsdale, working within the Curia, would take his own sweet time getting down to cases. Well, thought Cobb, let him set the pace.

Unaccustomed to silence from Americans, a people for whom he had little stomach, Lonsdale fiddled with papers for a moment and then, with a showy glance at his watch, bounced up from his chair.

"I say, ten o'clock. Spot of *espresso*, a lemon drink, a Cinzano?"

"Fine."

Lonsdale added a *berretta* to his black cassock with its monsignorially red buttons, clapping the stiff little hat rakishly on the side of his head, and, surprisingly nimble, led Cobb out of the office and down a confusing maze of corridors.

"Been at that desk since eight," he puffed. "They want clergy in early so as to give example to the civilians. Damned people will want their own trade union next. Worse than England."

Lonsdale led them to a sidewalk café on the Via della Conciliazione, glassed in for winter, heated by potbellied stoves. Some pretty girls and slim young men drank Coke and flirted. Older men drank coffee and read newspapers. There were no older women.

Both men ordered *espresso*.

"Hang about that office long enough and all sorts of people pop in. Nuns and other undesirables. Much easier chatting in a place like this."

Cobb wondered if he had been classed as an "undesirable" along with the nuns until Lonsdale realized who he was, that he had been summoned.

As if he had wondered aloud, Lonsdale said:

"Tell me about yourself, Cobb, where you come from, what sort of fellow you are."

Peter gave him a brief sketch.

"Convert, eh? Might have suspected so. There's a certain air about us."

An air, it was quite clear from his tone, of superiority.

The man was a rascal, Cobb concluded. He was tired of answering questions so he asked one:

"What brought you to the Church, Monsignor?"

Lonsdale laughed.

"Oh, it was Rome or pederasty, I'm afraid. Couldn't bear the society of women and my father kept pushing girls at me. Would have gone queer,

I suppose, so many men I knew at Oxford did, but the available boys I knew were all so . . . pimply. Took instructions at Farm Street, by the bye, from your lot, Jesuits. Ended up in a seminary."

His reply sounded scripted, rehearsed, the stuff of dinner-table *mots*.

"And your work for Cardinal Grassi?"

Lonsdale laughed.

"Ah, now, Cobb, you're the one we want to hear about. Not a tired old dray horse like me, chained to a desk. Your adventures in the horse latitudes, that's the stuff. This book of yours, your new celebrity, those exotic folk with whom you sported in the tropics."

The nasty edge had come back into his manner.

"I wouldn't call the people I wrote about very exotic. And when I was with them they did damn little sporting."

Lonsdale threw back his head in mock embarrassment.

"Oh, dear, I've said something to offend you."

Cobb bit off the retort. This wasn't going well, not well at all.

Lonsdale sipped delicately at his coffee.

Lonsdale's aristocratic drawl, half Oxbridge, half BBC Third Programme, his facile, self-deprecatory cynicism, his fatigue, were deceptive. Behind the bland blind of manner and wit resided a very clever and rather unhappy man. He was not a very pleasant person, not even a very good priest, but he was a successful one. Cardinal Grassi and other prelates for whom he had worked were aware Lonsdale would never be suspected of holiness, never threatened with beatification. But it was a large Church and there were plenty of men who would, while there were too few who could run an office, manage a staff, judge an individual or an issue, say no to a worthy applicant for favor, write a readable, persuasive brief. Grassi might not like Edmund Lonsdale. But affection was not essential in their relationship; he knew Lonsdale's worth. Lonsdale, who navigated through the subtler fens and bogs of Church politics, coped with trickier matters of personality, handled irksome cases like this fellow Cobb and his damned book.

Lonsdale's initial vagueness with Cobb had been a ploy. Cobb, who had more than a marginal brain himself, sensed this.

I know nothing of the Latinos, Lonsdale had said, dismissing half a billion people with a casually snob throwaway line. The truth was he knew a great deal about Latin America and its people. But it pained Lonsdale to tell the truth when it was not entirely necessary. Mendacity was his natural state. He asked Cobb to talk about himself, as if Lonsdale had brought nothing to their conversation. He had brought a good deal. He knew, for example, the reasons for certain turnings in Cobb's brief career in the Society of Jesus at which Cobb could but guess.

All Cobb's good intentions about permitting the conversation to develop naturally, at Lonsdale's pace, were impatiently discarded.

"Monsignor, perhaps you could tell me why you sent for me. Why am I here?"

Lonsdale shrugged.

"Isn't it every priest's dream, this Rome of ours? The Vatican, proximity to power, the pomp, the circumstance? Look around you, all these appealing young people. Doesn't all of this excite you, stimulate and uplift you?" He half turned in his café chair. "Regard San Pietro. Nothing like that in your jungle backwaters, eh?"

How differently could two men regard the same thing. Last night, alone in the piazza with his friendly, capering beggar, Cobb had been deeply moved to look up at the basilica, the lighted window off to its right, to think about the men who had lived in those apartments, the man who lived there now. Lonsdale's smooth insincerity cheapened the whole business. Perhaps Cobb had been fortunate spending the first years of his ministry in "jungle backwaters." If they had no San Pietro, neither did they have Monsignor Lonsdale.

"Monsignor, *why?*"

Lonsdale was not easily pressured, simple black-and-white answers did not come naturally. He was a man trained in diplomacy, a devious man, for whom charm and evasion functioned as did honesty in other men. He had taken the usual vows, as a priest he avoided the usual sins. This was no hardship for Lonsdale. At his age, in his state of health, the usual sins held little attraction. He preferred his work. It provided, he felt, as great a satisfaction as once had more fleshly pleasures.

"What, what?"

Cobb restrained his anger, or tried to.

"Monsignor, six or seven weeks ago certain letters were sent. My provincial in Boston, Father Hanlon, passed on to me instructions to be in Rome the first week of January, to report to you at the Vatican. You confirmed this in a letter direct to me. I still have no hint of what is wanted of me, why I've traveled four thousand miles, what I'm doing in Rome!"

Lonsdale waved to the waiter.

"Another *espresso?* My treat, of course."

Cobb shook his head.

The waiter went off to fetch Lonsdale's coffee. Beyond the misted glass of the enclosure real life went on, auto traffic, motorbikes, men and women bundled against the chill, here and there a child playing. Nice, Cobb thought, nice to realize there was a world out there on which Lonsdale had not yet placed his clammy grasp.

"Monsignor?"

Lonsdale looked at Cobb, steadily this time.

"My dear fellow, when I mentioned earlier there were those who found your little book naive, I was, forgivably, being kind. You're a young man, you have promise. One hesitates to curdle such promise with unnecessary strictures."

His voice hung in air.

"But . . ." said Cobb, wanting to have done with *politesse*.

"But your associations in Mirador, your little book, certain charges you have leveled, suggestions you have made carrying the slander that a duly authorized anti-Communist government and the Church, *this* Church, have conspired to murder nuns . . ."

"I never said the Church was involved in their deaths."

Lonsdale gestured impatiently, rattling his *espresso* cup.

"Then in the concealment of facts."

Cobb nodded. "Fair enough," he said.

Monsignor Lonsdale pursed his lips and went on, his tones oily and patronizing.

"Such juvenile fantasies on the part of young priests sent out to the tropical missions are not, unhappily, rare. A boy fresh out of seminary is caught up in the rustic romance of such places. He is flattered by the attention of the natives. He begins to think of himself as more important than he is. If he is a European or, worse, an American, he carries with him the crusading naiveté of the democracies. You do not run places like Bolivia or Mirador as one might Sweden. Permit a scabrous lot of *bandidos* spouting socialist rubbish to come to power in countries like that and you solemnize institutional chaos. Churches are shut down, priests are shot, and the commissars take down the holy pictures and replace the Virgin with Engels and Marx."

Cobb, angry but in control, said, "You're right about one thing. They shoot the priests."

Lonsdale smiled—until Cobb completed his thought.

"The government of Mirador is systematically killing priests and nuns and closing the missions."

"Undoubtedly there are excesses. In civil war one must realize that . . ."

Cobb interrupted. "Monsignor," he said, trying to stay cool, "you don't understand."

"And *you* do? You are the expert witness for whom Rome has been waiting? You the messenger sent from on high to instruct the rest of us in our ways?"

Cobb did not dare respond. He feared the words that might come out.

But suddenly he knew that behind Lonsdale's fencing there was menace.

His father had been right. His book, of course. Did Lonsdale know about the new book? Did Rome know? Kurt Salomon's warnings echoed in memory. Then, anger and pride overwhelming prudence, he blurted out:

"I was there. I know what happened. I know what's happening now. Those were Catholic nuns who died. Even after their deaths became known a Catholic bishop was still blessing the tanks and dining at the palace. Half the clergy in Mirador don't answer to Rome anymore, they pay fealty to colonels. What do you think the average, dumb, unlettered peasant makes of that? What does he think of his Church when he sees his bishops in bed with the *junta*? Do you wonder at the appeal of communism? Does it startle you that ordinary men turn from their Church in revulsion?"

Lonsdale fixed him with a dead eye.

"The party line, Cobb. Isn't that what it's called in your country? The party line . . . ?"

Sarcasm hung in the air. Peter struggled for control.

"It's called *truth*, Monsignor. And I thought Rome might wish to hear it for a change."

Lonsdale's pansified, upper-class voice drastically changed then. "Just where is your parish, Cobb? Who are your parishioners? What is your constituency? To which overworked, doddering episcopal vicar do you report?"

His old man's wattles shook, his suddenly young man's eyes blazed, feral and aggrieved.

Cobb did not enjoy being bullied. He had never, not since he was a child, permitted Charles Cobb to bully him. He was damned if this English fairy . . .

"Well, Cobb?"

Peter stood up. "Monsignor, if you wish me to say more on this subject I prefer it to be to Cardinal Grassi."

Lonsdale slapped a pudgy hand on his wasted thigh. His voice turned oily with charm. "Amadeo Cardinal Grassi will pray over you, Cobb, and mutter Italian wisdom, and may conduct you on a guided tour through his small but impressive collection of oils by Fra Filippo Lippi." His voice hardened. "But you will damn well answer to me on this matter and to me alone!"

Cobb turned and headed for the door. "Monsignor, if Cardinal Grassi wishes to see me I'll be at the Hassler."

Lonsdale's fury collided with his snobbery. "The Hassler? The Jesuits are putting their people up at the Hassler?"

Cobb smiled. "We *are* an elite corps, Monsignor. Or so it is said."

Lonsdale's lips moved silently, angrily, as Cobb left.

16

When **Peter** Cobb slipped out of the Hassler early next morning to attend mass at the neighboring church, Trinità dei Monti, there were children still asleep in the lee of the Spanish Steps, huddled in their sleeping bags and down jackets, blond-haired, tousled waifs from America and northern Europe, this generation's Children's Crusade to the Saracens, stranded midway between here and there, peddling their baubles, scrawling their pictures, smoking their dope. The church was damp and dark and Cobb prayed for them. And, as always, for his mother, for his father—with that secret delight of knowing how such a thing would enrage him—for his sister Jane, to whom he had spoken in Milan by phone the night before.

He phoned Hathaway at the Embassy and got an invitation to lunch. They met at Manfredi's.

"This place is called Manfredi's."

"I know," Cobb said, "I read the sign."

"Old Peter." Tom Hathaway seemed ridiculously pleased that Cobb was in Rome.

The restaurant was filled. Tables for two took three, tables for four took five or six. Everyone was talking, smoking, pouring wine, gesturing. Babel. Chaos. Bedlam with carbonara sauce. A fierce vitality, none of it forced.

"A dining room back home with this many people would be awkward," Hathaway said. "I suppose it's birth control does it. Italians are used to swarming all over one another. From the cradle."

"That's the one right-to-life argument the Church hadn't thought of."

It was Rome as he remembered it. Politics changed, individuals, but Rome and the Romans not.

"Well," Hathaway said, "I'm not sure I agree completely. There *are* differences. In *Corriere* the other day—they have their own 'Dear Abby,' you know—someone wrote asking what the protocol was for sending flowers to the hospital of someone who'd just been knee-capped. Did one or didn't one? You didn't have that sort of thing when we were here during college."

The women seemed as beautiful as ever. The young men as lean, as sleekly tailored. A pale woman with a *quattrocento* face waved to Hathaway.

The waiter came and they ordered wine and considered the menu.

"Now, Peter," Hathaway said, "you've got to get some clothes while you're here. That outfit you've got on went out with running-boards. I've got a marvelous tailor. Let me give you his address. This suit's his."

Cobb said it was wonderful.

Hathaway looked pleased. "There are consolations to living here," he said.

"I'm sure."

"My man does a very nice black suit," Hathaway said. "Some of the most elegant clerics in town . . ."

Peter laughed. "Tom, you don't change, do you?"

"Of course not. Why should I?" Hathaway asked, quite evidently pleased with the person he was and discerning no reason at all to change. And, as usual, he was in love. Also, as usual, there were, well . . . complications.

"It's not easy, Peter, not at all easy being a rogue. If you're as dedicated about it as I am, it's a day and night job."

"Your devotion to pleasure is most impressive," Cobb admitted.

Hathaway smiled, distantly, as if remembering long-forgotten flesh. Then, shaking himself back to the present, he said, "There's another girl now."

"I'd be disappointed in you if there weren't."

Hathaway leaned forward. Unlike the Miradorans he had a confidential voice, accustomed to conspiracy. His voice lowered now. Not for nothing had he spent all these years in the foreign service.

"A girl for whom I'd give my soul."

Cobb could not resist the laugh.

"Tom, you've traded your soul for too many things. There's nothing left. Mephistopheles isn't buying."

"Are you?"

"Uh-uh."

Hathaway ignored his response, went right ahead, as Cobb knew he would, as he always had.

"I want you to meet her. We'll have dinner together, the three of us. Unless"—his eyes crinkled in delight—"unless you want me to scout up a devout young thing for you."

"I'm in training, Tom, no girls, a few laps every morning, even cutting down on the beer."

"They'll canonize you yet."

Thinking of Lonsdale's trembling, petulant fury, Cobb said he didn't think so.

Hathaway waved his disclaimer away with a hand.

"Ah, what do you know? But listen, let me tell you about this girl."

And he did.

It was typical Hathaway. She was, again, typically, a princess. Young, beautiful, passionate, intelligent, and devoted to Hathaway. Also, unfortunately, she was married.

"One of those desiccated elder sons of a noble family. She was nineteen, he was in his mid-twenties. And of course the son of a bitch didn't think to inform her until after the ceremony that he was a homosexual. Prefers the drag bars off the Via Veneto to the nuptial couch. Bastard! And he had to do it right, too, saw to it that the banns were read, one of the more fashionable cardinals performed the marriage, got the kid well and truly hooked before he dropped his little bombshell. '*Cara mia*, I should tell you, now that we're happily and forever wed, that I really prefer a certain young boy with tight jeans and brilliantined hair in the Piazza Barberini.' Bastard!" he said again, his voice still low but hot with anger.

"You really have it, don't you," Cobb said.

"Yes, Peter, I do," Hathaway said, the mocking tone vanished.

Then, after a moment, he said, "Her name is Pia."

There was a pleasant reverence in how he said the name that touched Cobb. Hathaway might still be the rogue he claimed to be, the rascal Cobb remembered, but his feeling for this girl, love, infatuation, passion, whatever it was, was genuine. Hathaway might boast, or exaggerate, or equivocate. He did not lie. Not in this tone of voice.

He continued now, the words spilling out: "Her grandfather was one of the big *fascisti* of the regime. The King despised Mussolini; so did most of the royals. This one, the grandfather, didn't. Don't ask me the reasons. Pia doesn't know herself. The partisans lynched the old boy back in '45. Pia's father watched them do it. The family doesn't like to talk about it very much."

"Understandable."

"They've got a lot of money, textile dough from up north, and they've got the family name, and they've got the black sheep grandfather. So they worry about the Red Brigades a lot and now, to top things off, Pia's married to this fag and there doesn't seem any way out of it."

"Catholic?"

Hathaway shrugged. "Naturally. Under the law she could get a divorce. But she won't."

"Without knowing all the facts, Tom, it sounds as if there might be valid grounds for an annulment. After all, if the husband concealed his homosexuality, if he had no intention of consummating the marriage . . ."

Hathaway shook his head. "The new Pope has everybody nervous. No one knows yet which way he'll jump on annulments. The clergy Pia's talked with are all very cautious. They won't commit themselves to anything until Gregory gives a sign. Is he a liberal on such matters or a conservative or what? We just don't know."

"Well, don't ask me. I'm just a missionary in from the country. You probably know a lot more about Gregory and Church politics than I do."

"Oh, yeah," Hathaway said sarcastically, "simple little Friar Tuck in sandals and burlap. And staying at the Hassler."

"That's me," Cobb agreed pleasantly.

The waiter cleared away their pasta and fetched the veal and several people stopped by the table to greet Hathaway. Then, when it was quiet again, he asked, "Peter, just why *are* you in Rome? Trouble about the book?"

"Why do you ask that?"

"Hell, I dunno. I read the cover story in *Time*. I even read the damned book. If Gregory turns out to be the right-wing monster some of the smart boys are predicting, you could be in a little hot water."

An instinctive caution had taken hold of Cobb. Not even with his old roommate was he quite ready to speak frankly. The interview with Monsignor Lonsdale had shaken his customary self-confidence. Men like Lonsdale didn't take such a tough line on their own. And behind Lonsdale was Curia Grassi. And behind him, still insubstantial and shadowy, still a distant figure on the Boston Common, still an unseen force behind a lighted window high on the facade of the papal palace, was Gregory.

"Do you know a monsignor called Edmund Lonsdale?"

"Sure," Hathaway said, "English fairy. Works at the Vatican. Diplomatist, shrewd, travels in the better circles, plays bridge with the right people."

"That's the one. It was Lonsdale sent for me. I had *espresso* with him yesterday morning on the della Conciliazione."

"That must have been cheery. Did he say what he wanted?"

"All very vague," Cobb said, still cautious.

Hathaway was too good a diplomat to be fobbed off. He knew the impact Cobb's book and subsequent celebrity had already had. Questions had been asked in Congress. The nuns, after all, had been Americans. A subcommittee of the United Nations issued a statement. Amnesty International wrote letters. In the end the colonels who ran Mirador righteously called for an official inquiry. Lieutenant Montoya was called. Several of his men were brought in. The hearings were closed. And when they were over the government of Mirador issued a statement declaring the entire affair, while regrettable, remained a mystery. Bands of guerrilla terrorists had been in the area. Montoya had so testified. Perhaps the guerrillas could shed some light on what happened to the poor women. Mirador, unfortunately, could not.

On the assumption that Hathaway might know about such matters, Peter asked, "Is our government planning to do anything more about those nuns I wrote about? I mean, beyond sending a testy note."

Hathaway laughed.

"You jest. Don't you realize Mirador is one of our staunchest allies in the region?"

"I was afraid of that," Peter said.

Tom regarded his old schoolmate thoughtfully.

"Of course, if someone poured a little more oil on the fire you've started . . . some busybody, some troublemaker . . ."

"Yes?"

Hathaway shrugged.

"Then even a phlegmatic jerk like our glorious President might have to do something."

Cobb said nothing.

After a brief pause, Tom continued: "That is, if his own church didn't cut off his balls first. . . ."

Hathaway reached out to pour some more of the chilled Frascati then, permitting his warning to hang over the table like cigarette smoke, and Peter purposely changed the subject.

"Kiki's still in Boston. Married again. Dozens of children."

"Kiki with *bambini?*" Hathaway marveled. "Impossible."

Peter shook his head.

"Tom, nothing is impossible. *Nothing.*"

The next day was a feast of some local significance and it was announced in the papers that the Pope would give a benediction from his balcony. Cobb went to it. Standing there in the piazza he now saw Gregory for the second time, closer now, a white-robed, rather burly figure, waving to the crowd and making the sign of the cross above them. And, again for the second time, Father Peter Cobb, S.J., fell to his knees before his Pope, shivering slightly in the damp wind off the Tiber, and wondering if it was the wind that chilled him.

17

On the same morning Amadeo Cardinal Grassi received Edmund Lonsdale's memorandum about his interview with Cobb, Grassi had been handed an alarming statistical printout from the Vatican computers: more than forty priests, most of them young, many of them Jesuits, had applied to be assigned to missionary work in a single, minor Latin American country. Two dozen nuns had made similar applications, as had a number of seminarians who requested they be permitted to do their final years of theological study in that same insignificant Latin land. It was, of course, Mirador. And some of the applications cited as the inspiration behind their requests a book called *Speculations.*

Grassi mistrusted zealotry. He was suspicious of statistical aberrations. Not for years had anyone applied for service in Mirador. The place was a backwater. Now the Catholic religious were thirsting for the place. It wasn't healthy. It was unnatural. This damned fellow Cobb. And his book hadn't yet been published in Europe! Think of the sort of brushfires it could ignite among the Dutch, who were always trembling on the brink of heresy. Or the French, with their romantic notions of what the Church was and what it wasn't. Or in the gloomy provincial cities of Germany, ever ready to fall into ranks behind a new leader. Or here in Italy, in the name of God!

Normally the Cardinal was not a man easily panicked. He sat now, munching dry toast in his Vatican apartment, washing it down with steaming tea, breakfast coffee too strong a brew for his delicate stomach, and as he often did, considering how fortunate a man he was. Very few priests from the Red suburbs of industrial Turin become princes of the Church. Fewer still become members of the Curia, that government within a government that runs the Roman Catholic Church. A few years before he had been one of the men who maneuvered the first John Paul into office. The feat, elevating a relatively obscure prelate without ambition onto the papal throne, was an impressive one and had given Grassi a taste of power that had stayed with him, had become a part of him, hanging about him now as cigar smoke stays in the drapes. And as he took his meager breakfast he glanced over the memorandum submitted to him by Monsignor Edmund Lonsdale directly following his morning mass.

Lonsdale was a treasure. Efficient, suave, ruthless, his urbanity played a useful counterpoint to Grassi's own deceptive ingenuousness. Grassi was not simple but he seemed so. Lonsdale seemed complex and was. There were times when Grassi lost patience, when Lonsdale's easy, dissembling charm proved an unacceptable substitute for honesty, probity, truth. But you do not run governments, or churches, with piety. This business of the American, Cobb, for example. Carrot and stick, and who to play it better than Edmund Lonsdale.

Even to Cardinal Grassi, who had helped elect him, Gregory remained an enigma. He proposed "the option of love." Very well, it was in such obtuse and mystical phrases that Popes ought to speak from the Olympian heights of their office. It was for more practical men, men like Grassi and Lonsdale, to shape the policies that were the reality underlying the poetry. Grassi had already formed several papacies. He intended to participate in the forming of Gregory's. So he forgave much of what he disliked in Lonsdale, he made allowances. The man was a priest but no Christian, and Grassi knew something about Edmund Lonsdale few people did: that the monsignor was gravely ill. But there was still value to get out of him.

Grassi put aside Lonsdale's memo and picked up the telephone.

"Lonsdale," he said, "I want to meet this fellow Cobb. Informally. Can you arrange it?"

In his sparse Vatican cubicle Edmund Lonsdale pursed his lips.

"But of course, Your Eminence. Which night are you free for dinner?"

Cobb's life in Rome began to fall into a pattern. He got a phone call from Lonsdale, and grimly prepared for an icy chill or a stern lecture. Instead, it was an invitation to dinner, and the suggestion he do some sight-seeing, amuse himself, see some old friends until the time would be ripe for more "substantive" conversations about his status. Cobb, puzzled, accepted the dinner invitation and asked Lonsdale to arrange entrée to the American Academy, where he hoped to do some research.

"But, my dear fellow, of course. Nothing could be simpler."

Cobb, hanging up the phone, suspected that was the *only* simple thing he had yet encountered in Rome.

After mass each morning in the double-spired church of Trinità dei

Monti next door to his hotel celebrated by permission of the pastor, a cherubic sort with a brother in Chicago, Cobb changed out of his black suit into blazer, trousers and raincoat, and set off at a ground-covering lope to the Academy, bordering, as the guide books had it, the park of the Janiculum. The Academy was one of the few American buildings in Rome, a Stanford White design, with an excellent library of English-language books. Cobb's hotel Italian was improving but he was not yet ready to essay research in the language.

In *Speculations,* Peter Cobb had written movingly, eloquently, convincingly, of his friends in Mirador and of their courage and decency in the face of near intolerable horror and the provocations of the regime. It was a passionate defense of their right to revolt against an authoritarian government, an indictment of autocracy and a withering criticism of a Church that opted for neutrality, or worse, blessed the tanks that clanked out into the savanna to crush the rebels.

In *Speculations* he had written about others, his friends. And about Mirador. He had not written about himself, his role. His . . . war.

And now he would, in a book tentatively titled *Holy Wars.* It was a book that would, he intended, put the theological and philosophical argument that, under certain conditions and in extraordinary circumstances, it was not only permissible but right for a priest to wage war. *Speculations* had burst from him in poetic emotion. *Holy Wars* was to be a coolly reasoned tract, replete with historical precedent, convincingly wrought, rationally constructed.

And in it he would, in the eyes of many, perhaps in the eyes of his Church, indict himself. For in it he would admit (some would say "boast") for the first time that it was he who for a time had led the rebels against the government and had helped plunge Mirador into the bloody civil war that still raged.

This second book, Cobb understood, could destroy him.

And yet he must write it. He could not lapse silent. He must take the risk. Fame had provided the pulpit. He knew he was being arrogant, he even suspected uneasily that he might be wrong. But the urge within him to finish this book and to publish it was as strong as any need he had ever known. As strong as sexual desire. As strong as his love of God.

Cobb thought over and over again of his parish in the shantytown, of his Miradorans, of the whir-whir of insects in the soft tropic nights, the hot sun and the Pacific breeze, of the horror of Figueroa and the nuns, of the gallantry and the easy grace of Flor, of a small, insignificant and well-loved country so far away. And while he thought of such matters, at other tables in the same reading room arid intellectuals pored over manuscripts and scrawled at iambic pentameter and annotated notebooks and dreamed, as Cobb dreamed of Mirador, of other lands, real and imagined.

Like many of the Vatican's priestly bureaucrats, Edmund Lonsdale was a wealthy man. There was family land in Berkshire, vast estates in cattle and hogs and grain. Not that Edmund Lonsdale had ever farmed. His was a career of the usual venial sins at Harrow, of more serious peculations at Oxford, offset by a brilliant season in the Oxford Union, a brief flirtation with London, the near-suicidal remorse and self-disgust that led him to Farm Street, and to a conversion, also by Jesuits, not all that radically different from Cobb's own.

Lonsdale had for years occupied a large apartment off the Piazza Mattei, near the old Jewish ghetto from which, every *carnevale*, the adult males were driven to race the length of the Corso clad only in loincloths, while medieval Rome cheered and encouraged them on their way with sticks and slop buckets. On the day appointed for the dinner at which Cobb and Cardinal Grassi would meet, Lonsdale left the office early to supervise the preparations. His staff was accustomed to such evenings. But Lonsdale liked to be there himself, sniffing the corks, pushing a finger into the cheese, supervising the slicing of the ham.

Peter Cobb, Lonsdale's reconnaissance had demonstrated, was not a boy easily bullied. That came, he supposed, from having such a man as Charles Cobb behind him. Even Grassi knew of Charles Cobb. A difficult, not very sympathetic man, but one who demanded respect. Europeans both, it never occurred to either Lonsdale or Grassi that old Cobb would not be behind his son, supportive and manipulative. They knew nothing of the strained relations between father and son and so, having probed the younger Cobb inconclusively, they were now prepared to demonstrate to him some of the respect they would have shown his formidable father.

Edmund Lonsdale's dinner table was as meticulously crafted as a Fabergé egg. One Cardinal, Grassi, one young American innocent (or not so innocent, Lonsdale had begun to suspect), Cobb, one film director Visconti was dead, Fellini was filming abroad, this one would have to do), two countesses, one cabinet member, a newspaper editor (serious, not tabloid; Lonsdale wanted none of *his* table conversation bubbling up in a garbled version in the tuppenny press), a fashion designer and his lover, male, an aging Englishwoman of good family, and the Princess Pia Bartoldi. Was she coincidence, Cobb would wonder, or had Lonsdale somehow swiftly sniffed out his Hathaway connection?

"Everything I know about America is from *Time* magazine," Lonsdale was fond of announcing, as he did now over cocktails in the library of his flat to Cobb and the newspaper editor, the first of his guests. The remark was ingenuous. It was also untrue. Lonsdale knew a great deal about America and disliked most of what he knew. "It was in *Time*," he went on, "that I first read about you. Your book."

"*Time* was very kind to me," Cobb said, searching for the appropriate neutrality of tone to take with Lonsdale. Their first meeting had ended in rancor. He did not want to be responsible for a resumption of bitterness.

"Ah, so you write books," said the editor. "I too have written books."

"And brilliantly," Lonsdale, who had never read one of the editor's books, remarked with enthusiasm.

"Yes, well, one does what one can."

Cobb's generous smile launched the editor into a denunciation of the Italian reading public. Apparently the man's books had not sold very well. Neither *Time*, nor possibly anyone else, had reported on his authorship.

Amadeo Cardinal Grassi, one of the countesses, and the fashion designer and his friend arrived in a batch.

"You don't know Grassi?" the editor hissed at Cobb as Lonsdale bustled off to greet his guests.

"No."

"Don't be fooled. He's not stupid."

Cobb said he had not imagined that he was.

"Well, you know," the editor said, "some of these fellows, one tends to underestimate them." Then, quickly, "Not Lonsdale, of course. The instant you meet Lonsdale, you know he's *comme il faut.*"

They had been speaking English. Now, as Grassi was led to them, red-robed and gnomish, the newspaper editor shifted to rapid Italian. Cobb was missing most of it, but not the tone. One of conspiratorial deference. When it was Cobb's turn he bent to kiss the Cardinal's ring.

"So nice," Grassi said, in heavily-accented English, "very nice."

He smiled benignly. Cobb wondered if Grassi were accustomed to having Americans greet him with a slap on the back.

Grassi wagged a short finger at him. "We must talk, you and I," he said.

"I'd like that, Your Eminence."

"Good, good." Grassi beamed at him and then the second countess had arrived and immediately took him up in a flurry of complaining Italian.

The fashion designer had very little English but his friend made up for it. In twenty years they would be petulant, mincing, devoted, a reasonable facsimile of the aging queers of *La Cage aux Folles*, a film Cobb had seen in Boston. The designer rolled his eyes.

"Roberto once considered the Church," his friend said.

"Sì, sì."

"But his passion for cloth, you know." The friend waved an articulate hand. "A bolt of the right fabric and he would burst into tears from sheer emotion."

"Sì, sì," the designer said, his head bobbing.

Pia Bartoldi was a surprise. From Tom Hathaway's lovesick description Peter had expected a tiny Dresden doll, wide-eyed and vulnerable. Instead there was this tall, placid girl with long hair in a French braid, a smashing figure, and an assured manner. She looked Scandinavian or perhaps Dutch, rather than Italian.

"You are Tom's hero," she said. "I have heard so much about you."

"Tom remembers me as a boy," Cobb said honestly. "Until the other day we hadn't seen one another in years."

"But he remembers well," she said.

Peter liked her. There was a directness about Pia that was decidedly un-Roman. Apparently her marital difficulties were reasonably well publicized—as well as her relationship with Tom.

Pia was the most beautiful woman in the room. And that included the film director's companion, a young actress with an extraordinary body.

"The new Loren," the newspaper editor whispered to Cobb, his eyes glittering.

"Oh?"

Cobb was not sure whether this was sarcasm or lust.

The cabinet minister was tall, patrician, graying, the sort of man who might have worn a toga in the senate of Caesar's time. His wife was small and homespun. The cabinet member ignored her as he might a speck of lint on his sleeve.

"I know your father," he told Cobb, "an extraordinary man."

"He is," Cobb agreed, surprised. He remembered Charles Cobb's blanket dismissal of Italians as "a bunch of wops."

"The refinery project at Palermo. A shame the thing fell through. A most imaginative concept."

Vaguely, Cobb recalled some scandal or other involving one of his father's companies. Certain Italian officials had been bribed. He wondered if this had been one of them.

Lonsdale set a good table. The prosciutto was sliced so thin as to be literally translucent. There was a good Frascati. The goblets were Waterford, the china Wedgwood. Peter wondered at the source of his money. It seemed not to bother anyone else. Pia Bartoldi was at his right, one of the countesses, who had no English, at his left. No matter, she concentrated her conversational fire on the fashion designer's friend.

White-jacketed waiters served, their white gloves glistening against the dark blue china. As good hosts do, Lonsdale led the conversation, drawing out the cabinet minister on the latest terrorist outrage, the filmmaker on the recent scandal at Cinecittà, the fashion designer on the new hemlines.

"Poof," said Pia, her voice low but her young, open face denoting boredom. "Rome is such a village. One can predict the scenario."

Cobb laughed.

"Not me. They've had me off-balance ever since I got here. The minister, for example, knew exactly who I was. Knew my father. What does he do, get a briefing on the whole table before he accepts a dinner invitation?"

"Yes. From Monsignor Lonsdale. The man spends hours on the phone. I used to think we Italians loved gossip. Compared to Lonsdale we have taken vows of silence."

"So he filled you in on me. Filled everyone in."

"But of course. You are fresh conversational meat. Who wants to hear about my unhappy marriage?"

Her voice was light, casual. But when Cobb turned slightly toward her, Pia's face communicated concern.

"I liked your book. More than that, it touched me."

"Tom made you read it?"

"Forced me," she said, laughing. "Said you were the only great man he was ever likely to know and I'd damn well better read your book."

Her mimicry of Hathaway's hectoring tone was perfect.

"Missionary priests don't think of themselves as very great when they dine with *monsignori* and cardinals and cabinet ministers."

"Missionary priest? Poof," she said again, this time mimicking him. "Don't forget, I read your book."

Lonsdale even drew Cobb into the table's more general conversation.

When he heard his name, Cobb expected the edged, mocking tone he associated with their first meeting over coffee. Instead, Lonsdale was serious, apparently interested.

"These nuns," he began. "The Miradoran government's posture was that they were the unfortunate victims of some sort of battle, that they were caught up in a local unpleasantness and that their deaths were accidental."

"That's what they said in the United Nations," Cobb agreed. "My information was somewhat different."

Grassi was watching him, small eyes in a plump face.

"But naturally," Lonsdale said smoothly, "the insurgents needed a cause. This unfortunate incident was custom-made, was it not?"

"I agree it was unfortunate," Cobb said, his emotions very much in check.

"Fortunes of war," Lonsdale said smoothly.

"A terrible thing," one of the countesses clucked.

"Terrible," someone else said.

Cobb had the feeling he'd heard the words before. Only the accents were different. There'd been the same polite unconcern in the various Jesuit houses, in the common rooms of Harvard, in the television coverage from the U.N. during the General Assembly debate, in the buttery voices of talk-show hosts with their impatient. "But let's hear more about you, Father. And just how you became a writer . . ."

Pia seemed to sense his anger. She touched his arm. "They don't listen," she said.

He nodded. "I know."

There was veal with zucchini and a remarkable Bordeaux and then Lonsdale, without seeming to do so, was leading Cobb into the library. Grassi was already there, crouched comfortably in a leather armchair. Lonsdale closed the double doors behind him and left them alone.

A silver serving tray with coffee was perched on a small table. Cobb poured two cups.

Grassi pursed his lips as he sipped. "Very nice," he said, the same words he had spoken when Cobb kissed his ring.

Cobb remembered the thousands of cups of coffee he'd drunk in Mirador. With Joaquin, with Flor, with Figueroa. Strong and bitter, like his memories.

Unlike Lonsdale, Grassi did not fence.

"Monsignor arranged this dinner so that I could meet you," he said. "It was not purely social, of course."

"No, I understood that."

"My English is not sufficient for reading your book. Lonsdale summarized it for me. I have read several of the critiques."

"And?"

Grassi ignored the question. Instead he asked, "Is it to be published in Italy?"

"I believe so. The publishers say there are several European editions planned."

"Good. I will read it then."

Cobb felt he could speak directly to this man.

"Lonsdale thinks the book's thesis is naive. That I'm naive."

Grassi shook his head, the wattles moving. "No, I'm sure he doesn't think that. Not of the son of Charles Cobb."

141

Pia was right. Lonsdale's telephoned briefings had been complete.

Cobb had been sitting opposite the Cardinal. Now he stood.

"Those nuns were murdered, Eminence. Dr. Figueroa and I myself spoke with one of the soldiers. The man was drunk. Guilt-ridden. His story rang true."

"Ah, yes, and the poor doctor. He died?"

"No, he's still alive."

"Then the regime took no further action against him?"

Cobb gave a short laugh.

"They took his eyes. They destroyed his mind. What more had they to do?"

"They could have murdered him. They could have murdered *you*, Father Cobb."

"He was no longer rational. I was an American."

"So were the nuns."

Grassi gestured with his cup. "Ah, but your own government has been, what is the word, 'reticent'? on this entire affair. During the U.N. debate . . ."

Cobb shrugged. "The U.N. debate was a farce. It is Washington's policy under this administration to support any regime, *any*, that is against communism in that part of the world."

"And is not that the Church's position? To oppose communism?"

"Yes, but not to embrace fascism as the price."

Grassi put down his cup. "Cobb," he said, the small eyes keen, "these concepts you so casually utilize, 'communism . . . fascism,' they are not entirely unknown to us here in Italy."

"Meaning they are to me."

"Not necessarily. It is only that we have lived with them for the greater part of this century. Not simply as foreign observers for a year or two. My own father . . ."

"Yes?"

Grassi shrugged. "Ah, well, it's not a unique story. Imprisoned by Mussolini. Later, after the Bagdolio coup, arrested by the partisans and shot."

"But that's what I'm talking about, Eminence," Cobb said eagerly, "that's what the book was all about. The need to explore a middle ground between the two extremes. Never to permit the Church to be maneuvered into a position where its support, its blessing, is given either officially or tacitly to a government or a party or a movement that sanctions the killing of men like your father. Of men like Pedro Figueroa. Of mission sisters trying to teach children to read and write. We must find a course between the two evils. We *must*."

"Do you not think Rome is aware of this?"

"I assume Rome is 'aware.' But is Rome doing anything about it?"

Grassi made an impatient gesture. "You're a young man, Cobb. Obviously you're intelligent. You feel deeply. These are not bad things for a priest of God. But your vantage point is so limited. A few years in a small country and you think you know better than any of us, better than the Church itself, what our policies should be, how our attitudes should be fashioned. You see a world that is black and white. Rome sees a multiplicity of shades."

Cobb noticed that Grassi's English was not as crude as he pretended.

"There is good and there is evil," Cobb said dully, realizing how simplistic the words sounded. "Surely there is no confusion as to where the Church must stand on that."

"My dear fellow . . ."

Cobb went to the serving tray. Grassi nodded when Cobb offered to refill his cup.

"Eminence," Cobb said, "why am I in Rome? Am I to be silenced? Censured? What?"

Grassi smiled.

"If it were that, Father, it could have been done without this trip across the ocean, without my ever having to meet you, to have Lonsdale arrange this delightful dinner. The Church has a long arm. It reaches even unto America. To Massachusetts."

"Then why?"

Grassi set the cup down carefully on the table. He looked up at the much taller Cobb.

"Do not permit yourself to be used, Father Cobb. There are those who would make cults of books like yours. Faddists. Enthusiasts. They have no real understanding, only enthusiasm. Beware them."

"I don't understand, Eminence." He meant it. He knew he'd gotten fan letters. He knew nothing of Grassi's computer printouts.

Grassi waved a brown-spotted hand.

"We will talk again," he said, getting up heavily from the chair. "But we are being rude to Lonsdale and his charming guests. No?"

The two men, one tall and lean, the other gnarled and short, returned to the living room, where Lonsdale was serving brandy and telling a slightly naughty story.

18

"The chic thing, you see," Jane Orsini was saying, "is never to ski at home. Absolutely never! It's ever so much more fun if you're French to cross the border and ski at Cortina. Or for the Italians to drive up into France and ski at Megève or Val. The snow is always whiter, I guess. The Germans, of course, *zut*, the Germans ski anywhere."

"And push on the lift lines wherever they are," said her husband. "Have you any theories on why God made the Germans, Peter?"

Cobb remembered his two Germans at the mission in Mirador, their childlike obsession with soccer the only sliver of relieving light in the Teutonic gloom.

"No, Gigi, beyond the customary assumption they are a penance for our sins. It would take a more able theologian than me to theorize further."

Jane laughed. He was glad to hear it. She had not sounded happy in her rare letters, their phone conversation on his arrival in Rome had had a brittle, nervy quality, her soft, lovely eyes looked deep and tired. Gigi, if one could believe the stories, apparently led her a pretty miserable life. And, once again if the talk was true, if half the newspaper gossip was valid, Jane herself was playing overtime out of sheer self-defense. "Crazylegs" Cobb. He'd heard the talk. Who hadn't?

They were eating dinner at El Toulà. Not for Gigi Orsini the picturesque little *trattorias* that so delighted tourists or the flashier hangouts of the movie crowd to which Tom Hathaway was addicted. Not, in any event, when Gigi was with his wife and her brother, the so-famous American priest and writer. When Gigi was not with his wife, which was often, he was somewhat less selective.

They had the young lamb following a prosciutto sliced so thin the *Osservatore Romano* could be read through it. Since it was Thursday, the gnocchi was being pushed but Orsini, still lean as a boy, had waved it away.

"John Prince has just measured me for the cockpit of the new car. A single additional ounce of fat could destroy a year's work in the bloody wind tunnel."

Prince was the Englishman who built the cars that Orsini raced, and Gigi had picked up the slang.

"Wish I had his discipline," Jane said, looking down at what appeared to her brother a satisfactorily boyish body.

Gigi smiled. It was nice to be accused of self-discipline when you had so little. Especially by your own wife.

Jane was taking the children to Val d'Isère for a fortnight's skiing. Gigi would be unable to be with them, regrettably, since the South African Grand Prix was being run at the same time. Their married life, it seemed, was a series of such conflicts, a series of cumulatively punishing compromises in which Jane did the compromising and Gigi, well, Gigi did as he pleased.

"But you must come, Peter. You were always so much better on skis than I was. Why sit around stuffy old Rome emulating antique ruins when you can be getting some sun and some exercise?"

Now Cobb laughed.

"That was long ago and in another country. The last time I skied we were still wearing long thongs and skis were eight feet long."

Gigi's eyes widened.

"You're not serious, Peter. People in America, they ski like that?"

"Twenty years ago we did."

"Peter, do come," Jane said, "you've never seen the children and you and I haven't had a good old talk for eons."

"Yes, you must," Gigi said. Awfully convenient having a brother-in-law like this one to keep Jane occupied while he was away.

Cobb threw up his hands.

"I dunno, Jane. Love to spend some time with you and the kids. Love to get on skis again. But this damned business with Cardinal Grassi . . ."

"Oh, nonsense. You've been here a week already and nothing's happened. Trying to get things done in Italy is like doing the breast stroke upstream. And the Vatican, from what I hear, is more Italian than the Italians. Decades, entire centuries go by while people sit around reception rooms waiting to be seen. They develop green mold and put out shoots. Spiders weave intricate webs in their hair and termites eat away their shoes and things."

"Can you imagine Father?" Cobb asked.

Jane laughed again. "Why he'd just bite people and go all foamy at the mouth."

"But you should go skiing, Peter," Orsini said. "Really you should. Val d'Isère is bloody wonderful."

Orsini was afraid of Charles Cobb and wanted to get the conversation back to safer turf.

"Tom Hathaway's here, you know," Cobb said.

"No, is he? At the Embassy?"

"Practically running it."

"A regular little Clare Boothe Luce, I'll bet," Jane said.

In the end it was agreed that if he could slip away from Rome for a few days Peter would fly up to Geneva and make his way to Val d'Isère. Orsini said that "of course" the holiday would be on them.

Jane laughed again, rather triumphantly, her brother thought, even rather cruelly.

"Oh, Gigi, for all his vows of poverty, Peter is swimming in money. He makes us look like Sicilians."

For "us," Orsini read "you," which was as his wife had intended it. To retain sanity she used whatever weapons she had. Financial independence was clearly one of them.

There were, Peter suspected, others. And he felt more than marginally guilty about not having had, for so long a time, a good, serious talk with her. Instead now, even after all these years, it was just chat. Shallow, amused, meaningless. She was his sister and she was troubled. He was her brother, and more than that, he was a priest. It was not enough that he worry about her. He should damn well do something about it. He had a responsibility, God-given, man-given. Well, he thought, maybe at Val d'Isère, if I go there for the skiing. We'll talk then.

Good intentions.

The next morning Gigi flew out to Cape Town and Peter and Tom Hathaway took Jane to dinner. Pia Bartoldi was with them, every bit as appealing and likable as she had been at Lonsdale's table. Jane was pleasant, but reserved. A curious reticence. Cobb wondered, and disliked himself for doing so, if there had been anything between the young princess and Orsini. Hathaway seemed unaware of any tension at the table. Clearly, he was a man in love.

Jane was staying at the Excelsior. "I stare at the movie stars," she said laughing, "it so pleases them."

But when they had dropped her and she had let herself into the suite that gave onto the Via Veneto, she stood for a long time staring out onto the busy street, watching the traffic, listening to the horns, the occasional shout or laughter that floated up toward her bedroom. She undressed, carelessly tossing a Valentino suit across a chair, and then slipped into a nightgown. It was a clear, cold night, and the light of a full moon illuminated the darkened room. On the night table a white telephone gleamed dully in the half-light. The phone was there, beckoning. At the other end of it, she knew, at a certain number, at *several* certain numbers, there were men who would do for her what Gigi Orsini rarely bothered to do anymore.

Jane picked up a magazine and slid into bed. She tried to read. The print seemed blurred, the pictures banal. She shook her head angrily at herself and threw the magazine to the floor and switched off the lamp. At two o'clock she was still awake. There were sleeping pills in the bathroom. And there was the white telephone.

Finally she picked it up and, with a cigarette in her mouth, quickly dialed a local number she knew by heart.

"*Ciao*," she said, "it's me, Jane. At the Excelsior. Can you come over?"

At the other end of the line a man hesitated.

"It's a bit awkward," he said. "Freddo is here. He and his girl had some sort of fight. He's using my couch."

"Oh?"

There was a moment's silence. Then the man said tentatively, "He's not asleep yet. We just got in from a tour of the discos."

Jane's hand holding the phone tightened, nails digging into her palm. She knew what was coming.

"If you wish, I'll bring him along."

She nodded silently, and then, with a rush of words, as if wanting to respond without thought, Jane Orsini said, "Yes, bring him. Yes."

Papal audiences take on the personality of the particular Pope. This Pope, Gregory, relatively young, a physical, vigorous man, had already raised eyebrows on the *camerlengo*'s staff, the elderly ritualists whose function it was to organize such papal appearances, distribute tickets, herd the pious, sheeplike and awed, into the ornate rooms where audiences were staged. Gregory did not like to stand on platforms. Taller than most of those around him, bulkier, he preferred to wade into the crowd, shaking hands, touching, being touched, blessing, smiling, exchanging here and there a word, a greeting, a jest, all in a dozen different languages held together only by a grin.

"There's to be an audience," Lonsdale announced when he phoned Cobb at the Hassler. "Nothing special. Rather unwieldy. But you said you wanted to attend one. I haven't the foggiest when there'll be a more intimate occasion. Perhaps you'd better catch this one while you can."

Cobb said he would be there.

"Enjoy yourself," Londale said, his tone less cheery than the words.

He picked up his ticket for the audience at Lonsdale's cubicle. The monsignor was absent, off on some vital errand or other, but an envelope with Cobb's name on it sat propped against the IBM typewriter. Cobb shoved it inside the pocket of his black suit and, following the directions on a memo Lonsdale had pinned to the ticket, went out into the piazza in search of the appointed door.

The papal audience was scheduled for ten o'clock and by a quarter of the Sistine Chapel was filled. Perhaps four hundred men and women, half of them in clerical garb, stood shoulder to shoulder talking in hushed tones, some of the nuns fingering beads, many of those in attendance, both religious and laity, holding cameras. There was a touristy feeling to the assembly more than a sense of religion. This room, so obviously a small museum, a picture gallery, rather than a church, this crowd, excited, breathy, murmuring, glancing at watches. Why, then, did he not feel like a tourist? Why did he feel as if he were going to confession? Or as he had that day so long ago when he had taken Orders with mingled dread and joy, deep conviction and the suspicion of unworthiness, pride and humility clashing and confused?

At ten precisely two doors were thrown open. Beyond them stood a pair of Swiss Guards, extras in a Victor Herbert operetta, their silly, medieval pikes grounded. Between them then there passed a flurry of priests. And behind them, the Pope.

Gregory was a bigger man than he had anticipated.

The pilgrims, Cobb among them, fell to their knees. Even at that instant a few camera flashbulbs went off. Somewhere, a woman sobbed, perhaps a nun. Gregory, tall and bulky, white-capped, white-gowned, crossed the short interval of marble and mounted nimbly to a platform covered by a deep red carpet. He stood there for a moment, regarding his flock, nodding slowly, casually, as if he were counting the house, and then he raised a large hand and made the sign of the cross above them. Cobb, who had determined to keep his eyes on the Pope's face, bent his head with the rest of them.

"I propose to you the option of love," he'd heard Gregory say in a wet dusk on Boston Common, half a year and four thousand miles past.

He did not say this now, but it was what Cobb heard.

Cobb was still kneeling, head still bowed, when the Pope, his blessing given, began to speak colloquially.

"Come now, stand up, stand up," he said, the Latin becoming Italian and then French and then English and then something else. "You have come to see a Pope. Stand up, stand up. You can see nothing if you kneel."

All around him men and women were getting to their feet and Cobb rose with them.

Gregory waited until they were all standing, hushed and stilled. He nodded again, his broad, pleasant face split in a smile seemingly wide enough to encompass them all.

Then he began to speak.

If his mastery of languages was remarkable, his words were not. Yet his voice, in whatever tongue he chose, seemed to imbue the friendly, casual words with an importance far beyond their literal meaning.

"You are welcome in this house," he told them.

"A few months ago I was a stranger in this house. In this city. In this land. Today it is my home. One day, not too soon, I hope, it will mark my death."

There was a murmur of no's. Gregory raised both hands to still them.

"No, no, my friends. There is nothing terrible about death. Nothing to fear. It is life that presents problems, life that is difficult. Death is nothing. Death is but a passage to something better."

What was all this talk of death? Where was the traditional papal "we"? Nothing about Gregory was as Cobb expected.

Then, almost as if he were reading Cobb's thoughts, Gregory again extended his arms. "But on this lovely winter's morning," the Pope said, pausing with an actor's timing for the brief, appreciative chuckle of those who had crossed the windy piazza in the January chill, "why do we speak so seriously?"

He smiled again, this time more a broad grin.

"Let us instead say hello to one another. Let us embrace."

Gregory then stepped down from the little platform and into the mass of pilgrims, moving slowly through the crowd, turning this way and that, nodding, chatting, raising a right hand to form in the air a small cross. Behind and around him the priests bustled, busy and concerned. Gregory ignored them.

Cobb stood halfway back in the historic room, watching the Pope slowly move toward him. The crowd, docile until now, began like a field of grain to lean toward Gregory as if moved by the wind. At Cobb's side a priest prayed the rosary aloud, a woman, not a nun, wept, a mother held her child aloft, crying out in some alien tongue for recognition. Above them all cherubs swayed, Adam strove, the Deity held out an omnipotent finger, while prophets and sibyls bore witness, all in Michelangelo's astonishing gesture of turbulent serenity.

149

Gregory approached. Still smiling, bowing this way and that, not in obeisance but to bring his own head to the level of others, talking, gesturing constantly, reaching out and touching. Always touching. Always reaching out. The pilgrims gave way before him, slowly, stubbornly, as if wishing to prolong this moment of intimacy. Some of them fell again to their knees, causing Gregory to reach down, to raise them once more erect, the little priests attempting to aid him in his labors, but only succeeding in getting in the way.

Cobb could hear his voice now, murmuring, shifting easily, fluently, from one language to another.

"Hello, my brother. *Bonjour. Guten Morgen.* Good morning, sister. God be with you, my friend. *Ciao. Buenos días, mi amigo.* Hello. Good morning."

His voice, not amplified as it had been in Boston, nor as distant as it had been in the Piazza San Pietro, nor at one remove as when he stood on the platform in this room under Michelangelo's mad and wonderful ceiling, was low and resonant, a cheerful growl, intimate and warm. Peter Cobb did not fall to his knees; there was barely room. A nun in habit and a tall, middle-aged American in a double-knit suit, holding a camera, now intervened between Gregory and his mission priest of Mirador. Cobb felt his legs tremble. Gregory was greeting the nun now, a small woman who half fell, half knelt before him.

"*Buon giorno,*" he said, lifting her to her feet.

Now there was only the American tourist, raising his silly camera.

Cobb stood, rigid and yet shaking.

"Good morning, my good friend."

The tourist's camera, unused, fell from his hands to dangle on its strap.

"Holiness," the man muttered.

"Ah, yes, well."

Gregory's eyes were on Cobb's now. The tourist, blocking his path, fell to his knees to kiss the Pope's ring.

Gregory, smiling, moved slightly to one side, preparing to pass. Behind Cobb there was a press of bodies, of pilgrims eager to reach the Pope, to permit him to reach them. Peter could feel their pressure, leaning against his back, pushing forward, through him, toward Gregory.

The Pope had now at last extricated himself from the tourist's grasp and his hand rose, extending itself toward Cobb's, his pale blue eyes—they *were* pale blue—fixed on his.

At that instant, there was a loud clap.

"The audience is terminated."

A plump monsignor, officious and stern, glowered from the small papal platform.

Cobb's hand, as if possessing a will of its own, had come up. A few inches from Gregory's, it paused, the monsignor's announcement freezing it in mid-air.

Gregory looked at Peter Cobb.

He made a small gesture with his own hand.

Well, he mimed, and shrugged. These things happen. There are schedules to be kept, he seemed to say, without actually saying anything.

Reluctantly, it seemed, Gregory turned, and moved away.

Cobb fell to his knees. A trickle of sweat ran down the middle of his back, under the black suit he wore in deference to Gregory. And to their Church.

19

In Chicago a young Polish boy in the third year of his seminary studies, fretting privately about a homosexual urge, set himself aflame with lighter fluid after having typed a neat, six-page, and largely hysterical letter to Father Peter Cobb. A nun in Santa Fe startled passersby in a shopping center by crawling on bloody knees to a local parish church, chanting all the time the names of the three nuns slain in Mirador. In New York four Jesuit priests, eleven seminarians, and an editor of *America* magazine established themselves behind the blue sawhorses of the city's police department on First Avenue, across the street from the United Nations, and began a prayer vigil that they informed reporters was intended to force land reform on several Central American nations. The nations, of course, included Mirador.

Peter Cobb never intended any of this. He had written a small book about a small war in a small country. About some people he had once known.

Now, in the Hassler, the concierge handed him the day's bundle of mail. And now it *was* a bundle. No longer a slim letter or two. Somehow, they had tracked him down. Perhaps a little story in a newspaper. Perhaps the bush telegraph of zealots everywhere. Letters appealing for his prayers, his blessing, his guidance, his inspiration.

"I never wanted any of this. It's all bullshit. I never sought this crazy adulation. I don't want it now. I don't want it ever."

He told these things to himself, to his mirror, to the walls of his room. There was no one else. Jane wouldn't understand. Hathaway would retreat into cynicism. Lonsdale would sneer. And tattle. Grassi would make cathedrals of his fingers and lower his eyelids against the light. Against Cobb's eyes.

And those were the only people he knew in Rome.

He paged through the letters, tossing the torn envelopes into the leather wastebasket in the room, the crumpled stationery forming a small white alp in the basket. He read the letters. Wrenching, banal, passionate, idiotic, brilliantly wrought, foolishly phrased. Silly letters. Loving letters. All looking for something. For someone. For inspiration. For guidance.

Turning to him.

If only there were someone Cobb could turn to.

"Yes, Father," Cobb said into the transatlantic phone, "I've seen the Pope. And he hasn't bitten me. Or had me burned at the stake. Not yet, anyway."

Charles Cobb was calling from Houston. It was evening in Rome, following an afternoon spent taking notes in the writing room of the American Academy. Cobb senior, typically, had launched into the middle of things without even a conventional greeting. "I don't like it at all. Not at all. Something sinister as hell, those wops dragging you over there. Have you gotten in to see the Pope yet?"

Peter had the impression his father believed getting to see the Pope involved nothing more than calling his secretary and making an appointment, as one might do with Henry Ford or David Rockefeller.

But when Peter explained that his view of Gregory had been just that, a view and certainly not a personal interview, the old man seemed to accept it.

"Well, he's probably busy. Runs a big organization. Any of the bishops or cardinals giving you trouble?"

"Only in the sense they're all terribly vague as to why I'm here. No one tells you straight out what's going on. Some implied criticism of *Speculations*, of course, but I expected that."

There was a moment's silence and then Charles Cobb said:

"Peter, I have my interests in Latin America. You know that, of course."

"Yes."

"I can't be very specific but there's something going on. Between some of those spic colonels and your Church."

"Yes?"

"If I find out more I'll let you know." Then, after an instant, "Your man Gregory, impressive fellow?"

"Yes, Father. Impressive as hell."

"Well, be careful."

There was a brief exchange about Jane. Peter told his father with an assurance he did not feel that she was fine, that Orsini had been with her, that they had shared a pleasant meal.

"Orsini," his father said contemptuously, the name sounding more like an oath, and then hung up.

Cobb put the phone down and sat back against the pillows and the headboard of the big hotel bed, wishing he and his father were more forthcoming. He'd been shaken by his reaction to the Pope at the audience and he wanted badly to talk about it to someone. If Kurt Salomon were only here, he could tell Kurt. But Kurt was in Cambridge. Hathaway would laugh and accuse him of piety. Jane would listen solemnly and then say "uh huh" and change the subject. Lonsdale was, he feared, an adversary. There was no one to tell.

And if there had been, what was there to say? Cobb was a priest. Gregory was his Pope. It was only natural Peter's first close exposure to a Pope, *any* Pope, would stir powerful emotions.

But what Peter had felt in that crowded chapel was more than the weight of ages or the brooding presence of Michelangelo's masterpiece or an awe associated with authority. He had sworn a vow of obedience on the day of his ordination and he had lived by it. But obedience did not mean subservience or fear nor could it explain away the trembling of his legs, the difficulty he'd experienced in raising his hand to the approaching pontiff, or the nearly sensual relief he'd felt when the audience was terminated abruptly with a handclap and Gregory had stopped, and then turned away, just before reaching him. Peter had obeyed men for whom he had little respect, had done so because those were the rules and he had sworn to honor them. This, with Gregory, was of a different order of things, higher and infinitely more powerful. He was attracted and repelled in the same instant, drawn to the Pope and frightened away. Had he sinned, had he written a bad book, was what he felt in the Sistine nothing more complicated than the subconscious roilings of guilt, an unwonted acknowledgment of error?

Angry at himself, Cobb jumped off the bed and went to the dresser to tear open a pack of cigarettes. This was crazy! He had written a decent, serious book. He was in the right. He *knew* it! And, besides, Gregory had not even known he was there or who he was. To him, Cobb was just another young priest come to see his Pope. There was nothing more to it than that and he was a fool to be reading into the moment more than was there. He was no Savonarola and Gregory no high inquisitor. They were simply men whose eyes had met in a crowded room.

He lighted a cigarette and wondered where Hathaway and his princess were taking him to dinner.

The bomb went off during coffee.

Hathaway had reserved at Al Moro, in a slim alleyway off the Trevi fountain, where they ate baby squid and scampi deep-fried and went on to the specialty of spaghetti with egg and bacon, washed down by a splendid Orvieto. Pia was as jolly as if there were no husbandly skeleton lurking somewhere in the closets of her life, Hathaway was impressively informed on the latest opening to the left of this latest Italian cabinet, and Cobb had successfully, for the moment, shrugged off both the mystical experience of his audience and the exasperating hint by his father that, somehow, his summons to Rome was inextricably tied up with some new Church initiative to the fascist regimes that had killed and maimed his friends in Mirador.

"To bad you couldn't have gotten the Pope's ear, Peter," Hathaway said as the waiter took their coffee order. "One word from you and I'm sure Pia would have had her annulment."

"Just like that," Peter said.

"Nothing simpler, old boy. I know how you mackerel snappers all hang together on such matters. As bad as the Masons."

"Not that bad," Cobb insisted, "not a secret handshake in the lot."

Pia demanded to know about "mackerel snappers" and Peter told her.

"But fish on Fridays," she said, "why not? I love fish. It's a charming idea."

"Just proves how young you are," Cobb said.

And she *was* young. And in love. And in a rotten, stinking mess. When Hathaway asked Cobb's help he'd said no, that surely Pia had more influential contacts within the Church. Her appearance at Lonsdale's dinner table proved that.

Now, for reasons he did not even bother to articulate or to intellectualize, he blurted out, "If you really want me to, I'll look into the annulment situation."

Hathaway slammed a hand on the table, causing the silverware to jump.

"Peter, that's marvelous. I knew you would. Pia, it's as good as done. This man's not only a saint, he's a bloody genius."

"Nonsense, Tom," Cobb said, "these things are tricky. There are no guarantees. But I'll be glad to try. That is, if Pia gives me permission to discuss her marriage with the authorities."

Her face was grave. "Yes, Peter," she said, "I would be most grateful."

They were drinking coffee to the accompaniment of a long Hathaway account of a mission he had once undertaken to Libya to see Colonel Qaddafi when there was a commotion at the doorway.

"What the devil . . ." Hathaway grumbled, irritated that his story was being interrupted.

Cobb glanced toward the entrance. A waiter seemed to be arguing with a patron. Except the patron, in crash helmet and leather jacket, did not look like the sort of client drawn by Al Moro. Suddenly, the waiter wheeled, his face contorted in either fear or surprise, and he took a first step back into the restaurant.

Without thinking, Cobb grabbed Pia's forearm and yanked her toward him, shouting, "Tom! Down!"

He could still see Hathaway's face staring, uncomprehending, as the bomb went off.

The flame of the explosion and the roar of sound seemed to fill the small dining room, then the smashing of glass and china. The waiter who had turned was flung across a table and into a corner. The restaurant's electricity dimmed and then died, only to flicker back into life as an auxiliary generator cut in. Cobb lay atop Pia behind their table. He could see Hathaway's body prone between the table legs. Women were screaming and a deeper, masculine voice groaned heavily; someone else murmured a prayer over and over.

"Pia? You all right?"

"Yes," she said, her voice muffled from beneath him. Cobb crawled off her body and reached out to touch Hathaway.

"Tom?"

"Yes, yes. Okay, I think. Is Pia . . . ?"

"She's okay."

Cautiously, Cobb backed away from the table and got to his knees, then his feet. The warm, charming, talk-filled dining room of a few seconds before was gone. Through the blasted front windows came the night chill. He turned toward the kitchen. A chef and an older woman in an apron stood staring at their restaurant. The wreckage of the place was mirrored in the shock of their faces.

A few yards from Cobb a man's legs showed from beneath an over-turned table. A woman knelt by his legs, sobbing. He pulled aside the table and looked down. The man's face was gone. There was only blood and white bone and cartilage. He moved to another body. A girl. There was something wrong with her arm. He grabbed a napkin from the floor and dabbed at a bloody shoulder.

"Let me," a voice said behind him. Pia.

"Yes, if you can," he said.

She was pale but she was functioning. She reached past him and started to tear away the girl's dress.

"Good girl, Pia," Cobb said. "Good girl."

There were people standing now in the front doorway of the restaurant, their eyes wide, their mouths open.

"*Ospedale!*" Cobb shouted. "*Medico!*" A young man nodded and darted away. Somewhere, it seemed a long way off, Cobb could hear the wha-wha-wah of a police car or an ambulance. Without intending to do so, Peter, a stranger, had taken charge.

The young man in the leather jacket who had argued with the waiter lay on his back, spread-eagled on the cobblestones of the tiny street. His crash helmet had disappeared. Behind Cobb, in the restaurant, people were again on their feet, as Pia was, functioning. Amid them he could see Hathaway, a sappy grin on his face, his tie askew, his shirt splattered with something, blood or tomato sauce, the sleeve of his suit jacket torn. It was one of those suits of which he was so proud.

Cobb nodded at him and went through the shattered doorway to the young man on the ground. He knelt over him. He was very young, a boy really, and now his eyes opened. He saw Cobb.

"I'm a priest," Cobb said in one of the few Italian phrases he had really mastered.

"Sì, sì," the boy said. His chest seemed to be crushed. Cobb lifted what was left of the leather jacket. He could see rib and something he assumed was lung. He wished Figueroa had taught him more than the bandaging of limbs and the application of splints. This, this . . . chest, was beyond him. He closed the jacket again as the boy groaned, and began, very quietly, to pray the words of absolution. And as he did so, the boy gasped, "DeBragga, help me!" and was dead.

The police questioned them briefly before Hathaway, very official now, speaking rapid Italian and waving a diplomatic passport, got them away. Behind them the ambulances had left and they were sweeping up the broken glass and hammering plywood board into place. Three people were dead, another half dozen badly hurt.

"All for politics," Pia said bitterly. "All that for a stupid philosophy."

Hathaway, uncharacteristically somber, nodded.

"That's what most wars are all about," he said, "some lousy difference of opinion. Some arcane dispute over economics. Or to straighten a frontier. Or baptizing by immersion or by sprinkling the damned infant."

"Big enders and little enders," Cobb said.

"Three people dead," Pia said. "And for what?"

Hathaway shook his head.

"Did that boy say anything before he died?" he asked Cobb.

"No. Nothing. Muttered something about DeBragga."

"Don't know why you even bothered with him. It was his damned bomb nearly killed us all."

"Well, it killed him."

"Justice was served."

"I suppose so," Cobb said. In Vietnam, in Mirador, he'd become used to death. Here, in civilized Europe, death seemed more shocking because it was unexpected. Still, he was not as quick as Hathaway to make judgments. The police said the dead boy was a member of the Brigades. That, or an anarchist. They toss the words around so lightly, Cobb thought, as easily as did the regime in Mirador.

Pia and Hathaway dropped him at the foot of the Spanish Steps. The girl was still pale, but she had done well. Cobb was glad he'd promised to try to help. The marriage was clearly invalid. Perhaps there was something he could do. Hathaway looked at him narrowly as they said good night, the cab driver waiting impatiently.

"Don't waste any sympathy on that boy with the bomb, Peter. You'll find it's wasted."

"Sure, Tom."

"I mean it. This isn't Mirador, you know."

"Good night, Tom, Pia."

The cab made a short U-turn and roared away in the night. Inside the hotel the concierge handed Cobb his key.

"Another bombing tonight, Father," he said. "Ten people dead."

"Ten?"

"And hundreds hurt," the concierge added, inaccurately. "Madness, madness, and that fellow DeBragga issuing statements that only the Red Brigades can save Italy."

"Preserve us from intellectual bomb-throwers," Cobb muttered.

"Yes?" the man said, not quite understanding, his plump belly moving beneath the ornate uniform of his splendid office.

Despite the cold, Cobb threw open the windows of his room. Rome smelled as it had before, as sweet and elusive; the night sounds of traffic were as they had been before; the same moon hung over the Tiber. Yet something had changed.

It had begun the morning he faced Gregory. Tonight, looking down into that boy's face, his brown, frightened eyes nothing at all like the Pope's, he had again felt confusion, awe, a sort of fear clutching at him. Why? He'd seen death before. The bloody gore of terrorist acts; before that, in the war. It was all so strange. Cobb thought that, years before, he had come to terms with what life was, what he wanted from it, what it demanded of him. The answer, to every question, was God.

How simple he thought it would be, those afternoons in Chestnut Hill with Father Bergé, later, in the seminary, then, those first years as a priest in the missions. Like Voltaire, he had cultivated his garden. The world might be exploding around him, corrupting itself, polluting its atmosphere, but he had pulled over himself the covers of a child's bedroom, proof against all the boogeymen who ever lived or haunted the dark hours. Everything had seemed so satisfactory, so *right!* He had survived the war. A small smile: he had survived Harvard, perhaps a more perilous passage. All right then, he had endured both, not only survived but prevailed. And afterward, he had surrendered everything, renounced a life that, as the only son of Charles Cobb, could have been . . .

Chilled by the Roman night or by memory, Cobb slammed the windows shut, wrenched tight the handle locking them against the exterior darkness. He took the pack of cigarettes from his jacket pocket and threw himself on the bed, already turned down by the chambermaid, a chocolate mint in silver paper laid gently on his pillow. He started to light a cigarette. Then, childishly, he put the pack aside and took the thin wafer of chocolate from its wrappings and placed it on his tongue. A sacramental gesture. Empty, he knew. It was only candy. Sweet. Sweet tasting and meaningless.

In the morning, in the church of Trinità dei Monti, he consecrated, and then ate, and then distributed, other wafers. Not nearly as sweet. Infinitely more significant, desirable, vital, *important!* . . . that tasted like the unleavened bread they were.

Why was it he had no one with whom such matters could be discussed? Intelligently. Sympathetically.

As he walked down the steps from the church, the hippies begged coins, the sidewalk artists scrawled their bad pictures, the pretty, plump (or was she pregnant?) blond girl he had come to expect played her guitar. Again, badly. There were merchants of cheap leather goods, of watercolored pastiche, of Jesus sandals (which was how they cried their cheap footwear), of dirty pictures. A Turkish bazaar, translated here to the Eternal City.

At the foot of the Steps he turned toward the Vatican. The Academy was impossible today. How could he even hope to concentrate? Better to go to St. Peter's, to pray, if nothing else.

Fifty meters across the square he stopped to look back at the Spanish Steps and their scabrous, mendicant crew. There, at leasts, was life. Pitiful, starving, immoral, lost. But not alone! They had one another.

He had no one.

For the first time in many years, bar the occasional lusts of night, Peter Cobb badly wanted a woman. A woman to whom he could talk, vomit out his doubts, confess his fears. A woman who would hold and comfort him and confirm the reality of his existence.

20

Two days later there was another summons from Lonsdale.

"A dinner party?" Cobb asked, his voice innocent.

"No, no, my dear fellow. Instead, a task. For Grassi. A small thing but thine own."

They met at one of Lonsdale's cafés.

"So much simpler to talk, don't you think?" Lonsdale inquired pleasantly, snapping his fingers at the slim young waiter. "No curious nuns, no nosy monks."

Cobb ordered coffee and waited.

Lonsdale inhaled, his breath an ominous rale. But there was a smile on his pale face.

"His Eminence is planning a little trip. Thomas Cook and Company have been alerted, of course. No expense spared, none stinted. When my lud Grassi travels, we don't lay on tourist coaches and box lunches, you know. For Amadeo Grassi it is the Verandah Grill and an outside stateroom. Port out, starboard home. A certain style, a class, a cachet."

Cobb continued to wait. Lonsdale, like many priests with seniority, was inordinately fond of his own voice. In the parishes it made for windy sermons on Sunday. Here it made for chilled cups of *espresso*.

Lonsdale saw the boredom on Cobb's face.

"Dammit, Cobb, you listen to me, boy! You heed well what I say."

Cobb said, "Yes, Monsignor," and waited.

This is not going well, Lonsdale told himself, his heart beating overfast. This young man was obstinate and hard.

"Look, Cobb." Lonsdale's voice had lost its clever edge.

"Yes, Monsignor." So, too, had Cobb's.

Lonsdale picked up his cup. It rattled against the saucer. His hand, thin and trembling, seemed not up to its weight.

"Monsignor," Cobb asked, "are you well?"

This time there was neither mock innocence or stony indifference. Lonsdale, pale and wasting almost before his eyes, seemed to realize this.

"Cobb," he said.

"Yes, Monsignor?"

"It is Amadeo Cardinal Grassi's wish that you write a report for him. For his eyes only. Complete, honest, no poetry, no dialectics."

"Yes, Monsignor."

"You have lived there. Worked there. You understand the political situation. You know the people. You are of the Church."

"Mirador. He's going to Mirador?"

Lonsdale nodded, his hand momentarily steady, his eyes fixed, fierce and unyielding, on Cobb's.

"Yes, Mirador. The missions. Are they the rebellious, seditious nests the regime claims? Or are they awash with saintly nuns and little children at play and lepers miraculously cured?"

Cobb shrugged.

"A little of both, I'd say."

"Good," Lonsdale said, unexpectedly vigorous. "Then write it down. A report. A report for Grassi."

Cobb nodded.

"When?"

Lonsdale smiled through his pain.

"Ten days. You can take ten days."

"Here? In the Vatican?"

Lonsdale's smile faded.

"Any place you damn like, Cobb. But you hand me that report on Mirador in ten days."

There was no way for Cobb to know it but the thing had been arranged beforehand. By Grassi and Lonsdale.

Cobb frightened them. Oh, not that either would admit it. Behind them were pomp and ceremony and structure and the centuries. The whole panoply of two thousand years stood with them in serried ranks. They were the organization, they were tradition. They, not the damned, rebellious, arrogant, surly Jesuits, *they* were the Church.

And what was Cobb?

Still, he had written one book. He was writing another. And onto the tranquil surface of Catholicism he'd tossed a pebble. There were only ripples now.

"Get rid of him," Lonsdale had urged. "Shut him down. Turn him off. Distract him. Frighten him. Give him something else to do."

And Grassi, small and twisted, had nodded.

"Yes," he said, "give him something else to do."

And so they asked him to write a learned paper about Mirador.

Orsini's chalet was high enough above the village to constitute a decent climb on the packed snow of the roads, low enough to be isolated from the delicious lunches and the afternoon cocktails and the good restaurants and the better bars that made you think the French came to the Alps only incidentally to ski. Out of the valley funiculars climbed east and west to the height of 12,000 feet, a terrible and wonderful altitude if you were a skier and not precisely in condition. In the mornings you skied the west and in the afternoons the east, so as to have the sun always on the snow. Beyond, over the ridge, was Italy. Certain trails led across the border and it was advised in the ski school and the hotels that you ski with your passport in your pocket. Jitneys would bring you back around the mountain to Val and no one would make a fuss about the passports but it was advisable to have them.

Jane and the children and Jane's guest, a Contessa Massai, had driven up from Milan the week before and now Peter had flown to Geneva and then taken a train, then a smaller train, and, at a French town called Bourg St. Maurice, a bus for the last 40 kilometers over the pass through which Napoleon had once marched. Cobb found it pleasant to be in France again after so long a time, to be speaking French, to have quite decent wine served in *demis* on the train, to see the signs in French by the right of way and along the roads. There were avalanches along the road from Bourg, through the high villages where they herded goats and made cheese and swamped the laundry in big stone tubs in the middle of the main street—the women's arms beet red in the cold water. Once they were stalled by the snow and French army trucks came up with soldiers in their ill-fitting uniforms to shovel open the road.

"Peter, you are divine."

Jane leaned from the open window of the Mercedes at the hotel where the bus let them out.

"Not precisely an orthodox choice of adjectives, Jane."

He swung his bag into the empty back seat of the car and climbed in next to her.

His sister reached over and kissed him on the cheek.

"And I was afraid you'd arrive in one of the clerical dresses you fellows wear."

"Cassocks."

"That's what I said, cassocks."

He was wearing a trench coat over slacks and a sweater.

"The black shoes give me away though."

Jane giggled.

"Oh, Peter, I'm so glad to see you. I'm so happy you came."

He turned to look at her. She was watching the road that slashed through the town, spits of snow rushing at the headlights, but she was smiling.

In the morning he met the children, who were grave, wide-eyed, impressed.

Jane spoke to them in rapid Italian.

"This is your Uncle Peter. He is a priest and a great writer."

The children blinked. Cobb was not sure if it was the "priest" or the "writer" that did it.

The girl broke the silence first.

"Are you a friend of the Pope?" she asked. His Italian was up to that.

"Well, we are all friends of the Pope, I think."

"Me too?"

"Oh, yes. He loves children."

The boy joined in. "*Good* children," he said, "he only loves good children." He had a stubborn, defiant look on his face.

"A theologian," Cobb said. And then, "He loves all the children. Even those who are sometimes naughty."

The boy nodded, solemn as Lent.

"All right," Jane said, slapping both lightly on the bottom, "Uncle Peter must have his breakfast."

"They're fine, Jane. I like them."

"I'm glad. Considering all things, they're very good."

"And Gigi?"

"No sooner did we see you that night than he flew off to South Africa. The checkered flag waits for no man."

He had sat down at a small table spread for breakfast. He drank some coffee and then he said, "That bad?"

Jane shrugged. "Can't say I wasn't warned. Father delivered filibusters on the subject of marrying Europeans."

"Generalizations. They're what Father does best."

"Except in this instance he may have been correct."

The sun was coming in off one of the sundecks that girded the house on every side but the north, bouncing off the butcher-block surfaces of the

163

modern, eat-in kitchen, brightening Jane's face, which glowed under its mid-winter tan. She was smiling, she looked fine, yet there was a certain . . . tightness, a fatigue most people would miss but which her brother thought he could discern in her eyes, in her very bones.

"*Mangia, fratello mio,*" she said, leaning over to kiss his forehead.

"*Sì, signora, sì.*"

She slapped her head with the heel of her hand.

"Oh my God, Peter, I forgot. I *did* tell you we have a house guest, didn't I? Marella Massai?"

"Yes. Or Gigi did. In Rome, during dinner. The girl whose husband was killed. Did she come?"

"With us. You'll like her. She skis beautifully. I like her better than any-one I know in Milan. She . . ."

Jane broke off. The woman she had been describing came in through the swinging door to the dining room.

"*Ciao*, Jane," she said, and then, holding out a hand, she turned to Cobb.

"You're Father Peter," she said. "I'm Marella Massai."

He shoved back his chair from the breakfast table.

"No, don't," she said.

They shook hands. She had a nice cool hand. She was a tall woman, as dark as Jane was blond, with long hair falling straight down her back, a sun-burned face, large eyes in which he saw fatigue, gracefully prominent facial bones, a wide, straight mouth. They stood there looking at each other while Jane flew into her domestic bustle.

"Now sit down, Marella. Coffee? And, Peter, she's a *contessa*, you know, and must be treated with a certain deference. None of that American off-handedness you use with me."

But you're a *contessa* too, Jane," the Italian woman said, laughing.

"Doesn't count. It's Gigi's title. Mine on loan. Marella's a *real contessa* out of Burke's Peerage or whatever it is the Italians have."

"The Almanach de Gotha?" Peter wondered.

"We haven't had a king for ages," Marella said, "and we have more titles than ever before. Just like the old days when you paid someone a little money and your son became a *marchese* or your younger brother a cardinal. Oh, I shouldn't have said that, Father. I don't necessarily share the anti-clerical attitudes of so many of my compatriots."

Cobb laughed. "Actually, a pretty good system. Some of those boy car-dinals turned out all right. Others, well . . ."

"Isn't it too bad Father hates the Church so much, Peter," his sister said. "You'd be at least an archbishop by now with all his money."

They all laughed.

Well, thought Cobb, relieved that the Italian woman was not one of those heavy mourners.

A Scots nanny took the children off to a ski school nursery and the three adults spent an hour buying clothes and renting equipment for Cobb.

"Oh Peter," Jane said, "I like you ever so much better in powder blue. Can't you have your cassocks or whatever they are made up in something other than black?"

Cobb looked down at the quilted parka.

"Very elegant," he said. "They should see me at the Vatican now. There's a certain Monsignor Lonsdale who would start the defrocking procedures within the hour."

The cable car carried them to 9,000 feet and a chair lift took them to the high shoulder of one of the twin mountains flanking the valley. It was a clear day, cold, but with a hot sun and no wind, and they bought lunch in the summit restaurant and carried it out onto a broad terrace where slender Frenchwomen and deeply suntanned men drank chilled wine and stared at one another through mirrored glasses.

"Peter, smear some of this gook on your nose or by tonight you'll look like one of those boozy Irish priests."

Peter turned to Marella.

"*Contessa*, my sister has no respect at all for men of the cloth."

"But why should I?" Jane asked, mock-serious.

Marella laughed again. She forced the gaiety. Still, there was no mention of her dead husband, no sign of widow's weeds.

They skied the mountain twice that afternoon. Cobb had forgotten just how huge these European mountains could be. Each run took more than an hour. Considering how long it had been, he surprised himself by skiing reasonably well, falling only once when he left the packed *piste* and wandered off into deep powder. Jane had always been athletic and Contessa Massai was simply a superb skier. They were patient with him, waiting until he caught up. By the end of the second run he had his legs under him again. It was all coming back.

Dinner was pleasant, the children, as European children were, packed off early with the nanny, the table talk of skiing, the food excellent, the wine superb. Afterwards a maid cleared and they went in to sit by the fire. Light snow was falling beyond the big picture windows. He had been right to come, Cobb thought. How much better it was than to sit in the Hassler or in some café waiting for that damned Lonsdale to call. He could work on the report for Grassi just as well up here, leaving blanks for quotations and facts and research he could do later back in Rome in the libraries.

Jane had gone upstairs, her eyes tired beneath the cosmetic suntan. Marella Massai made no move to leave the big living room. She sat easily in a corner of one of the huge couches, light from the fireplace playing off the planes of her face, her long legs tucked up comfortably under the long, heavy fringed wool evening skirt she wore.

"More coffee?" Cobb asked, moving from his easy chair to the silver service on a sideboard.

"Absolutely not. One demitasse after dinner is sufficient to have me staring glassy-eyed at the ceiling until dawn."

He laughed, pouring himself yet another cup.

"I urge you never to spend any time in Latin America. Coffee is the national Coca-Cola. Children drink it instead of formulas." He took his coffee back to the chair. "It's been so long since I've skied I don't think anything could keep me awake."

"But you ski very well," she said. There was no flattery in the remark, none of the flirtation one got from American women. There was only a statement of what she felt to be fact.

"Thanks. Wish I could handle that deep powder the way you and Jane do."

"Jane is good. You ought to see Gigi. He simply flies."

"Gigi apparently goes very fast, whatever he does."

She nodded. "It's one reason I like Jane so very much. She has an ability to cope that one doesn't usually associate with American women married to Europeans." She paused. "That sounded rather superior and chauvinistic, I'm sure. It wasn't meant to be."

"No, it sounded as if you are just what Jane said you are, her best friend."

"Thank you," she said, inclining her head in a little bow.

He sipped the coffee.

"I've read your book, you know," she said. "Jane lent it to me."

Cobb laughed.

"I've warned Jane about that. Writers don't earn royalties on borrowed copies of their books."

"But you must forgive her. And I am grateful that she made me read it."

"She's forgiven. Actually, it's been sold to an Italian publisher. It won't be out here until next year, I'm afraid."

"It will be a sensation," she said. Again, there was no note of flattery in the remark. "Italians, even if they don't attend mass, are obsessed by the Church. And with our current 'opening to the left,' the political theorists are bound to debate endlessly your conclusions."

166

"And what are they?" he asked, not testing her but enjoying discussing *Speculations* with someone other than Edmund Lonsdale.

"Oh, that the Church should take a more activist role. Stop automatically supporting corrupt regimes simply because they're anti-Communist. Understand, just occasionally, the reasons behind terrorism."

Not knowing whether to comment, he was silent.

"You find it strange to hear me say it?"

"Well, yes, I do. I'd have thought you'd feel a lot differently. Considering . . ."

"Considering that my husband was machine-gunned to death?" The question was rhetorical. "Perhaps it's unnatural of me. At least," and for the first time a note of bitterness edged into her soft voice, "that's what some of my critics hold."

She had brought up the subject. Now he said, "Tell me about your husband."

She smiled. "A remarkable man. 'A future premier of Italy,' people said. That I didn't care about. It was Franco the man that I loved. It was funny. In public he was a dignified, serious presence, all dedication and probity, the very model of a modern major-general, one might say. A wonderful speaker, fluent, convincing, impassioned."

"And in private?"

She smiled broadly, the memory still capable of inspiring joy. "Oh, so funny, so full of mischief, always telling me impossible stories and insisting they were true. Not serious at all, not dignified. A man who loved jokes and small dinner parties in obscure little *trattorias* with three or four of our friends. At home, if I disagreed with him about something, if I said something stupid, he'd tickle me until the tears would come down my face. A boisterous, flamboyant man, more like an undergraduate than a somber, sincere politician of the Chamber, of the political campaigns. That was the side of him everyone saw and thought they knew. Only with me did he reveal the little boy he still was, the gentle, tender lover."

She stopped. Then, quietly, touchingly, she said:

"What a father he would have been. How fortunate would have been our children."

"I'm sorry." He knew it was inadequate, but such were the limitations of language.

"Yes," Marella said, "so am I." Her eyes were liquid. She fought tears and with rapid hand movements that masked nerves, she lighted a cigarette and inhaled deeply.

Then, as the smoke curled upward toward the beamed ceiling, she said,

"How is it you became a Catholic? Jane is such a . . . a WASP? Am I not right?"

He laughed, relieved at the change of subject, of tone.

"You haven't met my father?"

She shook her head.

"Jane says he is a *monstre sacré*. But she says it with love."

"True. A monster. But just how sacred, I dunno. After I converted, people wouldn't go near him for months, terrified he'd bite."

"But you did it anyway."

"I had no choice."

"Father Cobb, there is *always* choice. That is one thing I know about."

"Of course. But not when one is twenty years old and reading the philosophers at Harvard and boyishly infatuated with the ideal of perfect love. It would have been as impossible for me to walk away from the Church at that moment as it is for other men to walk away from a girl they love."

"And for you there were no girls?"

"There was one. Kiki Loomis. Wonderful girl. I'd simply decided there was at least for *me* a lot more to love than sex or even marriage."

"So you found God. You became a Christian."

"I thought so at the time. I was still a kid, I suppose, carried away by the romance of the thing. Boys my age were falling in love with girls. I fell in love with the notion of something infinitely bigger, more enduring, more important. But it was an immature sort of infatuation. I became a Catholic in Boston. It wasn't until Latin America that I became a Christian."

She said nothing. Her great, tired brown eyes communicated understanding, intelligence. She was not a chatterer; she lacked small talk. He went on.

"In the beginning it was an intellectual conversion, an intellectual vocation to the priesthood. I was still functioning on a rational, thoughtful level, just like any dedicated postgraduate student chasing after his Ph.D. God was a concept to be grasped, understood, reduced to logical phrases in an absolutely brilliant dissertation, defended with equal brilliance in my orals. I had not yet understood that you don't reduce God to size, you don't squeeze Him between the covers of books, that God doesn't fit on the carriage of an IBM Selectric."

"What's that, an IBM what?"

Cobb smiled.

"Marella, where have you been? No one writes books anymore without a Selectric. It's an incredible typewriter. Corrects your spelling, punctuates your sentences, practically looks things up in Fowler."

She laughed. She did not understand the allusion to Fowler but she let it go as unimportant.

"But this wonderful machine cannot capture God."

He shook his head.

"They're working on it. But I wouldn't lay odds."

"No," she said more solemnly, "I guess no one really captures Him."

"Anyway, Latin America changed all that. Here were these people I got to know, I lived among, a revolutionary, a country doctor, a nurse, and each of them in his own way with a better grasp on God than I had with all my book learning. A humbling experience. Joaquin was blowing up police stations and robbing banks and saying his prayers all at the same time. A Christian like Flor didn't have to try to intellectualize God: she was always *with* Him, instinctively, naturally, and without reservation or doubt, except as to her own lack of worthiness."

"Many of us have that, you know," Marella said quietly.

Cobb had a twinge of recognition. Lonsdale had said he was naive; Grassi presumably thought so. Now this Marella, who he had thought would understand.

"Look," he said, "I didn't mean to preach a sermon. You asked about my conversion and I told you."

"Father Cobb," she said with a gentle dignity, "do you always bite people's heads off for a remark?"

"*Scusi,*" he said, meaning it. "I'm sorry. It's simply that I've gotten defensive over the last six months. Especially the short time I've been in Rome."

"All because of a book."

He nodded. "A little memoir to friends I'd left behind. And you'd think I'd gone about tacking up theses to cathedral doors."

"Martin Luther is not my most attractive rebel," she said, smiling that he was forgiven, accepting his apology.

"Who is?"

"Oh, I don't know. Savonarola, perhaps."

"And we all know what happened to him."

Her smile faded. "Let's hope it doesn't happen to you, Father."

"You will get no argument from me on that, *Contessa.*"

"The name is Marella. And I hope we will be friends. As I am to Jane. As your friends in Mirador were to you."

"Good," he said, "I'd like that."

She smiled, the intelligent eyes no longer troubled. "That was what I liked best in your little book. The portraits of your friends."

Quite seriously, he said, "That is the heart of the book. The rest of it, well, your opinion or anyone's is as good as mine. Those 'speculations' were nothing more than a coda tacked on to the stories of Figueroa and the others. Odd, though, the coda is what people talk about. What stays with them."

"But, no, it is your friends that stayed with me. They always will."

He nodded.

"I'm glad, Marella."

She smiled. But as they shook hands he could feel hers trembling.

21

There was fine skiing for three days and then the foehn blew from the south, warm African air that picked up moisture over the Mediterranean to drench Italy and southern France. But at these altitudes it was snow, heavy, cloying, blinding. Cobb was happy not to have to ski for a few days, to read, to think about his report for Grassi, to get to know Jane's children. He said mass in his room each morning, alone. It was not required that he do so but it was habitual. A day begun without mass lacked center. Over dinner one evening, following a duty phone call from Gigi in Cape Town, Marella asked:

"Don't you miss saying mass, Peter?"

It had become "Peter"; they were at too close quarters, too relaxed for "Father" to be anything but stagy, awkward.

"Oh, but I do say mass. In my room before breakfast."

Rather shyly, she said, "Could I hear mass? It's always been a way to start the day."

"Of course. How thoughtless of me not to have asked."

The dining room became his daily chapel. Jane attended, at first out of curiosity. The children sat or knelt, still as perched birds. This was a new aspect of their mysterious uncle.

The girl was Fiona, the boy Charles, familiarly "Carlo," after his grandfather. Well-mannered, grave children, with Jane's blue eyes and giving promise of their father's extraordinary looks. Peter was surprised to learn they had been baptized Catholics.

"Gigi insisted," said Jane. "Typical of him. Never sets foot in a church but the children absolutely had to be baptized."

Marella laughed. "There are thirty million Italian men precisely like Gigi, I'm afraid."

Jane shook her head. "No one, I repeat, *no one* is precisely like Gigi."

Late in the afternoon on the second day of the storm the snow slackened. For the first time since it began they could see the roofs of the town, then people moving slowly in the street. Very few cars seemed to be moving. Jane said she was becoming claustrophobic.

"I'll buy dinner if anyone else is willing to venture out."

Cobb and the man-servant dug out the Mercedes and swept it clean of snow and he and Marella and Jane drove down into the town. Only the modern architecture of the chalets and the hotels and the shops spoiled the fairyland effect of a snowed-in Alpine hamlet. Shopkeepers shoveled the raised sidewalks clear and a small, yellow tractor with a floodlight crawled along the main street plowing a drivable path. Jane followed it and then, very competently, swung the big car into a narrow space between two buildings where wind had eddied out a bare spot clear of drifting snow.

"It's been so long since I've driven in snow," Peter said, "I'm impressed."

"Gigi taught her the trick of snow driving," Marella said.

"Oh, yes, he's taught me lots of tricks."

Dinner was in a bistro called Pierrot's, the usual wonderful food, the usual French din, girls with Paris chic and slim young men, everyone with suntanned faces and throats but pale hands from the ski gloves and mittens. Peter and Jane ordered "drys," Marella a Scotch-Perrier.

"I learned to drink in America," she said, "but the dry martini and I are mutually exclusive."

Their waiter was a professional, one of those small, tireless men who will wait on tables throughout eternity. No college kids here, ski-bumming for their rooms and their lift tickets as they would have done in the States. The waiter uncorked a chilled Moulin-à-Vent without asking. There was no *carte*, only a hastily recited list of the evening's specialties. They ordered *steak au poivre* and salads and Jane asked for a second "dry."

"What were you doing in the States?" Peter asked.

"I went to college there. Stanford. And I had a teacher in Sausalito I worked with for another year when I realized fate intended me to be a sculptor. I loved it. I think all Europeans love San Francisco. It's so much like home."

"Do you still sculpt?" Peter asked.

"I've not gotten back to it, not since Franco died."

"She's marvelous," Jane said enthusiastically. "She takes Giacometti a step further." She'd been arguing with Marella, trying to get her to sculpt once more.

"My friend Jane has never been accused of understatement," Marella said modestly. "I worked with metal and under his influence, but as for taking him a step further, hardly . . ."

During dinner Peter watched them. They were about the same age, one blond, the other dark, both slender, beautiful women. Marella, childless, had lost a husband, brutally, savagely. Jane had money, children, a handsome, dashing man. Yet it was Marella who tried valiantly to be vivacious, Jane who brooded. He did not like to impose himself into the situation with Gigi but she was his kid sister. He could still remember what she had said when their mother died. "Peter, we must *always* stick together!"

They had a second bottle of wine to finish the steak and then to drink with cheese. Then Jane ordered a brandy.

"Not me," Peter said. "My legs will be shaky enough in the morning and I want to try that trail into Italy."

There was a small dance floor and several couples were up now. A man who seemed to be someone Jane had met came to the table and after introductions were slurred asked her to dance. She still had that ineffable, lanky American grace. Peter liked to see her dance. He hated to see her unhappy.

Marella toyed with the last of the wine.

"You love your sister," she said. It was obvious she meant more than a simple statement of fact.

"Yes," he said, turning back from watching the dancing. "Eight years between us, but when our mother died we became quite close. Waging common war against Father, you know, siblings united against the world. We were always being sent away to different schools. But summers, the holidays, we made up for it."

"Jane has been very good to me. When Franco died . . ."

"Obviously you've been good for her as well. With Gigi away so much . . ."

She smiled away the compliment. "Sometimes I think it would be better for Jane if he stayed away."

"That bad?"

"You don't know Gigi Orsini very well. Spoiled, self-indulgent."

"There are those who say the same thing about Jane. Rich American brat. Playgirl. 'Crazylegs Cobb.' Latin Americans love gossip. Occasionally I'd see her photo in a magazine. Or my father would write a long screed about how it was all my fault. If I'd stayed home and played big brother instead of burying myself in a monastery, Jane would have turned out . . . differently."

"'Crazylegs,'" Marella said, "not too far off the mark, you know. Just look at her."

They watched her dance. So did most of the room.

Jane drove them home again, driving well despite the brandy. The village lay quiet under the carpet of new snow. Above them the mountains loomed darkly, and beyond them a clearing, cold winter sky. Marella said good night and went upstairs. Peter sensed she was leaving them alone. Maybe she only wanted to be alone with her grief.

"Want to talk?" Peter asked.

"Sure, what about? My wicked, wicked ways?"

He was not going to let a brittle response put him off.

"Why not mine?" he asked lightly. "Aren't I the one in trouble with the Vatican?"

"Oh, you. You're an angel. Whatever you've done. I'm the black sheep of the family. Hasn't Father kept you informed? He telephones me all the time. Long, pious lectures about my heritage, my breeding, about my letting the Cobbs down, letting Mother down . . ."

"No lectures from me, Jane. I thought we'd just talk."

Her lovely face tried to smile and then it crumbled.

"Oh, Peter, I'm so damned miserable."

She threw herself at him and he took her into his arms, an older brother, a younger sister, both transported back in time nearly twenty years.

The boy and girl, now the man and woman, talked until four. Jane brewed coffee and Peter chain-smoked and they both talked, not only about her marriage but about his vocation, about their distant father, their dead mother, their dreams, their illusions, their failures. It was as Peter had hoped, no one-sided homily from the pulpit.

"You can't know what it was like, Jane, those two pious old squareheads doddering around the place, arguing whether Pelé or Beckenbauer or some Spaniard I'd never even heard of was the greatest soccer player of our time. Outside, people like Joaquin were running wild, Pedro Figueroa was trying to steer a course between sanity and madness. In our own mission leprous parents were nursing children who would be lepers by the time they were twelve. The *junta* was butchering its own citizens and these two decent, mindless old men were jabbering *plattdeutsch* and discussing goals-against averages. Sometimes I thought I'd go nuts."

"Same here, Peter. I should have known what Gigi was, of course. About all those girls in the pits at the races in their tight jeans and their custom-made jump suits with Exxon and Firestone on the back. I'd *been* one of those girls, dammit. Whatever made me think I could reform him, how could I believe that the fact of a wife, a home, a child would miraculously turn him into a pipe-and-slippers type reading Dickens after dinner and early to bed with his dear, loving wife? I knew what the circuit was like. We lived together, you know, for a season before we married. I never told you that, did I?"

He shook his head.

"Lots of things I never told you. And they say confession is good for the soul."

"It is," he said. "Freud was a little late discovering that."

Jane laughed.

"And you don't charge seventy-five dollars an hour."

"My rates are negotiable."

She sobered.

"But *you're* not, Peter. You don't bargain or waver or trim. You're always Peter Cobb. The rest of us get confused about who we are and where we're going and what to do when we get there. You always seem to know."

She said nothing for a moment and then, "I'm not very good now, either. Gigi rubs his girl friends in my face. That's when he's here. When he's away, I'm lonely. I . . . I play around." Then the words came in a rush. "Not very nice hearing that, is it, Peter? That your kid sister is a tramp. A jet-set bum. An easy lay. A stock item in every gossip column in every cheap newspaper in the world."

"Feeling pretty sorry for yourself, aren't you?"

"Yes," she said, "yes, I am. Damned sorry. I've gotten myself into a stinking situation and my response is to make everything worse. Gigi hasn't done a thing to me that I haven't topped by doing to myself."

"Jane, Jane," he said, the priest and the brother in him touched by the sad despair in her lovely, familiar voice.

"I do these terrible things and I feel rotten about them and then I do them all over again. The other night after dinner with you and Tom and that girl of his, back at the hotel, I couldn't sleep. I called a man I know."

"Jane."

"Tonight, if you hadn't been there, I would have gone off with that man who danced with me."

"Look, Jane, you aren't my parishioner. You're my sister. I'm not going to tell you to go ahead and do whatever you want and the hell with guilt. And I'm not going to lecture you on sin or the sanctity of marriage or your responsibilities to your children. Or to yourself. You know all that stuff. Deep down, you know it. If you didn't know it you wouldn't feel so awful. You know these things instinctively. You've got the right stuff. Eventually it'll come out. I'll pray for you, if you wish. Probably even if you don't. But I'm not passing judgment. I don't have that right."

She didn't respond and then she got up and poured herself a brandy, not bothering to ask him.

"I dunno," she said.

"Most of us don't know very much," he said.

"Peter?"

"Yes."

"Pray for me, will you."

Peter did not ski in the morning. He stayed in his room, rereading what he had written for Cardinal Grassi. Not very satisfactory. "No poetry," Lonsdale had ordered, a straightforward report on the missions of Mirador and whether they were performing their function or serving as a boot camp for guerrillas. Or a little of both.

That was the problem. It *was* a little of both. He had a responsibility to write the truth and yet he feared Grassi would use any suggestion of mission complicity in the rebellion as evidence the local Chuch been radicalized. Cobb shook his head. Last night, with Jane desperately reaching out to him for help, he had mouthed platitudes and said everything would work itself out.

"A regular Doctor Pangloss, you are," he told himself contemptuously.

He'd failed Jane and now he dithered between his duty to Rome and his love for those left behind in Mirador. He rolled a fresh sheet of paper into the old portable and began, joylessly, to type.

Afternoon. Cobb and Marella Massai on a mountain.

A few hundred feet below the top of the lift they paused for breath and to permit the wilder of the mountain's young skiers to chatter past on the packed snow of the *piste*. This was France. Looking left they could see Italy. There were no frontiers, no sign posts, no garrisons, no *douanes*. Only the great Alps and the winter sky, blue and infinitely high. Leaning against a tree, his skis still on, Cobb ransacked the pockets of his anorak until he found his cigarettes. Marella, leaning on her poles, shook her head.

"You smoke too much, you know."

"One of my vices."

"The only one, I think."

"There's a monsignor called Lonsdale might differ with you on that."

"I consider him badly informed," she said.

Cobb laughed.

"Well, men are not angels. We deserve one vice, don't we?"

"Oh, yes. But a woman?"

He smiled.

"With women, who can quantify?"

There was a children's race and Jane had gone off to shepherd Carlo and Fiona. She'd insisted Peter ski with Marella. "You'd be bored to tears," she said, "and besides, the *bambini* all ski so much better than we do it's embarrassing." The reality was she suspected she had said too much the night before and she was uneasy about being stuck with Peter on a lift chair.

Cobb finished his cigarette and dropped it onto the snow, then pushed it beneath the surface and out of sight with the point of his pole.

"You're very neat," Marella said, watching him.

"Littering is the eighth deadly sin in America. The subject of countless sermons."

"Oh?"

"Absolutely," he said, and swung his skis around toward the *piste*. "And now," he said, "you will observe a theologically impeccable series of parallel turns not seen since the Reformation."

"Oh, I do hope so, Peter, I really do."

Marella cooked dinner that night.

"The least I can do in tribute," she announced. Both children had won medals in the competition.

"I think they give medals to everyone who enters," Jane said confidentially, "but don't tell Carlo. He wants to wear his on his pajamas."

"I wish I had a medal," Cobb said.

"You deserve one," Marella said, "that last tumble you took. A classic. You must have traveled ten meters through the air."

He was mock serious. "You should have been there, Jane. A truly historic moment. One instant my skis were flat on the ground, the next they were wrapped around my ears."

"But gracefully," Marella insisted, "never awkwardly."

Jane laughed. They'd succeeded in that, at least. Thank God for Marella, he thought.

There was braised cauliflower, an endive salad, and pasta carbonara for dinner, washed down by the Beaujolais *primeur* properly chilled in the refrigerator. They had ice cream and then, when the maid cleared the table and they sat over coffee, Jane said Marella deserved a medal as well. "The order of the Cordon Bleu."

"Yes," Peter said, "for an artist to cook like that . . ."

"Nothing," said Marella. "Being in France has inspired me. Back home I live on sandwiches and Fiuggi water. I wear filthy jeans and never go anywhere. The studio limits my horizon. No glamorous friends like Jane dropping by, no best-selling authors, no little boys with medals pinned to their pajamas. A terribly banal existence, I promise you."

"You must go see her, Peter. Just start dropping by the studio on transparent pretexts."

"Jane, you'll embarrass Peter. He's got more important things to do than watch me burning holes in girders with an acetylene torch."

There were two more days of skiing, another of snow, and then in heavy snow Cobb and Marella Massai hired a car to drive them down to Bourg St. Maurice and the train to Geneva. Jane and the children would remain in France for another ten days.

"I'll work on my suntan and read serious books and lose ten pounds," Jane assured them. "You'll both be so proud of me."

"But we are already," Marella said, meaning it.

Jane held her brother tight as they said goodbye, whispering to him, "Peter, all that rubbish I spoke that night. Don't brood about me. I'll be okay. Really I will."

"So I'm not to pray?" he said lightly.

"Just every so often. Mention me along with all the other sinners."

"You can count on it," he said, "and spare me the occasional prayer as well."

"I love you, Peter."

The French boy drove madly, if efficiently, through the blizzard, the car's yellow cones of light barely penetrating the snow that drove at the windshield.

"I hope he has snow tires," Peter said.

"I hope he has Michelins," Marella said.

The boy turned to grin at them. "*Ce n'est pas rien,*" he said.

"Sure," Cobb said in English, "just watch the road."

They were in Geneva at midnight. It was always a shock to be in Switzerland in winter and see the palm trees along the lake. Marella's train for Milan left first. Cobb's overnight from Paris to Rome would be another hour in coming. He bought them sandwiches and apples from one of the vendors on the station platform. Italian workers with cheap suitcases and bottles of wine under their arms jabbered happily and argued football. Cobb waved to Marella as she leaned from the open window of her compartment.

"It's been wonderful," she cried, happier than she had been since her husband's death.

"Yes," he said. "Yes, it has."

At eight in the morning he was in Rome at the ridiculous comic-opera railroad station Mussolini had built to congratulate himself on something or other.

The next day he was due to deliver his report on Mirador to Monsignor Lonsdale.

22

Lonsdale had not enjoyed a pleasant week. The cancer eating at his bowels was in no way improved by his compulsive appetite for good food and better wine. On Monday he had dined with one of the Borghese, "one of the more presentable Borghese," as he put it, on wild duck from the Venetian marshes. Odd, he realized, that he was not only able to continue to enjoy his meals but that he was almost constantly hungry.

"Monsignor," his doctor informed him, "you must follow a regime. You simply must! This is self-destructive. You are not feeding yourself, you are feeding a tumor."

"Yes," Lonsdale said, "I understand that."

"But you continue to do it."

"Yes."

"Monsignor, you wish to die?"

Lonsdale regarded the man tolerantly.

"Yes," he said.

The greatest publishing house in Rome is called Carletti Figli. Its specialty is the translation and publication of important foreign works. Carletti has for more than ninety years published Bernard Shaw, Hemingway, Brecht, Camus, Pasternak, Mailer. Important writers, important books. Books and writers that roiled the waters of Italian consciousness. Some would be best sellers, others not. But none would fail to have its impact.

Now Carletti was planning to publish *Speculations*.

There were no Carlettis left in the firm, not even any *figli*. When Lonsdale called there was only a little Jew from Padua with a spare beard and milk-bottle lenses to his eyeglasses.

"You have Cardinal Grassi's letter?"

"Oh, yes," the Jew said, "an honor. Such a man."

"Then you know who I am."

"Yes, Your Worship."

"And you know why I've come."

The publisher nodded.

"*And?*"

"And we are planning to publish Cobb's book. The galleys are being set now. The book was a best seller in America. It should be quite successful in an Italian translation."

Lonsdale nodded. "I'm sure it will be. A sensation. The Dead Sea Scrolls between hard covers. A television series. Fellini will want the film rights."

"Monsignor," the Jew said, "why this hostility? The author is an American. His story deals with an obscure Latin American country. The book came out months ago in New York. There are no secrets. Even *Time* magazine has written about it." He smiled disarmingly.

Lonsdale laughed. "Don't play the *naïf*, please. It is unworthy of both of us. Cobb's little book is . . . annoying. There are certain elements antipathetic to the Church for whom it could provide irritating grist."

The publisher shook his head. "Monsignor, we are publishing this book. The contracts have been signed. Checks have been sent to Father Cobb and to Dorset House. A subtle translation has been done. As I say, galleys—"

Lonsdale waved an impatient hand. "I know about the galleys. And I know about your checks. A few thousand lire would buy the Italian publishing rights to *War and Peace.*"

Carletti's man was silent. Lonsdale measured him and went on:

"The Church appreciates the profit motive. We're not Communists, you know."

"Naturally not."

"We'd not want your company to take a loss. A reasonable figure could certainly be paid."

The publisher held up a lean hand. "Monsignor, this is an exercise in futility. Peter Cobb's book will be published. We've sent out advertising. It's listed in our new catalogue. And, if by some misfortune, Carletti were not to come out with the book, someone else would. Rome *knows* about this book. *Speculations* will be published. By Carletti. Or by somebody else."

Lonsdale valued time too costly to waste it in useless recriminations. "I'm sure it will be a most attractive edition," he said smoothly.

"But of course," the man responded. "The truth is always attractive."

"Yes, isn't it," said Edmund Lonsdale, his lips pursed in irritated piety.

Cobb knew none of this. He appeared, at the start of the working day, at Lonsdale's desk.

"Here," he said, "no poetry."

He shoved a large Hassler envelope toward the monsignor. Inside, thirty pages of single-spaced type. Mirador. Reduced to fifteen thousand words.

Lonsdale made no move to open the envelope.

"Well," Cobb said, "what now? Back to Boston? Report to the Jesuit provincial? What?"

Lonsdale said nothing. Cobb had been summoned to Rome so they could keep an eye on him. He posed potential . . . *problems*. Grassi was alarmed by the passions Cobb seemed to be igniting in the younger clergy. Stall him, delay him, tire him out, keep him under your gaze. Those were Lonsdale's instructions.

Instructions he was not to reveal to Peter Cobb.

"Well?" Cobb asked again.

"Excuse me, Father," Lonsdale said, "my mind was elsewhere."

"This is what you wanted. You're finished with me now, aren't you? There's nothing more I can offer."

Again, Lonsdale said nothing. Peter stared down at him, puzzled, concerned.

"Monsignor?"

The Englishman looked up at Cobb. How unfair it was to have to fence with this healthy, confident young man when his own insides were in cruel rebellion.

"Nothing more. But . . ."

Lonsdale struggled for control. His face communicated pain. Then, with an effort whose cost only he could gauge, Lonsdale said, cold as January, "No, Cobb, we are not finished with you. Not yet."

Peter's shoulders slumped.

"Stay in Rome, Cobb. Stay in touch. This . . . this report of yours"— he touched it with a finger—"must be read."

Cobb had seen death. He made no argument with dying men.

"Yes, Monsignor. I'll stay in touch."

When Cobb left the little office, Lonsdale, gray-faced and hunched, was still sitting at his desk, the envelope unopened in front of him.

When he had left Rome for Val d'Isère and the week's skiing with Jane and Marella Massai, the papers had been full of the restaurant bombing. That was ten days ago. Now, there was nothing.

How quickly we forget, Cobb thought as he strode through a thin, chill February rain toward the American Embassy. Hathaway had called. It was important. Could they have lunch?

He had said little of the bombing to Jane or Marella. Jane had her own concerns; Marella would only be reminded of her personal grief. But if the newspapers had forgotten it in a flurry of other, more recent or simpler, trendier outrages, Cobb had not. In the smashed crockery of the restaurant, the cries of the wounded, and in the face of the dying young terrorist on the paving stones, there was Mirador, and all its tragic violence, calling him back.

There were marine guards at the Embassy but it seemed to Cobb that young, typically American secretaries and small, typically Italian clerks actually guarded the place. One of the Americans said, "I dunno," when he asked directions to Hathaway's office. One of the Italians got him there. Hathaway was smoking a pipe.

"Very preppie, Tom. I like that."

"My new image. Book-lined studies, pipe and slippers, the *Atlantic* opened and annotated on my desk. I'm considering steel-rimmed reading glasses."

"You don't need glasses."

"Oh," said Hathaway airily, "need has nothing to do with it. Image is everything."

Cobb flopped into a comfortable chair. Behind Tom's desk there was a framed, signed photograph of Bobby Kennedy. There was some sort of inscription but Cobb couldn't read it.

"Seditious of you to have Bobby up there these days, isn't it?"

"Career diplomats are supposed to be above that sort of thing. How was the skiing? You got a good tan."

"Fine. I've now fallen off half the Alps in France and several in Italy."

"Run into anyone I know?"

"No." For some reason he could not explain he had decided not to mention Marella.

Lunch was at one of those obscure little *trattorias* to which Hathaway seemed to have a private, arcane guidebook. The fish, he assured Cobb, came from the Adriatic. "It's very important to know that," he said, "they swim over from the Dalmatian coast, dialetically pristine. The Yugos are aware of just how a wavering party line can influence a fish's flavor. Something Italy has never learned."

The fish, Communist or Christian Democrat, was superb.

Hathaway leaned forward, forearms on the table.

"There was a bit of a stink while you were away. That boy. The one who threw the bomb."

"Yeah?"

"The cops came around a few days later. Wanted to know more about you. Just how much of a conversation you'd had with him before he croaked. Whether you'd met him before."

"My God, Tom, the boy was dying. I looked to his wound, gave him the rites. I told them all that."

Hathaway waved a hand.

"Hell, I know that. They're paranoid. Don't worry about it. I vouched for you. Told them you were very sound, voted for Nixon and everything."

"Thanks," Cobb said sourly. Tom ignored the note of annoyance and went on.

"They knew about your adventures in the banana republics. Seemed to have quite a dossier."

"They don't need one. It was all in the Rome *Daily American*."

"Sure," Hathaway said, "forget it. Dumb cops."

They talked about Pia, Cobb admitting he hadn't yet been able to do very much, and then they walked back in the surprisingly warm February sunshine until Cobb branched off to his afternoon's work in the reading rooms of the American Academy. He got almost nothing done. He'd dried up. The report for Cardinal Grassi seemed to have drained him of the urge to write anything more about Mirador. That night he went to a movie, dined on mediocre spaghetti in a workmen's restaurant, and slept badly.

If only Grassi and Lonsdale would have done with him and let him get on with the business of life, his work as a priest!

Cobb's report had surprised Lonsdale. He'd not expected frankness. It was his experience, gained through years of Church politics, that men told you what was in their interest, and not necessarily the truth. Yet Cobb, instead of weighting his report in favor of the resistance fighters of Mirador, as he'd done in *Speculations*, had admitted the missions, some of them, were working for the rebellion. He wrote about the priests who campaigned with the rebels, about the services they held in forest encampments, in mountain redoubts. About the nuns who nursed the wounded. About the guerrillas themselves who took weapons from Castro and the Russians as they took Communion from their priests and continued, despite everything, to think of themselves as practicing Catholics.

Lonsdale accepted the body of the report. He rejected its conclusions.

It was Cobb's thesis that the rebels were fighting a just war, that the regime was oppressive. And he ended, as he had in *Speculations*, with a plea that the Church hierarchy no longer support an autocratic regime simply because communism seemed the only alternative.

"There are alternatives. Men like Pedro Figueroa were not Communists.

They were good Catholics. And the Church turned from them."

Lonsdale wrote a summary of Cobb's report for Grassi to read. It would be what Grassi wanted to hear, shorn of Cobb's debatable conclusions. The Cardinal's mission to Mirador would be sufficiently complex without confusing the issue further. Lonsdale only hoped to live long enough to hear from the Cardinal's own lips just how successful that mission had been, thanks to Lonsdale's discrediting of this radical Jesuit and his oddly popular little book.

If only, Lonsdale thought, shivering, Cobb were just another penniless little monk and not the son of Charles Cobb. It was never wise to underestimate great wealth. Even when the son of that wealth had taken solemn vows of poverty.

Two days later the army of Mirador suspended operations against the rebel band headed by Joaquin Alfaro. Immediate tactical advantage, the *junta* decided, could constructively be sacrificed to ensuring that the visit of the papal nuncio, Grassi, would be a pleasant one.

Joaquin did not know this. The campaign had again shifted very much against his side. He only knew his battered little band had miraculously been granted the respite it so sorely needed.

While in Rome, a reporter named Darby was piecing together rumors that the Church was sending a very senior emissary to Mirador to see for itself just what was going on down there, and suggesting the presence in Rome of Charles Cobb's Jesuit son Peter, a man with strongly held convictions about Miradoran politics, might possibly be significant. Then, almost as an afterthought, Darby summarized what the Italian police were saying about Peter Cobb's "coincidental" ministrations to a dying terrorist in the *Brigate Rosse*. *Time* magazine, even on its "religion" page, delighted in marking such "coincidences."

Darby, well wired with his inspired Vatican leaks, his authoritative sources, wrote to his editor at *Time*:

"I don't want to overdramatize, but this guy Cobb is scary as hell. Hans Kung gets lots of publicity but no one but theologians knows what he's talking about, what the argument with the Pope is all about. Cobb's argument with Rome is simple. He wants the Church to get off its ass and *start* revolutions instead of hosing them down. A firebrand. And not just another Berrigan. Those guys didn't have a clue, for all their civil disobedience and Bill Kunstler-grandstanding. Cobb's *inside* the Church working out, not outside making faces through the window. He's written a best seller, he's got a rich old man, he's articulate, he's a matinee idol in a clerical collar. And now the talk is that he's hammering out another book that'll make *Speculations* look tame. A couple of the Curial smart boys, Grassi and a Brit named Lonsdale, seem to appreciate the inescapable fact that Cobb's dangerous. Everyone else is still drowsy, still worrying about whether sacramental wine ought to be dry or *brut*.

"I don't know whether Gregory even knows this guy's name. But he *will*. I think Cobb's heading for a showdown here in Rome. They're going either to listen to him or shut him up. And what that comes down to is Gregory. Is he going to buy Cobb's message? Or squash him? And don't buy that stuff about Gregory's being a benevolent, cheerful old pastor strumming his guitar and chucking *bambini* under the chin. This Pope is one tough son of a bitch."

BOOK V

———❦———

THE VATICAN

23

Gregory the Pope rose to the harsh buzz of an electric alarm clock on a night table to the right of his bed. Six o'clock. He pushed down on a button and the buzzing stopped. They used to send someone to wake him, one of the *camerlengo*'s men. It was a waste and he had sent out to buy an alarm clock. He had been Pope now for just over a year and he found many things about the Vatican and the life he was supposed to lead here to be wasteful and silly.

He kicked back the covers and stood up, stretching. Then, after rubbing a large hand across his face and running it once through his tangled, graying hair, he knelt at the side of the bed and prayed briefly, as he did every morning of his life, that this day would be blessed by God and that his actions would be motivated both by love and by justice. Love and justice, he knew, were not the same things. And he finished his prayer by asking that he be given the wisdom, when in doubt, to choose love.

There was in the papal apartment a large bathroom in old marble and, happily, with modern plumbing. He hung his cotton pajamas on a hook behind the door and stepped into the stall shower. When he was finished he toweled himself vigorously and, with a towel around his waist, shaved with a Gillette Techmatic razor. He missed the luxury of being able to skip the occasional shave, on a Saturday, for example, when he would enjoy the feel of the gray stubble on his big jaw and the flat planes of his face. Popes are to be clean-shaven, even on Saturdays.

He strolled out of his apartment dressed for the day, a simple white cassock over a cotton undershirt, a white skullcap, black trousers and shoes. One of his private secretaries, a Belgian, greeted him and together they walked to his private chapel. A young Swiss Guard with sleepy eyes saluted. At 6:30 he said mass. A half-dozen priests and two Guards made up the congregation. At a few minutes after seven he sat down to breakfast in his own dining room. He was a man blessed with a good appetite and on this morning he had two eggs, a small loaf of bread, split and toasted, orange juice and black coffee. Coffee was one subject on which he would not compromise. Gregory did not believe God or anyone else had intended *espresso* to be drunk in the morning. His coffee was brewed in a Chemex through filter paper.

The newspapers were neatly stacked beside his place. The Belgian secretary had now been joined by the *camerlengo*'s senior assistant and the two men sipped coffee and gave him an abbreviated verbal outline of the day's schedule. Gregory had the capacity to listen while he scanned the newspapers. As usual, there was trouble in the world. An editor had been kneecapped in Turin, an airliner had crashed in California, another Jewish dissident had been exiled to Siberia, another IRA hunger strike dragged on in Belfast. The African famine continued. An Australian election loomed. A blizzard had closed the passes from Italy into Switzerland and Austria. A cabinet shakeup had taken place in Belgrade. Gregory shook his head.

"Holiness?" the secretary asked, his intelligent eyes concerned.

"Nothing. The front pages. Depressing."

He pushed the papers aside. Later, when he was alone, he would sneak a quick look at the football news.

The secretary quickly moved to replace the newspapers with a slim stack of correspondence and several documents to be signed. He stood at the Pope's elbow, leaning over the table, earnest and informed, pointing out salient points and indicating certain passages. Thousands of letters arrived each day addressed to Gregory. Only a few ever reached him. He understood the necessity for screening. He only hoped the right letters were getting through.

By 8:15 he had finished breakfast and the early paperwork. There was considerably more reading to be done. He would tackle that in his study.

"Anything else?" he asked.

"Yes, Cardinal Grassi. He wishes an early audience."

"The subject?"

"His trip to Central America."

"Ah, yes, Mirador. Where the nuns were killed."

"Yes, Holiness."

"How long is it now? Two years? Three? And nothing done."

"Two years, two and a half. And, no, nothing."

At ten o'clock Gregory was in his study, sitting in a large, comfortable armchair, reading a report on the Church's finances in the Philippines. Stacked on the table next to him, just read, a long memo from the Sacred

Congregation analyzing Kung's latest theological excess. Gregory had initialed it without comment and put it aside. There was a knock and a priest-clerk announced the arrival of Amadeo Cardinal Grassi.

Gregory stood up.

"Yes, Grassi, good, good to see you."

Grassi bent low to kiss the papal ring.

"Thank you, Holiness. It is thoughtful of you to . . ."

"Not at all. Please sit down."

He respected Grassi. The man had a first-rate mind. Good politician. He had not warmed to him, for which he was inclined to blame himself. Well, that was chemistry, that was personality. He would not agonize over it. Grassi lacked the usual Italian gift for small talk and got immediately to his subject.

"I leave next Thursday for America," he said. "A day in Washington. A day in Mexico City. Then Mirador for a mass on Sunday. The next morning I meet with Portillo, who seems to be the senior colonel. His regime has been making noises about our missions there."

"Again? They've been complaining for years about our missions. Claim they're hotbeds of sedition and worse. And they kill off one of our priests every few months to make the point. Perhaps we should do a little complaining ourselves."

Grassi nodded quickly.

"As I fully intend to do, Holiness. In the strongest terms."

"Good."

Grassi went on. There was a question of reciprocity. At the same time the colonels were attacking the missions as guerrilla camps, they were hinting of permission to reopen a number of urban parochial schools closed down in the early days of the insurrection. "They suggest their willingness to finance whatever repairs and refitting have to be done."

"Then they want something, Grassi. Yes?"

Grassi permitted himself a small smile. "Naturally, Holiness. Which is the reason for my trip. To find out just what."

"Whose missions are they?"

Grassi glanced at his notes. "Maryknoll, principally, several Franciscan, two Jesuit."

Gregory nodded. "You'd better talk to all three before you go. Find out precisely the situation. If the missions are part of the rebellion you'd better know that before the *junta* springs it on you."

"I've already done that, Holiness."

"And?"

Grassi gestured with both hands. "Clearly there is some guerrilla complicity. How much is more difficult to determine. But there's some."

"Didn't one of the Jesuits, an American, write a book about it last year?"

"Yes, one Cobb."

"Well, you might read his book on the plane. Not that I'm endorsing the Jesuits, mind you, but it might be enlightening."

He said this with a smile. The Jesuits were not universally loved in the higher realms of Church politics.

"I shall, Holiness," said Grassi, as if the thought had never occurred to him.

Gregory stood and Grassi, understanding the audience was over, bent again over his hand.

When he had left the Pope pushed a button and a secretary hurried into the room.

"There's a book about Mirador," Gregory said. "A Jesuit wrote it. An American. See if you can find a copy for me."

"Yes, Holiness."

Gregory sank back into the chair and resumed wondering what he was to do about Hans Kung.

The snow that blanketed the Alps swept down the boot of Italy toward the south, whitening the mountains, raising the level of the Arno, and then, as it reached the latitude of Rome, turning into a heavy, wintry rain that swelled the Tiber and dripped from the arches of the Colosseum and glistened on the dome of St. Peter's Basilica.

Thank God for Burberry's, Peter Cobb thought as he stood in a doorway near the Quirinal palace searching fruitlessly for a cab and wondered about this strange obsession the Italian police seemed to have about his few moments kneeling at the side of a dying boy in the street before the bombed restaurant. Hathaway had called it paranoia, and dismissed it. The criminal investigation division did not. They had sent a car for him to the Hassler and for nearly two hours, over and over, he had again told them everything he could remember about the incident. A chief inspector chain-smoked brown cigarettes and frowned. In the end they let him go. But there was no car back to the hotel in the rain, only a request, quite polite, that he notify the authorities if he planned to leave Rome. That would be soon, he hoped. Three days had gone by since he dropped off his report to Lonsdale. Surely if there were questions or objections Lonsdale would have posed them by now. Perhaps he should call the Englishman to remind him he was still hanging around Rome, still waiting. The nightmarish thought occurred that Lonsdale might have forgotten all about him and his time in limbo would simply stretch on and on.

He wished Marella Massai lived in Rome.

He spent the afternoon at the Rota, the canonical tribunal where Catholic marriage problems were adjudicated. A cheerful monk promised to see what could be done about Pia Bartoldi's situation. His promise was tempered with a warning:

"I can make a beginning on the paperwork, Father Cobb. But with this new Pope, who knows? In a year there have been only a handful of successful prosecutions of annulment. And all those had been begun long before his reign. There seems a disinclination to move aggressively until Gregory clarifies his position. And, as of this moment, that position seems hard."

Cobb thanked the man. When should he check back?

"Oh, in a couple of months."

"That long?"

"Father Cobb, that would be very swift as things go today in the Rota."

On Wednesday evenings Tom Hathaway had people in for poker. "Why don't you come, Peter? All work and no play . . ."

Cobb said he would. He was lonely. The hotel room held no attractions. He had told Hathaway about his courteous reception at the Rota. But not about the freeze on annulments since Gregory's election. Pia would understand. Hathaway might not, might try to pressure her into something rash.

Hathaway's flat had a nice, masculine feeling. Darby was there, the *Time* magazine reporter. A marine major who commanded the Embassy guard, a novelist with a southern accent, and an American who worked for du Pont filled out the table.

"We play for lire," Darby said, "that way you win or lose thousands and nobody gets hurt."

"That's good," Cobb said. "Under a vow of poverty I'm not allowed to lose too much."

"Watch out for him, Darby," Tom said, "he's talking poor-mouth already. Count your fingers when you shake hands with a Jesuit."

There was American beer in cans from the commissary, and Hathaway's maid had prepared trays of open-faced sandwiches, salami, cheese, salmon, prosciutto. Cobb was in civilian clothes. He hadn't played cards in years, not since the seminary. He wore an open-necked shirt and a V-necked sweater under the old blazer. Hathaway had put out cigars. Cobb chain-smoked cigarettes and played cautiously. There was a nice, clubby note to the table. Chatty, growling conversation, concentration on the cards. After an hour Cobb was down 20,000 lire, about twelve dollars. But he was playing better, getting back his card sense.

The novelist dropped out and sat at Hathaway's battered upright, picking out old show tunes. Hathaway turned to Cobb and grinned.

"Nice, huh?"

"Yeah," Peter nodded. He meant it. It was nice to hear a piano again. His fingers itched for it. There was a feeling of community in Tom's apartment.

Cobb won a biggish hand with a flush.

"I warned you about Jesuits," Hathaway told the marine, who had raised Cobb twice.

"Ought to be a bishop after that hand," the marine muttered.

"Cardinal," Darby said.

"Hell," said Hathaway, "why be chintzy? Run the man for Pope."

"Job's filled," the du Pont executive reminded them.

"You met him yet, Father?" Darby asked.

Peter shook his head.

"I had a private audience with five hundred other people. Didn't get close."

"I would have thought after that book you wrote he'd have you up for cocktails."

"What book's that?" the du Pont man wanted to know.

Peter told them, briefly.

Good reporters like Darby knew how to play dumb, to pretend ignorance. "Is that why you're here?" Darby asked. "Isn't Grassi headed for Mirador?"

Cobb didn't like the direction the conversation was taking. He evaded the question. He didn't know, nor did Darby, that Darby's memo about him had been spiked by New York.

"I'm doing research at the American Academy for a new book. They were kind enough to arrange facilities for me."

"Deal the cards," someone said.

Darby wanted to give Cobb a lift back to the Hassler but Peter said no. He needed some air.

He didn't like the way the journalist had pressed him about Mirador. That was all he needed, to get his name in *Time* again.

But when the Italian magazines came out that week, there *was* his name. A reprise of the recent terror campaigns of the Red Brigades contained the fascinating and not quite accurate hint that a radicalized American priest named Peter Cobb, who had been expelled from "Argentina" for activities against the government, had been questioned by the Italian police about his mysterious links to the gang that had bombed the Al Moro restaurant two weeks earlier.

Gregory, who read everything, saw the item.

"Grassi, that Jesuit Cobb. Did you know he was here in Rome?"

Amadeo Grassi could not lie to his Pope, not even over the telephone.

"Yes, Holiness."

"But you thought it not of sufficient interest to mention it to me?"

"I know how busy you are, Holiness."

"I'm sure you do, Grassi," the Pope said.

The sarcasm hung in the air long after both men had hung up.

That evening, when Gregory had dictated his last letter, read his final report, dismissed his secretary, and settled into bed with a final cup of steaming herbal tea, he noticed an unfamiliar book jacket atop the pile of books stacked on his night table. There were always books there; the man read voraciously: history, theology, biography, poetry, economics, even the occasional novel an aide had mentioned or which had been reviewed intelligently in one of the many newspapers or magazines he skimmed; but this book had been shoved on top of the stack only that evening.

It was called *Speculations* and its author was Peter Cobb.

24

Cobb found it odd that the Jesuits had, so far, left him alone. It wasn't *like* them. From the instant his plane touched down in Rome he had expected, feared, a summons from the superiors of his Order. Surely some forbidding aide to the old Basque who governed the Society would turn up one day, glowering, displeased, threatening. None had. Was it the influence of Cardinal Grassi, a writ of hierarchical eminent domain, that determined Peter was Grassi's meat and not the Order's? Or were the Jesuits so concerned about their own problems—the running sore of conflict with the Vatican, the murmured Curial threats, the constant rumor that this Pope had lost patience and would finally crack down on the Society of Jesus—that Cobb was simply being overlooked?

Now, on a crisp morning came a young cleric to the Hassler with a pinched face and an envelope of Vatican stationery heavy as cardboard. *Not* the anticipated Jesuitical, but a papal summons.

"You are requested to accompany me, Father," said the young priest when Cobb had finished reading. "Is that quite convenient?"

It was not. Cobb was just back from morning mass at Trinità dei Monti, had not yet had breakfast, not yet read the morning papers. On his bureau was a sheaf of notes he had intended that morning to collate in the reading rooms of the library. It was quite inconvenient.

"Of course," Cobb said. Priests do not decline "requests" from Popes.

They crossed town by bus, standing, jostled by the usual morning rush-hour crowd on its way to work. His father would be surprised. C.C. would assume Vatican functionaries traveled in dark, powerful sedans. The note, the "request," was simple, to the point. Would Father Cobb call that morning on His Holiness in his offices at the Vatican? The cleric who brought the letter would accompany him and see to the rituals of entry. It was signed not by Gregory but by a monsignor with the title of private secretary. The note was in English, which Cobb found curiously comforting. Latin would have smacked of the inquisitorial.

The monsignor who sent the note shook hands briskly. An Italian but Americanized.

"You were at Harvard," he said. "I took my M.B.A. at the B School."

"Oh," said Cobb, wondering if he was supposed now to swap tales of evenings in Copley Square. But already the monsignor was leading him through corridors deep into the Vatican's bowels, past receptionists and Swiss Guards. At a large, off-white double door he paused and knocked. From inside, in Italian, came the single word:

"Come."

Gregory was seated. The room hung with pipe smoke. There was a desk, a couch, several easy chairs, bookcases.

"Holiness, this is Father Peter Cobb," the monsignor said in his good English.

"Good morning, Father, not too early for you, are we?"

Cobb approached and as he did so Gregory rose from behind the desk and walked a few steps toward him across the large room. Cobb went to one knee and dipped his head over Gregory's hand, his lips grazing the papal ring on the large hand.

"Good, good," said the Pope, "glad you could come. Now, Monsignor . . ."

The other cleric bowed his head and withdrew. Cobb heard the door closing firmly behind him. Gregory turned and walked to the couch where he sat down.

"Please, Father, take a chair."

Cobb dropped into one of the large, overstuffed chairs. He had still not said a word. Gregory began to say something and then halted, his face suddenly puzzled, questioning.

"But I know you," he said. "Met you somewhere. I know your face."

Cobb shook his head.

"No, Holiness. Two weeks ago, during an audience. I was just one of the crowd."

"But we met," Gregory insisted.

"No, Holiness. You passed very close to me. You smiled."

"Good," the Pope grunted, pleased.

Cobb remembered the instant, the emotion that had swept over him. Those same blue eyes smiled at him now, as they'd done in the ornate chamber of the papal audience.

"And Rome itself? The people you've met?"

"Rome is fine, Holiness. People have been most hospitable."

Gregory's eyebrows raised slightly. "Except when they are blowing up restaurants during the soup."

So he knew about that. Of course, he must.

"No, not then," Cobb said, wondering if he would be catechized further about the dying boy to whom he had given the rites.

But Gregory remarked, "We are both strangers in Rome. It still holds mysteries for me."

"And for me, Holiness."

Gregory smiled. "But you are a tourist. A visitor. They tolerate you. Tourists spend money. The hoteliers and the restaurateurs and the little old ladies who sell post cards welcome you. The shops lure you with clerks who speak English. The Romans are less enthusiastic about a foreigner who comes to stay, who is installed as their pastor. Hospitality in Rome is for those passing through."

Cobb recalled some of the verbal sniping at Lonsdale's table, with Gregory as its target. He pushed it out of his mind and said, "But I saw the crowd in the piazza when you gave your weekly blessing. There was a genuine warmth there. I could sense it."

The Pope shrugged. "I hope you're right, Father." Then, as if recoiling from what could begin to turn into self-pity, he said, "Your book. *Speculations*. I've read it."

"I'm honored," Cobb said, surprised and with sincerity and then, a natural caution asserting itself, a bit apprehensive. There were as many churchmen who hated the book, *and* its author, as there were who admired it. Into which camp would Gregory fall?

"It's been something of a sensation in America, I take it."

"Yes. Probably because it's so different. Not quite in the mainstream of what Americans are reading." It was his turn to smile now. "And it's short. A few years ago a man wrote a very short book about a seagull. It became an instant best seller."

Gregory did not smile.

"You have not written about seagulls, Father Cobb. This is a serious book by a serious man. I found it deeply moving."

Peter's heart leaped.

"I don't know what to say, Holiness. I'm . . ." The words would not come and he felt his face flush. He sat rigidly on the edge of the armchair, wondering what to say next, what Gregory would, or could say, more.

"Now you're working on a new book."

"Yes, Holiness."

Gregory essayed a small smile. "The publishers must sniff another best seller."

Cobb grinned. It was obvious the Pope was making a genuine effort to ease his tension.

"I'm afraid I'm going to disappoint them. Tracts don't sell nearly as well as stories about people. The first book had its memorable characters. The drama and tragedy of Mirador. And I was lucky."

"Ah, luck. How helpful it is to be lucky. No one beyond a small, provincial publisher was ever interested in anything I wrote until my election. Now they all want a volume or two. They send the most distinguished editors as emissaries. They write the most appealing letters. A Pope, it seems, is . . . what is the American phrase? 'a marketable commodity'?"

"Are you writing?" Cobb had begun to relax. The question was a natural one and it came easily to his lips.

Gregory waved a deprecating hand. "State papers. An encyclical. Hardly the stuff of best sellers. Nothing to arouse an editor's enthusiasm."

Gregory got up from the couch and moved to his desk. Cobb stood out of courtesy, but wondered if he were now to be dismissed. Gregory waved a hand at him and took up a pipe, tapping out the dottle.

"Do sit down. I want to hear about Mirador. About what you did there. What the others did. About your friend Figueroa. About the nuns."

His blue eyes fixed themselves on Peter Cobb's face, his chin firm, his mouth in a flat, pleasantly pugnacious set. This was not a man to whom you told lies, Cobb knew, even if he were not wearing the shoes of Peter.

"Well, Holiness, it's a long story."

Gregory nodded. "We have time, Father Cobb."

At the end of his long account, Cobb paused, his throat dry. He was an articulate man, he had lived the story, he knew what he wanted to say. He had told the truth as to his motivations. And, for the first time, he told of the degree of his involvement, the fighting, the anger, the passion he still felt about the events in Mirador.

Gregory leaned back, his strong hands pressing against the well of the desk, and he inhaled deeply, the big chest swelling under the white cassock.

"So you fought. You did not perform simply the function of a military chaplain. You commanded troops. Planned battles. Gave orders."

"Yes, Holiness."

"I'm not being unfair to you, am I, Cobb? That is the situation as I understand it from your own words."

"Yes."

For the first time Peter had the sense of being cross-examined. If he was to be convicted, he had convicted himself. Out of his own mouth. Gregory said nothing. Cobb waited.

"And you killed men."

"Yes, Holiness."

Cobb felt he should say something more, not as an excuse, but as an explanation.

"It was a reluctant thing. At the start, I was their priest, a fugitive like most of them from the regime, from the same assassins who took Figueroa. But their leaders were so . . . incompetent. Men and women were being cut to pieces. They weren't fighting a war. They were lining up at the slaughterhouse. Joaquin Alfaro was a child leading other children. I had the training. I had fought in a guerrilla war. I was there. They needed me. In the end, I agreed to serve them."

"To lead them," Gregory said, making the point as precisely as a lawyer.

"One serves sometimes by leading."

Gregory nodded. The analogy to his own situation, that of the papal definition, had been neatly drawn. He fell silent now. Cobb hesitated to say more, fearing still more explanation would become pleading. And pleading was something he would not do. He had told his story and now it was for Gregory to issue judgment. Or to hand down sentence. At last Gregory spoke.

"The just war. A concept over which theologians and philosophers have disagreed for a thousand years. The Crusades. The Hundred Years' War. The Thirty Years' War. The Kaiser's War. Hitler's. Korea. The Congo. Vietnam. The Israelis and the Arab states. In each of them, on each side, the absolute certainty of individual judgment that what was being fought was not only a just war but a holy war. Men are always so sure. And never more so than when they are wrong."

Cobb, his voice husky with emotion, said, "I was never sure. There was always doubt."

"But you resolved doubt. You acted."

"Yes, I did."

"And what does your conscience tell you now, Father?"

"There are still doubts, Holiness."

"And guilt?"

"No, I do not feel guilt."

The Pope rubbed a large hand over his eyes, as a tired man does.

"So many wars," he said, "and always for the noblest of motives. Populations decimated, cities burned, women widowed, children left fatherless, atrocities committed. And there will always be a voice raised in praise of a God who has blessed such enterprises."

The Pope paused and then continued: "In Iran, in the name of Allah, they are executing children. And the parliamentarians, clergymen all, pronounce such atrocities both lawful and holy."

"Northern Ireland," Cobb muttered, "assassination in the name of religion."

Gregory nodded. "Holy wars," he said, his face registering disgust. "How facilely we bless our own cruelty."

Cobb did not say anything. It was as if the Pope were talking more to himself than to the young American, as if he were calling up memories that filled him with revulsion, shameful acts he had seen. Or done? Was that possible?

Now Gregory made an effort, seeming to will himself back to *this* room, to *this* conversation, the past forcibly pushed aside, whatever unpleasant window it had pried open in his memory.

Peter wondered what it was he had seen, what remembered, just what had called up this angry contempt. The Pope made no effort to explain and the young American remained silent.

At last Gregory spoke. He seemed to have made a decision, passed some private judgment. Even his voice changed in timbre. Peter sensed the shift in mood and tensed.

"Cobb," he said, "we cannot permit Catholic priests to wage war. To lead troops in battle. To write books justifying such aberrant conduct. Do you understand?"

"Yes, Holiness."

His face was not communicating assent and Gregory knew it.

"Yes, but . . . ?" the Pope said.

"Holiness, I'm hardly in a position to argue a doctrinal point with my Pope."

"Why not? You haven't been reticent until now."

If he could not be frank with this man, then with whom? Cobb decided to plunge ahead.

"Until now, Holiness, this has been a conversation. An unexpectedly pleasant conversation between two priests. A moment ago I sensed that what had been a chat had turned into something else. You seemed to have come to a conclusion. You'd listened to me, given me ample opportunity to tell you what had happened in Mirador and why I'd done what I'd done. Then . . ."

"Then what?"

"Then you told me what I'd done was wrong. Aberrant. That it could not be tolerated. That to write in defense of such conduct was unacceptable."

"Yes, I said that."

"Then how can I continue to argue the case? You've ruled. You've passed judgment."

Gregory smiled. It was as if the pleasant tenor of their earlier dialogue had inexplicably been revived.

"And not 'sentence'?"

Cobb grinned in return, relieved. "For which let us be duly grateful," he said, wanting to sustain the suddenly lightened mood.

"Well, Father Cobb, it was not my intent to speak *ex cathedra* during an informal conversation like this one."

Cobb decided not to fence. More seriously now he said, "Whenever a Pope speaks, whatever he says, there is an element of *ex cathedra* to his remarks."

"I suppose so." Gregory too seemed to sober. "And have I been unfair?"

"No, Holiness, no one could say that."

Gregory nodded. "Good. And, now, Peter Cobb, speaking not as a Pope, not *ex cathedra*, may I ask you to abandon this project of yours, this new book, and not to make my papacy more difficult than it already is by encouraging *other* young priests to take up swords inappropriate to *their* vows and *my* wishes?"

Stubbornly, Cobb could not resist a jibe: "The Knights Templars wielded swords, Holiness."

"And are you embarked on a crusade to liberate Jerusalem, Cobb?"

"No, Holiness."

"Then?"

Cobb wanted to stand up. He suspected it was not polite to do so but for the first time he was angered. For the first time he sensed the steel beneath Gregory's velvet. "Are you ordering me to stop? Am I being silenced?"

Gregory too began to rise, then, restraining himself, slumped back into his chair. "If you are silenced, will you obey?" Gregory was thinking now not of Cobb's book but of his soul.

"Yes," Peter said swiftly, not having to think, "but only if the order comes from Your Holiness. Not from emissaries."

"Oh, then you've also begun to set ground rules for my papacy? *You're* to decide how and through whom my orders are given? Isn't that a somewhat impudent posture for a young priest to be assuming?"

"Impudent, perhaps. Certainly imprudent. But I don't pose the condition out of disrespect, either for Your Holiness or the hierarchy."

"Then out of what, Cobb?"

Peter feared he was making a fool of himself. But the words tumbled out.

"Your Holiness, Cardinal Grassi and Edmund Lonsdale and men like that have closed minds. They can't possibly know about Mirador or its people or the regime. Grassi'll be down there for a week getting guided tours from the colonels. He'll come back with a suntan and not a scintilla more knowledge than he had when he left Rome. I think it's important that the Church know what's going on. Not out of Baedekers or from the *junta's* public-relations men, but from someone who's been on the ground, who *knows*."

Gregory's voice was icy, controlled. "And our bishop in Mirador? Is he also bearing false witness?"

Doggedly, suspecting he was beginning to sound strident but not willing to give up, Cobb said, "Yes, yes he is. Maybe out of the noblest of motives. To protect the local Church from being completely shut down by the regime. But he's playing ball with them, yes."

"You're talking sedition, you know."

Cobb put his face in his hands for a moment, overwhelmed by a sense that this conversation with his Pope, which had begun so pleasantly, so promisingly, was deteriorating into squalid, destructive wrangling. He took a breath and then said:

"Holiness, you said that *Speculations* made sense. Why not give me a chance to finish the second book, the chance to make sense once again? I want the Church to know what I know. Then, if you think it's rubbish or heretical, tell me so and I'll burn it. I *won't* publish. Let me make my summation to the judge. Not here, talking off the top of my head, but cogently, sensibly, on paper. Let me submit to you a reasoned argument. Then, of course I'll accept your judgment."

Gregory stared at him.

"You'll obey."

"Yes, Holiness."

"Though you've established yourself, to your own evident satisfaction, as the only true authority on the subject?"

"That's not so, Holiness. But no one can possibly know what happened in Mirador who has not been there, has not been in battle, who has not fought."

"And are you so unique, Cobb? Has no man ever done what you have done? Seen what you have seen? Been where you have gone?" Sarcasm edged his words.

"No, Holiness," Cobb said, once again calm and sure of himself, "I only know what *I* have done."

"Fought?"

"Yes."

Gregory fixed Cobb with those penetrating pale blue eyes and then rose, waving a hand in curt dismissal. And as Peter got up, bowed, and started for the door, Gregory spoke one brief, final sentence, so softly he might have been speaking to himself, so softly Cobb was not sure he had heard him correctly.

Peter Cobb had finally met his Pope.

In Boston, in the distance across a rainy field; in the Piazza San Pietro, a tiny white-robed figure on the purple-draped balcony; in the Sistine audience, a man whose eyes he'd met, before whom he'd knelt. Now, for more than an hour, Pope and priest had talked, and the priest was miserable and confused, sensing that in justifying himself he had strayed into defiance; confused because the Pope had left him dangling awkwardly in mid-air.

It was, as the Roman table chat went, as if Gregory wore two faces, one up close, the other, distant: the charismatic, simple, even saintly pastor of the world; the complex, shadowy, devious church politician. They had spoken for an hour, for more, and still Cobb did not know if he had been censured, silenced, condemned, or bullied. The Pope had praised his first book, had warned him about the second. He did not know if he was to see the Pontiff again. Or report to Lonsdale. To remain in Rome or to fly home. Gregory had seemed on the verge of issuing a command. Cease and desist. Cobb was not sure what his response would have been, how he would have reacted, but at least he would have known where he stood and from that base of knowledge could have made a decision of conscience. Instead, Gregory had pulled back abruptly from the brink, had retreated behind a puzzling mask, his anger tempered with caution.

Cobb did not know, could not even speculate, what was to happen now. He was still mulling over the sentence with which Gregory had dismissed him, a sentence he now was quite sure he had heard correctly:

"Others," the Pope had said, "others have fought as well."

25

Others *had* fought as well.

Gregory himself had fought.

For a thousand years armies had marched across his country on their way to somewhere else. And always had his people fought them. Usually they lost. But always they fought.

Gregory too had fought.

Only then he was not Gregory. Not the Pope. Not even a priest.

His name then was Stefan. His family's name was Holstowski.

His father was Holstowski the gamekeeper, a gamekeeper as *his* father had been before him.

The family lived on one of the great Polish estates east of the Silurian lakes, north of the Pripet Marshes, astride the traditional invasion route over which armies had always marched. It was on their lands that Viktor Nevsky had fought Teutonic knights. Here that Gustav the Swede had marched. Here that the Austrians had come. The Lithuanians and the Baltic knights. The Prussians. The Tsar's men. Napoleon had passed here, victoriously headed east. Here Napoleon had passed again, with the tattered remnants of *La Grande Armée*, with Maréchal Ney fighting his despairing rearguard actions along the thousand miles of death and defeat and retreat.

A dark and bloody land, its soil ripe with death, its bleak forests alive with game. Holstowski, the father, had been gamekeeper to his majesty Nicholas II, Tsar of all the Russias, which included in those days the province of Poland.

Nicholas was never the hunter his own father, the giant Alexander, had been. But as a gentleman of his time and class was expected to do, he hunted, throwing open the vast reserves and hunting lodges to the royal and aristocratic layabouts who adorned the Petrograd court and who every year at the appropriate season moved themselves and their entourages into the countryside to slaughter birds, stags, bears, wolves, boars, elk and lesser game.

When the 1914 war came, Holstowski volunteered for the army, offering his thirty assistant gamekeepers as well without bothering to consult them. He and they were Polish Catholics; their Russian overlords were Orthodox, but Holstowski was a Tsar's man and loyal. His gracious offer was considered, and bluntly rejected. It had been determined, "at the highest level," that for the morale of the court, for the regal symbolism the people "expected," the tradition of the hunt should be continued, regardless of the war. Holstowski and his thirty men would be moved further east, to yet another half-million-acre hunting preserve in the foothills of the Urals.

And with Holstowski went his plump bride of the Silurian lakes and their young son, Stefan.

When the Revolution exploded and the first, garbled reports reached the Urals, Holstowski counseled caution. He was a peasant, as were so many who had raised the Red Flag, but he was a Tsar's man. When Denikin raised his first White banners and word of the counterrevolution reached their Ural enclave, Holstowski sent runners, and on their return with assurances of welcome, he packed up his thirty men, their wives, children, baggage and beasts, and in the middle of the mud season marched them all an astounding 700 miles in four weeks to the encampment where the White Army had erected its Romanov banners. No one in the Urals attempted to bar Holstowski's departure. They were relieved that he had gone.

Denikin's men marched and countermarched across half of Asiatic and some of European Russia, fighting, burning towns, freeing prisoners, hanging members of the soviets, skirmishing, blowing bridges, dynamiting railroads, killing and dying. And then, on a gray afternoon in late July, with thunder rolling down the river valley, a detachment of the Czech Legion smashed into the city of Ekaterinburg. Too late. The Tsar Emperor, the young prince, the Tsarina, the daughters were all dead. It was after that, Stefan Holstowski could recall his father's saying later, that the true terror of the civil war really began.

Stefan Holstowski would listen wide-eyed as his mother boiled tea and his father's cronies leaned heavy forearms on the kitchen table and nodded understanding of old Holstowski's wartime tales.

"When Semenov caught the partisans he shot them. No discussion, just up against the wall. When he took a Red town he lined up every fifth man and shot him, whether he was a Red or not. It didn't matter to Semenov.

Kalmykov killed everybody, women, children, everyone. They say he killed forty thousand. I don't know. But I heard forty thousand. When the Reds caught one of Semenov's officers—he was a man I knew—they took a hot iron and branded epaulets on his bare shoulders. They hated epaulets, hated any symbol of the Tsar, of the past.

"Semenov discovered new ways to kill. He drove some prisoners out on a frozen lake with whips and then broke the ice around them. They all froze to death in the water. And on the shore the Orthodox priests held up icons above their heads and chanted the prayer for the dead."

He laughed bitterly.

"A *very* religious war," he remarked sarcastically, and around him men muttered agreement. Then Holstowski went on, his son there at his feet watching him with riveted attention.

His wife objected. Drying her hands on her apron, she said, "This is terrible, do you have to tell such things? In front of the boy?"

Holstowski looked at her. "You were there yourself, woman. So was the boy. War *is* terrible. But I tell the truth. Better to know the truth and never to forget. You remember, boy, you remember?"

Stefan, proud to be noticed, nodded vigorously. He did remember. Some of the dead put away under the snow had been children, had been his playmates.

When the civil war ended, more in exhaustion than in clear-cut victory, the Poles under Pilsudski sued for peace with the Bolsheviks, and the Holstowskis and the survivors of the thirty gamekeepers and their families who had marched out of the Urals were repatriated to Poland. Holstowski knew how fortunate they were, how easily they could have been sent to a Siberian camp with other veterans of the White Army. The fact that they were Poles, foreigners, and that Pilsudski held so many Red prisoners to be exchanged saved them.

Now they were home, and for the first time in generations, Poland was a free and independent nation.

In the new prosperity of the twenties, with a government of colonels and capitalists, Holstowski prospered. Stefan grew as strong and as broad and as physically tough as his father. There were no other children. The rigors of war and of winter marches had left his mother barren. She insisted, when he was old enough, that her only child become an educated man. And in Poland, in those days, education was the province of the Catholic Church.

The years of rootless wandering, of peril and deprivation, of intimacy with death and suffering and violence during the civil war, had bred in

Stefan a self-reliant hardiness that, now that he was in school for the first time, seemed to meld with an extraordinary curiosity about ideas. He had always lived with people and with things: guns, trees, railroads, tents, snow melted for drinking water, bandages and the groans of the dying. Rarely, around the campfires of Denikin's bands, did the tired guerrillas discuss abstract concepts. Now, in school, his intellectual horizons were suddenly, shockingly expanded, not by degree but by geometric bounds.

In 1939 Stefan, the gamekeeper's son, was granted a full scholarship at the great University of Wroclaw. A blue suit had been purchased, lodgings had been arranged, books had been packed. Holstowski had taken his son aside to warn him of the perils of cities. His mother had baked little cakes and wrapped sausage for the trip. An old typewriter had been lubricated and serviced and now, blue and heavy and smelling of light oil, it stood proudly on a table inside the front vestibule of the Holstowski house. A sturdy suitcase bulged with clothes. And a Bible. His mother's.

In a shaded copse on the outskirts of their town a pretty girl named Anna, shy but not that shy, kissed him full on the mouth in the privacy of a tree on which he had the summer before carved their initials.

"You will miss me, Stefan, you *will*, won't you?"

He could feel her strong young body through the peasant blouse and the flowered jumper and said, solemnly, and quite meaning it, "But I could never forget you, Anna! Never."

Classes at the University of Wroclaw were to begin on September first.

But 1939 was also the year when Colonel Josef Beck, the Premier of Poland, was to permit hubris to maneuver him into a test of wills and of national strength with a neighbor to the west, the Chancellor of Germany. The excuse for their disagreement was a Baltic port called Danzig, later to be known as Gdansk. It was a dispute Beck could not win, that his neighbor, Adolf Hitler, could not afford to lose.

And so, two days after young Stefan Holstowski arrived wide-eyed, excited, and slightly awed at his university, war began.

The war lasted a few days. Not even long enough for the patriotic enthusiasm of young men like Stefan Holstowski to be channeled into practical use. It was not that the Poles did not fight. Charges by cavalry armed with lances against Guderian's tanks proved that. Colonel Beck's army was still waging war with the same weapons, the same tactics Pilsudski had used against the Red Army in 1919. They had no chance.

The Germans swept across the country. Wroclaw fell on the fifth day. Holstowski and his classmates huddled in the cellars of the old university buildings as the Stukas roared overhead. They emerged in the morning, dazed and frightened, to the clank of tanks rolling over the cobblestones of

Wroclaw's streets. They knew the tanks were German. The few Polish tanks had been wiped out in the very first battles on the frontier.

Poland lay as devastated after a month of fighting as Europe had been at the end of the Thirty Years' War. Germany occupied two-thirds of the country, the Soviet Union the rest. Politicians and other personalities had been arrested, more than a million Polish soldiers were penned behind barbed wire, public life was suspended, shops and businesses remained shuttered. In fields ripe for harvest the grain moved heavily, listlessly, in the wind; old women in shawls knelt in churches where no priest dared pray.

In the universities administrators and professors went into hiding or were trucked away by bored German soldiers while students like Stefan Holstowski wandered aimlessly from dormitory to empty classroom, wondering when they themselves were to be arrested, sent home, or recruited into the labor gangs already at work improving roads and rebuilding smashed bridges. What of their families, their homes, their friends? No one knew, there was no way to know.

"Holstowski! There's some girl here looking for you."

The shout echoed through the stone stairwell of the dormitory. Stefan leaped off the narrow iron cot where he'd been reading a textbook. At the foot of the stairs, looking up at him, was Anna Leskva. He bounded down the steps three at a time.

"Anna! How did you get here? How are things at home? What's happened?"

He threw his arms around her before she could answer.

"Oh, Stefan," she sobbed into his chest, her knees sagging with fatigue. He could feel her strong back under his hands, could feel its bone-weariness.

"Yes, Anna, yes. Softly, slowly, take your time."

Gently, he led her up the old stairs to the dormitory common room. A few weeks earlier, introduction of a female into his quarters would have been grounds for immediate dismissal from the university. Now . . . who was there to judge, who to dismiss?

"Your parents are well, Stefan. When I was certain my father was dead, that there could be no mistake, I went to your mother. There was no one to stop me. Men were running here and there in the town, trying to put out fires, carrying wounded people to the hospital, searching for their children. Some soldiers came through in trucks, heading east, away from the fighting. A policeman tried to stop them. They ran him down.

"I walked through the forest to your house. It was so beautiful there after the smell of the smoke, the noise, the horror, the bombs. I frightened a deer. It ran from me as if I were the dangerous one.

"Your mother and father were arguing. He was in his hunting clothes and had several guns laid out on a table. A shotgun, I think, and a rifle. Also a large knife in a sheath. He kept saying he was going, your mother kept saying, 'No, Holstowski, you stay. You stay here. For Stefan to come home to.'"

Stefan nodded. "The old man was going to the wars again," he said, half to himself.

The next morning, before dawn, Stefan and Anna began to walk across half of Poland, two children going home.

26

Holstowski was to be a gamekeeper again. This time, for the Germans.

The forest to which the Germans sent the hunter Holstowski and his wife and their boy and the young orphan Anna was known by various names. Mostly, it was called Vlatin.

It was hard against the demarcation line where the Nazis stopped and the Russians began. In October, less than a month after the fighting ended in Poland and while the western front was still dozing through the so-called "phony war," Goering motored east to see his new toy. Holstowski was summoned. He knew who Goering was and ground his teeth at being assigned to take him on a guided tour. But the *Reichsmarschall* was so obviously enthusiastic about this new terrain and the stag and bear and boar and other wildlife that abounded in it that Holstowski found himself treating the German as he had twenty years before treated Tsarist courtiers he disliked but with whom his work brought him into contact.

Twice more that fall and winter Goering came back. Others came as well. It was a cruel winter for Poland. But the Holstowskis lived well. The gamekeeper was providing a service to the Germans and they considered themselves a fair people. They paid him well, there was always plenty of food, he and his wife and their children (Anna was now considered a member of the family) were exempt from the petty tyrannies military occupation forces routinely imposed on subject populations. Then, in late May, Goering and a large entourage arrived once more, bibulous and jolly, crowding the lodges and even spilling over into foresters' huts from which the inhabitants were forcibly ejected.

"This time," Goering announced jubilantly to the gamekeeper, "this time we're after bear. Let's find a good one, Holstowski, and not some mangy creature still drowsy from hibernation. A nice . . . fat . . . roly-poly . . . Russian bear."

Holstowski nodded and said, "Your Worship," and before a week was out Goering and his party had a score of bears. On the night before he was to return to the west, to Germany, Goering, excited by the success of the hunt, abrim with good fellowship, pressed some money into Holstowski's hand.

"My dear fellow," he said, "I may not be back for a time. But don't worry. Your livelihood is guaranteed."

"Thank you, Your Worship."

"But hark to this, Holstowski. There could be difficulties. You know how things go in wartime?"

"Yes?"

Goering nodded.

"Well, I can't say more. But if there is any trouble, you get your family out. You're a clever fellow and a woodsman. Get them into the deep forest and hunker down until it blows over. Then you can go back to your place. You'll know when. I can't say more. But these Russian fellows, well . . ."

"Yes, Your Worship," Piotr Holstowski said, without knowing what the devil it was Goering was trying to tell him. But he was a man who listened to advice. Listened, and remembered. Even when he did not fully understand.

The trucks began to roll past Holstowski's house a week later, just after midnight, grinding along the narrow dirt roads in low gear. Holstowski was immediately awake.

"Stefan," he said softly, shaking his son by the shoulder.

"Yes, Father."

"Come. Get dressed."

The boy sprang lightly from his bed. In the kitchen he could hear his mother opening cupboards. His father had gone to wake the girl, Anna.

Stefan could hear the trucks now. He dressed, without being told, for the forest: boots, corduroy pants, a flannel shirt, a sweater, an old hunting jacket with big pockets and cartridge loops. As an afterthought, his guitar. He went into the kitchen to lace his boots. His father was drinking tea.

"This is what that fellow Goering must have meant," Holstowski said. "Help your mother fill rucksacks with food."

"Yes, Father."

Anna came into the kitchen now, her face dull with sleep, tugging a belted robe tight around her small, solid body.

"Girl, get yourself dressed. Then help my wife pack food."

"But . . ."

"Now hurry!" he snapped. The girl darted from him like a rabbit.

212

Beyond the house the trucks rolled.

What happened at Vlatin has been written and argued about for forty years. The trucks that woke Holstowski carried troops. He was himself never sure if they were Russian or German. Or perhaps both. The ten thousand Polish officers who came to Vlatin did not ride in the dubious luxury of army trucks. They were marched there, from a score of prison camps. The troops in the trucks were a reception committee. Of a very special sort. They were there to await the Polish officers, who began to arrive at dawn. By then Holstowski and his family were kilometers from their home, deep in the spring woods.

The forest was as beautiful as Stefan had ever seen it, the trees already heavy with leaves so ripely green as to be almost blue, a low sun climbing in the east, its rays slashing through the branches, the underfooting dry from a rainless week, pine needles cushioning their tread as they moved. There seemed to be no game. In the distance they could still hear the trucks, grinding uphill in low gear, and beyond them a murmur that might be human, but which even Piotr Holstowski with his hunter's ear could not define.

By mid-morning they were within a kilometer of the paved, provincial road.

"Stay here. Rest," Piotr said. "Stefan, go up to the road. Quietly. Do not be seen. Then come back and tell me what is there."

"Yes, Father."

The boy looked at his mother and at Anna. The two women had thrown themselves down on the pine needles, exhausted by old Piotr's unforgiving pace. Stefan dropped his rucksack and began a silent space-covering dog-trot through the trees. He was proud that his father had sent him, that old Piotr had not gone himself. It showed confidence.

Within fifteen minutes Stefan was back. The women sat up, their faces alert, expectant. Piotr took his son's hand and drew him aside.

"What did you see?"

"Troops. Russians. Also some Polish police. No Germans that I could see."

"Yes?"

"Father . . ."

"Yes, what else?"

"Thousands and thousands of men marching. Prisoners. Polish soldiers. Most of them seem to be officers. I could see the shoulder boards, the insignia. Thousands of them, shuffling along. Some of them look in pretty bad shape."

Piotr nodded.

"That sound we've kept hearing . . ."

"Father, it was the prisoners. Groaning, crying, whispering to one another. From here a low growl like a wounded beast. Up close you can distinguish individual sounds. The guards say nothing. They just prod them along, keep them moving."

"No trucks?"

"Not for the prisoners. Every so often one goes by. They are filled with troops."

"From which direction are they coming?"

"East. Same as the prisoners. They seem to be hurrying past them to get there first."

"Get where, boy?"

"I don't know, Father. To wherever it is they are all going."

Piotr said nothing. Then his son asked, "Where *are* they going, Father? Where are they taking our officers?"

"I don't know, Stefan," he said, and reached out to muss his son's hair affectionately with a large hand.

He did not know. But he suspected.

There was no question now about their getting out of the forest. Not even Piotr's forest-craft could take the four of them through the long, never-ending line of march, past the guards and through the exhausted, plodding prisoners. Holstowski remembered Goering's words. Whatever was happening, and with a clammy chill down his back he was beginning to think he knew, posed a very proximate danger to the Holstowski family.

Piotr walked back to where the others sat resting.

"Come," he said, "now we march west."

He had made a terrible error. Because it was Goering who had given him that shadowy warning, Holstowski had assumed the danger came from the west, from the German side. Instead, it was out of the east. The Russians. Well, Holstowski knew Russians. By God he knew Russians. There never was a Pole who didn't.

All that day they went west. Twice they stopped, swung wide to avoid patrols (unsure if they were Russians or Germans), and went on.

That night they slept rough. Old Piotr sniffed the wind. Rain was coming. That afternoon they had skirted back past their house. Troops had already taken it over. Trucks and motorcycles were parked all over the large yard. Signals technicians seemed to be rigging wire. The troops were Russians but Holstowski spied several Wehrmacht officers among them. Liaison, he supposed. They seemed to be using the house as a command post for whatever this mysterious maneuvering was all about. The devil take them all, Holstowski spat out silently into the pine needles. And that girl as well. That damned Anna.

"Stefan?"

"Yes, Anna?"

They lay on the needled bed of the forest a meter from one another. Beyond them Stefan's parents lay close together, back to back. Anna's voice was hushed.

"Your father resents my being here. He thinks I am a burden."

"No, Anna, that's just his way. He . . ."

"I know he does, Stefan. There's danger and he feels responsible for me. Now it isn't only you and your mother, but a stranger that he has to worry about."

"No, I'm sure . . ."

"No," she said firmly, "it is I who am sure." She gestured with a bare arm above the blanket bundled to her throat. "Does he not realize I crossed half of Poland on a bicycle to find you? That I have seen my own father dead? That I am not a child but a woman who has seen war and who has survived?"

Solemnly, Stefan said, "He knows that, Anna. We all know. Please, we are very happy that you are with us. We *all* are."

"You, too?"

"Of course, Anna. What a thing to ask."

She lay still for a moment, and then she said, "Stefan, at the university. Did you ever think of me?"

"Of course."

"I mean of *me*. Not just of home or your friends. Of *me*?"

"Yes, Anna."

She sensed the restraint in his reply.

"As a girl? Or just as a friend?"

"Well, as both."

"Good," she said, satisfaction evident in her voice, so much so that the boy was disturbed.

Stefan lay very still in his sleeping bag. The girl was so close he thought he could smell her hair. Even in the dark he could envision her, the round, pretty face, the chubby arms and legs, the solid body, the spray of freckles against the first spring tan, especially at her throat. He had trained himself *not* to think of her, not to conjure up her image as he fell asleep. He could hardly forget her. He never *could*.

"Good night, Stefan."

215

"Good night, Anna."

But it was a long time before he slept and, even then, his dreams were ripe with her.

They were on the move again before dawn. Piotr hummed tunelessly to himself as he marched. The others straggled behind him, Stefan to the rear lest one of the women fall behind.

By nine in the morning they were approaching the western limits of the Vlatin. Now was the time for caution. There seemed to be military patrols everywhere. Whatever was going on in the pine forest, neither the Russians nor the Germans wanted witnesses. Twice they took wide detours to avoid what seemed to be construction work, heavy bulldozers excavating trenches. Piotr shook his head at that. Here they were on what was virtually the German-Russian demarcation line and for both Germans and Russians to be cooperating in the building of fortifications held no logic. Why would they help one another throw up barriers when they, Germans and Russians, faced only each other across the line? And the Polish military prisoners? They seemed to be part of the feverish activity as well, wielding shovels and clearing underbrush. Not even in the chaos of the civil war had old Holstowski encountered anything as odd.

A small stream, running high and muddy after the spring rains of a week before, barred their exit from the forest. They threw themselves down on the ground a hundred yards back from the bank under the trees and rested while Piotr searched the opposite bank with his field glasses.

"Stefan?"

It was Anna.

"Yes?"

"I did well. I didn't hold you up, did I?"

"No," he said, "you were fine, Anna. Fine."

It was true. What a fine, strong girl she was. No whining complaints, no girlish temperament. Only a slick of sweat on her forehead and dampness on the back of her flannel shirt to show how hard they had marched, how far they had come. Her cheeks glowed. And her breasts moved rhythmically from the exertion of the march.

"Stefan!"

"Yes, Father."

"Come here."

The old man handed his son the field glasses and the two men lay side by side on the pleasant-smelling, pine-needled ground, staring across the stream toward its western bank.

"I see nothing, Father. No movement, no one."

"Good. But I must be sure. Once across we are out of the Vlatin. There is a town eight or ten kilometers further. Gradovice. We have friends there. I want you to cross the stream and reconnoiter a kilometer or two to the west. When you come to the district road check it out carefully. Then come back. I don't want to take the women across until I am sure."

"Yes, Father."

He noticed his father was no longer referring disdainfully to Anna as "that girl." He had accepted her as one of them. She had done well. Even Piotr recognized it.

Stefan kissed his mother's cheek and received a pat on the head and a whispered "Be careful." Anna smiled and then surreptitiously threw him a kiss. As he entered the cool water of the stream he could feel his face burning.

It was chest-high in the middle but the footing was solid. On the other bank he trotted quickly into the cover of the trees and was gone. The sun was now well up and he could feel the clothes already drying on his body.

In less than an hour he had reached the district road and scouted the terrain. A farmer's cart passed, pulled by an ancient horse. No other traffic. The way to Gradovice seemed clear. Good. Everything appeared normal, almost as if there had been no war, as if somewhere behind them in the Vlatin those mysterious maneuvers were not taking place. Stefan got to his feet and started back to the east, to his family. And Anna.

It was then that he heard the shooting.

Piotr Holstowski had died as violently as he had lived. The ground around him was blood-soaked. Underneath his body when Stefan turned it over there were three bloody fingers. Piotr's rifle was still hot, its chamber emptied. In his hand still, gripped tight in death, a hunter's knife, keen-edged and bloody. He must have killed a number of them before the last bullet crashed through his jaw and out the back of his head. There was only one other body in the forest clearing, that of Stefan's mother. She was also shot. Stefan straightened her skirts and sat heavily on the ground, sobbing. Anna was gone. So too the bodies of whatever enemies had done this and had been killed or wounded by his father. There were signs everywhere of booted feet, of heavy bodies being dragged away.

For perhaps five minutes the boy mourned. Then, thinking only of Anna, he arranged the bodies of his parents side by side and covered them both with evergreen boughs he hacked from the trees with his long knife.

They were dead. There was nothing now but to pray for them. Anna was still alive. He had to think that. And if she was alive there was always a chance he could rescue her. He got heavily to his feet, took one last sorrowing look at the green mound of pine boughs, said a brief prayer, and set off at a lope along the trail the murderers had left behind.

He never caught up with them. But he found Anna. She was dead.

They had stripped her naked and raped her. When they had finished their sport she had been disemboweled. Stefan hoped she was unconscious by then. Surely he would have heard her screams, even in the noise-deadening forest.

He covered her with what fragments of her shirt and trousers remained, and erected a little mound of boughs over her body. He knelt and prayed again.

Then, knowing it was foolish, that he would surely die himself, he continued east, following the trail of those who had killed everyone he loved.

So it was that Stefan Holstowski, just eighteen years old, witnessed the great massacre of Polish officers, ten thousand of them, in the forest of Vlatin.

For most of that afternoon he lay under a fallen tree on the slope of a hillside, watching the killing. Watching Russian machine guns mow down his countrymen. Watching the bodies tumble or spin or drop heavily to the ground at the brink of the long trench the Poles had themselves helped dig. The officers were marched up, a hundred at a time, opposite the flatbed trucks on which the machine guns were mounted. The prisoners stood there, confused perhaps. Then came the order in Russian and there was no more confusion. Then they *knew*. One or two cried out "Long live Poland!" Others tried to salute. A few to run. The bullets caught them all. And the bulldozers would clank up heavily to push the bodies into the long trench and then another hundred Poles would be prodded forward.

Stefan watched it all.

Finally, it was over.

The Russian troops rolled the last few bodies into the trench. Their officers stood chatting, smoking cigarettes with the handful of Germans. On the side of the hill Stefan slid his Mannlicher into position. He adjusted the sights and aimed.

The first bullet smashed through the head of a Russian captain. The second killed a German major. The third shattered the arm of a machine gunner on one of the trucks who was attempting to swing his gun toward the hillside.

Then Stefan was gone, a swift ghost melting into the dusk.

That night, hidden under boughs in a damp gully, Stefan wept for the first time. He had lost a family. Anna. The leaders of his defeated country. In the morning he was on the move, out of the forest. Within a month he had joined up with a few like-minded stragglers. Within a year Germany attacked Russia and in the ensuing chaos they became a formidable guerrilla band. By 1945, when the war ended, he had become its leader. He had become Grigor, the deadliest of killers. And, as he stood for the first time in his life in the ruined capital of Warsaw, he knew the killing was over. He had never found the men who killed his mother, his father, and Anna. He never knew if he should blame the Russians or Germans. Cheerfully, he had killed both.

Early in 1946 he entered the old monastery at Cracow. Only his confessor ever heard the story of Stefan's war. Not even the old priest ever heard the name "Grigor," the code name he carried in the war; the name he would take as Pope.

27

This Pope's first anniversary in office was drawing close and *The Times* of London, another institution that spoke *ex cathedra*, sought to sum up Gregory. It asked of an unnamed but very senior bishop who'd worked with him the straightforward question. "Do you like the Pope?" And the bishop had answered, "Gregory leaves me perplexed."

Which was how Cobb felt when he received a second, even more unexpected summons to the presence. Would the Pontiff remember his defiance or would he be forgiving?

Gregory received Cobb in his study, a warmer, cozier room full of books and deep chairs, magazines and pictures, with two large windows that gave not onto the piazza but onto the Vatican gardens. Shut out was the tinny sound of Roman traffic. Gregory, puffing a large-bowled pipe, again rose to meet Cobb. Peter went to his knee and kissed the papal ring. It was odd. Cobb had expected that particular ritual to bother him, smacking as it did of times long past. Yet, with Gregory, he found it instinctive, natural.

"Now," said the Pope, when the two men were seated, "what is happening in Rome? What is the talk?"

"I'd think Your Holiness would know that," Cobb said, surprised.

"If I were an Italian it would be one thing. Poor foreigner that I am even my own people tend to shield me. How could a Slav possibly understand the subtlety of Roman gossip? They fear to upset me. They've not yet quite figured me out."

"I'm not sure Rome understands anyone who's not a Roman. And I'm not sure we will ever understand Rome."

Gregory noted with amusement how the young American had slipped into the first person plural, linking himself with his Pope.

"A universal Church with a hundred nationalities and a thousand tongues."

"Once there was one, Holiness."

"Ah, yes. Do you miss Latin?"

"Only the ablative," Cobb said, risking a joke. He was relieved that Gregory was so genial.

It drew a smile. Then, "No, seriously."

Cobb leaned forward. He was beginning to sense Gregory's shifting moods. And he was happy not to be defending his Miradoran thesis.

"At first I thought the idea of the vulgate was terrific. I suppose most people my age did, clerical or lay. What a wonderfully simple way to break through the apathy of millions of nominal Catholics out there for whom the Church had lost relevance. Just speak to people in their own language."

"Only it didn't happen that way."

"No, Holiness. In throwing out Latin we lost something else. A sense of community. Oneness. Maybe even the sort of secrecy fraternities have that makes them popular. A feeling that one . . . *belongs*."

"You sound like Archbishop Lefebvre."

Cobb smiled. "Hardly that. I miss Latin. I'm not prepared to go to war over it."

Gregory seemed to seize on that. "And for what would you go to war?"

Soberly, Cobb said, "Only something very serious, Holiness. I don't go to war lightly. Anyone who does is a fool."

Gregory nodded. "I agree." Then, lightly, "What news of the rialto? What's happening in this great world out there beyond my prison walls?"

Clearly the Pope wanted to know. Cobb racked his memory for things he'd heard, the current rumors, the notions floating about, the latest topic from dinner in Val d'Isère, things Tom had told him, what Jane had said, what Lonsdale's dinner party had produced.

"The Brigades, of course. The economy. Inflation. Just what this American president is up to. The latest divorce. The latest film."

"And . . . ?"

"Well, there's talk about you, of course."

"I still possess novelty value."

"There's curiosity. Confusion. They . . ."

Gregory's question was quick, pointed. "Confusion about me or about my policies?"

Cobb composed his reply thoughtfully.

"I think there's confusion about you. A new Pontiff. Not Italian. Relatively young and unknown. To me this seems natural. Even in the States we're curious about Your Holiness. As to your policies, perhaps confusion is the wrong word. It's not as if you'd put forth a number of *dicta* and then backed away from them or temporized . . ."

"As Paul did."

Cobb nodded. "Pope Paul *did* confuse people. I was a seminarian. It was all too much for me. One day hard line, the next day soft."

"But Jesuits enjoy that sort of thing. Keeping things simple and consistent gives your typical Jesuit no room for philosophical maneuver."

"Holiness, I was a seminarian in my twenties. I was still trying to fathom the *Summa Theologica.*"

"And now?"

"These days I enjoy having a certain latitude."

"As with your book."

"Yes, Holiness, as with my book."

Gregory reached for a box of old-fashioned kitchen matches and amid clouds of smoke relighted his pipe. Cobb tensed, waiting for the authoritarian words he feared would come, about a book the Pope would tell him he must not write.

Instead, "Tell me about your friends in the Red Brigades."

Cobb shook his head.

"No friends of mine, Holiness. One contact after I gave the last rites to that boy. A silly phone call. I hung up. Nothing since then. My Red Brigades connections seem to exist only in the minds of the police."

"Good," Gregory said. "We cannot have our priests engaging in terrorist conspiracies."

Cobb was unsure whether the Pope meant more by that than a reference to the Brigades.

"Mirador was very different, Holiness," he said quietly, trying not to sound defensive.

"I'm sure it was, Father." And Gregory the Pope put his pipe down and leaned forward, looking into Peter's face.

"Cobb, Mirador is not the world. Even less the universe. It is a minor Central American oligarchy serving as a microcosm—for larger countries, bigger problems. More complex interrelations between repressive regimes and their rebellious populations. You think Mirador is complicated. Don't you?"

"Yes, I do."

Gregory shook his head, the thick gray hair cascading over his broad forehead. "Cobb, compared to the Balkans, Mirador is a study in civics."

Cobb took a chance then, risked the rapport that seemed to be developing.

"Holiness, Mirador may be small. But it matters."

"Of course it matters. Small is not nothing. A matter of degree, not of significance."

"No."

Gregory pushed his ashtray away and formed his hands into a single fist in front of him. "Cobb, last Christmas, you may have heard, the Russians were making ugly noises about invading my country. Perhaps my compatriots were to blame. We are a difficult, annoying people. But the Russians were massing on the border. There was a rumor—who knows how it began—that if the Russians came in, I had warned them I would fly to my homeland and lead the resistance against them. That I would die fighting for my country. You heard that?"

"A wild rumor. But, yes, I heard it."

"Well, it was all very romantic. A marvelous story. Very flattering to me. The warrior Pope, a man larger than life, a hero. I would go down in history."

Gregory shook his head. "A fool, I would be a fool. To die is nothing. You have fought in wars, you know that. To live is the thing. To do one's duty. To do the job. Not to make glorious gestures. If the Russians were to invade my country I would speak out. I would bring every pressure to bear. I would pray. And I would weep. But I will not throw myself under tanks. What can a middle-aged man do better than a twenty-year-old boy with a rifle? Nothing! My responsibility is no longer simply to one troubled *mitteleuropean* country with a history of intransigence. Armies have been marching across my country since Napoleon. Since before him."

He unclenched his hands.

"Cobb, do not throw yourself away for Mirador. There are larger tasks."

Tom Hathaway gave Cobb dinner at a *trattoria* in the Trastevere. The princess Pia was in the country.

"So you've met him. Actually sat down and talked with him."

"Twice," Peter said.

"What did he say? How did he look? Did he raise holy hell with you?"

"Tom, I dunno. We talked. He listened. I listened. It was except for the furnishings and the honor of the thing rather like being called in by your faculty adviser at college. He even smoked a pipe."

"An intellectual."

"No, impossible to categorize. Oh, he's a brain, all right. I've read enough of his stuff to know that. But he's a street-fighter too. And subtle as hell. The Curia is kidding itself if they think this man is some unlettered, obvious character from the boondocks who'll go all to pieces if they toss a double meaning at him."

"No Polish jokes," Hathaway remarked.

"This man may singlehandedly render the Polish joke obsolete."

A waiter came and they ordered. Hathaway refilled their glasses with a Ruffino.

"What did he say? About you. The book."

Cobb thought for a moment.

"I kind of think that our conversation was privileged, Tom. I hate to be stuffy. And he didn't tell me not to repeat it. But I just think . . ."

"Sure, sure. I know." He paused. "But, listen, did you mention Pia?"

Guiltily, Cobb said, no, he hadn't.

"Hey, Peter, I understand. I mean, what the hell. This is the goddamned Pope you were talking to. Don't worry about it. Really."

But I do, Cobb wanted to say, and, God forgive me, I was so concerned with my own problems, so awed, it never occurred to me to ask.

"Sorry, Tom."

Hathaway waved a hand.

"Hell, I understand. But she's such a great kid and I love her so very much . . ."

Peter did not tell Hathaway of the Pope's final words:

"You must come back again, Father. I want to talk to you about America."

"It would be an honor, Holiness."

"And more about Mirador. Where you fought." Cobb was unsure whether he heard sarcasm in the papal voice.

Marella was in Rome.

"Have lunch with me, Peter," she said over the Hassler's telephone.

"With pleasure. Is there something wrong?"

"Yes. No. I'll tell you when I see you."

They made a date in a restaurant so obscure not even Lonsdale would know of it.

She was late. But when she walked through the door of the restaurant, bundled in furs, her breath turned to vapor by the damp cold of the wind off the Tiber, heads turned from pasta and antipasto to look at her. Cobb was glad he was wearing the old tweed jacket and a turtleneck. No reason to commit scandal by wearing a Roman collar.

"Beautiful as ever," he said.

She reached out a long hand.

"And you, solemn as ever. Solemn as the Colosseum's stones."

"No, never solemn. It is forbidden to Americans."

"Then dignified."

"Dignified I can accept."

They sat and he waved a menu at the waiter. She ordered a Cinzano and took off her fur hat. Her dark hair tumbled down, soft and wavy.

"You've seen *il papa*."

He gave a short laugh. "There aren't very many secrets in this town."

"There are none. *None!*"

She did not laugh. Her face was sober. "Peter, you are in trouble?"

He shook his head. "No. Or at least, I don't think so. Why?"

She shrugged, very Italian, the face communicating less than the shoulders. "There's talk. You and . . . well, the friends of that boy."

"The Brigades?"

"Yes," she hissed, "and do not speak so loudly."

Cobb exhaled impatiently.

"Marella, half of Rome seems intent on involving me in some crackpot conspiracy and the other half wants to arrest me as a conspirator. And all I'm trying to do here is write a book and eat a little pasta."

She laughed.

"Rome cannot resist an intrigue," she said. Then, more seriously, "But do not think of *them*"—she stressed the word—"as comedians. My husband once laughed at them, you know."

"Sorry."

She shook her head.

"It's all right. I can talk about it. Now."

Peter reached a hand across the table to touch the back of hers. It was still gloved but that made the gesture no less intimate.

"No," he said, "let's talk of cakes and ale . . ."

". . . and cabbages and kings?"

"Yes."

"And Popes?"

"No."

"Ha!"

"Hathaway's reaction exactly. He doesn't seem to understand that when a priest is summoned by his Pope, it isn't like being asked over for cocktails by that nice couple in the house across the hedge."

"What is it like?" Her lovely face was serious, wanting to know.

"This may take some time," he said just as seriously. "Let's order first and then we can talk."

He told her no more than he had told Hathaway about his actual conversation with the Pope. Confident of her greater tact, he spoke more freely of his own reactions to Gregory.

225

"A hard, secure man, capable of gentleness but in no way soft. No sentimentality. Crisp, rational, but not cold. Very, very intelligent. And a lot more subtle than some people around him seem to think."

"People like your Monsignor Lonsdale?"

"Exactly. Lonsdale seems to believe Gregory can be conned. Sweet-talked and led around by the papal nose. It looks to me as if it would be very risky to underestimate this particular *papa*."

"And your book? Your future?" she asked, the concern tangible in her voice.

Cobb shrugged. This was moving close to the area of his conversations with Gregory he felt to be sensitive, even privileged.

"You know, vague discussions, nothing very precise."

Marella sensed his reticence. In response she shifted the talk completely, telling Peter about a conversation she'd had several days before with his sister.

Peter looked thoughtful. It was he, and not Marella, who returned to the subject of his two papal audiences.

"I just had the feeling that if I talked to him"—it wasn't necessary for either of them that he say just whom he meant—"about Jane, about my father, about my own doubts and concerns, that he would have been of tremendous consolation. Not that he would have handed me a package of solutions neatly wrapped, but that he would have said something that was of help. And that just having talked to him would have made me feel a lot better."

"Like a good therapist."

Peter smiled. "Well, I suppose so. But there are damned few shrinks in this world for whom I feel a genuine affection."

"And you do for Gregory."

"Yes."

It was true. The Pope had all but ordered him to trash his new book, had bluntly informed Cobb the Church could not, would not, tolerate having its priests functioning as guerrillas, had seemed on the verge of silencing Peter, of taking even more drastic action against him. And yet . . .

That night, before he slept, Peter prayed for Gregory. Not as the Pope, the institution, the way priests traditionally did, but for the man. A man he was coming to like. Not that he understood Gregory. Not yet. But he knew that what he was beginning to feel for him was something very special.

Gregory had been a priest for more than thirty years. He had his own theories about where the Church had begun to go wrong. He had watched it happen. He was living now with the consequences. Popes do not publicly criticize their predecessors. This did not mean they did not make judgments. Gregory had his theories: the authoritarian Pius had given way to the liberal John. Had John lived and not died agonizingly of cancer, perhaps he might have exercized control over the whirlwind he'd set loose at Vatican II. But he had not. And Paul was not the sort of leader to rein in wild men or curb excess. He was decent, dedicated, weak. John Paul had died before either he or the Church had a chance to test one another. Gregory was the heir to theological anarchy.

There was no way of knowing how many years he would have to reverse the process, to reestablish stability. Nor what breed of man would succeed *him*. He knew from the first day, from that moment when the white smoke curled upward from the Vatican chimney, that it was up to him to stop the rot. To stop it *now*.

He had called in a secretary and begun to dictate. In Brazil a "people's church" had become the latest vogue. A "church" that side-stepped the usual table of organization, that ignored its bishops and archbishops, that now had gone direct to Rome, petitioning the Pope to bless its works, to encourage its membership, to smile benignly on its good intentions. And they *were* good. The "people's church" was doing good work among the very poor, whom despair was driving from the Church. How tempting to wish the "people's church" well and to encourage its growth. Instead, Gregory dictated:

> This so-called "theology of liberation" cannot be accepted. It undermines the traditional and correct authority of the bishops who are the Pope's appointed representatives. How easy it is to recognize, it is in fact impossible not to recognize, that this concept of a "people's church" will be unable to avoid infiltration by strong ideological connotations along a certain radical political line, of class violence and the acceptance of violence as a way of achieving certain determined ends. It is absurd and dangerous to think such a "church" has validity outside the authority of the bishops. I therefore call on all of you, priests and people, to abandon this concept and to unite behind your duly appointed bishops and archbishops.

He signed the pastoral letter "with filial love."

And when it was read from the Brazilian pulpits a week later, four hundred priests, most of them young and working among the poor, defied his orders. In Rome cardinals clucked and Curial savants wondered. But Gregory stolidly refused to be moved. Better to lose four hundred, better to lose four *thousand* priests, than to temporize, than to permit the rot to go any deeper.

He had been handed a Catholic Church that was falling apart. It was his responsibility to pull it together. Reading four hundred Brazilian priests out of the Church was a painful decision. But Gregory had been making hard decisions ever since that afternoon in the forest of Vlatin. He would go on making them. Those priests, many of them, were fine men, sincerely motivated, doing good work. But in their zeal they were pulling the buttresses of the Church down upon them. It had taken two thousand years to construct this Church of theirs. Gregory was not the man to stand by idly while the well-intentioned demolished a structure of which God Himself had been architect. He would not permit it! Not the Brazilians or rebellious Jesuits or Hans Kung or anyone.

And certainly not a Peter Cobb, as much as he liked him.

28

Spring arrives early in Rome. The Mediterranean is a few miles to the west and the Mediterranean washes against Africa. In Holy Week on the day the Pope washed the beggars' feet, the temperature reached eighty. The rooms Peter Cobb had taken in a crumbling, faded orange villa down a cul de sac near Borgo San Pio were heavy with the promise of summer. Working on his book at a table in the kitchen, which was the coolest room, he wore khaki pants, a threadbare Lacoste shirt that had once been navy blue, and his feet were bare against the cool tile of the floor.

"Padre!"

The old woman who ran the place, part concierge, part janitor, part spy, banged on the double door of his apartment. "It is the post. A letter from America."

It was from C.C. Which was odd. His father communicated by telephone, by cable, by private jet. Not a long letter but it was in his father's own hand.

"Helen," it said, "is ill. The doctors believe it to be cancer. She is in Memorial here in New York for tests. She is being very brave about everything, even cheerful. Your mother was like that. I cannot believe there is a God. No decent power could possibly take pleasure from punishing two such women so terribly. No God could drive me to despair twice in one life in precisely the same way. I will not ask you to pray for Helen since the fault must be that of this God to whom you pray. But I wanted you to know. And to think lovingly of her, as I know you do."

It took Peter two hours to get through on the telephone.

"How is she?"

"Home," his father said, his voice tired and older than Peter remembered. "It's cancer. They plan some more tests. There are certain . . . treatments. She's here now, resting. Next week I'll have more information."

"Tell her I send my love."

"Tell her yourself. I'll get her."

His father put down the phone and after several minutes he heard Helen Gatewood's voice.

"Hullo, Peter," she said. "Isn't this stupid of me, causing all this row."

At least *her* voice sounded the same.

"Terrible," he said, trying to match her tone, "always making trouble."

"Raising hell."

"I don't see why he puts up with you."

"Or I with him," she said, laughing.

In the end Peter said, quietly, solemnly, "Helen, he told me specifically *not* to pray for you. I'm afraid I'm going to disobey him yet again."

"I know, Peter," Helen said, just as solemn, "and you know that I'll forgive you even if C.C. won't."

"Yes, Duchess, I know."

There was a brief silence.

"Pray for me, Peter."

After he had hung up the phone Peter lighted a cigarette and sat back on the old couch that dominated the living room and thought about his mother. And Helen. And his father. Especially his father. How terrible cancer was. And how more terrible to have to face its vicious, wasting horror for a second time and without any sort of emotional anchor except C.C.'s own strength. Even the strong break.

I wish, Peter Cobb said silently, I wish he believed in something. *Anything!*

His father had said he did not want Jane to be told. No point in upsetting *her*. When there was more definitive data from the doctors he would tell her himself. Peter thought he was wrong, that the old man tended to carry too much on himself, burdens that he ought to share. But that was the way he was, how he lived, how his entire life had been structured.

In the end Peter put on a pair of sneakers and walked down the street to the local church. It was late afternoon and still hot in the streets, jammed with office workers returning home. Inside the church, which was dedicated to some obscure local saint of whom Cobb had never heard and who he suspected had never really lived, it was dark and quiet and smelling faintly of dust. He knelt in a side pew in front of a garish altar and prayed for Helen, that the cancer was not really cancer; that if it was, it could be cured; that if it could not be cured, she would not suffer. He prayed then for his father. And for Jane. And for himself. If only he could ask Gregory to pray as well. Surely a Pope's prayers had a better chance of being heard in the celestial hubbub than those of a troublemaking Jesuit in sneakers and tennis shirt.

Then, more soberly, he remembered Helen Gatewood's placid, lovely face and her tenderness toward C.C. Cobb, a man who rejected tenderness and worshipped power and who was now powerless and needing love. "Oh, God," he prayed, "she's a good woman. A loving and giving woman. Help her now in her hour of need. Help us all."

Night had fallen as he left the church. In the rear pews old women in black lifted their shrouded heads in curiosity.

His book was finally going well. And he thought he knew why. Gregory had twice summoned him and twice let him off. Savonarola had not been as fortunate. The third time Peter might not be as lucky. So he plunged ahead, the words and the arguments pouring out, sure, almost arrogantly sure that he was right and that what he was writing would have an impact, would make its point, would change attitudes. Get it done now, get it finished. Before anyone stopped him. Before, as with the Brazilian priests, he was forced into a cul de sac from which there was no retreat but only the options of surrender or defiance.

He had moved to an old apartment, in a house whose glories had died in a century past. Marella had found it for him. He was grateful. Here there was none of the artificial gaiety, the forced congeniality of staff, the small intrigues that had begun so to depress him at the Hassler. Here, other families lived, real families. Here the old woman sulkily mopped the marble vestibules and randomly carpet-swept the worn stair, fetched him his mail and his morning papers and fresh bread, greedily snatched at the crumpled lira notes he pushed at her, scowled her thanks, and pried. He liked that. He liked her nosiness. And the weekly drunkenness of the man who lived above him, the clatter of children playing in hallways, the shouts of women and the occasional curse or sob or slammed door.

It was a place where he could be alone but where he was not lonely. It was, he supposed, a home.

On Easter Sunday he took Marella to the Piazza San Pietro. It was his practice now, unless he was visiting the Vatican, to wear civilian clothes. Even to attend mass. A warm April sun washed the great square. Around them milled the thousands of pilgrims and Romans for whom this morning was, traditionally, part holy sacrifice, part Mardi Gras, part Broadway opening.

Gregory was a distant figure in white on the platformed altar erected for the Feast, as tiny and as far off as when Cobb had first seen him that dank afternoon on Boston Common when he had stupidly, stubbornly, refused to kneel, and then *had* knelt. There was no question of kneeling now. They were too hemmed in by the crowd. Was it possible that was only six, seven months ago? Cobb half turned to watch Marella's face. In profile it was so solemn, controlled, lovely. Her lips moved in prayer.

There was Easter dinner in the country. She had a car, a little mini-Cooper which she drove as adeptly as she seemed to do everything.

"These people are great friends of mine," she'd said. "You'll like them."

He did. As he liked Marella. And when she had dropped him that evening at his apartment he took her slender hand in his for an instant and then, very quickly, he squeezed it tight and turned away.

He could hear the rapid put-put of her car's engine as she drove off and he leaned heavily against the door of the old house, thinking. Then, heavily—perhaps it was the big meal they had eaten with her friends at Ostia, perhaps it was the weight of a relationship he suspected was starting and which he could not permit to ripen—he walked up the stairs. Perhaps it was just the long day and the unfamiliar early heat of a Roman spring.

But when he unlocked the doors of his suite and stepped inside and turned on the lamp, Italo DeBragga was waiting for him.

He was tall, broad but not heavy, with thick blond hair going gray and a mustache gray already, and he sat easily in one of Peter's two beat-up old chairs, his blue eyes on Cobb's, his mouth softened into a half smile.

"I am DeBragga, Father Cobb. Of the *Brigate Rosse*."

"Oh?"

"My apologies for having let myself in while you were not here. Forgive me my trespasses."

"As we forgive those . . ." Cobb muttered. DeBragga! That boy who died bombing the café had said his name even as he bled to death.

"Just so," DeBragga said. His English was excellent. As it should have been. The man had spent four years in the States, in the Embassy in Washington. "You know who I am."

"Of course. Your name is in the papers nearly every day."

"And on the walls of police stations."

Cobb nodded. Then, shoving the keys into his pocket, he walked past his uninvited guest toward the kitchen, with a show of casualness he did not feel.

"I'm going to make myself some coffee. Do you want some?"

"Yes, please, that would be very nice."

DeBragga seemed very confident of him. He made no move to accompany Cobb into the depths of the apartment. Peter wondered if there were accomplices. In the bedroom, perhaps. The kitchen was empty. On the old table the sheaf of manuscript seemed untouched. That signified nothing. The man might have been here all afternoon and half the evening. He could have read it all.

While the water was heating, DeBragga sat chain-smoking cigarettes. Peter went back to the living room and sat down facing him.

"Well?"

"Yes, of course, you deserve an explanation, Father Cobb. There are several matters which brought me here. First, to thank you for your kindness to that boy."

"As I've already told the police, I was simply fulfilling a priestly function. There was no political motivation."

"Naturally. I understand. Yet you *were* kind and I have thanked you for it. Then there is the matter of the police. Through no fault of your own you have been the victim of certain . . . harassments. No?"

"Yes. Nothing intolerable. More a waste of my time and of theirs."

"Still, my information is that you have behaved properly. Offering nothing more than answers to questions. Nothing more than a factual account of what happened."

The kettle was boiling now and Cobb got up. "I knew nothing more. I wasn't protecting anyone, there was nothing more for me to tell."

DeBragga's voice followed him down the corridor.

"And that regrettably awkward telephoned attempt to recruit you to our cause?"

"I told the police about that, too."

DeBragga entered the kitchen behind him. He smiled.

"As you should have. The man who contacted you was a fool."

"I wasn't able to tell the police much. Just that the contact had been made."

DeBragga waved a hand. "Don't concern yourself. I'm not here as an enemy or a threat."

Cobb looked at him. "It's instant coffee, I'm afraid."

"*Va bene.*"

As he poured, Peter asked, "Why *are* you here?"

DeBragga reached for the cup. "*Not* to recruit you, Father Cobb. But perhaps to persuade you."

Peter picked up his cup and the two men returned to the living room. Extraordinary, Cobb thought. Here he was chatting and drinking coffee with the most notorious man in Italy, perhaps in Europe, the infamous Italo

233

DeBragga, the intellectual, the poet, the diplomat-turned-terrorist suspected of being the mastermind behind the abduction of Aldo Moro, of a score of assassinations, of a hundred raids, attacks, outrages. The dialectician of the cause, the aristocrat-become-killer, a man with the manners of the drawing room and the ferocity of the jungle.

"Persuade me of what?"

DeBragga sipped at the hot coffee as if gathering his thoughts. Then:

"Father Cobb, I am neither a romantic nor a fool. I have no enthusiasm whatsoever for enrolling you as a courier or a driver of getaway cars or, forgive me, a political assassin. But I have read your book about Mirador. I know something of your current researches in the various libraries of this bookish city. I am aware that within your Church . . ."

"Is it not also yours?" Cobb interrupted.

"Once it was. No longer."

Cobb said nothing, his point made.

"Within your Church, formerly mine, there is a certain antipathy toward your point of view. Certain powerful forces are at work which would silence you, banish you, erase you forever from the public consciousness. Is this not so?"

"My views have not met with universal approval," Cobb conceded.

"Fine—we need not fence. You have met with His Holiness."

"Yes."

"These were substantive discussions?"

"I'm not at liberty to say."

Cobb tensed, despite himself. Until now the conversation had been amiable. But this was the first question he had refused to answer. DeBragga quickly relieved his apprehension.

"No matter. I assume that they were. Pontiffs do not in the nature of things summon young Jesuits to chat about the quality of the linen in the altar cloths."

Cobb said nothing.

DeBragga continued. "Do you have *any* vestige of sympathy for the cause of the Red Brigades?"

"No."

"Then you support the fascists?"

"No."

DeBragga gestured impatiently. "Father Cobb . . ."

"Look, Signore DeBragga, you're too intelligent a man not to understand it is possible for a reasonable man to reject both extremes. Certainly this is not an either/or situation. Black or white. There are many things the Italian government does, that my own government does, that my *Church* does, that I find repugnant. But that hardly arouses me to take up an automatic rifle or to roll grenades through the doorways of *trattorias*."

"Nor do I want you to. There are plenty of my countrymen who can do such work and do it well. Father Cobb, I want you to write about the Brigades, not to put on their uniform."

Cobb put down his cup. "I don't understand. Write what?"

DeBragga sat forward, the languor shed now, eagerness in his voice.

"You are a famous man. You have a following. A respect. Your credentials are impeccable: a Jesuit who has not abandoned his Church but who has had the courage to write an important book critical of the sort of fascist regimes against which we fight. Obviously, you're no Communist. No terrorist. You have those bourgeois characteristics which make you irresistible to the masses. The Brigades have done excellent work and yet are perceived as butchers. We have presented ourselves badly. We are seen as interested solely in the destruction of society. This is not correct. We wish to change society. It is hardly the same thing."

"You don't convince too many people of your reasonableness when you bomb a railroad station on a holiday weekend, a station full of workers and peasants."

"An outrage was necessary. Apathy is our fiercest foe."

"And to kill Moro? Why was that essential?"

"Impact. It was necessary. I regretted it but it had to be done."

Cobb shrugged. "The end justifies the means."

For the first time DeBragga lost control. "Oh, come now, Cobb. Let's not adopt superior airs. It's not as if all your time in Mirador was spent in the baptizing of babies and the blessing of lepers."

Cobb felt a chill. The man was uncomfortably close to the seat of his own doubts.

DeBragga seemed to be making an effort.

"Look, Father, this is a battle being waged for men's minds. For their souls, if you insist. Right now it is being fought with bombs and nine-millimeter pistols. We are ready now to move to another stage. To attempt to convince Italians in more subtle ways that the country must be changed, that this government must be gotten rid of, that parliamentary democracy has run its course. To have a man like you writing intelligently of us, not propaganda, but thoughtfully, exploring the programs we propose . . ."

"And would you call a halt to violence if I did?"

DeBragga was silent. Then he stood up.

"You know that I can't. Not yet."

Cobb remained seated. So this was the intellectual soul of the terrorists. His rhetoric would have embarrassed the Yippies of the sixties. And they wanted him to become their Tom Paine. No thank you, Cobb thought, thank you very much but no thanks.

It was hopeless, he knew, but he could not permit DeBragga his empty conceits. There were, dammit, vast differences between Mirador and the Europe of the Social Democrats.

"Look, you didn't come here to debate and I'm hardly in a position to try convincing you of anything. But to draw analogies between Mirador and Italy simply isn't logical. You don't know anything about what's going on down there. You say you read my book. Fine. But I suggest you didn't understand a word of it."

DeBragga's handsome, ruddy face seemed to redden. Cobb went on, damned if he was going to be bullied.

"Here you have a functioning democracy. Your people, if they get the votes, could conceivably form a government. It might not be a government I liked or the Vatican liked or Washington liked. But you could do it. Don't you understand there is absolutely no possibility of such a thing happening in Mirador? *None.* The *junta* threw a bone to the electorate a couple of years ago. Land reform. It sounded fine. Agricultural do-gooders flocked into the country from the American Midwest. One night in the best hotel in Mirador City three of them were having dinner. Some soldiers walked in, pulled out machine pistols, and killed all three of them at their coffee. The soldiers just strolled out again. The *junta* didn't even make an effort to solve the crime."

"It happens here as well. In Italy . . ."

"Wait a minute. I'm nearly finished. Out in the provinces some of the peasants took the land-reform burlesque seriously. They became very enthusiastic. Finally, it seemed, they might actually own some decent ground instead of swamp or hard-scrabble. They petitioned the local land baron. He said, fine, come into the district capital and fill out certain forms. The peasants came in. It was like a holiday. They had to walk twenty miles but they came. Wives and kids came along. It was a fiesta. They all wanted to be there for the great moment when they, too, would own a bit of ground."

Cobb paused.

"A platoon of troops met them on the outskirts of the district seat. They killed eighty of them. Perhaps a dozen got away. I treated three of the children who escaped. One of them died with me. One lost an eye. The third survived. He was twelve years old. He is fighting now with Joaquin's band. Such things do not happen in Italy, Signore DeBragga. They happen every day in Mirador."

DeBragga regarded him with, for the first time, cold dislike.

"There are subtler methods of subjecting peoples, Father Cobb."

Now, remembering Marella's dead husband, remembering that blasted railroad station in Turin, remembering Moro dead in that automobile, Cobb permitted release of his own anger. He got up to face DeBragga.

"I don't think we have anything more to say."

"Don't be too sure, Father Cobb. Many of your fellow priests are sympathetic to the ends I pursue."

"Please leave."

DeBragga looked pained.

"Signore DeBragga," Peter said, angry now, so angry he forgot the possibility of a gun, "please get the hell out of here. We have nothing more to discuss."

DeBragga shrugged and got up.

"I'll go. Thank you for the coffee. And don't use the telephone. It is not operating. It will be restored to service by morning."

Cobb nodded coldly.

DeBragga went to the door. For a giddy moment Cobb feared some last, histrionic gesture, the pulling of a gun, a demand that he go along.

Instead, DeBragga gave a courtly half-bow and, without another word, left.

Italo DeBragga would now ignite a spasm of violence the length and breadth of Italy. And in his arrogance he wrote letters to the nation's leading newspapers to announce his intentions:

"Because of the intransigence of the government and of certain personalities, the Red Brigades reluctantly conclude there exists no longer any possibility of a peaceful settlement. Therefore we shall resume our campaign to drive this perfidious regime from power and to establish a true government of the people. We call upon His Holiness, Pope Gregory, to convince the civil authority that its continued oppression of the Italian people and its denial of their legitimate rights are doomed, in the end, to failure."

Uneasily, reading the communiqué in that morning's *Corriere*, Cobb wondered if he was one of DeBragga's "intransigent personalities."

In the Vatican Curial hackles were raised at the man's presumption. To call on the Pontiff to bless his wickedness! How presumptuous. This DeBragga was not only a killer, he was a *poseur*. A fake.

Gregory had his own, less simplistic view of Italo DeBragga. For De-Bragga had written yet another letter, this one shorn of pomposity, yet every bit as dialectical. In this letter, delivered by hand to one of the papal secretaries, one intellectual, DeBragga, addressed another, Gregory the Pope.

"Holiness," it began:

> I hope that in the generosity of your soul you will find room
> to forgive me for the audacity of my public statements earlier
> this week in which I was so bold as to address a personal ap-
> peal to you to bring your inarguable talents to bear on the gov-
> ernment. Obviously, this was a tactic intended to attract at-
> tention. In that, it has apparently succeeded. I am now at-
> tacked more for my discourtesy than for my knee-cappings.
>
> Holiness, I am aware of rumors about your youthful en-
> deavors in Poland. I also understand fully that your present
> role demands a certain adherence to traditional values and the
> status quo. If indeed it is true that during the Nazi occupation
> you fought for your country's freedom, perhaps you will find
> it in your heart to understand what it is that we in the Brigades
> are trying to achieve. Many of your young priests, while per-
> haps disagreeing with our tactics, share our aspirations. We
> must rid Italy of a government that does not work. We must
> provide a people's alternative.
>
> I do not ask for your blessing. I appreciate such a thing is
> still not feasible under the present circumstances. But I ask
> you to understand our motives are not destructive but positive.
> There is much hatred in the land and, inevitably and sadly,
> men must die in order that the nation live.
>
> You may be interested to know that some time ago I ad-
> dressed a similar appeal to one of your priests, an American
> named Cobb. And as young men will, he refused an appeal to
> reason, and ordered me from his quarters. This is the sort of
> stubborn negativism against which I struggle. And against
> which I now send this appeal for understanding to you, Holi-
> ness.

Gregory put down the astounding letter. Against all odds, he chuckled.
"Well done, Cobb," he said half aloud, as delighted by the young priest's
courage as he was puzzled by DeBragga's impertinence. What "understanding" could there be between an urban terrorist and the Bishop of Rome?
Without knowing it, Gregory and Cobb had both rejected DeBragga's appeal with virtually the same response.

That Sunday morning, speaking from the balcony of St. Peter's, Gregory
scrapped the usual pastoral sermon to the tourists and spoke instead directly
to the Brigades. His message was plain: Expect no sympathy from me, he
said. We do not treat with terror.

His remarks disappointed the Left and pleased everyone else. And on Monday morning, during the rush hour in a dozen Italian cities, nearly a hundred Italians, most of them civilians, some even of the Left, were killed in attacks by the *Brigate Rosse.*

On Tuesday the forty-fourth Italian government since World War II fell and both the right wing and the Communists demanded an end to gentlemanly coalition. Either concessions must be made to end the terror or a brutally efficient government would be installed with the will and the muscle to smash the Brigades forever.

Intellectuals shook their heads and blamed it all on Gregory. This was what happened when you elected non-Italians to fill the shoes of Peter, when you permitted Popes to meddle in Italian politics. If only he'd demonstrated more mature judgment and not incited DeBragga . . .

29

Jane Cobb sat in the front row at Giorgio Armani's fashion show on a straight-backed and decidedly uncomfortable little gold chair, smiling pleasantly at the *paparazzi* who would fire off their motorized Nikons at her and at Giorgio's other faithful clients until the first lanky model undulated through the pearl gray drapes and down the long runway. Jane smiled but she was not happy.

C.C. had finally taken her into his confidence. Helen had cancer. Her father had broken the bad news to Peter a month before. Now, thirty days later, to her. As if she were a child, as if she were a distant, somewhat cretinous relative. It was insulting. Patronizing.

Her mood was not improved by a hangover. Or by her husband. Gigi was in Buenos Aires, the Argentine Grand Prix. A week of time trials and practice and the race itself this coming weekend. Yesterday, in the *Corriere della Sera*, the photo. Gigi, smiling broadly, nearly as broadly as the girl with him. She was one of those interchangeable pit-crew blondes, perhaps twenty years old. God, Jane thought, I don't mind if he fucks them if only he wouldn't pose with them for the damned cameras!

The hangover, in part, derived from Gigi's callous stupidity. She had flown down from Milan to Rome yesterday at noon. The afternoon was a haze of shopping and martinis. The night . . .

One of the usual young men had taken her to several of the usual places, had danced with her at the usual discos, had provided her the usual pills, had done the usual things to her body, had let her do the usual things to his.

"Crazylegs" Cobb. She was paying for it now.

Suddenly the *paparazzi* fell away from her as the first Armani model bounced through the gray drapes.

Jane Cobb recoiled. The girl could have been the blonde in the photo with Gigi.

Next to Jane an aging film actress murmured her delight, seeing the dress and not the girl.

Peter Cobb regarded his sister that evening across the veal piccata and the bottle of Frascati. They were dining, her invitation, in the inevitably chic little restaurant off the Via Veneto and, again inevitably, at the best table in the room. Around them the hum and bustle of a Rome which might be nervous about the state of the lira or the political situation or the forays of the *Brigate Rosse*, but which was very confident of its own rung of the social ladder. A rung, needless to say, near or at the very top. A plump man with silver hair, a pretty girl, a younger man who decorated apartments, a rather famous film director, all of them had stopped at the table to greet Jane and to whisper later whether she really expected any of them to believe this solemn young man was her brother.

"My set. My friends. Nice, aren't they?" Jane said brightly.

"They're okay, I guess. I prefer your friend Marella."

Jane laughed.

"And so do I. But I promised to show you *tutta Roma*, didn't I? And to shovel some food into that skinny frame of yours. My God, Peter, don't they feed you anymore? Are you on bread and water?"

"Sure. I'm fine. And you're pretty skinny yourself, kid."

"That's diet. And exercise. So the fashion magazines won't banish me to Elba."

The food *was* incredible. Peter gave his sister that. He didn't like the way she looked, diet and exercise notwithstanding. There was a tightness about her eyes, her mouth. An artificial energy he didn't like. Drugs? He didn't know. They had skirted serious talk all evening. She'd told him about Giorgio's new clothes, he'd chatted about Easter dinner with Marella. She was still angry with their father over having confided in Peter and not in her. Peter had told her nothing of his visit from Italo DeBragga.

Nor had he told anyone. The police would be interested, of course. Perhaps it was his duty to let them know that the most wanted man in Italy had passed an evening drinking instant coffee in his flat. Certainly Cobb felt no debt to DeBragga. He did not even like the man. All the journalistic glamour of the intellectual-turned-terrorist tended to fade when you saw the man up close, when you listened to his shallow self-justifications, the banality of his polemic arguments. Still, Cobb had decided against notifying the authorities. He was opting out, adopting the neutral stance, as he had done for so long in Mirador—before the killing of the nuns and before what happened to Dr. Figueroa.

241

He had come to what he considered a reasonable compromise with himself. If the police called him in again, he would tell them the truth. He would offer nothing. But if they asked if the *Brigate Rosse* had made further contacts, he would tell them. Probably they would be furious that he had not notified them immediately. But he was not going to become a police informer. As to the Vatican, he would say nothing. And if Gregory asked?

Highly unlikely. He hoped he wouldn't ask. Cobb knew that Gregory was not a man with whom you fenced. You told him everything.

"Any word from Gigi?" Peter said.

"Oh, you know, the usual cablegram. 'All goes well. Weather rotten. Keep your fingers crossed for Sunday.' Gigi is not a man to compose long letters."

He had also seen the photo in yesterday's paper. But Jane did not mention it and he would not.

She was staying at her usual hotel and he walked back with her. The April night was soft, hinting of summer. Only once did her composure crack. They had an *espresso* in the lobby and when she had signed the check and the waiter padded silently away on the thick carpets, she said, almost to herself, "Oh, Peter, it's a stinking life sometimes."

He tried to take her hand. "Look, I'm supposed to know about such things. Be able to help . . ."

She pulled away, shaking her head violently. "No," she said, "I'm sorry, Peter, but you can't. Maybe no one can."

She strode away from the table across the lobby toward the lift, leaving him behind. His last view of her face was of eyes liquid with tears.

Upstairs, in her suite, Jane Cobb, known as "Crazylegs," gobbled a handful of pills and, an hour later and still unable to sleep, picked up the telephone and began to call the discothèques in search of someone, anyone, who would come and make love to her.

Cobb read himself to sleep with the late edition of one of the Rome dailies, a paper whose front page was devoted mainly to the latest *Brigate Rosse* outrage, the maiming of a magazine editor that afternoon, a sixty-year-old man who had had both of his kneecaps shattered by gunfire. And where were you, Signore DeBragga, when he was shot? Cobb asked himself.

Almost unnoted in the same newspaper was an AP dispatch from Mirador. A government sweep in Isulutan province has resulted, said the wire service, in some 800 civilians being killed. The regime insisted they were all guerrillas and that the death toll was "only" 350. Washington sources, a sidebar noted, tended to credit the regime's claim.

Cobb put the paper down, said a brief prayer, and at last fell into a troubled sleep.

At the Vatican that same night, Gregory had sat late at his writing desk, tapping out on an electric typewriter the notes that would be edited and hammered into a pastoral letter—a letter, he knew, that would please no one, especially not in Latin America where in ten days' time it would be read from all the pulpits during Sunday mass. He wrote:

> Workers have the right to organize and to demand an end to social injustice and political repression. But there must be moderation in these efforts and these demands. Nonviolent dissent. The clergy is authorized to support such nonviolent efforts but must stay out of practical politics. In no case, whatever the provocation, must priests or bishops support actual combatants or encourage revolutionary activism. Their efforts must be restricted to the support of legal opposition.

And just what *was* legal in a country like Mirador? That was a question Gregory knew he could not answer. Cardinal Grassi had returned to Rome after his fact-finding mission with a hodgepodge of contradictory conclusions. Worthless! He should have known better than to send one of those old, Curial warhorses to investigate anything. He had learned more from a few chats with young Cobb, even given his political bias. Grassi had been a waste of time. And time was what Gregory did not have in dealing with the explosive conditions in a Mirador, or a dozen countries like it.

Oh, he knew already what the critics would say to this latest papal communiqué. That he was urging the authorities to introduce reforms and at the same time assuring them he would use his influence to keep the peasants peaceful even if they did not.

It was a dilemma not even the Vicar of Christ felt himself capable of solving.

Marella Massai wiped the sweat from her forehead with the back of a forearm and stepped back to look at the twisted, amorphous metal skeleton that stood in the center of her studio and which she was twisting, hammering, melting into a shape she could already see in her mind's eye but which would have been totally mystifying to the casual observer. She had risen before dawn to start work, resenting even the time it took to make coffee, to shed her nightgown for jeans and a denim workshirt and a rag of bandanna to pull her hair back from her face and to keep it out of her eyes. Once again,

243

after a long hiatus, she was anxious to work. These early morning hours, before the heat of the day, before the intrusion of telephones and of a maid wanting the day's instructions, were the best time. The emptiness of those months following her husband's murder, months during which she never even entered the studio, seemed to have fled as quickly as it had come. But with less reason. She *knew* why she had stopped working. Sudden, violent, senseless death. She was far less sure why she had resumed her work. What was the inspiration? Was there one? Was it simply she had been idle long enough, that sufficient time had passed, that the need to create that resides uninvited in the marrow of the artist had naturally manifested itself?

Or was it the troubling, pleasant discovery of a new friend called Peter Cobb?

She remembered now the pressure of his hand on hers that Easter Sunday night. He had liked her friends in Ostia. They had liked him. Even the drive back into the city along the clogged weekend autoroute had been relaxed, casual, striking just the right note. She had driven. There was none of the customary Italian machismo about Peter, no need to demand that he take the wheel, that he supply the lead, that it be *his* friends and not hers to be visited. Perhaps that came of being a priest. Perhaps it was his Americanism. She was unsure.

She was unsure of a lot of things about Peter Cobb. And about herself. She was only glad that he was here. In Italy.

She pulled the pair of old work gloves on her hands, stepped up again to the metal sculpture and resumed twisting a stubbornly straight rod into an acute angle.

Tom Hathaway was in bed with a girl. Not Pia. Not his future wife.

Things were not going well for Hathaway and his love. Being together and not being able to make love was even worse than being apart. The damned Church! How unfair it was that a nice girl like Pia could have her entire life screwed up by a bastard like that fairy husband of hers and the Church not understand.

Beside Hathaway the girl stirred. She was a Florentine who'd been taken up by an assistant director and was now script girl at Cinecittà. The assistant director was filming in Sweden, the girl was lonely, Hathaway had run into her at a diplomatic cocktail party.

Tom looked at his watch. Five o'clock. It would soon be dawn. The girl moved again. He reached over with one hand and gently slid it between her ripe thighs. She murmured something and moved toward him.

God, but he wished it was Pia.

Edmund Lonsdale laughed appreciatively. The *marchesa* at whose table he was dining on this particular spring evening was a notable bore. But by some fluke this dinner party had come off rather well. Even the parliamentarian with the cadaver's face had proved rather good value with his store of ministerial gossip. Perhaps, Lonsdale thought with his usual self-knowledge, he recognizes a fellow fascist.

"Monsignor, your glass?"

He passed the Waterford goblet a few centimeters to his right so that a celebrated novelist could reach past the intervening young woman and pour. An excellent claret. Lonsdale smacked his lips in appreciation. Save that wop stuff for the pasta shops and the tourist hotels. He drank off a bit of it and then, quite content, told yet another outrageous story that had the table applauding.

How good life is, thought Lonsdale, for those of us who have come to terms with it.

But it was not only the wine and good fellowship which had Monsignor Lonsdale in such a buoyant mood. His spies had informed him of a tentative, yet promising, relationship that seemed to have sprung up between his least favorite young cleric, the American Cobb, and a recently widowed Italian woman of impeccably good family.

There was more than one way to drive a wedge between this damned Cobb and His Holiness.

The woman might be just the tool he needed to break up the unseemly intimacy of Pontiff and priest. Her name, Lonsdale had been told, was Marella Massai. She was a *contessa*.

30

It was on the fortieth lap of the Buenos Aires Grand Prix, when he was running in third place, that Gigi Orsini's Lotus hit an oil slick and spun out of control, turning over twice before finally coming to a fiery stop in a hedge of acacia. He was twice given up for dead, once in the ambulance, the second time in the emergency room. A quickly summoned Dominican murmured prayers over his body while the doctors stripped the metallic crash suit from his body, pulling away at the same time great patches of burned flesh that fell away like suet from a grilled mutton chop. Beside the Dominican a blond girl sobbed histrionically, already seeing herself on television and in the photo magazines pale and black-gowned at the graveside of her lover. She was wondering just which black dress would be most photogenic when the doctors hustled her from the room so they could operate.

It was after midnight in Rome when Gigi crashed, and not until noon of the next day that his wife Jane could be found and notified.

"I hate Sundays," she had told herself that morning when she woke, uncharacteristically alone, in the large bed of her hotel suite. Sunday was race day. It was on Sundays that racing drivers died. They died on other days as well, of course, during practice, or testing a new car or new tires or a new track. But Sunday was the deadliest day.

It was also a day on which the shops were closed. Jane called Peter's number, then, after the telephone had rung only once, hung up. Why turn his day sour as well as her own? No shopping, no Peter, and an entire race day stretching endlessly, morbidly ahead of her. If only the children . . . and then she remembered the children were at home in the north. Where she should be. And not here in seductive, wicked Rome.

She breakfasted alone on the sidewalk in one of those vast outdoor cafés on the Piazza del Popolo. "Breakfasted." There *were* consolations to living

246

abroad. No one in Rome "brunched." Early in the afternoon she dove into a darkened movie theater to half watch, half ignore the latest work of genius by some Italianate American, while around her in the dim rows Roman swains groped in the bodices of giggling shopgirls.

It was dusk when she emerged. The bar of the Excelsior was nearly empty. Fine weather had, it seemed, called all Rome to frolic in the country. Jane looked at her watch. The race had not yet even started, if her somewhat vague calculation of transatlantic time was correct. The bored barman became more sprightly when she took one of his stools. He knew who she was, not the name, but the face. She tipped well, he was sure of that.

"Uno dry," she said, and the bartender beamed his pleasure and began to mix a dry Tanqueray martini. The potted palms, the smoky mirrors, the marbled floor, the deep, plush banquettes, the tiny, polished tables with their phony gilt edges, the taste of the martini, even the after-shave lotion wafting across the burnished hardwood from where the barman stood—how familiar it all was, how . . . comforting. On racing Sundays she wanted familiar things around her, familiar but not intimate. On Sundays no intimacies, thank you, no whispered confidences, no assurances of, "I know how you must feel, my dear. Those tiny cars, going so fast."

Banality was what she wanted on Sundays like this one.

And, oh, yes, one other thing.

At eight o'clock, quite drunk, she asked for the telephone. The barman placed it in front of her and then, thoughtfully, moved himself and his bar rag a few discreet paces away.

"Oh—" She nearly said, and just caught herself, You can listen, my poor, dear man. It's all frightfully innocent, I assure you.

She had trouble getting the number. And then she did.

At midnight, she was in bed. She was no longer alone.

The thing had taken some arranging. Dear Peppo, so gay, so clever. Always prepared to attempt the satisfaction of a whim, even one as *outré* as this latest notion of hers. To become, for one night (she assured him *this* particular night only), a whore. To work in a bordello, not for the money, they both understood that, but for the . . . novelty. She told Peppo she was bored, she didn't want to call anyone she knew, she wanted sex. It was all so simple. She did not explain about racing Sundays. The madam of the house was a gem. She looked Jane over carefully, received again the hushed assurances of Peppo that she was neither crazy nor a junkie who might cause trouble or upset the clients, and she was assigned a bedroom.

Once inside, Jane slumped heavily against the door. What a damnfool thing to do, even as drunk as she was. What a shameful, destructive act!

Then, frightened, embarrassed, drunk, she stripped off her clothes and slipped into the theatrically filmy peignoir the establishment provided. She propped herself up on the oversized bed and regarded her image in the circular mirror above. Oh, she whispered, don't let anyone come. And then, irrationally, Make them come quickly. She looked at her watch. The race must be started by now. She reached down to the handbag she'd prudently shoved out of sight under the bed and felt about until she found her Quaaludes.

She felt better after that and when the first of the night's clients had arrived, she greeted him with more than a simulated passion that would have, had he understood English and known who she was, explained quite explicitly why she was called "Crazylegs." All the man knew was that she was beautiful, she was "English," and that whatever she was asked to do, she did with an erotic avidity.

After him there were two more, and then, toward dawn, a man and a woman.

That, she decided, after gulping another handful of Quaaludes, was the part she liked best, the man watching while she and the other girl made love. It was then she could really forget it was racing Sunday.

It would be Peppo, the helpful faggot who had arranged Jane's *Belle de Jour* sexual fantasy fulfillment, who had taken her to the bordello, who would hear the first flash on the radio of Gigi Orsini's crash and would realize that somehow, someone must get her the hell out of there and back to her hotel before the gutter press found her. Even in panic, Peppo thought clearly. The "someone" must be her brother, Father Peter Cobb.

He reached Cobb by telephone, the number given him a few days before in case he needed to reach Jane the night she dined with Peter. Peppo put the situation plainly, quickly.

"Okay," Cobb said immediately, "I'll meet you there. Give me thirty minutes."

"Father Cobb," Peppo said tactfully, "you realize what I have told you? The sort of establishment this is?"

"Just get going," Cobb ordered. "Thirty minutes."

The two men met on the sidewalk in front of the place.

"Father Cobb," Peppo said apologetically, his soft hands making small, helpless circles, "I am so sorry."

"Sure, sure," Peter responded impatiently, "now let's get hold of the madam and get Jane the hell out of there."

Cobb was neither reckless nor stupid. He knew that of all the world's press, of all the cheap-shot artists and *paparazzi* and sensationalists and gaudy headline writers, none so revels in scandal as the Italian. They have it down to a fine art. Compared to the Italian scandal sheets, Fleet Street conveys a gray dignity. Compared to the Italian, the American supermarket tabloids are restrained to the point of constipation. Peter knew the risks he was taking. He could see the headlines now. Angrily, he shook off his reservations and he and Peppo entered the bordello.

By the time they had threatened and bribed and raged and smuggled her out of the place and back to her hotel, the lobby was besieged by the press. Jane was drunk, she was drugged, she had been screwing for nearly ten hours, but when she stumbled through the press of reporters and photographers and *polizia* into the lobby of the hotel on Peter's arm, Jane Cobb's face was pale, beautiful, and composed.

"*Cara mia*," Peter muttered as he forced her, still clothed, into the shower, "I don't know how you do it."

An hour later, totally sober, eyes slightly reddened but otherwise clear, dressed in a navy-blue Ungaro suit, her hair neatly tied in a French knot, Jane Cobb Orsini met with four members of the press selected by lot (after several fist fights) in the sitting room of her suite, and answered questions.

Her brother, Peter Cobb, sat next to her and said nothing.

And when all the questions had been asked—when had she last heard from her husband, had there been intimations of disaster, had their marriage been happy, had she known the blond girl who was with him at the track and in the hospital, would she fly to Argentina, where was she when the news exploded—when she had answered or tried to answer all those questions and the press had finally been ushered out, she slumped against Peter's chest and, for the first time, began to cry.

"Oh, Peter," she said, "I'm so ashamed. So damned ashamed."

He held her and stroked her hair. "It's okay," he said, "okay."

She sobbed aloud. "And I dragged you into this sordid mess. A priest. And you had to go to that awful place . . ."

"Jane, come on. Any Jesuit who's worked the waterfront missions of a Latin America port knows all *about* bordellos. That's where our parishioners are . . ."

She hiccupped then, half an inadvertent laugh, half a renewed sobbing. And he continued to hold her and remembered a day many years before when she had broken a necklace their mother loved and how he had held her much like this and stroked her hair. Yes, he'd said then, and yes, yes, he said now, and felt her body trembling against his, racked with sobs, the same, unhappy little girl, twenty years and four thousand miles from home.

249

And then she told him about racing Sundays and he listened, and then in his turn talked and she listened. And he knew that for the first time in a long while he was acting as a brother. And a priest.

Gigi Orsini did not die.

"Pity," the cynics said.

"A miracle," said the doctors.

"*Che bella fortuna,*" said an Italian teammate to the blonde he had inherited from Gigi and who was now sharing his bed in the Amigo Hotel in Brussels where he was preparing for *that* week's Grand Prix race.

And the blonde, cheated of her graveside scene, murmured, "*Sì, caro,*" and did things with her mouth to distract him from such a morbid subject.

They flew Orsini to Houston after a week. That was where the best burn center was located. C.C. Cobb had seen to it.

The old man's initial reaction, over the transatlantic phone to Peter, had been typical.

"So Stirling Moss finally bought it."

"He's not dead, Father," Peter said patiently.

"From the dispatches here in New York it seems academic."

"Well, there's always a chance."

C.C. paused. He was thinking of Helen Gatewood. "Yes," he said, more subdued, "I suppose there's always a chance."

"Of course there is."

Then, briskly, all business, Charles Cobb asked, "What is it, burns? If it's burns there are places that specialize."

"Yes, Father. Your staff should be able to find out. Can you do that?"

"Of course. Have you talked to Jane?"

Peter said nothing about how they'd had to track Jane down at the bordello.

"Yes, she's upset, naturally. But she's hopeful. Gigi's crashed before."

Old man Cobb grunted. The sound could have signified anything.

But if Peter was evasive and his father grunted, it was Jane Orsini who now *acted*. She shook off the shame of what she had done as she shrugged off the shock of her husband's crash and the flaunted infidelities that had preceded it.

"But you're magnificent," Marella told her, and meant it, "the way you've pulled yourself together."

"Of course," Jane said. "Aren't I C.C.'s daughter?"

She flew out of Leonardo da Vinci to Houston with both children, confused and slightly frightened, firmly in tow. Peter and Marella saw her off.

"But, Peter," Marella said, "I wasn't just trying to cheer her up, you know. She really is quite incredible. I'd be in a nursing home at this point full of Valium."

Cobb nodded. He knew, better than Marella could, how much truth there was in his sister's flip remark that she was C.C.'s daughter. As he was his son.

With somewhat greater panoply, Gregory the Pope was also traveling. To central Africa. One of those brief pontifical explosions of energy that had begun with John XXIII and which Curial Rome feared would never end. It was one thing to minister to a Pope enthroned in the Vatican, quite another to shuffle along in his wake in the heat of an equatorial noon while a hundred thousand black men chanted "welcome" in the same words they had used a century before to their tree gods.

Gregory himself did not wonder about the efficacy of such exhausting labors. He understood the importance of communication. A hundred pastoral letters read in ten thousand pulpits on a year of Sundays would not have the dramatic impact of a single white-robed figure standing among them whose right hand slowly, precisely, made the sign of the cross. The Nigerians, he knew, were Moslems, polygamists, animists. Perhaps five million of them were Catholics—and most of those polygamous. Still, Gregory knew he could reach these people, across the years and across the miles and across the barriers of culture and language and pigmentation. He could reach them because he must. Because it was his work.

Edmund Lonsdale did not accompany the Pope to central Africa.

"A narrow escape, that," he admitted over a brandy and soda to an amiable Benedictine. The two men were watching television.

"Here's to him," the Benedictine said, raising his glass in marginal tribute.

"Ah, dear, yes," Lonsdale said, more enthusiastically, "just because I didn't want to go doesn't mean I don't wish him well."

Cobb also watched the Pope's progress on television, remembering a rainy afternoon in Boston when he, like this ocean of black faces, had turned toward Gregory in mingled curiosity and wonder, remembering, as the thousands of Africans fell to their knees, how he had once knelt on the wet grass of Boston Common and had rededicated himself to this man who was his Pope.

While in Houston, in a room that smelled of carbolic acid and the faint odor of frying veal, Jane Cobb Orsini sat in a chair by the side of her husband's bed and wondered whether she, or he, or both of them were to blame for the wreckage of their lives, the destruction of what they had once had, the aimless, empty paths along which they raced to desolation.

There were several magazines in her lap, unread. The children were at the hotel. A nanny had been swiftly recruited. C.C.'s local corporate flunky had turned out efficient. There was nothing for Jane to do but to watch over her husband and to wait. The doctors pursed their lips and said nothing, eloquently. Jane wished Peter were here. At least they could talk, joke. Remember happier times, when there was still love between her and Gigi. If Peter were here, he could say a prayer. It might help. It couldn't hurt.

A magazine slid off her lap and noisily clattered to the floor. She reached down to retrieve it.

If only she could pray.

At the end of that week she asked the doctors if Gigi could be moved again. He did not seem to be progressing. Perhaps in Italy . . .

The Texans shook their heads.

"But there is a burn center near Rome," she said. "My father's staff have checked. It's . . ."

The doctors shook their heads again. Orsini was a dead man if he was moved again. Shock would finish what the flames had begun. Besides, they assured one another, although they did not say so to Jane Orsini, what the hell did the wops know about burns, anyway? Now if it were delivering *bambini*, that would be different. . . .

While back in Milan in her studio, Marella Massai hacked away at raw steel and suffered for her friend Jane Orsini. No one, not even Jane, knew how close to a total psychological collapse Marella had been last winter when Jane insisted she come up to Val for the skiing. She kept things to herself, Marella did, she did not cry aloud. Jane had saved her. Jane and her kids and the mountains and the unexpected pleasure of her brother. Peter Cobb was a decent, disinterested man, who wanted nothing from her but her friendship. Not her body, not her mind, not her connections. Simply and wonderfully, all he had wanted was her company. She owed so much to Jane, she owed much to Peter. Now Jane was in trouble. She wished she knew what to do to help. Peter, she suspected, was headed for trouble. Just what, she had no idea. But there was an openness about him, a vulnerability that she feared for. She wanted to see him again. And again. If she were more of a romantic, she'd suspect she was falling in love with him.

Impossible! she thought, picking up her acetylene torch.

31

The papal jet crossed the Mediterranean, banked slightly, and prepared to begin the long descent to Rome.

Gregory puffed his pipe and stared through the window at the sea. How lovely it was. Blue skies, white clouds and beneath it all, the lovely mirror of the sea. How simple if things were as tranquil down there as they seemed at this altitude. To his right, a few hundred miles south, Libya and mad Qaddafi. Beyond, to the east, Egypt. Then Israel. And beyond that, hostile Islam, the Persian Gulf, Iraq and Iran, tearing at one another's vitals. Behind him, blotted out by the afternoon sun, Morocco and the desert war that had gone on, it seemed, forever, that would go on, it seemed again, forever.

His pontifical mission had gone reasonably well. Gregory was a practical man. He anticipated no miracles and had witnessed none. Four countries in nine days. Perhaps two million people had seen him, heard his words, knelt for his blessing. Laughing people, laughing as they surged toward him, even as the mounted police tried to beat them back. The police laughed too, as they brought their batons down on the heads and shoulders of the crowd. To the Moslem officials he had been friendly, ecumenical. Surely there was a common language of love, decency, honor, even between men of such disparate faiths. To the black Catholics he had preached the same things: love, decency, honor. But to them he had also been stern. They must abjure polygamous relationships. One man, one wife. How odd it must sound to a people who had counted wives as chattels, to whom wives were wealth for ten centuries—more.

Gregory's message would have been more popular had he skirted the issue. He could not. If they had their duties, so had he.

A fifth African nation had been on the original schedule. It had been scrubbed. A religious war had broken out, a civil war. Dispatches were sketchy. But it was said ten thousand men had already been killed. Ten thousand. The number of Polish officers who had died in the Vlatin more than forty years ago. Men still dying by the tens of thousands for causes most of them only vaguely understood, but which were no less passionate and sanguinary for their confusion. So he had not gone to that country. Too risky, the experts said, too full of danger, of potential embarrassment. There might be . . . an incident.

Gregory the Pope nearly permitted himself a grim smile. He wondered what they would think, these cassocked *monsignori* and bishops and red-hatted cardinals, if they could see the boy he was in the forest of Vlatin, lying on that hillside with his parents and Anna dead in the trees behind him, drawing a bead on Russian officers with the old Mannlicher. He was older now, and a Pope, and he knew it was right and proper that they shield him from violence, even from "embarrassment." But there had been a time . . .

The plane banked again and the descent into Rome began.

It was full spring now, the middle of May. At night, after Peter had finished work, he would walk out into the neighborhood and stop by this or that *trattoria* for dinner, a half bottle of cheap wine, and sit there alone, eating, drinking, reading the newspaper, half watching, half listening to Rome. Sometimes he wrote letters in longhand, partially as an escape from the disciplines of the typewriter. He wrote to his father, long, cheerful, somewhat thoughtful letters, full of unimportant news and full of assurances of his belief that Helen would get better. He did not really believe this but it was what he wrote.

His father never replied.

And in his book Cobb wrote:

> When the State and established society conspire to deprive the people of their vote, their land, their right to organize, to publish, to debate, and other rights, the Church has the *duty* to protest. And when those protests are ignored or paid lip service, to go beyond protest. How much beyond is for each bishop to decide. And if the bishop rules, thus far and no further? Therein lies the dilemma of the priests of Mirador. And of a hundred other places in a hundred other times. When does legitimate protest by a priest become intransigence? When does intransigence become disobedience? I will give you an example: when the bishop of the diocese of Mirador City blesses the tanks of the Miradoran National Guard which will then roll into the countryside to support the land barons

in putting down revolt, then I say the bishop is no longer legitimate and the priest who disregards his instructions commits
neither sin nor offense.

There *are* just and holy wars. Mirador is but one of them.

He pushed the sheaf of paper aside and lighted another cigarette. He
had just reread what he had written. It had no passion, none of the poetry
of his first book. It was didactic, stiff, hortatory, cold. It was a tract he was
writing. He'd heard better stuff, more inspirational words from the pastors
of rural parishes during Lent.

Fame had provided him a pulpit and he wasn't doing a damned thing
about it. All the talk shows and the cover stories and the critical adulation,
all the passion he'd whipped up in the eager hearts of other young clergymen, the pathetic hopes of those he'd left behind him in Mirador, the admiration of men like Kurt Salomon, the uneasy, curiously respectful hostility
of a Lonsdale, in itself a sort of tribute, this unexpected intimacy with
Gregory himself, all these had given Cobb opportunities few priests had
ever had. He'd been singled out for some great and meaningful role. He
hadn't sought it, it had been thrust on him. But since it had happened, he
had a duty to fulfill his destiny.

Instead, this dusty, empty pile of manuscript. Where had anger flown,
art fled, power eroded? Mirador had receded in time, in distance. He could
still feel crackling within his soul resentment of the injustices he had seen.
He could feel it but he was no longer writing it. He could hear Figueroa's
screams but there was no pain on his pages.

In all these weeks since he had come to Rome he had but twice acted
like the priest God had chosen him to be: when he blessed the dying terrorist in the gutter outside the bombed restaurant and when he had rescued
his own sister from the bordello and the yellow press. A dour cloak of failure
draped his shoulders. . . .

A message had come to Gregory from the east. From Poland. From an
aging and sober archbishop of the Baltic province of Gdansk, where the
shipyard workers had launched Solidarity at the very fag end of the seventies,
to report that the natives had again become restive. Difficult. Potentially
dangerous. Gregory might not know Mirador or its people. He knew Poland
and the Poles.

What was happening now, or what was threatening to happen, was, on
a scale a hundred times as large and a thousand times as perilous to the rest
of mankind, what had already happened in Mirador. There were clearly
differences. In Mirador the enemy was a fascistic *junta*, in Poland, a Marxist

regime. Both of them, coincidentally and unhappily, were staffed by colonels. In both countries the working classes, the peasants and the factory hands, had allied themselves with whatever was left of the intellectuals. In both countries the Church was a potentially powerful Third Force.

Gregory was in his personal suite. He preferred the apartment to the office when there were confidential matters to be discussed. It must be the Slav in him, he acknowledged, suspicious, secretive, conspiratorial. He felt conspiratorial now, leaning forward, elbows on sturdy knees, as he listened to old Plitzka. The archbishop, fifteen years older than his master, held a tall glass of Pilsener in a large paw. The two men had been talking for nearly two hours. In Polish. Easier for Plitzka, Gregory told himself. Also less likely to be overheard and understood.

"Go on, Plitzka. Another beer?"

"No, Holiness. I'm fine. Where was I?"

Gregory remembered when he was a young priest and Plitzka terrified them all. Shrewd, tough, brutally frank. Well, he was still shrewd. His assessment of the Polish situation jibed with other whispers from the east, other emissaries. "What will happen if the regime cracks down yet again?"

"Oh, yes. This time, I fear, nothing will hold them back. The young ones who took over for Walesa, they are less thoughtful, more impetuous. They . . ."

"And the Russians?"

"Ah," said Archbishop Plitzka, "they'll come in, of course. Shoot everyone they don't hang. It'll be jolly."

"Ha," the Pope said. In Poland you needed gallows humor. Otherwise you had only the gallows. Or so the saying went.

Plitzka went on. "And, as usual, the Church is in the middle. If we support the workers against the regime, the Russians will come in and we'll lose everything. If we sustain the regime, the workers turn against us and stop going to mass. The young priests are for the workers. They don't reckon the risks. They're all hotheads. Crazies. No one thinks anymore. No one sits down to think."

"And you, Plitzka?"

"Well, Holiness, I think we must aid the workers. And try to save what we can when they break the eggs."

"You think we can save anything then? After the Russians come?"

"Something, perhaps. We survived 1939. We survived the Russians. This too shall pass."

Gregory nodded and then stood up. He wished he could believe Plitzka.

"Thank you, Your Excellency. My secretary will take you to your quarters. Perhaps you will do me the honor of lunching tomorrow."

Plitzka, bearlike but trembling, fell to one knee. "Holiness, I am sorry to burden you like this."

Gregory helped the old man back to his feet. "Excellency, burdens are why I am here."

He rang, a secretary came, and the old Polish prelate limped heavily away down the carpeted corridor. Old. It would be for the younger Bishop Kronk to see this through.

"God bless, Plitzka," Gregory murmured, and then shut the door firmly behind him. He wished he could as easily close off these concerns about a new paroxysm of destruction that seemed about to overtake his country. Then, remembering he was the Pope, he resolved to worry no more about Poland than he would any country.

"Ha," he said again, half aloud, not much chance of that. A Pole was a Pole, whether you sent him into space as a cosmonaut as the Russians had done or elected him Pope as the Italians had.

It was then that Charles Cobb decided to come to Italy.

Helen Gatewood sat propped up against pillows in the townhouse she now shared with C.C. on East 62nd Street in Manhattan, trying not to feel sorry for herself, trying harder not to feel the pain.

What rotten luck.

If Peter's correspondence with his father was a relentlessly one-way affair, his and Helen Gatewood's was decidedly a dialogue.

"I've never been much of a Catholic," she wrote, "and yet I believe in good and evil, reward and punishment. And it occurs to me what's happening is very clearly punishment for my being with your father. This 'living in sin,' as the more quaint among us put it. Do you think so?"

And Peter had replied:

"No, I don't think so at all. When my mother was dying and after she was dead, you saved my father's life. I really believe there are infinitely more credits against your name than debits. You've given yourself fully. What more has any of us to give than that?" Then, jocularly, to lighten a cheering letter that was threatening to become morbid, he added, "Besides, Helen, Father is impossible now. Just think what a mean old son of a bitch he would have been without you."

Then in a postscript, "For God's sake, burn this before the dear old fellow sees it. Love, Peter."

In one of her letters she expressed a desire to see him and Jane again. That she meant "for the last time" went unsaid.

"I'm not all that weak, you know," she wrote, "and there are many days when I'm positively boisterous. I don't think there's any great advantage to dying at home when you can die on holiday, do you? I liked Italy the one time I was there. And I do love you both. And Jane's children . . . I barely know them at all. What do you think? I promise not to be a burden."

Peter replied immediately. "A terrific idea. I'd do it, Helen, barring an absolute veto by the medics. It's spring now and quite lovely and there are good doctors here. But can you get the old man to agree? You know his less-than-enlightened attitudes toward what he so charmingly calls 'the wops.' "

Whatever C.C. thought of "the wops," he had never been able to say no to Helen Gatewood.

Cobb functionaries were sent ahead to prepare the ground. Cobb affiliates were alerted. Cobb executives examined houses, measured windows for new drapes, interviewed doctors, inspected hospitals, conspired with officials in Washington, bribed Italian bureaucrats, purchased a certain style of hospital bed that Helen found more comfortable and flew it from New York to Rome.

Finally, on a fine day in May, Charles Cobb and his dying mistress boarded a jet at JFK in New York with a doctor, two nurses, and four flunkies in attendance, and eight hours later landed at Leonardo da Vinci.

By an enormous exercise of will, Helen Gatewood was able to walk off the plane, past the specially ordered wheelchair that awaited.

"I'll be darned if I'll be an invalid before I have to," she declared, and Cobb, his face stern, patted her arm and said quietly, "No, no, Helen. You'll walk. We'll walk together."

Watching them come toward him at the customs gate, Peter for the first time in his life thought of his father as old. He hadn't seen him since that dinner in Boston at the Ritz six months before. It was Helen who was ill. But his father looked awful. They were both paying the price of her cancer. Peter lifted a hand to wave a greeting. Helen waved back; C.C. did not. Instead, he turned to one of his aides and snarled, in a voice that carried through customs, "And get on that luggage right away before the damned dagos steal it all."

"Hello, Helen; welcome, Father" was what Peter said. What he was thinking was Well, we don't change, do we? Any of us.

But they *were* changing, all of them. They just didn't know it yet.

32

They were moving Gigi Orsini outdoors for the first time. Jane bustled in front of him and behind and to both sides at once, getting in everyone's way.

"Not so fast. Hurry. You'll bump into that door. Be careful. Faster."

More than two months had passed since the crash. She seemed somehow to be taller. She was certainly thinner. But her eyes were clear. And when she was not frowning at the quality of the care her husband was being given, she smiled a lot.

Gigi had been home from the hospital for a week. There were other operations still to come, more skin grafts, plastic work, an annoying patch behind his knee and another on his chest that continued to drain. But he was alive. He might even walk again. People still did not like to look at him, of course, because his face was no longer there.

"I can still see his face," Jane told herself furiously, "and if I can still see it, then it's *there*." Various surgeons gave her various responses when she asked about rebuilding his face. Not that it was so important to her, because she could still visualize Gigi the way he had been. But for the children. It was not right that children fled, terrified, from their own father.

The attendants positioned Gigi's wheeled cot on the patio of the big house according to Jane Cobb Orsini's instructions. In the shade, of course. But facing Como and the Alps beyond. His eyes had been damaged but they functioned. He could not speak. There was one hole where two nostrils used to be. His nose, that elegant blade of cartilage, was gone. He could hear. But the exterior ears would have to be recreated of living flesh from other parts of the body. One hand was a claw. The other, incredibly, had healed almost completely.

"Now, that's fine, isn't it?" Jane bubbled. Then, to the nurses and servants, "All right, you can go now. Thank you, thank you. Please go."

She pulled a rattan chair across the polished red tile of the vast patio and sat down next to her husband. His eyes rolled toward her.

"Yes, Gigi," she said to those eyes, "you rest. I'll stay right here. Don't worry. I won't leave."

His eyes flickered up and down in assent.

The brain still functioned.

Jane had not gone to Rome to greet her father and Helen Gatewood.

"I just can't, Peter," she told her brother by phone from Turin and the hospital where Orsini had been flown after she persuaded the Houston doctors to let her take him home to Italy.

"He'll just vegetate here," she had pleaded to the Texans. "In Italy, well, maybe there's a chance he can walk again. Talk. There's a very fine burn center in Torino. Turin. They know what to do. Oh, I know you're wonderful here, but for Gigi, Italy is home . . ."

The blond, red-faced Houston surgeon to whom she was talking shook his head. My God, he thought, this magnificent animal of a woman. With all that money. With all her connections. With those legs . . . and she can't wait to be alone with this slab of barbecue meat.

"All right, Mrs. Orsini, no way we can stop you if you insist. I think you're makin' a mistake. But I sure understand how you feel."

"Thank you, doctor. You've been sweet."

He blushed.

"Everyone has. Everyone's been just wonderful."

She meant it.

Jane could not explain the euphoria that had swept over her when she realized that her husband would live. Malicious folk smiled knowingly and remarked that now, at last, Jane had Gigi just where she wanted him: helpless and so ruined no other woman would ever want him again.

Such folk were wrong. Whatever residual anger she had toward Gigi for his wastrel ways, his infidelities, his selfish, vagabond life as a race driver, had been swept away by the violence of the crash, by the severity of his burns. As for her own guilt, the shame of what she had done in that bordello in Rome, in a score of other bedrooms with a score of other men . . . and women . . . all that, too, was sluiced away. Jane had but one role now: as Gigi's wife, to nurse him back to health and to care for his children.

Even her father and Helen Gatewood came second.

The sun dipped now toward the Alps and began its descent into France. Jane leaped to her feet, reaching out a hand to Gigi's claw to let him know she was not leaving, and shouting in Italian at the house:

"Come quickly now. Do you want your master to take a chill in the dusk?"

Gigi's eyes rolled up toward her face.

"Tomorrow, darling, we'll come out earlier. And stay longer. The air will be good for you. I know it, I know it."

She walked beside the wheeled bed as they lifted it and turned it toward the double doors that led from the patio into the house.

Helen had gone to bed and Peter and his father sat easily in the library of the *palazzo* C.C.'s people had leased for him, drinking brandy and talking as men do late at night when the women are asleep.

"She's better, Father. I can see an improvement after just a few weeks."

"I wish I could see it. I keep remembering her as she was."

"She's been through a lot. Chemotherapy, the drugs."

"I know, I know."

Peter had dined with them that evening. Again, he remarked to himself his father's age. C.C. sipped at his brandy, absentmindedly swirling it gently around the snifter.

"So Ascari will live."

Peter knew whom he meant. "Yes. The burns are terrible but he'll live."

"Rotten shame," his father said. Peter chose to think C.C. meant the accident, and he simply nodded. C.C. went on:

"That bastard lives and Helen dies. Where's the balance? Where's the grand design in that?"

"It's a design we don't understand, perhaps. Besides, Helen hasn't died. There's always a chance. And as for Gigi, that doesn't strike me as living as much as it is subsisting."

"Splitting hairs."

"It's the Jesuit in me, I guess."

"Ah, yes. The Jesuits. They've left you alone, apparently."

"Yes, Father, and that's puzzled me. Not like the Jesuits to let one of their own stray like this. I guess they feel the Vatican itself is watching over me with sufficient fervor."

"Perhaps they've sufficient troubles themselves," C.C. remarked, his intelligence services as efficient as ever.

"Oh?" Peter knew his father well enough to know he did not drop casual remarks on important matters without there being something behind them.

C.C. shrugged.

"There's some talk of papal irritation with the Jesuits. Your man Gregory seems a bit annoyed at whatever they're up to."

"And what are they up to?"

His father barked a brief, joyless laugh.

"That's a bit odd, isn't it? Your asking me what's going on in your own Church, your own Order? How the devil should I know? A pox on both their houses."

261

33

Mirador! Across the miles and across the months it came again to Peter: the sleepy lapping of the warm Pacific against golden beaches; the drone of insects in the tropic night; the cry of market women and the low laughter of cool cafés and beer halls; the shrieks of plumed birds and the scurrying rustle of a scorpion across a rattan carpet; the smell and sound and tactile memory of it; all awakened in a letter from Flor Duarte. And there was something else, a hardness he had not heard in her voice before:

> We are a real army now, Peter. You would be proud. Did you know we have tanks? Castro sends them. More and more of his advisers are with us. They don't give orders, not yet. But you can sense their impatience. We use them and they use us. A mutual deception. And there are more and more Americans on the other side. To one who has read history the whole affair is redolent of Spain in 1936. Well, we have had our share of Guernicas.
>
> I am sorry not to have written more. But one has duties. Joaquin, of course, spits at the mention of you. I do not. I hope that whatever you are doing, wherever you are, you are happy. If this reaches you, think well of me, despite everything. And of Joaquin. Whatever he says, I know you helped us create what we now have. I only wish you were still part of it.

She signed it, "with love."

Her letter had come with the morning's post. The old crone had brought it to him. Now Cobb sat at the kitchen table sipping a third cup of early coffee and considering, with a sense of depression, the stack of typescript piled neatly alongside his typewriter. His role was ministering to souls, to those who, like Flor and Joaquin, needed him, whether they realized it or not. Instead he had become a scribbler of books, a dialectician, arid and self-important. Living graciously in Rome. He did not regret the first book. He had something to say and had said it as best he could. The book had worked its impact. He wondered if Flor had seen his book. Of all the critics, her praise would have meant the most to him. For she had been there. It was, in large measure, *her* story. But this second book . . .

Cobb pushed at the impressive pile of typing paper. It did not move. It had grown too heavy. Sheer bulk of pages, he knew, did not make a book.

He got up and took the coffee with him, turning his back on the typewriter and the manuscript. Better to get out, to walk, to go somewhere, anywhere, get away. Get away from the vague sense of guilt Flor had reawakened in him that he was needed in Mirador rather than here, that it was his ministry that mattered and not his writing.

Gregory also had his correspondents in Mirador. And, for quite different reasons, their letters left him vaguely uneasy.

It was Peter Cobb's book which had heightened his curiosity about Mirador and specifically the role his Church was playing there. The mission of Cardinal Grassi had been less than satisfactory. A more skeptical observer should have been sent, someone who knew the region. Grassi had come back with a fairy-tale version of reality. The local bishops had demonstrated their piety, white-robed children had sung, little girls had handed him flowers, and the colonels of the *junta* had charmed him with their reasonableness. Well, so be it. Gregory was not a man to spend his energies in fruitless regret. He had sent out other emissaries. Less august men, younger, immune to charm. It was their coded communiqués he was now reading and which disturbed him as Flor's letter had disturbed Cobb.

Peter's restless lope through morning Rome had ended with *citron pressé* in a café near the American Embassy. On an impulse he went into the café and telephoned Hathaway.

"Buy me a cheap lunch?"

"Hell, buy you a good one. Meet me at Alfredo's at one."

They had a corner table. Geneva, Tom said, had been the usual waste of diplomatic time.

After they ordered they talked of Charles Cobb's precipitate descent on Rome.

"Poor Italy," Hathaway remarked, "your father will be a one-man army of occupation in a country that's been occupied too many times already."

"Goths, Vandals, Huns and now C.C." Peter agreed. "Hardly fair, is it?" Hathaway leaned closer.

"How's his lady friend? She really in bad shape?"

"The Duchess? Well, I guess so. Cancer. The doctors in New York didn't provide much encouragement and so C.C. put his people on it and they came up with some sort of new treatment over here."

"Miracle cure?"

"No, I don't think it's anything crackpot. Not another ground-up apricot-pit formula. But even if it were, Helen would have been willing to make the trip, C.C. never gives up on anything without exploring all the options, so here they are."

The two men dug into their meal. Americans raised in boarding schools and accustomed to the manners of the university dining room do not pick delicately at their food.

"How's Pia?" Cobb asked between mouthfuls of a superb squid salad.

"Oh, you know," Hathaway responded, uncharacteristically vague.

"Now what does *that* mean?"

Hathaway continued to eat and then, doggedly, he answered, "It means *your* goddamned Church and *her* goddamned religion have screwed us up rather thoroughly and for the moment I'm not seeing her."

"I'm sorry, Tom, really I am."

"Not your fault, Peter."

"Well, you asked me to help and I haven't accomplished a damn thing."

"It was a long shot. I think we both knew that."

"Still, I'm sorry."

"Sure, forget it. We simply decided it hurt more being together and not being able to do anything about it than being apart."

Castel Gandolfo is an ugly, useful estate in the Alban Hills where, since 1927 and the Vatican Concordat, Popes have fled the heat and found rest. But Gregory was not resting. He was having his vigorous morning swim. The year before he had had them repair the swimming pool, replace the old tiles, flush the thing out.

It was after his morning swim that Gregory buried himself amid papers in a small, pleasant, den-like room lined with books and read and thought and wrote and read again. There were a number of areas of concern for the Pope this spring. Africa he had taken care of. Not that he had solved it; far from it. He did not expect a nine-day tour of four nations to have been much more than a showing of the flag. But he wanted himself on the record. There was nothing more he could do with Africa for the moment.

Then there was Kung. Fortunate for Gregory, fortunate for the Church, that theology was so boring. If more people read Kung, the problem would be all the greater. Kung was an irritant. Everyone talked about him and nobody read him. Perhaps the best way to handle Hans was to ignore him. Why draw attention to obscure enemies?

But Gregory could not ignore his other problems. To do so would be an abdication of responsibility. From the beginning, ever since the moment the white smoke issued from the chimney, there had been the matter of the Jesuits. Testing him, always testing, arguing, evading, bobbing and weaving their devious way through the rules. He was not the first Pope the Jesuits had ever tested. He would not be the last. Gregory knew that. He also knew that if he did not pull the Jesuits up very short, and soon, his writ would be run. He'd be too old, too tired, too weak to confront them. Popes came and went. The Jesuits remained. Rebellious, difficult, arrogant. No, there could be no more delays. Now was the time for the Jesuits. He had been working for a year toward this moment.

Then there was Mirador. What a mess. How pleasant it would be to declare neutrality, to curl up in the comfortable sort of isolationism so many Americans affected before the Second War. How attractive. How . . . impossible. This Cobb. Curious, wasn't it, how important a Jesuit's ideas had become in Gregory's consideration of the Mirador crisis? Not that Cobb made Jesuit policy. A cog in the machine. That was all. Cobb, the Jesuit, the expert on Mirador, was not even aware that his Pope was about to act on both those troubling areas of concern.

Perhaps, thought Gregory, perhaps it would be interesting to have young Cobb on hand next week when Gregory the Pope summoned the Society of Jesus to his presence.

34

With young men, modern men like Cobb, even an obsession has its limits. Perhaps that was why his book was grinding down. Mirador was too far away, in miles and in time. Its beauty and its horrors were both slipping beneath a horizon of distance and time, over a year now. Flor's letter revived it. Briefly. It was not that Peter had become callous or bored. It was simply that other people, other things, obtruded on his awareness: Jane's patient, admirable nursing of Orsini; C.C.'s devotion to the Duchess and her near-saintly acceptance of pain and proximate death; the shadowy, veiled threat of the menacing DeBragga and the continued snooping of the Italian police; and, far from least, the decidedly not shadowy figure of the Contessa Marella Massai.

It had all begun innocently with Marella. Jane was her friend, she had lost a husband, brutally, shockingly. They'd skied together, chatted in the Alpine nights, she'd heard his mass, had knelt and received the Eucharist from his hands. Begun innocently, still innocent. Until now.

"You're just kidding yourself if you think this thing isn't dangerous," Peter now told himself. He'd no damned business playing around with a single, attractive woman like Marella. Unfair to her, unfair to him, unfair to his Church. The temptation was there, the pull was powerful. Oh, not just the physical side, though he could not deny that part of it, but the rest of it. He was alone in a foreign country, she was a friend, a confidant, a good listener, a pleasant companion.

Peter decided, not for the first time, against seeing her again alone. Too hard on him, too hard on her. In that, Cobb was not being egotistic. His instincts were precisely accurate. Marella felt herself drawn to him as powerfully as she had once been drawn to Franco Massai. And, tossing in her bed in Milan, she told herself for perhaps the dozenth time, "I won't call him. I won't go to Rome. I won't see him again unless Jane is there." And she meant it.

Then, as people do, three days later she was on the telephone.

"I've got to be in Rome. My agent is talking about a show. There are a million details. When I have them arranged will you drive out into the country with me? I'll provide the picnic."

And as men do who are frustrated in their work, who are looking for things they cannot precisely define, as men do who are alone and lonely, Peter Cobb said yes.

Marella had hired a car, the usual nervous little Alfa Romeo, and when she picked up Cobb at his place she had the top down and a wicker picnic basket on what passed for a back seat.

"You are to lunch today, dearest Reverend Father Peter Cobb, more splendidly than any Roman since Claudius."

She slipped lithely behind the wheel. "Now get in. You've moldered too long in this dull city."

Like most Italian women of her generation and class, she drove well, piloting the little car in and out of the chaos of a Roman rush hour. Soon they were on the *autostrada* headed east, away from the sea, up into hills that genuflected to the real mountains beyond. After an hour she pulled off the highway and turned onto a two-lane road that began to climb sharply toward the Apennines, the craggy spine of Italy.

"Do you want to drive for a while?" she asked.

"Nope. Except for trucks and the occasional jeep I haven't driven for years. This buggy is out of my league. I'd probably put us into the ditch."

Not for the first time she noted Cobb's almost total lack of typically male ego. How unlike the men she knew, had grown up with. There was nothing in Cobb demanding that he take charge. It wasn't weakness or lack of ability, she knew. It was strength and the confidence of that strength.

"Don't you want to know where we're going?"

"Nope," he said again, comfortably slumped down in the seat of the little car, "I assume you and Thomas Cook and Son have everything arranged."

She drove east into the high hills.

As she drove she half watched Peter's profile to her right, so close she could reach out a gloved hand and touch him. Or he could touch her. He never had, absent the casual handshake or brushing against each other on a lift chair or passing something at table. It is a ridiculous life we lead, she thought. Only an hour or two ago in Trinità dei Monti he had stood on a consecrated altar and re-enacted the daily miracle of the bread and wine. Now he was here, sitting next to her. A priest. A holy, perhaps even saintly man, and she had fallen in love with him. How inconvenient, her more sophisticated Milanese friends might have said, how awkward of you, Marella.

Well, it was. Damned awkward. And not only that, but stupid. I am not, she told herself firmly, the sort of woman who seduces priests. It is ignoble! It is wrong! All very well to make such sensible moral judgments; it was something else to live by them.

Did he know? She glanced toward him as if fearing he could read her thoughts. But his face was averted, watching a farmer's boy barefootedly kicking an ancient mare into a reluctant trot. She turned back to the wheel and the winding road ahead. He *must* know she loved him. How could he not?

It was nearly noon. A bright summer's day with the sun hanging in a cloudless bowl of blue. But at this altitude, more than a thousand meters up, it was cool even with the sunshine. They were both wearing sweaters now, as they climbed the hillside above a crumbling village toward a crumbling ruin even higher up. Peter was wearing one of Franco's old pullovers. She'd brought it for him. Wearing her husband's sweater, picnicking with her husband's wife. Widow! She hated the word. She was still Franco's wife. Only now there was no Franco. There was only . . . Peter Cobb.

She wore walking shoes and wide-waled corduroy pants and a mauve handband that kept her dark, wavy hair out of her eyes. Cobb carried the wicker basket and walked behind her as they climbed toward the ruined church she'd promised him. Not as slender as Jane, taller than Flor, she moved as well as either of them. No city girl, this. Not the way she covered ground, not the way he remembered her on skis. He could feel sweat trickling down his back, could feel the dull, pleasant ache in thighs unused to climbing. A year ago he would have sprinted up a slope like this one with a rucksack on his back and a BAR in his hand. He climbed behind her and watched the lovely, metronomic movements of her haunches.

They reached the old church just before one.

"Isn't it lovely?" she said, waving a hand proudly around the ruin as if she had created it just for him.

"Lovely," he agreed, "if a trifle beat up."

It was that. There was more ruin than church. Tumbled walls, covered with moss and vine, no roof; the floor, if there ever had been one, covered with velvety grass and wild flowers. There were flowers everywhere, clinging to the crumbled walls, issuing from every crack and fissure in the stone. There had once been a *campanile*. Now there was only another pile of gray stones a few feet higher than the rest of the place. Marella grinned at him and threw herself down on the grass inside the ruined outline of the church's walls.

"It isn't blasphemous, is it, to have lunch here? Tell me it isn't."

"Of course not. And if it is, I hereby issue a dispensation. Retroactively."

He dropped to the turf beside her and pulled out a handkerchief to mop his brow.

"And I was cold when we started. Some shape I'm in."

"You're in lovely shape," she said, smiling.

"Yeah, just like this place. A couple of medieval ruins."

He was glad he had come. It was a magnificent day; the old church crouched on a hillside above a tourist-brochure valley complete with stream; the blue Italian sky vaulted high above them. Rome was hot and noisy and dirty and full of intrigues and jealousies and vague menace. Here there was only Marella and himself and this fine archeological relic.

"Happy?" she asked.

"Yes."

She broke out the lunch, cold pheasant with a stiff mayonnaise sauce, salad, scampi, bottles of mineral water and wine, crisp, small loaves of fresh bread, three cheeses, two of them fine, one of them wonderful. When lunch was finished he lay back against the grass.

"I can hear Gregorian chants coming right out of the ground," he said.

"Before Gregorian chant was invented, there was singing here. Hymns and holy men and people worshipping."

"You're right," he said, "in my country a building fifty years old is granted landmark status. We forget how really old Europe is, Italy is."

"It's old, and in some ways it never changes."

There was a different tone to her voice and he said nothing, waiting.

"You know how we have the custom at New Year's in Italy of throwing old crockery out the windows when the new year begins at midnight?"

"Yes, I think I've heard that."

Her voice now was *very* solemn. "Well, last year was the first New Year I'd seen in without Franco since we were married, and obviously I didn't feel much like celebrating. But at midnight I went out onto the terrace of my apartment to watch and all around me, in my building and the other buildings, people were tossing old dishes and cups and saucers into the street and laughing and calling out to one another, you know, 'Ciao!' 'Happy new year!' that sort of thing. It was very warm for January first and I stood out there watching and listening. In an apartment across the way—an apartment belonging to people I actually know, very nice middle-class people with the politest children—I could see in through the open windows that the children, all in their teens, were having a party. And I thought, how nice. How very nice. And then they began singing."

She paused.

"They were singing all the old fascist songs. From the time of Mussolini.

These nice, well-brought-up, polite children of my friends. And I thought, well, we don't change much, do we? and shivered and went inside and locked my windows against the night and the sound of their singing."

He waited for a moment and then he said, equally solemn, "The Red Brigades and the old fascism."

"Yes," she said, "pulling Italy apart once more perhaps."

They talked about Mirador after that, Peter telling her things he had not told her before, things he had not told anyone.

"You miss it, don't you?"

"Yes," he said. "It was where I was happiest, where I worked best, where I contributed something."

"And you don't feel that way here? In Rome?"

"Only when I'm with Gregory. During those few hours I feel as if what I do and what I think or say is important. Otherwise, no. Absolutely not. A fifth wheel."

"Peter, we need fifth wheels. Spare tires. You put yourself down unnecessarily."

"Maybe. But it's how it seems to me."

She turned on him now, almost angry.

"Well, you're wrong. What about me? When you and Jane took over my care and feeding at Val I was a neurotic basket case. When you were finished I was back functioning again. Not great, but doing more than just existing. I even got back to work. And now here I am in Rome arranging a one-woman show with my agent. My God, Peter, you think you've played no part in helping me get back at least to the point where I am now?"

"It was Jane," he said, fearing he was being stubborn. "You and I were just guests. Jane worked the miracles. Or you did it yourself, pulled yourself out, more likely. I was there for the skiing and just happened to be one of the spear carriers in your recovery."

"Oh, Peter, it was more than that. More than I can say. . . ."

"Well," he said, uneasily.

Then, once again very much under control, Marella said, as polite as a schoolgirl, "Peter, I am very grateful to Jane. But I will never be able to tell you what you've done for me."

Later on in the car, heading down out of the hills and back toward Rome in the fast fading light of a summer evening, he knew that if he reached out an arm to drape it casually around her shoulders, they would have ended their day by making love. He watched her lovely Tuscan profile and then wrenched his eyes back to the winding road before them. And did nothing.

35

From around the world they came. The successors to Loyola and Regis and Xavier and Isaac Jogues and Marquette. The Jesuits. The Society of Jesus. Other great orders of the Church took their names from men: Dominicans, Franciscans, Vincentians, Benedictines. Only the Jesuits took the name of God's only son for their own.

And now they came to Rome. More than a hundred provincial superiors and other leaders of the Order. Their Superior General, aged and sick, remained behind in Madrid. Too ill to travel, they said. Privately the Jesuits believed Gregory the Pope had tactfully donned the velvet glove. Why humiliate the poor man with a summons to Rome when he had already been all but stripped of authority and a special papal delegate installed to function as his interim successor?

The rest of them came, as ordered. Secretly and individually. There was to be no fanfare. No press conferences were to be held. No torchlight parades. No whispered confidences to the religion editors of *Time* or *Figaro* or *Stern*. Gregory had laid down the ground rules and, as their host and their Pope, he expected them to be obeyed.

To Father Falcone, the delegate he'd installed to manage the Order, Gregory was specific:

"I want you to meet with them first. At the villa. Not here at Castel Gandolfo. Not at the Vatican. I want them brought down a peg before they meet with me. And make it very clear to them, Father Falcone, this is not a conference. Not a conversation. I am not interested in their views. I expect to address them, to answer no questions, to get their obeisance, and to give them a brief blessing. Is that understood?"

Falcone, himself a Jesuit, bowed his head.

"Yes, Holiness."

Gregory got up and went to one of the French doors looking out on the gardens of the Castel.

"You're a good man, Falcone. If you were ten years younger I'd give you the Order. But don't worry, I'm not that cruel."

Falcone smiled. "I know that, Holiness."

"I believe you do." Then Gregory's face again hardened. "But understand this: no dialogue. I am not meeting with the Jesuits to hear of their construction of the world and its problems, their vision of the Church, their definition of their own role. I am meeting with them to tell them *my* pleasure. Not theirs."

"I understand."

"Good, then let's have some lunch and you can be off to beard the lions."

Four days later the hundred most senior Jesuits in the world gathered in the Sistine Chapel at 10:00 of a cloudy Roman morning to meet with their Pontiff. They had heard mass together at their own headquarters near the Vatican and had strolled across the piazza for their private audience. Falcone had met earlier with them at a villa outside the city. He had read a message from Gregory, had made it clear there was to be no debate. "This is not participatory democracy," Falcone had told them, "nor is it intended to be."

Only Falcone's great age and the affection many of the men in that room held for him stilled the anger. Falcone did not feel like a traitor. He had a higher loyalty to Gregory than to his Order. But he knew that many of his fellow Jesuits did not feel that way. No matter. He was beyond ambition. He read the Pope's message, answered one or two procedural questions, and left. Behind him the Jesuits muttered. Now the fencing was over. Now they would hear directly from Gregory.

The Pope kept them waiting. The President of France was in Rome. He met with the Pontiff over breakfast. Politics. Gregory pressed a second cup of coffee on his guest. No, he smiled, there was no hurry. No pressing engagements. The Frenchman also smiled. He knew about the summons to the Jesuits. So did all of Rome. Such matters may be arranged in secret; they are rarely held in secret.

"Confidentiality," remarked the Pope, "is alien to Italians."

The Pope and the President of France understood each other. Each governed the ungovernable. They did some business and then the Pontiff rose. He was now an hour late for the Jesuits. An hour would make them nervous. Much more than an hour and they would turn surly.

Father Falcone had sent for Peter Cobb the day before.

"His Holiness requires your presence tomorrow morning. Be at my office in the Vatican at nine."

"Yes, Father."

Falcone looked up from his desk.

"That's all," he said.

"Yes, Father." Cobb did not move. "Can you tell me what will be required of me?"

"Only your presence."

Peter knew about the Jesuits' having been sent for. Despite all of Gregory's strictures, he knew. He was only puzzled about his own role in the affair. You do not invite forty-year-old Jesuit missionaries to convocations of Jesuit provincials and the hierarchy of the Order. No Jesuit, no matter how senior, held any grander title than "Father." There were no *monsignori,* no bishops. There were all just . . . Jesuits. At least that was the theory. Cobb understood the convention. He did not delude himself that the Order was any more democratic than the Church itself. Gregory wanted him there. He would be there.

Others also knew the Jesuits had been summoned. That evening over the dinner table of one of his inevitable countesses, Edmund Lonsdale found it difficult to restrain his delight. "The Jesuits are, of course," he declared sonorously to an audience of pederasts, aging noblewomen, and pseudo-intellectuals, "what we have in the Church instead of the *Brigate Rosse.*"

The epigram drew the muttered applause it deserved and then a movie producer asked cynically, "But what can Gregory do to them? Popes come, Popes go, but the Society is with us always."

Edmund Lonsdale nodded.

"I am sure His Holiness will prevail," he said piously. "The forces of right, you know."

"But who is right?" the countess demanded. "Personally I can't stand Jesuits and I detest this Pope."

"Perhaps they'll destroy one another," said a young playwright with a pleasant lisp.

Lonsdale said nothing. If only they would, he thought. How delightful it would be.

Father Malachy Hanlon, the Jesuit provincial of New England, shifted his backside impatiently on what he considered a damnably uncomfortable chair in the front row of the Sistine Chapel and glanced impatiently at his Rolex oyster. Eleven o'clock. An hour after the Pope was scheduled to address them, an hour and a half since Hanlon and his fellow Jesuits had filed into the Chapel and taken their places. Next to Hanlon a Basque Jesuit blew his nose. Behind him two Frenchmen gossiped. Down the row Hanlon could see the elegant Creeley of San Francisco raise a quizzical eyebrow. Where the devil was the man? If he was going to chew them out let him arrive and be done with it! This waiting was worse than the Chinese water torture.

At that very moment Gregory the Pope strode into an anteroom of the Sistine and surveyed the small entourage who would accompany him into the audience. They were all standing. Gregory looked around him and nodded. Falcone, the old Jesuit, several members of the Curia, a Jesuit cardinal, several *monsignori*, and Peter Cobb. Gregory nodded again. There was no small talk.

"Well," he said in Italian, "let's go."

They fell in behind the Pope roughly in descending order of seniority, Cobb at the end. For a giddy moment Peter thought of a matador's suite and wondered why there was no music. Would Gregory earn an ear? Or would he be gored?

There was, of course, no contest.

"Fathers," said Gregory as the assemblage rose to greet him, "let us pray together."

Cobb had seen Gregory many times before. In the pulpit or on the balcony. In the foggy distance on Boston Common. Across the vast reaches of the piazza. At audiences. Up close, sitting in an easy chair across a room. He thought he was familiar with all his moods, his gestures, his fluctuations of style. And of substance. He had never seen *this* Gregory.

The Pope did not pace. He stood in the middle of the floor of this moderately large and arguably overdecorated hall and lectured the great men of the Society of Jesus as if they were schoolboys. Or enlisted men.

"Fathers," he began, "for four hundred years the Society of Jesus has done great and important work. It has opened India to Christianity, tamed the forests of North America, supplied martyrs to the shoguns of Japan. It has educated our boys and our men, staffed our retreat houses, written books, converted English intellectuals, raised money . . . and spent it . . . healed the sick and prayed over the dead. Good, significant work. The Church today would be a different sort of organization had Loyola and his little band not formed their brotherhood."

The Pope was speaking in Italian. Now, he shifted to French. Later, to English. He would conclude in German. It was a virtuoso performance. But in whatever language, the lash of his words conveyed the same message.

"But all that is history. I will not bore you with references to other times. To *other* difficulties the Society has had with Rome. You were not born then. Neither was I. So we won't waste time on regretting the past, to wringing our hands over what might have happened before and why. Suffice it to say this is not the first time a Pope has met a group of Jesuits in an adversary situation. Only this time I am the Pope and you are the Jesuits in trouble."

Gregory glanced down at a sheet of paper he held in his left hand.

"Fathers. I have too much respect for your intelligence to deal in equivocation or euphemism. Your Society is famed for the subtlety of its intellect. You are . . . the elite. The best we have. The first legion. Caesar would have gloried in you. Napoleon would have assigned you to Maréchal Ney at Austerlitz. And"—his voice lowered ominously—"on the way back from Moscow." He waved a hand as if in dismissal. "But you know that. A corporate ego has never been lacking in your ranks.

"Nor, without reference to such of my predecessors as Clement XIV, is it necessary for me to remind you of the unhappy consequences when your Society and a sitting Pontiff have been unable to agree on a matter of substance."

The men in the Sistine shifted uneasily in their seats. Having told them he would not rake up the past, Gregory had thrown in their faces the despicable Clement, who had disbanded the Order for meddling in secular affairs. Clement remained such a *bête noire*, even now, that there were Jesuits who solemnly refused even to enter the Church of the Holy Apostles, with its monument to Clement.

Gregory paused to permit the stir to subside.

"Fathers," he said, "I will put the case against you. Not as individuals but as a Society. And then I will tell you what I plan to do about the situation."

Hanlon was not the only Jesuit to notice that Gregory was not even pretending to use the formal papal "we." "Goddamned ego," Hanlon muttered to himself through clenched teeth, "not even the pretense of civility."

Gregory knew what they were thinking. Cobb, standing well to the rear, was reminded of an animal trainer, goading tigers to leap through hoops. Gregory had everything but the whip and the chair.

"Fathers," the Pope resumed, "there are three areas of concern. The first derives from the apparent attitude of some elements of the Society that it, and not the Vatican, determines Church policy. The celibacy of priests, the question of the ordination of women, the various rulings on birth control, abortion, homosexuality. The list goes on. Second, an insistence on taking controversial positions in the political realm. One can be a Catholic liberal. One can be a Catholic conservative. What is not possible is for a priest to become a politician, to hold elective office, to join guerrilla move-

275

ments"—Cobb's palms went damp—"to subordinate his priestly functions of spiritual guidance and education to social activism. It is no coincidence, I feel, that your Daniel Berrigan is a Jesuit. Thirdly, there is the seeming inability of you, as the provincials and vicars of the Society of Jesus, to control the membership of your own Order, to maintain discipline in what was once, and could be again, the most disciplined company in the body of the clerical Church."

The men to whom he was talking, most of them old, all of them accustomed to deferential respect, had stopped shifting in their places. Now they sat stunned, silent, stiff.

"The first two are sins of commission. The third of omission. It weighs more heavily on you than the other two. For young men, even more mature men, to break a rule, to be insubordinate, to be carried away by their emotions, erroneously to interpret theology or even the simple rules of conduct, all this is understandable. What is intolerable is your failure to attend to these mistakes on the part of those who look to you for guidance. I see around me in this room an extraordinary group of men. Intelligent, learned, dedicated men.

"Some of you, I fear, rebellious men."

For the first time there was a murmur in the great room. Standing to the rear but hearing, seeing everything, Peter Cobb closed his eyes. He literally feared Gregory had gone too far, that surely one of these men would stand and hurl defiance, that he would perforce be witness to a historic religious schism.

But no man rose.

The Pope paused, as if his own words had shocked and in a way even surprised him with their anger, the bitterness of phrase, the unrelenting ferocity of criticism. He was, after all, their father. Their brother. Their fellow priest. And then, as if he had shrugged his shoulders against softening doubt, against papering over differences, he steeled himself and continued. This time, without meaning to do so, in colloquial English:

"Fathers, what in the name of God has happened to you? Where have you gone wrong? When did the Society set itself up as a papacy in exile?"

When these rhetorical questions had gone unanswered, as they had been intended to do, Gregory spoke again, this time hurrying out the words, flat and unaccented, as if wanting to get a distasteful business out of the way once and for all.

"I have not yet decided, Fathers, what to do with your Order. For the time being Father Falcone will continue to represent me as your leader, spiritural and temporal, in the regrettable absence of your revered Superior

General, who has my love in his illness. I will study the position. One or more of you I may call to my office to discuss details.

"I *may* name a new Superior General . . ."

There was a collective gasp. Jesuits elected their own Superior Generals! Popes did not!

". . . or I may, under certain conditions, permit you to elect one. For the time being, nothing is to be done without Father Falcone's assent. You are to remain in Rome. And"—his cold gaze swept the room—"what has been said in this room today is privileged. I want no headlines."

He turned then, without a final blessing, and swept out.

36

Cobb broke a rule by drinking alone that night. He felt knocked out by the events and emotions of the turbulent day. He could still hear Hanlon's snarled, angry words, "What in hell are *you* doing here, Cobb?" and his own stunned, stupid inability to answer intelligently, or even with a suitably equivalent snarl. Perhaps Jesuits had been chewed out as viciously before. Maybe Clement XIV had been as nasty when he banished them. But no one could have been any tougher than Gregory. And for Cobb, the youngest man in the room and a Jesuit, to be there as witness was an emotional burden—no, more like a shock—that he would never, never forget.

The old villa was still. He half lay, half sat on the battered needlepoint of the couch sipping cognac in the darkened room. What, he wondered, was the mood in that sprawl of buildings on the Borgo Santo Spirito where the Jesuits had their world headquarters? They had been told to cleanse their house or to lose it. They had been threatened with displacement by the hated *Opus Dei*. They had been asked, no, ordered, to prepare a new vow of fealty to the Pontiff. And he had been conscripted to witness their shame. It was his own Order the Pope had flayed. Where did his loyalties lie? Well, at least on that question he was serene in self-knowledge. There was only one Pope. There were many Orders. The Society would have to make its accommodations. It would not be the other way around. Not with a man like Gregory.

Cobb drained the glass. He got up and wandered into the kitchen to put it in the sink under the faucet. He flipped on the ceiling light. There, on the kitchen table, mocking him, was the pile of typescript of his book, a book that he had begun with such passion and on which he now gazed with mixed apathy and irritation. What had ever possessed him to think he was capable of composing a persuasive treatise on such a vast, complex subject?

He was no theologian. His first book, he now felt in this mood of depression, had been a lucky fluke. This second attempt was clearly beyond him.

He switched off the light and pulled back the curtains that masked the kitchen window. Out there was the city of Rome, warm and beckoning. Somewhere, through the open window, a radio played. A popular song. A woman's voice. From a parked car across the street he could hear murmured conversation. A laugh. It was after midnight but still the air held the whiff of a pungent pasta sauce. Italy. How odd that all the Cobbs were here at the same time. Jane nursing her destroyed Orsini, C.C. here with Helen, Peter under summons by a Pope seemingly intent on bringing his Order to its knees.

With his chastisement of the Society of Jesus, Gregory seemed to Cobb a more ferocious figure, not the cheery, avuncular man he'd thought he was getting to know. Cobb and a few others had accompanied Gregory back to his apartment from the Sistine Chapel. One by one they had been dismissed. Now Gregory and Cobb were alone. Disquieted, Peter wondered if he too should leave. But the Pope made no move to dismiss him. And he began to probe Cobb with a little catechism.

"You think I was hard on your friends? Unfair? Dictatorial?"

"Hard, yes. Unfair? I don't think so."

"And dictatorial?"

"I'm sure not, Holiness."

Gregory's face was flint. "You're wrong, Cobb. Popes *are* dictators. There was no democracy at work in that room just now. No sweet reason. No temporizing. That's all past. For a year I've waited for you Jesuits to clean your own house. You didn't."

Cobb sensed uneasily he might have stressed the "you." "No," he admitted.

Gregory raised both hands slightly, palms up. "What was I to do? Did I have options?"

Before Cobb could answer, Gregory slashed through the air with his right hand, answering his own question. "No, I did not. Nor could any Bishop of Rome. I regret the necessity of what I had to do today. But it *was* necessary, that's the point. I know there were decent, just men in the Chapel this morning, men that I hurt with my words, with my actions. I regret those hurts. But if children are entitled to their tantrums, parents are entitled to punish. No more holding of hands, Cobb, no more."

"No, Holiness."

Gregory seemed to relax. "We must all, after all, save our souls, Peter. The saving of souls is why we're here. Our own as well as others'."

279

"I know that."

"Sometimes we lose sight of the basic truth. We become distracted."

Cobb was sure this was meant for him, that it was not generalization.

Gregory picked up his pipe now and began to pack it. "What shape do you want the Church to have, Peter? What directions should it take?"

"I don't have strong feelings on it, Holiness."

Gregory raised his eyebrows. "I had the impression you held strong feelings on everything."

He seemed serious. Cobb had too much respect for him to fence. "Well, on some things I do, I guess. I think the Church can be better than it is. That its priests and its bishops can be better. That they . . ."

"And its Popes?"

"Well, yes. If the Pope isn't a great man you can hardly demand greatness of deacons and nuns and parish priests, can you?"

"It is for all of us to demand greatness of ourselves, isn't it?"

Cobb nodded. He'd started to respond to Gregory's question about the Church. Now he'd been diverted. Gregory erected directional signals and then took away the road maps.

"Look, Holiness, I came to Rome full of myself. Highly inflated. I'd done a small book that critics called important. My head was turned. I was intent on changing a world, reforming a Church. *My* Church. Seminarians and men working in the urban ghettos and nursing sisters in the cancer wards read my book. They began writing me, began telling me that what I'd said about Mirador was meaningful to them. I got my name in the papers, got myself on television. All that got me started writing another book. More ambitious. Perhaps too ambitious."

"And . . . ?"

"And I met you. I realized I didn't know it all. That maybe there were some things, many things, I didn't know."

"Even the great questions unsettling the Church today?"

Gregory was mocking him now, Peter was sure. Gently, but mocking. He resumed his catechism.

"Women taking Holy Orders. Homosexuals. Celibacy. Abortion. Birth control. You hold strong opinions on them?"

Cobb shrugged. "I could accept women priests. I would remain celibate myself but I could accept married priests."

"What else? What of the other great questions of our time?"

"Well, I'm equivocal on birth control. In Latin America I know a lot of priests who routinely prescribe the pill to slum mothers. Women who are already old at twenty-five, who've already had six or eight kids and no visible husband or means of support. Those priests seem to sleep well at night, to have no problems with their consciences."

"We cannot endorse such things, Peter."

"I know that. I'm saying only that, among other things, I'm not sure."

"You're not doubting your faith."

"No, only how it is sometimes administered."

"Abortion?"

"I am against it, Holiness. Which brings us back to birth control. Permit the pill and you obviate the pressure for so many abortions."

"Hmmmmm." The sound was unsettling.

Then Gregory asked, "Before Mirador, you'd seen war, had you not?"

"Yes. In Vietnam. I was a marine."

The Pope nodded. "A marine, now a Jesuit. There's a symmetry to your life. And you fought?"

"Yes."

"There are always millions of men wearing uniforms. Not too many actually fight. There's a difference."

"I know it. The marines have a delightful expression for soldiers who don't fight. 'Rear-echelon pogues.' Please don't ask me what a 'pogue' is, I don't know. But I always liked the contemptuous sound of it."

"I too," said Gregory. "And your Marine Corps, not very democratic, was it? No show of hands as to whether an order was to be obeyed or not?"

"No, not at all. They said 'go,' and you went."

Gregory smiled. Then, "Peter, the analogy is imperfect, but there are parallels between your description of the Marine Corps and how our Church functions. There are tables of organization, there is discipline, there is an ultimate authority. In recent years much of that has been jettisoned. For good reason, of course, very good reason," he said with a throwaway gesture of his hand quite effectively dismissing those "very good reasons." He went on.

"It has gone too far. There are cracks in the walls that took two thousand years to construct, cracks, perhaps, in the very foundations. I am not unaware of the talk. I knew when I was elected what my reputation was, what expectations I raised. And if I have disappointed some of you, well, I understand that. If I seem intransigent on such matters as divorce and abortion and the pill and celibacy for priests, I am not so out of insensitivity. I am so because I do not think the Church can withstand many more of those fundamental retreats from what we have for so long held, without toppling the entire structure around our ears."

He paused, then said with a half smile, "It is, after all, my own soul at

281

hazard here. You have your responsibilities. I would hate to see you put your own eternity at risk by not living up to them. No more than I care to throw the dice with my own fate by not acting as I believe in all conscience I *must* act as Pope."

Despite the smile, Cobb sensed warning in the Pontiff's voice.

"I too listen to my conscience, Holiness. I may be wrong, but I act out of belief in the right."

"Good, good. You must. We all must."

He lighted the pipe and went on:

"You must understand, Peter, there has to be, must be, a balance wheel to all this. Let liberal Popes who come after me redress my sins of reaction. John flung open the windows of the Church, thinking, perhaps, one day to adjust them. Paul lacked the will or the way. They stand open today, and a wind sweeps through the Church threatening to pull it down about our ears. I believe in change, progress, reform. But we have had too much of it too soon. It is for me to solidify matters for the moment. It is an old Church. A few years' retrogression might provide the stability on which later progress can be soundly based."

Gregory looked closely at Cobb's face, seeking something there. Agreement? He was not quite sure he had it. Love? Loyalty? He was quite sure of those. He knocked the ashes out of a dead pipe and went on.

"I do not, Peter, to paraphrase Churchill, intend to preside over the dismantling of the Catholic Church. And if that loses me the *love*"—he stressed the word—"of some of my priests . . . or all of them . . . I must accept that loss in return for their obedience. *God* judges Popes, the Jesuits don't."

Late that night, mercifully, cognac and fatigue took hold and Peter Cobb finally fell asleep, Father Malachy Hanlon's furious face haunting him, memories of that extraordinary morning in the Sistine Chapel still roiling through his troubled mind.

Gregory, he was sure, did nothing simply for effect. He'd kept Peter behind when the others left, for a reason. Why? A warning to behave? A concern for Cobb's soul? In a strange way—and Cobb recognized the impertinence of even thinking it—Gregory had seemed to be asking the young man's blessing on what he'd done to the Society.

37

Then, one morning later that week, unasked, unheralded, old man Cobb
arrived at his son's doorstep.

"What do you know of a priest called Guglielmi in a place in Sicily I
can't pronounce and of a child who inspires miraculous cures?"

"Not a damn thing," Peter confessed. "Come in and have breakfast
and tell me about it."

His father's face was gray, lined, older than he could ever remember it.
C.C. seemed to have aged since their last meeting, only ten days or two
weeks before over dinner. Now the old man fell heavily into a chair and
looked around the room with eyes that just missed being blank.

"Terrible place," he said. "Can't you find better quarters?"

Peter ignored the question but from the kitchen, where he brewed the
coffee, he called, "How's the Duchess? Any change?"

C.C. mumbled something he could not hear. When the coffee was
ready Peter carried two cups into the living room.

"Now," he said, pulling up a chair, "what's all this about?"

Helen Gatewood was worse. That was what it was about. The vaunted
Italian specialist had been as useless as those quacks at Memorial in New
York. The cancer was slashing through her body inexorably, destructively.

"These dagos don't have a clue. Helen's so goddamned brave, so willing,
so cooperative. And they poke and prod and go right back to that same tired
regime they tried and that failed in Manhattan. Chemotherapy. Same
damned thing killed your mother. Burned her out and killed her."

The fury and the helplessness seemed to overwhelm him. Peter tried to
break the mood.

"What's this about the priest and the miracle cures? Where'd you get
that?"

The old man shrugged. A familiar look came over his face, sly and knowing. "Everyone knows about it. But the Church is trying to shut it up.
They don't want to turn the place into another Lourdes."

"Father, I'm out of my depth. Tell me what you know. If I can help, you know that I will. I love Helen too, you know."

C.C. nodded. He knew. He and Peter were communicative in their fashion. No needless words. C.C. took a deep breath and began.

"There's this child, a peasant boy, in some godforsaken village in the anal cavity of Sicily. The wretched child was apparently born retarded. Cretinous, a harelip, some such business. Mongolian idiot, I suppose we'd say, gibbering and twitching. Then . . . one day, without any explanation at all . . . no rational explanation, the local priest, a guinea, of course, name of Guglielmi, reports the child is speaking in tongues. You know, in languages other than his own . . ."

"Yes, Father, I know what that means."

C.C. ignored the ironic interruption. "And that isn't all. The blind, the deaf and the halt are brought in. The boy drools on them and, *voilà!* they are made whole. Guglielmi decides he has a good thing going here. Poor region, poorer parish, and suddenly he's found the alchemist's stone. He begins to take out ads. 'Come and let this miserable idiot but smile upon you and thou shalt be healed.' All nonsense, of course."

"Of course."

"No rational man would be gulled by it for a moment. The sort of rubbish the fakirs have been peddling for years. Necromancy and con games. What's kept clergymen in business for millennia. Witch doctors. Nothing more."

"I'm sure you're right, Father."

Cobb finished. Then, staring defiantly at his son, he said, "A charlatan, right?"

Peter nodded. "I'd say so. Wouldn't be the first one."

"You don't believe in the boy."

"No, of course not, not on the basis of what you've told me."

C.C. got up and walked to the window. "Peter," he said, "I want to take Helen to Sicily to see this child."

Charles Cobb regarded his son through narrow eyes. His voice was tough, skeptical.

"You think it's all nonsense, don't you?"

"Yes, I guess I do."

"And we shouldn't go?"

Peter had been waiting for the question. He knew his father was on alien turf, that he wanted guidance, that he wanted his son's blessing. C.C., with no faith in anything or anyone but himself and the system within which he had for so long flourished, was crying out for help.

And Peter responded.

"Father, it may all be hysteria or a con game or some extraordinary set of fortunate coincidences. If you're asking me if it'll work, I don't think it will. If you're asking me should you go, should you try, is it worth the candle, then I say, yes, go! And I'll go with you."

For the first time since his son had been a small boy, Charles Cobb opened his arms to embrace him.

Sicily in midsummer was a vast kiln. Charles Cobb's chartered jet landed at Palermo where a large, shiny black Cadillac limo met them. Helen had been reasonably vigorous during the plane ride. Now, in the heat bouncing up at them off the tarmac, she was near collapse. Peter and his father and the chauffeur had to help her into the car, very nearly carrying her thin body. The driver had been given instructions beforehand. Peter sat up front with him holding a map on his lap. He had little faith in Sicilian rental cars or their drivers. They drove out of the airport and skirted the city, picking up a road to the southwest. The windows in the car were opened a few inches. Peter looked back over his shoulder. Helen's face was as gray as the dust of the roadside.

"Okay, Duchess?" he mouthed against the sound of the wind and the motor.

"Just fine, Peter."

She didn't look fine.

The chauffeur was very proud of the car. He smiled as he drove, gunning the engine unnecessarily as if to demonstrate its power.

Peter tapped his arm. "Is there air-conditioning?" he asked.

"Oh, yes," the driver said. He made no move to switch it on.

"Will you activate it?" Cobb said.

"Oh, yes," the driver replied, and moved a lever on the dash. Cobb imagined he could feel a puff of fetid air.

"Shouldn't you close the windows?" Cobb asked.

"Oh, no," said the driver. "Is too hot."

They left the highway after an hour and headed due south. There were hills now and the road climbed into them, carving slow arcs against the hillsides. A plume of dust like the rooster-tail of a racing speedboat rose behind them. C.C. sat erect, stoic, his thin lips pressed together, his face dry despite the heat. Helen, mercifully, slept.

Santo Stefano was an old town piled on a hill, houses like square-cut boulders littering its sides. The streets wandered this way and that as if, many years ago, an earthquake had pried them up and then, tiring of the sport, had dropped them randomly back again. The church was old, rather pretty, and to Cobb's eye, clearly lopsided, leaning perhaps five or six degrees out of plumb. The driver, looking dubious, parked the car on the side of the church that had shade. Helen stirred in the back seat.

"Stay there, Father," Cobb said, "let me see if I can raise this priest of ours."

C.C. nodded. He looked very old and exhausted.

Father Guglielmi was not the scrofulous mystic Cobb expected. Instead, a spare, small man with graying hair and a spotless cassock and crisp white collar greeted Peter in the tiny rectory just off the church itself. He offered Peter a chair and then a glass of water. Peter thought of his father and Helen sitting in the car in the heat.

"No, thank you. You see . . ."

Guglielmi made a gesture with his hands. "A hurry, you're in a hurry. To see the 'saint,' of course."

"Yes, Father. A friend of mine, a lady, is very ill. She and my father are outside, in a car."

Guglielmi nodded. "And they think that if they visit this child . . ."

"Yes, that's what they think."

"And you, you do not believe in the child."

Cobb did not want to be rude. "I don't really know. Newspaper reports about such matters are notoriously vague, inaccurate."

"And you don't believe in miracles."

Cobb shrugged. "I believe there *have* been miracles. That there are things we cannot explain. That God moves in strange ways . . ."

"You evade a 'yes' or 'no' answer."

"I don't know enough," Cobb said.

"You mean you don't *believe* enough."

"Perhaps that's it," Peter conceded.

"Then why did you come to Santo Stefano, Father?"

"Because a woman I love very much, whom my father loves, is dying of cancer. The doctors say there is no cure. My father is a wealthy man. No expense has been spared. No specialist has been overlooked. No treatment. She continues to worsen. The child of Santo Stefano is . . . seems to be . . . their last hope."

Guglielmi nodded. ". . . a last hope. A hope in which you do not believe."

"Does it matter, Father, what I believe? If *they* do, isn't that sufficient?"

"Perhaps. There is no exact science here, you know. No precision. No rational explanation. People come to see the child. They pray. They touch him. They go away. Some of them later announce they are cured. From the others there is silence. Who knows? Who can say?"

Peter looked into the Italian's face.

"Do *you* believe, Father Guglielmi?"

Guglielmi got out of his chair. "Come, it is hot. We must not keep your father and his lady waiting. I will take them to see the child."

The two priests walked through the church and into the side street where the big car sat, its shiny black surface covered with gray dust.

The child of Santo Stefano was a mongoloid.

Helen Gatewood stood between Peter and C.C. in the cool, dim bedroom of the small farmhouse where the child lived, leaning against both of them heavily, despite her wasted frame, nearly sagging. "This is grotesque," Peter told himself. He refused to look at his father, the cold, efficient, rational Charles Cobb, fearing the revulsion, the anger he was sure he would see in C.C.'s face.

The child sat in a large armchair, his large head lolling to one side on his tiny shoulders, his mouth agape, his slit eyes flickering this way and that, watching, capturing each of them. Father Guglielmi had gone first, greeting the child's mother, whispering a few words, gesturing toward the Americans. The woman nodded and went back to her laundering. The child and his "miracles" were things she did not understand. People came, a little money changed hands, they saw her child for a few moments, they left. On feast days the villagers prayed at a small shrine that had been erected in the front yard, the gaudy statue of a madonna. Drying, faded flowers in bunches lay on the bare ground around the statue. The woman paid them no heed. When her child was born the villagers had thrown rocks through the window, had shouted "monster," had whispered obscene things about her and her baby. Then, after the first "miracle," the rocks had become flowers. She dealt with both hatred and worship with the same cold contempt.

Father Guglielmi spoke.

"Miss Gatewood, if you wish . . ." He gestured with a hand, gently, almost gallantly.

"Yes, Father," Helen said, her voice soft and fading like the flowers in the yard. "Thank you."

C.C. and Peter held her arms as she stepped forward toward the child. When she was at the chair in which he sat she paused, and then, reaching out one thin, pale arm, she touched his small, bare, rather filthy foot. Peter shot a sideways glance toward his father. Tears ran down C.C.'s face. But on Helen's tired, wasted face there were no tears, no revulsion.

She was smiling.

38

When the Cobbs returned from Sicily there was a message for Peter. From Italo DeBragga: "Perhaps you can help me."

The sweat of the south, the strain of the trip slid from Peter's shoulders. DeBragga was a killer, he was cynical, he was a chilly intellectual who'd made Cobb an unacceptable demand for aid. Cobb had all but thrown him out of the house. Now, once more, DeBragga was asking for help. Again cynically? Peter didn't know. He only knew that DeBragga had once, long ago, been a Catholic. In a sense, he was still of Peter's flock. And they had one element in common: DeBragga's obsession for changing a government, Cobb's with changing a Church. Their methods were different, their ends the same.

A car whisked Peter to the rendezvous, a banal little *trattoria* in the suburbs. DeBragga sat behind a vase of dead flowers and a bottle of Valpolicella. The proprietor lurked nervously in the background, honored by DeBragga's custom, terrified by his proximity.

"Well?"

DeBragga smiled. A less confident smile. Tighter, slimmer. Something had happened. Had the terror gone too far? Bouts of conscience? But when Cobb entered and took the other chair at the table, DeBragga began to preen.

"Ah, my dear chap, my personal conduit to His Holiness."

Cobb cut him off. "I thought we'd dropped all that fencing the last time. And as for the Pope, your last exchange of communications with him ended up with a hundred people murdered. I don't think he's much in the mood for any more of your philosophizing. Too many people lose their lives."

Some of the cockiness seemed to go out of the man. Two thugs—Peter assumed they were his bodyguards—sat at a table near the door. A half-dozen other tables stood empty. There were two cars parked outside.

DeBragga leaned forward. "All right, I regretted that. I understand your anger. And Gregory's. But that isn't why I asked to see you," he said.

"Then why?"

DeBragga licked thin lips. "Simple. You're a priest, I'm a Catholic. Or I used to be one. I want to confess myself to you."

Peter gave a short laugh. "Oh, come on, DeBragga. There are a million priests in Italy, some of them I'm sure quite sympathetic to your cause. Why me? Why an outsider?"

Some of the old shrewdness reappeared in the terrorist's handsome, tired face. "Maybe because then you won't be able to testify against me. Seal of the confessional and all that."

Peter shook his head. "When they catch you, DeBragga, there'll be no shortage of witnesses. They won't need the little I know about you to send you up."

DeBragga slammed a hand on the table. Cobb could see the proprietor give a small, nervous jump.

"All right, then, I'll tell you, Father Cobb. I really do want to confess. There are things I want to get off my mind. And . . . there are small, subtle instincts that tell me my time may be growing short. The police, the army, they're not all fools, you know. One day one of them . . . well, it isn't only that. Within the Brigades there are stresses. Younger men, the young lions of our organization, feed on their own ambition. To you I may appear a wild man, a killer. To some of my younger colleagues I seem conservative, even obstructionist, an old fogey not sufficiently aggressive either in tactics or strategy."

Cobb sensed a degree of honesty in his words. What degree, he was unsure.

"All right, you have a fear of death. You want to confess. Fine. But why me, why not one of your own priests?"

"They're Italian, Father Cobb. They talk. For word to get out that I was belatedly finding religion, it would mean my death. Suddenly, violently, painfully."

Cobb remembered the people dead in the railroad station, remembered Moro, remembered Marella Massai's husband.

"You wouldn't be the only one to die like that, DeBragga."

"I thought you were a priest, that your business was saving souls."

"I am. And it is."

"Well, then, help me save mine."

They were speaking intensely, but in low, guarded tones. By the door the thugs continued to laze. The restaurant owner nervously polished glasses behind the bar. There was no one to hear. Yet they spoke quietly.

"DeBragga," Peter said, speaking carefully, wanting the words to be right, "you know that for a valid confession there must be a genuine act of contrition and an equally genuine intention not to sin again. There can be no question of my giving you absolution without this. If you leave me and go back to the Brigades and the killing, well . . . just forget it."

"To the Brigades, yes. I must go back. You do not send in letters of resignation, you know. But as to killing, no, it has begun to make me vomit. On that I can make you a promise."

"These promises aren't to me, DeBragga. They're to God."

"Yes, I remember that much of my catechism."

Peter heard his confession in the kitchen of the place. DeBragga seemed sincere. Well, it wasn't for priests to ascribe motivation, to issue judgment. He had said his sorrow was genuine, his repentance real. Who knew? Men who dwelled in the neighborhood of death had been known to experience spasms of honesty.

When DeBragga left the place, ordering Cobb to stay behind for fifteen minutes and then to call a taxi, he turned to shake Cobb's hand.

Peter had instinctively pulled back. And then, without analyzing it, he accepted the man's hand and held it for a moment.

"Good," DeBragga said. "You're losing your arrogance, Father Cobb. Maybe one day you will be a true priest."

Charles Cobb was giving a little dinner party.

"We're going home, Peter," he told his son on the telephone. "I want you to come for a decent last meal. Helen and I owe you a great deal for guiding us to that godforsaken hole and that extraordinary boy. I'm calling Jane in Milan as well. She deserves a break. Nursing that poor son of a bitch can't be much fun."

Peter noted that Gigi was no longer "Nuvolari" or "Ascari" or "Stirling Moss." He was "that poor son of a bitch," which in the lexicon of his father was progress.

"Of course I'll come. And you're right about Jane. If she gives you any trouble let me know and I'll add my voice. I really want to see you both before you leave. The Duchess still okay?"

"More than okay, Peter."

"Great."

C.C. suggested if Peter had any friends he wanted to bring along, he should do so.

"Well, Tom Hathaway's around. You remember him. And he's got a girl."

"Ask them. Please do. The more the merrier."

290

*   *   *

"Peter, that's damned nice of your old man. But I haven't got the heart for it."

Cobb and Tom Hathaway were having lunch in one of those obscure *trattorias* in which Tom seemed to specialize and Peter had just conveyed C.C.'s invitation to his farewell dinner.

"Might be good for you to get out," Cobb said. "For both of you."

Hathaway shook his head vigorously. "Nope. I'm not seeing her anymore. It's just too damned painful to be with her and to love her as I do and not be able to do anything about it. My God, I used to think I understood how people felt about things. How smart I was. What a wise-ass. Trouble was I'd never been in love. Never knew a thing about it. All those romances I had and I never knew a damned thing."

"What can I tell you, Tom? Pia's an adult. She's a Catholic. What choice has she got? It's tough on you . . ."

"Peter, you don't know what tough is."

"But think about it from her point of view. She's made a decision not to marry you unless she gets an annulment and she isn't getting one. Not now, anyway."

"Screw the annulment. I want her on any terms I can get. Marry her. Live in sin. Or not live together and just see one another a lot and become lovers. I don't care. I don't really care anymore. I just want her and I can't have her and it's your bloody Church and her bloody stubbornness that're to blame."

"Well . . ."

Hathaway refilled their glasses.

"So tell your dad I'm out of town or something and thank him for me and tell Helen how happy I am for her."

"I will."

Tom shook his head again, this time slowly.

"I wish I could tell Helen and C.C. one more thing, too. How damned lucky they are to have one another."

"They're getting married, you know," Peter said.

Hathaway laughed, bitterly.

"Isn't everyone? Everyone but me . . ."

"Peter? You old hermit, how are you?"

It was Jane. Calling from Milan.

"I'm fine. How's Gigi coming along?"

"Oh, you know. It's hard, it's painful, but he's alive. Let us be duly thankful . . ."

"And you?"

"You wouldn't recognize me. Suntanned from spending so much time with him in the garden. Haven't had a drink in weeks. Wear my hair up in a bandanna when I play nurse. I'm as dedicated as that girl Hemingway fell in love with in *A Farewell to Arms*. If I could quit chain-smoking I'd run for saint, I'm so good."

"Good. You flying down for the party?"

"Oh, I dunno. I'm so happy for Helen and Dad but I don't think I really want to hear any more lectures from him about Gigi and what a rat he is."

"Jane, I think you'll find he's changed. Father, I mean. You won't recognize him."

"Ha."

"No, I mean it. Ever since Sicily, he's . . ."

"Peter, what really happened down there? You know I don't believe in miracles. Yet something happened."

"Something did. I still can't explain it. Father insists it was a miracle, pure and simple. If Helen would let him I think he'd be putting up plaques and statues of obscure martyrs and virgins. All that old cynicism is right out the window. To me, *that's* the miracle. Even more than Helen's remission."

"But what was it, Peter?"

"Sis, I wish I could tell you. I wish someone could tell me."

In the end Jane said she'd fly down for C.C.'s dinner.

Charles Cobb rubbed his hands.

"Well, Peter, look at her. By God, look at that woman. If she looked any better I'd be shopping for chastity belts. All these dagos dashing around Rome in their tight pants and Helen an unmarried and highly desirable woman. By God, she ought to be locked up."

"Charles, don't be a fool. I'm an old woman barely out of a sickbed."

"Rubbish," C.C. said pleasantly, "you're just reaching your prime."

They were having drinks in one of the huge sitting rooms of the *palazzo* Cobb senior had leased. A white-gloved waiter served cocktails from a silver tray. Two maids passed *hors d'oeuvres*. Jane Orsini sat curled up in a corner of a velvet couch, her long legs tucked under her, her nose sunburned and peeling, her cheeks and arms darkly tanned, drinking a Perrier and not saying much.

At the table, Peter sat between Helen and Jane. At the head of the table Charles Cobb rattled on, the torrent of words gushing forth as if he had been suddenly released from a lifelong vow of silence. They were all turned toward him, listening. All except Jane. She stared ahead at a tall, graceful candle whose flickering flame seemed to hold her mesmerized. "Jane?"

"Yes, Peter?"

"All right?"

"Of course."

She reached out to touch his hand.

C.C. continued to talk. Peter was no longer listening. He was remembering again the feeling of another hand touching his. Marella's.

". . . mind you, I'm far from sold on organized religion as such. All that damned bureaucracy. All those rules. Fish on Fridays and ashes on Wednesday and selling indulgences and tossing holy water around and all that secret mumbo-jumbo being jabbered over the sick and the dead. Bad as thirty-third degree Masons, all that nonsense. But by God, any religion that can produce a man like that Father Guglielmi and little boys that can cure with a touch, well, there's got to be *something* to it. There's got to be some damned thing."

"Father," said Jane, "as a student of comparative religion, you make a good oil baron."

C.C. looked stern. "There's nothing says capitalism and religion are mutually exclusive. Why, that damned Vatican is rolling in money. My advisers tell me the Pope makes D. K. Ludwig look like a mendicant. He's got more old masters and uncut diamonds than a museum. Than Cartier and Harry Winston put together. And I'm not saying there's a thing wrong with it. Too damned bad some of our distinguished Protestant clergymen hadn't the good sense to buy appreciating collectibles when the market was low, instead of tucking away their money in an old wool sock under the kitchen floorboards."

Jane laughed. "Father, I don't think your definition of what makes a good religion is precisely what the theologians intended. Is it, Peter?"

"What?"

After dinner they drank brandy and the men smoked cigars. C.C. was more somber now, more the old C.C. Helen sat close to him on a couch.

"I hope you'll come to New York for the wedding," she said.

"Couldn't keep me away," Jane said.

"If I can, I will," Peter said.

"It'll be a real wedding," C.C. promised. "Church and organ and choir and all."

"Which church, Father?" Jane asked.

C.C. looked pained.

"Catholic, of course. Who the hell d'you think cured Helen? Wasn't Billy Graham."

Before the evening was over old Cobb took his son aside.

"Peter, you planning on staying in Rome forever?"

"No, Father."

"That book of yours coming along?"

"Yes. I'm plugging away at it."

His father was silent for a moment. Then, "You thinking of quitting?"

"Quitting what? The priesthood?"

"Yes, I heard you had a girl, someone called Marella."

"I like Marella very much, Father. But I'm a priest. I signed on for life."

"Well, Peter, I've been a son of a bitch for life and now there seems some risk I may not be one anymore. Nothing's forever, you know."

Peter shook his head.

"Some things are. They may be inconvenient or they may hurt, but they are forever. They are if they're worth anything."

39

Full summer gripped Rome in a vise. The rich had fled to the sea. The poor
swore and sweated and drank. Tourists wondered why they had left their
comfortable homes to suffer such discomfort. Only the Germans in their
ridiculous shorts seemed content. It was the nature of man to suffer and
they snapped endless photographs of themselves doing just that. Gregory
remained at Castel Gandolfo, with his court. Those left behind, minor
bureaucrats, janitors and nuns, alternately cursed the heat and prayed that
their misery was somehow being translated into actual grace, that in this
hell of a Roman summer they were totting up spiritual credits against a
purgatory yet to come. Peter Cobb, inured to the humid furnace of Central
America, ate and drank frugally, lived in a cotton shirt and khaki trousers,
and sought out the shady sides of streets. And in the summer of his dis-
content, Marella arrived back in Rome.

"I'd given you credit for more sense," he told her when she phoned his
apartment from the airport.

"I know. Not that Milan was much better. God, but it's hot."

"You should have gone to Como."

"Two days only," she said. "My agent and I must talk again. September
isn't that far off. We've got to decide some matters concerning the exhibi-
tion. Look, this phone booth is an oven. Will you have dinner with me?"

They met for drinks at eight in a sidewalk café on the Via Veneto, just
down the street from the Excelsior. Peter got there first and ordered a beer.
The waiter had just come on, relieving the lunch and afternoon man, but
already the armpits of his white jacket were darkly moist. The glass was
wonderfully cold and Peter passed it across his forehead before taking the
first sip. The crowd was mostly tourists, older men and women exhausted
by the day and wondering if it was safe to leave this pleasant sanctuary for
the dubious alleyways in search of pasta in the *trattorias*. Boys cruised slowly

past on their motorbikes or in open cars, watching the girls. The *paseo*. Just like Mirador before the war; only the duennas were missing. Two Swedish girls who might have been airline employees giggled encouragement to the boys. They were very tan and wore mini-skirts. He watched the byplay with amusement and then Marella was there.

"Where did you get that tan?" he said. "You look wonderful."

She did, too. Hair more closely cropped, turning her long neck even more swanlike, her face and arms and bare shoulders very brown, the sea-blue of her silk print dress startling against her skin, her bare legs brown as well, her slender feet curiously elegant in espadrilles.

"I must have a drink and I'll tell you everything. What's that, beer? Wonderful, I'll have one." All this without a breath as she flopped into a chair next to him and then, birdlike, reached over to kiss him lightly on the cheek.

"Welcome," he said, catching the waiter's eye and motioning for two more beers.

"Well," Marella said, "first, the tan. I'm working on a very large piece. Too large for the studio, so I've borrowed some dear man's garden and work outdoors. I wear shorts and a halter and sweat like a pig while I hack away at the steel and trample the poor fellow's lawn into dry hay. I assure you, when he sees it he'll never again encourage the arts."

"So the Vandals have again descended on poor Italy."

"With a vengeance."

The beer came and silently they toasted each other.

"Oh, but that tastes good. I drank an entire bottle of Fiuggi at the hotel while I unpacked."

"Good," he said.

She drank down half her beer and then sat back. "Now, finally, I can relax."

"You should. You work too damn hard."

"You should talk. You're so pale, Peter. Can't you cheat a little bit on your book and get down to the beach for a few days?"

"I have to stay in Rome. What I should do is get back out on the river. For a month or so there I was rowing every morning. Then, well, things got complicated."

"I know. I'm still thinking about Helen and your father. What an extraordinary thing."

He shook his head. "Extraordinary isn't the word for it."

"What really happened? Your father's convinced it was a genuine miracle? Do you believe that yourself?"

"It doesn't matter what I believe. The fact is that it happened. My father believes it. Helen believes it. And she's the one who's got cancer."

"And now . . . it's still in remission?"

"The doctors say so. Oh, they make no promises. No money-back guarantees go with it. But there certainly has been a change, and for the better. We flew down there, we looked up this Father Guglielmi, he took us to the boy, and *violà!* That was weeks ago and Helen hasn't had a chemotherapy session since. No pain, no weakness. The doctors stroke their beards and look sage and confess that cancer is a very strange malady indeed that no one really understands and that we should just accept the accident of apparent remission and let it go at that. Old C.C. is ready to build a cathedral for Guglielmi and Helen just smiles and says she knew all the time that if she kept praying . . . and fighting . . . something would happen."

"I'm so happy for them."

"Oh, yes, and they're really getting married. C.C. is finally going to make an honest woman of her, the Duchess keeps saying. They're flying back to New York next week. I'm invited to go over for the ceremony."

"Will you?"

He shrugged. "I haven't got the foggiest. I'm under orders to hang around here."

"The Pope?"

She asked the question in a voice tactfully low.

"Yes," Peter said. "He and the Jesuits are still at swords' points. No one knows how it'll end. He seems to have some exotic notion he can use me to good effect."

"Well, why not? You're a Jesuit. He obviously trusts you."

Cobb laughed.

"But *they* don't. I'm the pariah, the traitor in their midst. My former provincial from Boston, an old tyrant called Hanlon, is over here. He damned near has apoplexy every time he sees me. Some of the others seem to feel the same way. I was there, you see, when Gregory humiliated them. They can't forget that. And they're not likely to forgive."

"What ever happened to Christian charity?" Marella said.

"Jesuit provincials have always felt that was for other people."

The sun had gone down now behind the hotels and the office buildings and the wide street was now totally in shadow. It was still hot but it seemed cooler.

"Another?" Peter asked.

"Yes, just the one more and then I'm buying you dinner. You look as if you need a meal."

"Fasting and good works." He laughed. "The secret of my success."

They sipped the beer and Marella asked about his book.

"Nearly finished."

"But that's wonderful."

"I guess so. A year ago that same man Hanlon warned me in Boston that I was a priest first and an author second. I laughed at him then. But sometimes I think in his mulish way, maybe there was something in what he said."

She smiled. "Peter Cobb having doubts . . . ?"

"Sure," he said, trying to be light about it, "even me."

She saw through the bantering.

"Oh, Peter," she said, sounding empty and sad. She reached out to cover his lean hand with hers, a small, brown hand on his, larger and pale.

"So tan," he said, looking down at their two hands.

"Yes," she said. And then, remembering she had promised herself not to do this, she pulled her hand away. The mood of intimacy was broken. Both knew the break was deliberate. After an instant, Cobb continued:

"And defying Gregory or just ignoring his wishes . . . I haven't felt very good about that."

"You love him, don't you?" she said.

"Yes."

"And not just as the Pope. As your superior."

"No, that way too, but as a man. Even when I don't understand him."

It was dark now and cooler and he paid and they got into a cab and Marella told the driver where the restaurant was.

He was a different Peter. From the moment she had seen him in the café, while they sat there drinking beer, and later at the hole-in-the-wall restaurant she'd winkled out for their dinner, Marella knew that. A different Peter, somehow softer and yet even more determined than when she had first met him months before in the Alps.

A different Peter as well in his attitudes toward other people. Not that he'd ever been callous; it wasn't that. He'd never been cold or unfeeling. Only . . . controlled. But he seemed to have relaxed control, to have closed the distance between himself and those he loved. Jane. His father. Funny, foolish Tom Hathaway. The Pope. The Gregory he loved, even when he didn't understand him. Only toward Marella had Peter Cobb kept his distance.

If she were a different sort of woman, she told herself now as she lay abed in her hotel, if only . . . but she was what she was. There could be no cheap tricks, no subtle seductions. And Peter was what *he* was. Perhaps it was just as well she'd played fair and hadn't tried to exercise the sort of wiles other women used. With Peter, she felt, they would not have worked.

That did not mean she didn't want him. Oh, but she wanted him. No man since her husband had made her feel this way. She remembered now the look of his hand, the touch of it, as she covered it with her own on the table of the café on the Via Veneto. To have a man like Peter so close and then not to be able to do anything about it, not a damn thing . . .

If Marella had been able to read his thoughts at that very moment, her hunger and frustration would have been even more painful. Peter was not in bed. He was seated at the old kitchen table working on his book, an untidy pile of manuscript which to his eye seemed already to be curling and yellowing.

He tried to write. But Marella intruded. Visions of her face, her strong, tanned hands, her body, kept materializing on the blank page before him. And as he scribbled sentences and discarded them, Marella was there with him. To continue to see her was foolish. He remembered their picnic. An innocent thing. Yet he was behaving like a schoolboy.

He had no business being with her. He should have told her that when she called, should have told her that a long time ago. Wasn't fair to her, wasn't fair to him, the sort of emotional roller-coaster they were both on was too tough, too punishing. She needed a man. Not a frocked capon. As for him, Peter knew just how dangerously close he was to falling in love. It was impossible, forbidden, *wrong*! But there it was. All around him there were people in love. Whatever their problems, his father and the Duchess, Tom and his girl, Jane and that damned Gigi, they had someone to hang on to, to reach out for, to curl close to. He had no one. No, that was not precisely correct. There was someone. And he was cold-bloodedly turning away from her. Or he was trying to do it cold-bloodedly.

What choice had he? He'd taken vows that no man, not even Gregory, could put aside.

BOOK VI

POLAND

40

Couriers came to Castel Gandolfo. Even when the Pontiff was officially on vacation, the great bureaucratic machinery of the Vatican continued to grind. There were six hundred million Roman Catholics. Four hundred thousand churches. Six hundred thousand schools. Hospitals, seminaries, missions, offices, convents, rectories, dioceses, archdioceses, colleges and universities, Curial courts and the vast Vatican itself. But there was not only the Catholic Church to administer, to lead, to inspire, there were Catholicism's relations with other churches, with other, secular governments, with Christian nations and with Moslem, with Judaism and with Buddhism, with democracies and the totalitarian regimes, with constitutional monarchs and with military *juntas*, with benevolent Switzerland and atheistic Russia. And now couriers came bearing news of the Pope's homeland.

"So we poor Poles are to be disciplined once again," Gregory said that night over dinner.

He sat at the head of a table of nine men. Facing him, this latest and most distinguished courier from Warsaw, Kronk, now the archbishop and the bearer of bad news. With him, old Plitzka, aged and wise. To the Pope's right, his Secretary of State, a shrewd, aging Italian who spoke from the corner of his mouth, as men do who keep secrets. To his left the *camerlengo*, an Italian, and his court chamberlain, another Italian, whose gaunt frame belied his enormous zest for spaghetti. Three of the other four men were senior cardinals, invited out of a sense of their own importance. The last man was Falcone, the venerable caretaker Gregory had installed to watch over the Jesuits.

"So it seems, Holiness," Kronk said, his face grave even as he nibbled at the delicious, chilled antipasto that seemed to his alien tongue the most civilized thing about these damned Italians. Kronk was Gregory's protégé, a tough, pragmatic fellow who understood communism and knew how to work with the regime. Not the most senior churchman in Poland, but the one closest to Gregory.

"What do you think, Kronk, will the Russians come in? Or are we to have another episode of self-punishment?"

"The latter, I'd think. I don't believe we'll see the Russians in Warsaw again unless the regime can't handle the situation."

The Secretary of State asked a question, the corner of his mouth working to form the words. "Are we wise giving so much encouragement to the union movement? If we stir them up again and they go into the streets like this and the troops come out against them, what can we do? We tell them to be strong, to be independent, and then we fold our hands in prayer and leave them to their own slim resources."

"As the Americans do," noted one of the cardinals.

"As they did with the Hungarians in '56 and the Czechs in '68 and the Poles once before."

"The Americans *always* speak loudly, no matter what the first Roosevelt said."

Gregory listened.

"Well," said Kronk, "let's not turn this into an American problem. It's our problem, in Poland, and I for one want to know where I take the Polish Church if the troops come out. Do I resist or do I bless the tanks? Or do I find some middle road?"

"A middle road, of course," said the *camerlengo*. "Extremes are to be avoided."

"Easier said than done," a cardinal said piously.

Gregory remained silent. A few years ago, as a bishop, he would have spoken out. In those days he was seen as a radical, a young priest thrusting the Church, and himself, into every situation where a decision cried out to be made. Well, that was how young men were. Even when they'd been consecrated bishop. He was older now and, he hoped, wiser. And as Pope his was the final authority. It was all very well for Kronk, or these cardinals, or anyone else to urge desperate measures. They were subject to his veto. If *he*, the Pope, decided to take action then action would be taken. There were no balance wheels to govern his power. That was why he sat and listened, and was silent.

Kronk, his protégé, noted the silence.

"Holiness, I need advice. I can't simply go back and fold my hands and say mass. All Poland knows I'm here. They'll be expecting something when I get back. A pastoral letter, some sort of guidance. If the Church doesn't provide it, then who will? And where does that leave the Church?"

One of the younger Italians exploded.

"My God, Kronk, stop thinking like a Pole. The Church has problems everywhere. Right here in Italy. You act as if the diocese of Warsaw were our *only* concern. That sort of provincial thinking is not worthy of you."

Kronk snarled a low, inaudible word or two. Then, struggling to control himself, "You don't have the damned Russian army outside the walls. You don't have a union movement intent on corporate suicide. You don't have thousands of your people penned by barbed wire in football stadiums. I know there are other problems. But no one elected me Pope. I'm just a poor, ignorant Polish priest concerned about my parish and desperate for guidance from more sophisticated men."

"He's right," said the Secretary of State soothingly, the diplomat who would have felt at home in the U.N. as much as in the Church.

The young Italian cardinal was not to be muted. Gregory's silence encouraged him.

"I am most sensitive to your problems, Kronk. I simply refuse to see the Church become so obsessed by one local difficulty that it can no longer function effectively in its universal mission."

"Which is?" Gregory asked, perhaps surprising even himself.

The men at his table turned toward him, then, slowly, to the Italian.

"Holiness, there is no reason to redefine it. Our role is, as it always has been, the salvation of souls. Everything else is incidental."

The Pope showed nothing in his face. Kronk seized upon the Italian's response.

"Yes, my dear Cardinal, and how are we to save Polish souls if we abandon the Poles? If we stand aside piously fingering our beads when more of our people are arrested, if our churches are nailed shut, if our pastors are silenced? How effective do you then think we will be? How the devil can I isolate myself from the struggles of my flock and expect them to listen to me when I lecture them on faith and morals? You permit a break between Church and people and you risk losing an entire nation. And remember, please, through all its travails through the centuries, Poland has remained Catholic. Because its priests and its people have been one."

Well said, Kronk, Gregory thought to himself. It was not precisely what the Pope's response should be but it was exactly what the Archbishop of Warsaw should be saying. Bravo, Kronk! Well done. But still, the Pontiff said none of this aloud.

Two nuns were serving dinner. They re-entered now, smoothly, efficiently clearing the antipasto plates and replacing them with dishes of spaghetti carbonara. What a great honor to serve such holy men.

When the sisters had again left the room the *camerlengo* asked, "Holiness, may I raise another matter?"

Gregory smiled.

"This business of the Jesuits. You've left them in a sort of limbo. Not a day passes when some Jesuit or other doesn't grab my cassock to ask what's happening."

Another of the Italians laughed, then, bowing slightly to Falcone: "When have Jesuits not been grasping at cassocks and demanding information? With all due respect to you, Father."

Falcone returned the bow.

"It is very natural, their curiosity. I myself have been importuned."

". . . And you tell them nothing," the *camerlengo* noted. "Or at least that's their complaint to me."

"It is not my role," Falcone said quietly, and Gregory, again silently, blessed him for his reticence. That was why he had put Falcone in as caretaker. He was not a man who talked.

But now the young Italian who had argued with Kronk took up the affair.

"Well, who can blame them? If I were a Jesuit I'd want to know what was happening."

"It's all incidental," said the Secretary of State. Not even his diplomatic tact was capable of preventing the retort, "Only the salvation of souls should occupy their time."

Gregory dug into his pasta and listened and said nothing of substance.

The next morning as he swam laps in his pool and mulled over the dinner conversation of the night before, how some men had spoken sense and others had made fools of themselves, Gregory prayed that, somehow, he would be given the wisdom to make the decisions for which others waited. Of course he must do something about Poland. Kronk was right. But what to do? What to say? How far could he go in encouraging the Poles and yet not risk an open and complete rupture with the Warsaw government and beyond Warsaw, the Russians? He did not know. Nor did he know just what he *was* going to do about the Society of Jesus. Falcone was clearly, and was intended to be, but a temporary overseer. A new Superior General must be named. But this time, one loyal first to Rome, and secondly to himself and his Society. Could he trust the Jesuits themselves to elect such a man? Then there was Mirador, about which young Cobb, and not only Cobb, was pestering him. He had reports from Mirador, confidential reports that corroborated much of what Peter Cobb insisted was the situation. An entire country, a Catholic country, was at risk. Support the guerrillas and lose a government's benign favor. And lose more than that if Castro and not the nationalists was the real power when the civil war ended. Yet . . . to continue to smile on the regime would push the rebels in their thousands away from the Church and into the eager embrace of communism. It was so easy to declare neutrality. So easy. So impossible. One had to take stands. But where?

That evening, as he read the texts of the latest U.N. debate on Israel, a courier arrived.

Gregory thanked the young monsignor who fetched him the sealed envelope. He opened it, read it carefully, and tossed it on the end table next to his easy chair. He reached out for his pipe and filled it carefully, tamping down the tobacco with a strong, thick finger and then lighting it with an old-fashioned kitchen match. Then he picked up the dispatch once again and reread it through.

Well, he thought, Kronk was right. He would have to do something about Poland. And soon. The Kremlin, he was confidentially and authoritatively informed, had told Warsaw to crack down and crack down hard. And this time the Polish military regime was to order any church closed and any priest detained who argued the toss.

"Detained." What an innocent word to convey such terror. The Nazis, Gregory seemed to recall, used such euphemisms.

41

Gregory had returned to the Vatican. To go into seclusion. September had come and with it the entire world seemed to have shaken off summer's indolence and to have gone mad. But Gregory's seclusion was not retreat. He was preparing to act. He wanted first to think. About Poland. About the Red Brigades. About the Jesuits. And Mirador. And Hans Kung. And a thousand other concerns that cried out for decisive, intelligent, *correct* action. For three days he received no one, ate sparingly, prayed, meditated, read. Especially did he read. Long, dry-as-dust reports on the military government in Warsaw, the rebellious mood of the Society of Jesus, the latest splinter sect of crazies hoisting the banner of Archbishop Lefebvre. And in the course of this reading, belatedly he came across in his correspondence file a letter from Peter Cobb.

"Holiness," Cobb had written, "although it is obviously but a minor item amid the many important concerns of your papacy, since you expressed interest in the book I was writing, I think you should know that I have now finished writing it, and I will so inform Monsignor Lonsdale, who was kind enough to discuss it with me on several occasions."

Gregory permitted himself a smile. He knew something of the verbal grappling that had gone on between Lonsdale and Cobb. He enjoyed Cobb's polite understatement.

"I will submit myself to the Society for reassignment now that the book is behind me. Of course if your Holiness should require my services in any other matter, Mirador, for example, I will respond at any time. My personal wish would be to return to Mirador in a missionary function. I will, however, go where I am sent. Your Holiness has my gratitude for his kindness and my continued devotion both as a priest and as a man."

Gregory reread the letter and then put it aside.

Cobb found Lonsdale at a corner table in his favorite *trattoria.* He was shocked at the man's appearance.

"Yes, yes, Cobb, sit down. I know I look awful. See it in your eyes. Not even Savile Row can camouflage it."

Cobb pulled out a chair.

"What is it? No appetite?"

Lonsdale barked a laugh.

"I'm the gourmand I always was. You'll see, I'll demolish the *scallopini* before your very eyes and eat half your *pesto* as well. Goes through me like shot through geese. Damned intestines are going, bottom of the stomach gone. Doctors say they simply don't understand why I still have an appetite." He threw up his hands and several rings flashed in the restaurant's lights. "Well, let's be thankful for small favors."

A waiter came and Cobb ordered as Lonsdale poured them each a glass of Rubbianco.

"And now, Cobb, now that you've won . . . ?"

"I don't understand. Won what?"

"Oh, don't fence. Damned Americans don't do it very well. Reason you're such rotten diplomats. Can't understand why your country is so noted for its poker players. You show everything in your faces."

"Really, I don't understand."

Lonsdale leaned forward, his slack jowls quivering as he moved. "Your book, dammit. You take on the Jesuits and the Vatican and the Pope himself, none of whom want you to write the bloody thing, and you sail blithely ahead as if you had sense and write it and no one says bugger-all. You've won, Cobb, don't you have the sense to know that?"

Cobb shook his head and smiled. "It's odd, but I don't feel I've *won* anything. It's finished. It's over. And now I'll go back to my work. I just wanted to tell you that. And to apologize for my arrogance. You were just doing your job when you tried to shut me up."

"My God, a penitent Jesuit. *Quelle merveille!*"

Cobb let the sarcasm slip by. Why leave enemies behind?

Lonsdale waved at a passing waiter who nodded, promising to be back.

"And your next assignment, young Cobb? Some grand appointment in His Holiness's retinue? The house liberal, the Vatican's boy wonder?"

Cobb shook his head. "Mirador, I hope. The missions."

Lonsdale slumped back. He understood good men and bad men, honest men and venal men. He did not understand men without ambition.

"Well, well, well."

Peter felt good inside. It was the first time he'd ever really stopped Lonsdale's flow of caustic eloquence. A small victory but a sweet one.

The waiter came then and Lonsdale was as good as his word, ordering an enormous lunch and wolfing it down. But when the meal was over and they walked together to the door of the place, the waiters bowing and pretty girls regarding the two clerics curiously, Lonsdale's movements were slow and unsteady. Cobb got him a cab, helped steady him with an arm as he climbed in.

"Don't come to the office anymore, Cobb. If you want to see me I won't be there."

"Oh?"

Lonsdale shook his head. "They'll know where I am. But don't come. I really don't think I want to see you again. I don't enjoy being reminded of my defeats."

He closed the door and the cab rolled off into the Roman traffic.

That afternoon Cobb wrote to Father Hanlon, the New England provincial, at his temporary headquarters in Rome. More formally he told him what he had told Gregory and Lonsdale. He asked that he be sent back to Mirador, to the missions.

His father and Helen Gatewood had flown home. Jane was back in Milan. Marella? Well, he was not going to call her. Leave the games-playing to the Tom Hathaways of this world. No, that wasn't fair. Tom had quit playing games, and where had it gotten him? And how much help had Cobb, his best friend, his pet priest, provided? Not a damned bit. That night Cobb dined alone, at home. Something cold and a beer. He watched television. It was odd not to feel guilty about the typewriter standing there silent and unused on the kitchen table. For the first time in two years he was not writing. In a way it felt good. In another, empty. Television was all about the Red Brigades. And Poland. Depressing. Cobb hoped Hanlon would act quickly on his request. He could smell Mirador, hot and steamy and sweet.

During that same night, as Cobb slept, the Polish military government arrested 1200 dissidents. Including Archbishop Josef Kronk.

Gregory came out of seclusion.

The contemplative man gave way to the man of action. The Vatican became the funnel of a tornado. Men and cables were dispatched to the United Nations, to Washington, to Warsaw, to other churches, to the Kremlin itself. Demands were issued, support was asked, punishment was threatened. An audience with Hans Kung, painstakingly arranged over a period of months, was abruptly canceled. "Tell Kung to go to the devil,"

Gregory snapped, "which is where he's destined in any event." A United States senator from Illinois with a Polish surname telephoned from Washington. As an aide held his hand cupped over the phone Gregory asked, "Is he on the foreign relations committee? Does he have any muscle?" and was told no. Gregory ordered, "Tell the senator I'm saying mass." A Polish émigré group erected "Solidarity" banners, blood-red and wind-rippled, in the piazza of St. Peter. They announced a hunger strike against the Warsaw regime and sat down to gnaw their kielbasa and drink Pilsener. A deranged nun poured gasoline over her head and set herself aflame in the street outside her convent. There were reports miners in Silesia had again sealed themselves inside their mines and were systematically destroying machinery. A member of the Warsaw regime denounced Kronk as a "dangerous *provocateur*." *Pravda* noted Kronk had two years ago visited the United States. The appropriate conclusions were drawn. Dr. Billy Graham issued yet another clarification of his statement asserting there was religious freedom in Russia. *Time* magazine prepared a cover. The President of the United States told his Secretary of State to call in the Polish ambassador and "tell that Commie puppet we won't bail out their goddamned loans this time around." The Italian Communist Party wrangled over what its response should be and ended up by saying nothing. Gregory listened to his advisers and, like the Italian Communists, said nothing. Not publicly.

Behind the scenes he said and did a great deal. His intelligence services inside Poland assured him Kronk was alive and well and enduring a reasonably comfortable sort of house arrest. The regime knew the danger of creating martyrs. "Why," said Gregory's informant, "they haven't even cut his phone. They listen in, to be sure, but he's on the telephone."

Gregory grunted and said nothing.

For the first time in his papacy, Gregory really *was* unsure. Every instinct of body and soul cried out for his personal intervention in the Polish crisis. In his mind, there was confusion. Among his advisers, chaos. The older, phlegmatic men of the Curia protested purely narrow, national concerns were distracting him from his appointed, universal role. He was the pastor of the world, not of Warsaw.

Still uncertain, vacillating, he summoned his Secretary of State on the third morning of the crisis. The Secretary was a sensible fellow. But after a half hour's chat, Gregory had still not decided. As the Secretary left, a monsignor handed Gregory his appointments calendar for the day. Near the top, the name of Peter Cobb, S.J. Oh, yes, Cobb's letter, about Mirador, about his desire to return there. Gregory had asked Cobb to drop in. That was before Kronk's arrest. Now, distracted, Gregory began to run a pen through the name, to cancel what was hardly a priority item. Then, abruptly, he told the monsignor, "When Cobb arrives, send him in."

Peter Cobb stood across the room from where Gregory sat behind the huge desk in the papal office.

"Sit down, Cobb. I won't keep you long."

Peter took a straight-backed chair. There was a crisp, businesslike edge to the Pope's voice and he suspected this was not going to be the sort of rambling discursive chat they'd had so often when the two men took easy chairs and slumped casually into them.

"Yes, Holiness?"

"I read your letter. Thank you. I won't pretend I'm pleased you've finished your book. Perhaps, a few years from now, we'll both feel differently about it."

"Well, I'm glad it's done. There were times when it seemed I was playing author instead of living as a priest."

"Your father? And his lady? Is that what you mean?"

"Yes, them and other members of my family. Friends. And strangers. Service to others, abnegation of self . . . these were the essentials when I took my first vows. I seem to have drifted away from them. It wasn't a good feeling. Here were all these others, who weren't priests, trying hard, very hard, to fulfill their roles, their destinies, if you will, and I was poring over manuscripts in Vatican libraries and tapping away at an old typewriter as if I were . . . I dunno, Jacques Maritain. Well, I'm not. I'm a Jesuit priest. For better or worse, a missionary. My job is working with people, helping them find their God. If I do that, I'll find my own. That very basic truth seems somewhere along the line to have eluded me."

"But not now."

"No, now the book is a *fait accompli* and I think I'm back on the track. I hope I am."

Gregory got up and went to one of the tall windows behind his desk. With his back to Cobb he asked, "And do you think I should visit Poland?"

"I'm sure you've thought it through and that you'll make a measured response to what happened to Archbishop Kronk."

Gregory wheeled.

"Dammit, Cobb, don't fence. You're not one of my Curial diplomatists. What do you *really* think?"

"Well . . ."

"Go ahead. If you think it would be a flamboyant, theatrical gesture inspired by narrow nationalistic concerns, say so."

"No, I don't think that."

"Then *what?*"

Cobb knew he had no choice but to tell the truth.

"I'm alarmed by it. I think it's dangerous."

"Ha! Two assassination attempts right here in Rome. One of them by a disgruntled priest. And you think *Warsaw* is dangerous?"

"Yes, I do. And I don't mean only physical danger. Suppose some untoward incident occurs. Perhaps the regime will attempt to embarrass you. So many things could happen. It's not only you that's at risk, it's the papacy itself. Its dignity, its prestige, its . . ."

"Cobb, for goodness sake, I may once have mentioned to you that only one of my first fifteen predecessors died in bed. A Pope dies. A Pope is murdered. A Pope is made to appear ridiculous. But the papacy goes on. The Church goes on."

"They arrested Kronk. They could arrest you."

Gregory laughed. "Don't underestimate them, Cobb. They're not stupid. They're subtle people. A few of them brilliant. Don't forget, I *know* them. I've coexisted with them. I saw them come to power. I've negotiated with them, dealt with them, fought with them. I've won my points, lost my points. Of course there are the mindless bully-boys who'd as soon crack my head as spit in the holy water. And the dialectical zealots who deal only in the arid realms of theory. No, I know these fellows. If I simply give them Kronk's head without a battle, what comes next? They close the schools, disband the convents, draft the priests into the army? Eh, what next if I do nothing?"

Cobb thought for a moment. Then, almost to himself, "So a churchman joins in opposition to an illegitimate regime . . ."

"Yes, Cobb," Gregory said solemnly, "but there is a difference between Poland and Mirador. I would carry no guns, mobilize no battalions. I do not plan again to become a guerrilla."

"But you fight."

"Yes, in my own way, I fight."

Cobb said nothing for a moment. Then, "Holiness, if it is not impertinent, I think you have made up your mind. I think you are going to Poland, no matter what."

Gregory looked at the younger man and grinned.

"And you disapprove?"

"No, Holiness, I approve with all my heart. My Mirador, your Warsaw, they are both trips worth taking, once the risks have been weighed, the potential for good assessed. Of course you should go. And again, if it is not impertinent, my prayers go with you."

"Prayer is never impertinent, Cobb, not even for Popes."

Gregory got up now and perched on the edge of the big desk, his white cassock tucked under a big thigh.

"Well, Cobb, if I'm going to Warsaw, as you seem so sure, I don't have much time, so I'll make this brief. I think I can talk straight with you. You keep your mouth shut, you don't conspire or politic. You and I have things in common. Far more than most of the saintly dandies who run this Church of ours. They're good men, most of them, but with limited vision. You and I have lived in the world, we understand power, we've been to war. I once loved a young girl. Perhaps you have. We've never enjoyed the luxury of insulation from temporal problems. At twenty I was killing men. I should have been in the university. The war took that away from me. At twenty or twenty-five you were in Vietnam. Last year you were in Mirador. You have had two wars, I only one."

"And now you go to war again."

"Let's hope not. But war or peace, I go not as a soldier but as a priest. Not to fight but to pray. It is God's strategy, not the Pentagon's or the Kremlin's. There is a difference, Cobb, believe me, there is."

Cobb thought for a moment and then he said, "Holiness, you have so little time. You said so. May I remind you that in my letter I said that I hoped to return to Mirador? Not as a soldier, but once again as a missioner?"

"Mirador," Gregory repeated the word, as if testing its sound.

"Yes, Holiness. A place where I can do my work. Where I can make a contribution consonant with my abilities. Where there is need of priests. And of so much else."

"A backwater."

"I suppose. But not to me."

"Cobb, here you are in Rome. The center of the world, at least for you and me and every other Catholic. A great city. Where great decisions are made which have their impact, inevitably, on backwaters like Mirador and a thousand other Miradors. Does none of this tempt you, this being at the seat of authority, of possibly working here? Is not that work more important? Cannot a contribution made here also be 'consonant with your abilities'?"

Cobb had the uneasy sense he was sounding stubborn, insensitive.

"There are so many who can and do fill such roles here. There are so few who can do in Mirador what I believe I can."

"To train a dissident militia?"

Cobb shook his head. "To serve a people, Holiness. My soldiering is over. I could never fight again. I still see that officer crucified in the church-yard of Coptacl. I will always see him."

"Good," Gregory said. "Such things are forgotten too easily. They are worth remembering."

He was silent for a moment and Peter took advantage of the moment to ask, "Do I have your blessing to go?"

"Peter, you have always my blessing. But for Mirador, no."

Cobb slumped back in his chair.

"I *am* going to Warsaw, Father Cobb. You will be one of those who go with me."

42

No one could complain that once Gregory made up his mind he wasted any time. He had the *camerlengo* summon his senior advisers. They were barely seated in the baroque conference room adjoining his private office when he said, "Well, my good friends, you will have to run the Church without me for a time. I am going to Poland."

They knew he'd been considering it. But the abruptness of his announcement startled them. The Secretary of State, a man who would be called upon to work out details of the venture, asked questions. When would he leave, when would he be back?

Gregory grinned broadly.

"Don't worry, I'll be back within a week. Sooner, if the Russians put a boot to my rear end."

Gregory did not permit the meeting to drag on. When he'd finished what he had to say, answered a few questions and ignored others, he ended it simply by getting up and walking out of the room. Behind him his advisers shook their heads.

The papal secretary was waiting.

"Jean, I'm taking a little trip. I may want you to go as well."

The young priest stared. "In the midst of all this trouble, Holiness?"

Gregory nodded. "Yes. Please ask the operator to put me through on the telephone to Archbishop Kronk. I wouldn't want Poland to learn about my trip secondhand."

Within moments the connection had been made and Gregory picked up the Vatican's white telephone.

"Kronk," he said, "how are you?"

"Well, Holiness, although a trifle circumscribed in my activities, you understand."

"Of course. Listen, Kronk, I have something to tell you. It is for the moment strictly confidential."

"Yes, Holiness. But the telephones . . ."

"Yes, yes, Kronk," Gregory said quickly, purposely missing the point, knowing the phones must be tapped, "it's always better to say important things in person. But there is a question of time."

Kronk, still trying to stave off what he feared might be a compromising remark on a tapped phone, interrupted. "Holiness, you don't understand. I . . ."

Gregory broke in.

"Kronk," he said firmly, "please shut up and listen. Here is what I am going to do. . . ."

Thus it was that the Warsaw regime, and the world, learned that Gregory the Pope was going to Poland in three days' time.

He had not asked permission. He had not first informed the host government. He had not asked the Curia to smile on his initiative. He had not given a speech outlining his reasons. He did not seek the blessing of the United Nations. He did not even tip off the American president in advance.

He was simply . . . going.

The Poles did not know what to do about Gregory. He was a loose cannon rolling uncontrollably around the decks of the regime. Gregory was wrong: he'd told Cobb some of the Polish colonels were smart, very smart, that no one should underestimate their subtlety, their intelligence, their sophistication. Well, the intelligent ones, the subtle ones must have been on vacation. Gregory's plane landed in Poland and for the next thirty-six hours there was holy Catholic apostolic chaos. Even Gregory shook his head. He was proud to be a Pole and this, this was an embarrassment.

The world saw it all on television. The Poles were stupid even there. They could have cut off the signal any time they wished. But having bragged to a dubious world that Poland was free, that the "detention" of Kronk and a handful of "troublemakers" was but simple prudence and not an assault on civil liberties, they feared that a television news blackout would contradict their boasts. And so a world watched as a bulky, middle-aged man in white robes simply strolled through nearly forty years of rules and fiats and Marxist-Leninist dialectic and emerged, untouched, on the other side.

The papal jet was originally to land at the principal Warsaw airport. Gregory's ETA was eleven in the morning. By dawn 300,000 Poles were already there, at the airport, with thousands more coming in every hour. The regime, panicking, issued orders. The plane must land instead at the small military airfield west of the city. Fine, said Gregory, we wish to do nothing to inconvenience our hosts. His "hosts," of course, wished him in perdition, or anywhere other than Poland, but it would not do to say so. Word was quietly passed about the change in arrival site, no announcements were made, but by ten o'clock several hundred people were lining the access roads leading to the secondary field. How they had gotten there, what bush telegraph had informed them, no one could say. They were simply there.

So were the troops. And the police. And representatives of the regime, a regime at the moment very much divided. Kronk, some felt, should not have been arrested. He was a subtle, adroit man who had for several years now not only headed his Church in Warsaw but had been the balance wheel between the rash and the prudent. "Our role," Kronk had said, "is to preach the gospel and teach religion. Beyond that, charity. To work for the poor, the orphaned, the imprisoned. Our role is not that of toppling regimes or winning elections." Archbishop Kronk was so cautious, his critics had it, that he might as well move in and join the regime. "He'd make a fine colonel," a radical young priest snarled. "He's even got the makings of a belly." But if the undeniably chunky Kronk was the regime's pet prelate, as the cynical insisted, he could also, like a favorite pet, scratch and bite and foul the living-room carpet—as he had now done, leading to his euphemistically termed "protective detention."

The morning was cloud-filtered, mild, the grass verge of the tarmac rich green and damp from a dawn rain. Everyone was still watching the wrong airport. The Polish TV cameras were still focused on the main airport and its mass of stolid, waiting faithful. In Warsaw, at the headquarters of PRV, the national broadcast authority, calls were placed, calls were received, the argument went on. Was it better for the world to see the vast crowd waiting vainly or to televise the much smaller numbers who had come so mysteriously to the military field?

It was ordered. And a few minutes before eleven in the morning the papal jet, with its yellow-and-white flashings, tore through the scud of low cloud, banked once, and landed smoothly on the long, military runway. The plane taxied behind an army jeep to a halt in front of a corrugated shed. A wheeled gangway was rolled up and after a bit of confusion, with the jet's door being opened once, then closed, finally reopened, the Bishop of Rome stepped out.

Rome television, everyone's television, in fact, was picking up the Polish signal. And now, at the instant Gregory emerged, the scene shifted from the swaying, patient crowds to the empty military tarmac. No explanation was given. In Rome the news commentator got it all wrong. This was, he said, a more secure part of the main airport, chosen, he smoothly assured his audience, for purposes of security. The cameras followed the Pope as he descended the gangway steps and then, in a gesture become familiar, fell to his knees to kiss the soil of Poland, his own native land.

A military officer, unsure perhaps of the protocol, saluted. Several priests bustled up, their skirts flapping. They were shoved aside by Communist Party functionaries anxious to get their rear ends on television. The first official to reach Gregory seemed undecided between a handshake and a bow and compromised with a sort of shuffling obeisance that was half wave, half curtsy. Gregory moved toward the man and embraced him, bearlike. The functionary beamed.

The Italian announcer babbled on, giving the record of other historic arrivals at an airport which, of course, was not what his television picture was showing.

Gregory was now the hub of a knot of men, clerical, lay, military. There seemed, on the screen, to be some sort of discussion going on. The Pope was nodding vigorously and smiling all the while. Obviously *he* knew where he was. His pilot would have had to be given the altered instructions. Were they laying down ground rules for his entry into Warsaw? Was he asking where Kronk was? Or were they simply discussing protocol, who would exit the airport first? The Italian announcer gave a brief rundown on the history of the wrong airport.

Peter Cobb stood by a few yards from where Gregory and the Poles seemed to be negotiating. There was no point to joining the conversation. He wouldn't have understood a word of it. Fewer than two dozen were in the papal entourage. Gregory had decreed it. "This *isn't* a state visit and I want to make it brutally clear that it isn't."

As if to underline the unofficial, unceremonial aspect of his journey, Gregory's small party were young men, young as churchmen go. They'd been told to limit themselves to one suitcase each. They'd been told to prepare for rain, to prepare to spend time outdoors, to wear comfortable shoes.

Now, the incomprehensible jabber of Polish became louder. Gregory was still talking. Around him several clergymen and perhaps six or seven officials were shouting, throwing their hands in the air. One military officer turned away in irritation, only to be pulled back into the huddle of disputatious men by the belt in the back of his coat. A plump man in the square fedora of a socialist functionary shook his fist at one of his colleagues. Gregory continued to talk. Peter had the odd sensation the Pope was enjoying himself. He wanted to light a cigarette. But the Polish policemen and soldiers were watching, curious, the television cameras, and he jammed his hands into the pockets of his black suit and waited.

At last the thing seemed to have been arranged. Gregory had won the toss, or so it appeared. Only Cobb had no idea what the toss was. Now the Pope shook several hands in the knot of men with whom he'd argued, both clerics and Polish officials, and broke through their ranks to head for where Cobb and the others waited. Beyond the wire fences a caravan of official cars and army trucks and olive drab buses waited.

"Well, Fathers," Gregory said in Italian, his voice booming, buoyant, "get your bags. We're going to Warsaw. And we're going there like pilgrims. We'll walk."

He took two days to get there. It was only fifteen miles and Gregory was not a man who strolled. He stepped out vigorously in that first mile and he was still maintaining a good pace in the crowded, narrow streets of the old city during the last mile. But it was not only Gregory who was staging a march. With him, it seemed, was half of Poland.

At first, there were only a few: the clerics who had greeted him at the airport and the security forces, the troops and police and official functionaries assigned by the government to ensure against trouble, to protect Gregory from aberrant attack, to protect the state from a zealotry they feared he might whip up. Outside the barbed wire and the fences and gates, the few hundred civilians alerted to his arrival by some vague, inexplicable, extrasensory impulse cheered their Pope, fell to their knees, accepted his wave of blessing, and fell in behind his protective entourage. Like a snowball rolling downhill, the hundreds soon swelled. By mid-afternoon they had become thousands, by nightfall a hundred thousand. All night, while Gregory slept in a peasant's barn down a dusty lane just beyond the highway, the faithful hurried to join the throng. They came with babies on their backs or in carriages, they came in wheelchairs, they came on canes and crutches, even on litters. They limped, walked, trotted, ran, crawled.

"To Gregory!" went the cry. And the government, awed and even frightened, did nothing to stop them.

The Pope said mass the next morning at six in the scruffy yard in front of a cottage. There were now perhaps a thousand priests in the caravan. They concelebrated the mass and distributed Communion. When hundreds of the soldiers and police knelt to receive the sacrament, bureaucrats shuddered. What was it about this man that, in less than twenty-four hours, was reversing the flow of forty years of history? By eight, they were on the road again, now half a million strong.

Peter Cobb marched with him. He and a half-dozen of the younger, burlier clerics who'd flown in with Gregory from Rome constituted themselves as a sort of Praetorian Guard, fending off the overenthusiastic, accepting the boughs and flowers handed him from out of the crowd, steadying his elbow when once or twice on the rough cobble his ankle turned or his foot faltered. Cobb kept watching Gregory, who was grinning broadly, forever saying a word or two in response to a shout or a prayer from the multitude. In one big red-knuckled hand, Gregory hefted a shepherd's crook. With the other hand he signaled blessings as he went, a Pied Piper marching ahead of five hundred thousand of his children.

That first night they had stayed in a barn, the Pope and his courtiers. The bureaucrats scuttled back in their cars into Warsaw and more hospitable shelter. The vast crowd, of course, simply lay down in the fields and tugged coats and shawls closer. Inside the barn, once the officials and a few stubborn enthusiasts had been chased away, Gregory helped the others as they erected a crude table from barrels and boards. His face was sunburned now, especially the prominent nose. Gingerly he touched it with his big fingers.

"Well, Fathers, here we are prepared for martyrdom or worse and not one of us thought to fetch a tube of sunburn lotion."

They laughed and Gregory laughed with them and at himself. He looked across the rough table at Cobb.

"I know you Jesuits are accustomed to better things, Peter. But cheer up, tomorrow—Warsaw. A splendid city. You'll have linen on the table once more."

Cobb joined in the laughter. The food was rough, the barn smelly, their feet hurt, Gregory was not the only sunburn case. But the hearty camaraderie reminded Cobb of times in the Marine Corps, of the best times with Joaquin and Flor and the guerrillas. They were alive, they were accomplishing something, they were headed for Warsaw and for Kronk. There was, to Cobb, a sense of participation he had not felt about his own Church for a long, long while.

They would sleep rough that night, on the dirt floor of the barn. Gregory knew the worth of a dramatic gesture.

The men in his entourage marked out their own bits of turf. Peter looked across the big, smelly space by the light of lanterns and saw Gregory kneel briefly and then spread the blanket the farmer had supplied. When he was seated, tugging at a shoe, Cobb, on impulse, went to him.

"Holiness, if you're not too tired . . ."

"No, Peter. What is it?"

Cobb squatted on his heels like a cowboy next to the sitting Pope. "That book of mine, the thesis about just wars."

"Yes?"

"Well, I've decided not to publish it. When I get back to Rome it'll make a good fire against the chill one of these nights."

Gregory pursed his lips. "That's quite a change. For six months now people have been trying to get you to abandon this project."

321

"Yes, they have."

"And you sent them all to the devil," Gregory said, smiling.

"Well, let us say I declined their advice."

"And mine."

"Yes, Holiness. And that was toughest of all to do."

"But you did it. You told us all, in the politest of terms, to cultivate our own gardens, that you had something to say and that you were going to say it."

"Stubborn," Peter conceded.

"Well, you're young. To the young is permitted much." Then, tugging off the other shoe and balefully regarding a black sock through which his big toe had worn a hole, he said, "Why are you giving up now? What changed your mind? None of *us* could."

"You convinced me, Holiness."

"I? But in Rome you were adamant. Whatever eloquence I have was brought to bear. To no avail. That damned book of yours was an obsession and nothing anyone might say was going to dissuade you."

"I know. But this trip's changed all that. You've changed it. Who knows what's going to happen tomorrow in Warsaw? But you took the risk of coming here. You *acted*. You didn't sit back there in Rome writing pastoral letters or sending telegrams to the regime. You got on a plane and came to Poland. You *did* something."

"My critics hold that this sort of personal diplomacy is foolish."

"Well, perhaps it is. We'll know tomorrow."

"But even so, this dubious venture of mine convinced you to abandon your dream?"

Peter nodded. "Yes, because you were going to the people. Preaching. Taking your ministry to the church militant. I realized that's what I ought to be doing. Not writing polemics and dickering with New York publishers and negotiating with Curial censors. I'm not a writer, Holiness. I'm a *priest*. And I haven't been functioning as one."

"And you are now?"

"Yes, I am."

Gregory smiled. "We *both* are, Peter."

Cobb lay down. He had come so far, he had worked so hard, now he was giving it all up. He tugged his raincoat around him when he felt the first bite. He knew fleas, oh, God, how he knew fleas. Somewhere over to his right in the dark he heard a hard slap and a muffled grunt. Gregory. Peter grinned. He knew it had been worth giving up the book. Worth making this damnfool trip, all of them marching off in sandals like Peter the Hermit

322

confronting the Saracens. And unlike the Hermit, they just might pull it off. But whether they did or not, the important thing was to be part of it. He was at peace, and very happy.

Not even the fleas could keep him long awake.

This is more like it, Gregory told himself as he strode into the first of the sprawling residential suburbs of Warsaw and the green countryside began to barter its trees and low hedge for billboards, shops and the dreadful project apartments that ring every European city, west and east. Kronk was still a few miles, perhaps a few hours away. No longer so far. Ahead of Gregory a phalanx of motorcycles with red revolving lights rolled slowly through the crowd, forcing it back to the curbs so that Gregory and his by now enormous following could pass. Every so often Gregory would toss a look back over his shoulder. He could no longer see the end of the line, he had no way of knowing how many people there were. No one knew. There were too many to count.

As Gregory passed a tavern men held beer glasses high and shouted to him. He waved back.

"Good beer?" he shouted.

"Yes, Holiness, good Pilsener! And cold."

Gregory waved again and marched on. And the mass of people marched behind him.

In Rome and in a thousand other places church bells pealed out in celebration. The entire Roman Catholic Church seemed to be on the march. An Iron Curtain had been torn apart as if it were cotton lisle.

Gregory did not delude himself. He was no hysteric. He knew he'd not yet solved anything. With Cobb at his elbow, the Pontiff said, "Well, Peter, an adventure, eh? A romantic escapade. An escape from paperwork and administration and all those things we all must do and which we all hate."

"I know, Holiness, maybe it's just being away from Rome. This country of yours, I'd not expected it to be so green. And despite the regime, not shabby or threadbare."

"Ah, well," Gregory said, "we are, after all, entering the capital. Up north or in the mining towns near Czchow, you'd see differences."

The crowd was not docile, nor was it especially orderly. There was too much enthusiasm for that. But the authorities had no problems. Perhaps the huge march, the passion incited by Gregory, would pose long-term problems later. The march itself, none. Troops and police and paramilitary levies flanked the line of march, now more a surging sea than a line. But a good-natured sea. Every so often a woman or a girl would dart out of line and run to one of the troops, to shake his hand, to kiss a cheek, to hand over a flower. The troops, boys, most of them, at first shambled uneasily, embarrassed, from one foot to another. Then they relaxed, grinning, waving back, sometimes tossing the flower back to the crowd where it would be caught by another hand and again passed on.

Now in Warsaw priests stood in cassocks and broad-brimmed straw hats against the sun. There were women in aprons, children kicking soccer balls, sedate gentlemen in decent suits, young couples walking hand in hand, a child slung across the mother's back or perched on the father's shoulder, plump functionaries in flat hats, nuns telling the rosary as they went, farmers in from the country in their denims and neck cloths, pretty girls flirting slyly with the soldiers as they passed. All of them, around and flanking and following Gregory as he walked into Warsaw, crossed the Vistula, walked toward confrontation with the central government, walked toward an imprisoned Kronk.

Gregory did not know it, not yet, but he had already won. The government had caved in.

"What are we to do?" asked a choleric general rhetorically that morning as the Supreme Soviet met in plenary session to consider the situation. "Shoot the Pope down on the steps of the cathedral? They did that to Becket a thousand years ago and the damned English are still muttering about it."

No, they could not shoot Gregory. Obviously. Nor could they stop him. Not with a million people being swept along in his wake. Gregory, at this point, was more a force of nature than a mere man. Perhaps, had they acted sooner, at the airport, for example . . . But they had not. The government had been indecisive. Now, decisions were demanded. The people were watching, the opposition. Moscow was watching. The world. Gregory could not be stopped. But what of Kronk? It would no longer be simple to move him; the cathedral where he served his house arrest had become itself the hub of a vast sea of humanity. But it could be done.

"Think of it," a commissar declared, rubbing pudgy hands, "Gregory arrives and there is no one there. Think! Embarrassment, confusion, a loss of face, eh?"

The hard men who ran the country and answered only to themselves . . . and to Russia . . . pondered and grappled and argued and, in the end, surrendered.

"Kronk! Who the hell is Kronk? Forget him. Let Gregory have him. In a day the mob goes home. In a week the excitement is over. In a month they ask, 'Kronk who?' "

Not all were convinced. But this is how it was decided.

And Gregory continued to march toward Kronk, the million or more marching stride for stride with him.

It was symptomatic of the regime's paralysis in the face of Gregory's bold stroke that the government television continued to transmit, step by step, his defiant journey. At any moment a single, low-level technician could have thrown the switch that would have erased Gregory from a hundred million television screens. It all would have been so simple. Kill Gregory's image and you kill Gregory, that was the way they should have reasoned, that was how they should have acted. But they didn't. In a confrontation between one man and a supposedly monolithic society, it was the society that had crumbled and was fading away, an elaborately crenelated sand castle on a rising tide. And the regime's own state-controlled television apparatus catalogued his victory and its own defeat.

Peter Cobb shook his head, marveling to see the cameras. "Why the hell are they flagellating themselves this way? How can they permit Gregory to rub their noses in their own shit?"

It was late afternoon now, nearly six, but the sun still beat down hotly on the huge square in front of the cathedral of St. John where the Metropolitan of Warsaw, Archbishop Josef Kronk, waited for his Pope. By God, Gregory had pulled it off, the Italian anchorman announced. Sure, the Poles were stupid. At every option they'd chosen wrongly. But give Gregory some credit. It wasn't all blind faith and mystical inspiration. These were his people, this was his country, this the regime with which he'd coexisted, and even prospered, for so long. He knew them, he knew his country, his knew his people. Their flaws, their weaknesses, their superstitions, their vanity, their fears. Knew them and played on them.

"Oh, now, what's this?" the Italian anchorman demanded rhetorically.

The great doors of the cathedral were swinging open. Could it be Kronk? Was it possible?

"Kronk! Kronk! Kronk!" the crowd in the square chanted.

43

And it *was* Kronk. Big-bellied, slightly stooped, balding, the Metropolitan of Warsaw slipped through the doors of the cathedral and took several steps forward across the broad stone veranda that fronted the church. He had not been seen since his arrest. There were rumors he had been mistreated, that he had himself gone on a hunger strike of protest, even that he had died and that the authorities had concealed his death. None of the rumors was true. He was free, he was alive, he was . . . "Kronk! Kronk! Kronk!" The crowd surged toward him.

A mob is a frightening thing. Even a mob such as this one, more than half women and girls and children and motivated not by hate but by love and a deep religious conviction, a love of church, a love, even now, even after Kronk's captivity, of country. The mob's motives were of the purest. This did not make the mob any less terrifying. Even the most stolid, experienced policeman or soldier fears a mob. But on this day, in this particular quarter of the capital the soldier in charge of security around the cathedral was neither stolid or experienced. The major given the assignment had become sick. A virus. His replacement, an eager young captain anxious to impress, wanting to make his mark, would now make it. Disastrously.

"Kronk! Kronk! Kronk!" the people shouted as they swept forward toward the steps of the great church across the cobbled square. The few policemen who got in the way were swept along with the crowd. They were not attacked or threatened or seized but simply disappeared into and became a part of the mob. The young captain, standing halfway up the broad, long flight of steps leading to the veranda on which Archbishop Kronk now stood, his arms stretched out to the people, looked nervously to one side and then the other and then behind him. A few soldiers, a squad of police, nothing more. Far to his right and to his left the water cannons were parked. Waiting. In the alleys and the avenues leading into the square, armored

326

cars and companies of troops. Waiting. The crowd continued to move toward the steps, toward the cathedral and Kronk, toward *him*.

He panicked.

Snatching at the walkie-talkie slung around his shoulder he barked into it the order for the water cannon to fire, for the troops to move into the square behind the armored cars. No one had told him to do this. The regime had decided against a confrontation with the crowd, with Kronk, with this damned meddler Gregory. But men under stress do not always remember their instructions. Kronk had come out of his prison, the mob was pushing inexorably toward him across the square, brushing aside the screen of police and soldiers, and the young captain forgot what he had been told to do on this day and he did, instead, what years of indoctrination had taught him was right: to quell the mob, protect the State, maintain authority.

The first, heavy streams of water slammed into the crowd on its flanks, sending men and women skidding sideways with its force, tumbling their legs from under them. A child fell and was snatched up, only to be dashed again to the stones when its father was hurled to his side by the trip-hammer force of hydraulic pressure. Men and women screamed and grabbed at one another to escape the pounding. But this was still only at the very edges of the great crowd. Toward the center they were not even aware that the order had been given or that the cannons had begun to fire. There, they pressed eagerly forward toward the cathedral and . . . "Kronk! Kronk! Kronk!"

Behind the water cannons came the armored cars and the men. They moved slowly into the square. The captain retreated up the steps toward the top level where Kronk stood. He had his pistol out now. He was not actually aiming it; he would not have known where or whom to shoot first. But it was out, held in his hand at belt level.

"A gun!" someone shouted; a hundred someones shouted. "Save Kronk!" a man yelled, and then a hundred voices took it up: "Save Kronk!"

The archbishop, whose eyesight was no longer that good, did not see the gun. He heard the shouts and interpreted them simply as a sort of cheer over his apparent release from arrest. "Good," he said, nodding his head and smiling broadly, "good."

Men in the front rows of the mob saw him smile, saw him nod. A signal! They sprinted toward him across the last fifty meters between them and the cathedral steps.

"Good," Kronk said again, extending his arms in a welcoming gesture, as the men came on, really running now.

The captain was now but a few paces from Kronk. He could hear the archbishop's voice behind him. Hear him saying "Good, good!" He wheeled,

327

intending to tell Kronk to shut up, to stop inciting these crazy fools coming at them both across the square. But what the front rows of the crowd saw was the pistol, raised toward Archbishop Kronk.

It was not really aimed; the officer had no intention of firing. He was gesticulating with his right arm and the pistol happened to be in his right hand. From the crowd a bottle was thrown. Then something else. Then a dozen somethings. A small, green apple hit the captain squarely between his shoulder blades. He whirled, the pistol coming up. It was inadvertent. But the crowd didn't know that. A tall, red-headed laborer, who'd carried his tin lunch box to the demonstration, swung it once around his head and let it fly. It smashed into the young captain's face, breaking his nose and slicing into one cheekbone. Stunned, he turned slowly away from the square and toward Kronk. The archbishop started to say something and then he saw the young officer's bloody face.

"My son . . ." Kronk said gently. Only the captain heard him. And then the mob was up the stairs and the young officer disappeared beneath their feet.

It was at that moment that Gregory entered the square.

Peter Cobb moved closer to Gregory now. If there was to be trouble, this was where it would happen. If there was violence, then here. Cobb took one of the Pope's forearms, another young priest took the other. And they pushed ahead.

To the millions far away watching on television, Gregory was but a tiny white figure marching along at the head of a vast multitude of followers that dwarfed even the thousands waiting for him, some of whom were now grappling with police and soldiers inside the square of St. John. The Polish television cameras, watched over nervously by a senior official of the Ministry of Propaganda, had shifted abruptly from the flanks of the crowd and the cathedral steps, where fighting had broken out, and had resumed following Gregory's progress toward St. John's. So while the TV cameras were studiously ignoring the violence in the square, Gregory's arrival, as yet unnoticed by the waiting faithful, was the focus of the television coverage, as he had been for nearly every moment since his plane landed at the military airport. Now, again, Gregory was center stage.

Not even he knew about the fighting that the young officer's panic had ignited. The square was so large that at the end which he would now enter, the crowd itself was unaware of the violence. There, Gregory was the focus of excitement. The water cannons, the armored cars, and the steps of the cathedral now running with the blood of a stupid young soldier were too far away. Now, in the square of St. John, there was a new chant:

"Gregory! Gregory! Gregory!"

As he pushed his way into the square, behind Cobb and his other young men, the faithful fell back against the stubborn pressure of those jammed behind them, and dropped to their knees, blessing themselves, holding up small children and calling out for his blessing. Gregory knew this was why he had come. This! Not the release of poor Kronk. That, possibly, could have been negotiated quietly with the regime through diplomatic circles. Gregory understood politics. No, it was not Kronk he had come to save. It was the Polish people. All forty million of them. He was a realist. He knew the Communist house of cards was not about to come tumbling down simply because a Catholic prelate had flown here from Rome.

Gregory stepped into the square itself. The crowd fell back, a human corridor formed itself. Ahead of him, a long way off, the facade of the cathedral, so loved, so well remembered, loomed above him. He could not see Kronk, did not know he was there, knew nothing of the captain's stupidity. Or his death. Suddenly, without knowing why, Gregory badly wanted a pipe. If only he could smoke one now . . .

He could not. And of course he *would* not. He took a deep breath and, after a momentary pause, began to walk across the great square toward the church and, he hoped, toward his servant Kronk. "The servant," as Gregory put it, "of the servant of the servants of God." He was aware of shouts and salutations and murmurs of encouragement from behind him and from either side. Straight ahead, the crowd fell away. Gregory stepped off.

Ahead of him, perhaps six or seven hundred meters away, Kronk stood alone in the crowd, a solitary figure surrounded by devout Catholics eager to express their love, their fidelity, Catholics who had just trampled a young countryman into bloody gruel. Tears flowed down Kronk's cheeks. He wanted freedom; he had not wanted death. Liberty, but not at any cost. Gregory, at the other end of the square, knew nothing of this. Nor, as yet, did he know that the water cannons and the troops and the armored cars were pinching into the square from either side. Not knowing this, he continued to walk straight ahead, toward the doors of the distant cathedral, toward, he hoped, Kronk.

"Gregory! Gregory! Gregory!"

Cobb remembered Gregory on Boston Common, how small he had seemed, how far away. And how the distance had closed in Rome, in the piazza, then, later at the audience, how large the Pope had grown. He knew him now, as he had not then, knew the granite that underlay the marbled charm. Now, standing next to the Pope, Cobb knew his true size.

329

At the cathedral end of the huge square they now heard the chants for Gregory. And, as if ordered, they began to pull back, forming in front of Kronk a rough corridor of humanity roughly conforming to that created in front of Gregory. At last, the way was clear between the two men. Gregory, whose eyes were better, saw Kronk, and instinctively, as he hurried forward toward him, he raised his shepherd's crook. As if on a signal, thousands in the crowd fell to their knees on the cobblestones, and swiftly out from the center of the square, as if rolling across a placid pond, other thousands knelt, and other thousands, until, it seemed, everyone in the square had knelt in prayer.

And then a strange thing happened. The troops and the water cannons and the armored cars which had, seconds before, been battling on the fringes of the crowd, suddenly faced no resistance. There was no one to fight. And the cars rolled to a halt, the troops stopped where they were, and the water cannons were turned down to a trickle that became, in the vast silence, a drip, drop, drip, drop.

It was then that Gregory reached Kronk. Cobb was still hanging on to one white-sheathed papal arm and sensing this was the time, he released it. The Pope opened both arms to Kronk and embraced him.

At that instant a single gunshot crackled across the great square and Cobb, moving instinctively, grabbed Gregory's arm and started to pull him down. He felt the arm tense beneath his hands.

"No," Gregory said firmly. "I think we shall stand."

Cobb released the Pope's arm and looked around. He and Kronk and Gregory were the only people standing in the square. And Gregory was saying something to Kronk in Polish. Irrationally, Cobb decided he knew just what he was saying:

"I propose to you the option of love."

Kronk hosted dinner that night in the archdiocesan palace.

"Well, Cobb, no fleas tonight, eh?" Gregory demanded over the soup.

"Holiness, I don't expect to miss them."

"Good man, Cobb, good man."

Peter knew he was saying more than that. There had passed between the two men that afternoon in the square when the shot was fired something no one can understand who has not been under fire. And who has not flinched. Neither of them had. It was yet another thing they would have between them always.

That night, after dinner, at Kronk's request, Gregory led them in prayer in the chapel of the palace.

"Oh, Lord," he prayed aloud, "thank You for giving us back our dear Kronk. And for our safe arrival. And for good companions on the journey. May we act wisely whilst we are here and leave Poland better than we found it."

Cobb bowed his head and felt the thrill go through him at the words about good companions. He knew Gregory meant him. And he knew in justice that he *had* been a good companion.

In the morning Kronk and the Pope received emissaries from the government. The negotiations had begun. Cobb was excluded from these meetings. He had neither the language nor the diplomatic skills. Instead, a young priest assigned by Kronk took him about the city on a tour.

That evening, he was summoned to Gregory's quarters.

"Good, Peter, good. Here, sit down." Gregory waved his pipe. "Please smoke if you wish."

"Thank you." Peter pulled out his cigarettes.

"Good. Peter, before we left Rome for this quixotic venture you asked to be assigned new work."

"Yes, Holiness, the missions of Mirador."

"No. Not Mirador. I have another job for you. More difficult, more important."

There loomed before Cobb the awful possibility Gregory was about to assign him to some minor bureaucratic job in the Vatican. The sort of flattering "inside" post for which more ambitious men maneuvered. To become a member of the Pontiff's personal entourage, to become, Cobb recalled with a shudder, another Edmund Lonsdale.

Instead of any of this he said, "What your Holiness asks, I'll do."

"I know that, Cobb. And in this job such an attitude is essential."

Cobb waited. The Pope got up and went to his chair behind the big desk. He took a pen and began to scrawl a brief note on papal letterhead. When he was finished he pushed it across toward Peter.

"Father Falcone has suffered a mild stroke. They telephoned me this evening. He will be unable to function for a time."

Gregory continued. "Take this note back to Rome to Father Hanlon, your American provincial. Remind him it is confidential. I've said so in the note but remind him anyway. When I get back from Poland next week you and I will speak again. I'll formalize all this then. In the meantime, do nothing but wait. Keep all this to yourself, all but what I've told Hanlon here."

Gregory gestured and Cobb picked up the heavy sheet of stationery. The note was written in English.

Effective on my return from Poland Father Peter Cobb will replace Father Falcone as my personal legate to the Society of Jesus. His authority will be considered as mine. I will personally notify other fathers of the Order on my return. For now, this directive is to be kept confidential.

It was signed "Gregory."

With a shaking hand Cobb put the page back on the leather-topped desk.

"Holiness, there are ten thousand men and a hundred reasons why I cannot take on this responsibility."

Gregory looked at him coldly. "*Non serviam*, Cobb, from you? No, I don't think so. And there is one man who says you *must*. And will."

Cobb was not yet ready to concede. "Holiness, this isn't rebellion or false modesty or anything else. I've been a priest for many years. I've never administered a parish, never mind a province. And now, the whole Order? I'd botch it up totally. If the Church thinks it's got troubles with the Society now, just wait until I get in there for a few weeks."

Gregory rose once again. Now, no longer as cold, he half smiled. "Perhaps that's what you Jesuits need. More confusion and less organization."

Cobb laughed, despite himself.

Gregory made an expansive gesture with both big hands. "You see, Peter, you've begun already to come around to the notion. Lightning hasn't struck, no nuns have begun speaking in tongues, the ceiling of the Sistine has not fallen."

"Not that we've heard."

Gregory came to him now and put a big hand on his shoulder.

"Peter, administration is a knack. You have it or you don't. In Mirador you ran a small army. But it's not an administrator I need for the Jesuits. I need a man. Someone who can take orders and who can give them. You have something in your belly that enables you to disagree with a Pope and to debate an Edmund Lonsdale and still you have the selflessness to put aside an important book and to decide, all on your own and without pressure, to get back to first principles, to get back to ministering to souls. Those are no bad qualities for a man to have who is asked to grab hold of a dissident religious Order and yank it firmly back into line by the nape of the neck."

"It is my own Order that dissents."

"Yes? You think an outsider would be a better choice?"

"Yes, I do."

"You're wrong. Can you imagine my putting a Dominican in there? No,

Peter, you set a thief to catch a thief. And a Jesuit to discipline a Jesuit."

Cobb shook his head again.

"Holiness, there are so many things I don't know. Precisely what it is you want from the Society . . ."

"Obedience, loyalty, devotion, and their best, most inspired work."

Cobb listened intently, as if committing the words to memory. Gregory noticed it.

"Don't worry. I'll be back in a week. Or less, if the Russians insist. We'll have plenty of time to talk. You can take notes then. For now, what I've just said is sufficient. Get your colleagues to give me, and the Church, the sort of intelligent love you yourself demonstrate, and I'll be satisfied, and both the Church and your Order well served."

In the end, as Gregory knew he would and as Cobb was sure he would not, Cobb bowed his head.

"Yes, Holiness, I will do it. Please pray for me."

"I will Peter. And you for me . . . here in Poland."

Peter Cobb knelt to kiss his ring. By midnight he was airborne, back to Rome.

Father Malachy Hanlon had installed himself and his staff in a Jesuit school and faculty house in the Trastevere.

"Cobb? What's he want?" he demanded of the young priest who came to him the next morning in the comfortable living room he had taken over as his own.

"He says it's a message from Warsaw, Father."

"Smarmy bastard," Hanlon muttered. "All right, send him in."

For several minutes Hanlon railed at Cobb from his chair about the disloyalty of the young, the ingratitude of inferiors, and what he called the "papal ass-kissing" of Peter Cobb in particular.

Finally Cobb threw himself into a chair.

"Father Hanlon, please don't say anything more until you've read this. Things are going to be difficult enough as it is."

He pulled the Pope's letter from an inside pocket, got up, handed it to Hanlon, and went back to his chair.

"What's Gregory done? Pardoned you for your errant ways, Cobb? Is that it? We're to take you back if you promise to sin no more, to keep your damned face off television and out of the newspapers? Promise him you'd write no more books, is that it?"

"Please read it, Father. It's a confidential matter between you and me and His Holiness."

Hanlon stubbed out a cigar he was smoking and pulled the letter from its envelope.

Thirty minutes later, when Cobb left, Hanlon's large, beefy face was still pale and slick with sweat.

44

In Poland, Gregory continued to shake a regime and inspire a nation. Television followed him into the mines, the shipyards, the steel mills. Everywhere he went he carried his shepherd's crook, everywhere he waved his blessing, everywhere the crowds cheered and fell to their knees in silence, everywhere the government men sheepishly trailed along. Watching on Rome television, Peter Cobb, who had himself been there three days before, shook his head. The man was incredible. Infallible! Well, not quite that. Not in this stubborn insistence Cobb become the caretaker pro tem of the greatest religious Order in the Catholic Church. There, Peter was quite sure, Gregory had erred.

But priests do not disobey Popes. For two days Peter had been poring over entire sheafs of documents, reports, analyses, memos, Curial investigations, dossiers. A papal aide had sent them to his apartment by private courier. The man had arrived in an undistinguished car, wearing undistinguished black clothes. Thank God, Peter thought; what would his landlady have said if a Swiss Guard had marched up with the papers in one hand and his halberd in the other? The papers were a portrait of the Society of Jesus in the nineteen eighties. Cobb sat there, wishing he were a lawyer. The documents limned out, and then shaded in with cross-hatched detail, nothing less than a grand jury indictment of the organization to which he had dedicated most of his adult life.

"Jesus," Cobb breathed after several hours with a particularly noisome batch of dossiers. No wonder Gregory had moved in, had sent the Superior General on sick leave. There seemed not one but a dozen different Societies of Jesus, each of them its own feudal feifdom, arrogant, secretive, rebellious. Not so much a conspiracy as a pattern. The entire Order had gone off the tracks. Each superior, each provincial, indeed, each Jesuit, seemed to be writing his own theology, making his own rules, establishing his own church. It was as if ten thousand Luthers were nailing their own *défis* to ten thousand doors at Wittenberg.

335

On the afternoon Gregory arrived in Cracow Peter received a phone call from Father Hanlon.

"Look, Cobb," the New Englander began without ceremony, "this is as painful for me as it is for you. But I'm damned if I know what to do. Obviously you took me by surprise the other day. I'd made plans to go back to Boston. Am I supposed to hang out here waiting on your pleasure or what? And just how long am I to remain silent as a clam about your new celebrity?"

Hanlon's irritation amused Cobb. And he noted that for the first time the older man was not addressing him as a slightly retarded juvenile. The anger in his voice was a sort of tribute to Peter's maturity. Hanlon, finally, was treating Cobb as an equal. Not liking it, of course, but doing it.

"Father, there's nothing I can tell you. Except that what we discussed the other day is still confidential. I'm in the dark myself. I suppose we'll all be until His Holiness gets back."

"Damned foolishness," Hanlon muttered.

"I'm sure you're right," Cobb agreed cheerfully.

Hanlon continued to bluster. Cobb blandly agreed that the situation was unfortunate. Hanlon, it was clear from the documents the Vatican had supplied, was one of those who would have to go. Why irritate the man further when in a short time he would be stripped of his enormous power and humiliated? Cobb chilled the resentment he still felt toward the provincial and promised to contact him once he had instructions.

"Good of you," Hanlon said sourly.

Peter resisted the retort and hung up.

On television Gregory was entering the shipyards of Gdansk.

"What an incredibly dramatic gesture," the Italian television anchorman announced enthusiastically. "What a stroke of theater!"

And it was.

The world watched as Gregory reconquered Communist Poland.

When Peter Cobb said mass that morning at the damp, narrow side altar of his neighborhood's poor parish church, he felt a surge of love and of pride welling up within him, as if he too were still with Gregory on his private crusade to the infidels, tramping the dusty roads of Poland.

When he got back to the apartment there was a message.

> If it is not too inconvenient, could you call on me? It would
> be an act of charity of which I would not myself be capable.
> But I think you are.

It was signed, "Edmund Lonsdale."

Lonsdale was dying. He had, typically, the best private suite in the best hospital in Rome, the Ospedale Salvator Mundi, and the nuns who fussed with his pillows and freshened his water pitcher were the youngest, prettiest sisters on the nursing staff. Lonsdale held out a hand to Peter, so thin the blue veins were as easy to read as freeways on a road map of Los Angeles.

"Ah, Cobb, how good of you. After all the trouble I gave you, you came."

"Yes, Monsignor."

"I knew it. And not to gloat, either, I'll wager."

"Of course not. How are you?"

Lonsdale waved a feeble hand.

"Tolerable. There's no pain. A blessing, that. I've never been much for suffering. They never would have made a martyr out of me. One hint of the thumbscrews and I'd have cheerfully gone over to the other side. Whatever side it might be."

"I'm sure not," Peter said, unconvincingly.

"Oh, but you're wrong. And you know you are. There are men who fight and there are men who compromise. I've always been the latter. Would have made a good politician, you know, if I could have stood having all those grubby people around me. Kissing children, visiting pensioners, shaking hands . . . wouldn't have been worth a damn at that sort of thing."

Cobb pulled a straight-backed chair up closer to the bed and sat down.

"Is there anything I can get you, anything you need?"

Lonsdale laughed, the sound rattling emptily within his shrunken frame. "Another five years?"

"Well . . ."

Lonsdale, with considerable effort, pulled himself erect in the bed. Even that small exertion brought sweat to his wasted face.

"Cobb, there's so much to say, so little time in which to say it."

"Take your time, Monsignor. Don't tire yourself. I've no place to go."

Lonsdale laughed again. "But I do. That's the joke."

Cobb said nothing, but waited. It was obvious Lonsdale had something to say, something that seemed to him important.

Finally, the older man began. "Cobb, I've given you all variety of hell ever since you arrived in Rome. I did it because I thought you needed to be taken down a peg or two and I did it because I enjoyed doing it. Bit of a bully in me, I imagine. Not a very nice thing to have to admit but when you're dying the temptation to be honest is very nearly irresistible. When cancer has eaten away half your tripes, it tends to focus your vision rather remarkably."

"Isn't there anything that . . ." Cobb started to say. Lonsdale waved an impatient hand.

"No, don't be tactful now, don't cosset me. The nuns do sufficient fussing. They think I'm a very holy man, that I must be, seeing that I'm a monsignor. Ha! If only they knew."

"Perhaps they do," Cobb said. "We're supposed to love *everyone*, you know."

"Yes, yes, a worthy thought. And one which *you* undoubtedly believe. Not me. I can't abide people I don't genuinely like. 'Love thine enemy'? Not for me, I'm afraid. Not at all."

Cobb nodded but said nothing.

"Look, young Cobb, just sit there and listen to a dying old man have his say. Don't try to reform me. Too late for that. Just listen."

"Yes, Monsignor."

Lonsdale took a deep breath and resumed. "You and Gregory, Cobb, you're dangerous people. You really believe all this nonsense we preach. Love, self-abnegation, loyalty, discipline, goodness. God knows where you get the strength, but you have it. And you flourish. Damned hard on ordinary folk like myself. We bend with every breeze and find rational justification for having caved in."

For the first time Cobb spoke from the heart, interrupting the old man. "If you knew how many times I've bent, how many stupid, selfish things I've done . . ."

"Shut up, Cobb. Don't be simplistic. You know what I mean. Of course you're not perfect. Who the devil is? That's not what I'm saying."

There was a noise at the door and a young nun, smiling, stuck her head inside the room.

"Out! out!" Lonsdale shouted. The girl fled, terrified.

Lonsdale smiled. "Nice to see authority still has its privileges somewhere. Even if it's only in the vestibule of death."

Only Lonsdale, Peter thought, could essay such a ridiculous *mot* and very nearly carry it off.

Lonsdale beckoned Peter closer to the bedside.

"I hear things, Cobb. I'm not supposed to but I do. You can't have spent all these years listening at the keyholes of power and not." He paused, cleared his throat with difficulty, and then, his voice lower, conspiratorial, he went on. "They have plans for you. Gregory has been asking questions. I don't know precisely what, but they have something in store. Some variety of august appointment."

"Oh?" Cobb said, his manner innocent. Not even to a dying gossip was he about to whisper confidences.

"Quite. My spies are exasperatingly vague. Sorry about that. But it's something big. Have they told you anything?"

338

"Like everyone else I've been caught up in the Pope's trip," Cobb said, evading rather than lying.

Lonsdale waved a feeble hand. "Yes, yes, such excitement. Well, if you've no information, I have very little of value to add."

He fell silent, as if he had lost the train of his thought. Cobb waited, and then, sensing there was more, he said, "Yes, Monsignor?"

Lonsdale nodded. "Well, then, one thing. Not so much information as advice. Heed me, Cobb, heed me well."

"Yes?"

Lonsdale waited for a moment, as if wanting to get the words right, and then he spoke.

"Whatever this appointment is, no matter how attractive a situation it seems, turn it down. If it involves your becoming one of us here in this vast, purple bureaucracy, say no. I don't care what honors it may bring, what rewards it promises, what power and influence it offers. However eloquently it is proposed, you must say no."

Curious despite himself, Cobb said, "Why?"

Lonsdale closed his eyes and then, opening them, he continued. "Cobb, I am a vain, silly, sybaritic old man. The sort of person you young fellows laugh at behind our backs. I contribute nothing, I comfort and console no one, I chatter eloquently about trifles. I am a venerable cipher. Yet once . . . once, I had potential. Once, long ago, had I gone that route, I might have been of use. I was not unintelligent. I'd not yet become cruel or cynical. I might have run a decent parish, presided over a reasonable diocese. Instead . . ."

"Yes?"

"Instead, I became what you see before you. A shallow, empty man weighty with honors bestowed for reasons so obscure even I cannot remember their provenance. A clerical capon, valued for my dinner conversation, for my gossip, for my witty dissection of this or that rival for Vatican favor."

Cobb knew Lonsdale's self-appraisal was as accurate as it was pitiless. He wanted to remonstrate, to comfort the dying man. But as he began to speak, Lonsdale's face stayed the words.

"No, no, Cobb, don't be polite. Spare me your generosity. I know precisely who I am and whence I came. It is too late for regret, far too late for reformation. As a young man I could have gone in another direction. Could have served instead of being served. But an appointment to a Vatican ministry came available and I took it. The pomp, the circumstance, appealed to my vanity. In this old city where even Caesar was ambitious I slaked my ambition. Had I remained in England . . . in some obscure country parish . . ."

His voice changed, became sly: "I tried to fix you, you know. Did my best."

"You mean about Mirador? The book?"

Lonsdale waved a feeble, impatient hand. "No, don't be stupid. It was more than that. It was nothing as honorable, I assure you. Decidedly more venomous. I told my Jesuit friends about your curious relationships here in Rome. Your flirtation with Italo DeBragga . . ."

"DeBragga? I barely saw the man. He came to me and asked me to write some nonsensical propaganda favoring the Brigades. I told him to go to hell."

Lonsdale's mouth assumed a sickly, pussycat's smile.

"But they weren't to know that, were they? The Jesuits. How could they? All they knew was what I told them. About his cozy little chats at your flat."

"Not very cozy."

"Don't quibble, Cobb. I was out to torpedo you and I wasn't about to permit factual niceties to get in my way. I even indulged in a little tattle about you and the charming Contessa Massai. . . ."

Peter shook his head. How could he indulge anger at a dead man? "But why did you hate me? What did I mean to you? We'd never even seen one another before I came to Rome . . . came to your office at the Vatican that morning . . ."

"And off we went for our morning coffee, like two old sophisters renewing acquaintances."

"I don't understand," Cobb said dully. "Why would you try to ruin me?"

"Oh, dear fellow, how blind you are."

Peter shook his head in confusion and said nothing. How could you bully a dying man into telling you something he didn't want to say?

Lonsdale made a croaking noise and Peter looked up. The man's pale face was an unexpected pink. Cobb grabbed the glass of water on the night table and held it while Lonsdale sipped, greedily.

"Thank you. I was choking there for a bit."

Tears ran down Lonsdale's face, not of remorse or pain, simply a reflex to his choking spell. Cobb did not know this.

"Monsignor?" he asked gently.

Lonsdale paused, and then, with a fatigued patience, he said, "Cobb, you're a young man. Talented. Possessed of a certain flair. You have courage. Intelligence. Worst of all, a rustic brand of integrity. No, take that back. Worst of all, you're *young*. A life ahead of you. A career. Recognition. Achievement. Fame. Honors. Respect." He took a deep breath and then went on. "Can you possibly conceive of just how difficult it is, it might be, for a man like me to accept a boy like you? By God, don't you see, Cobb? Don't you understand?"

His withered body shook with the violence of the question.

At last Cobb *did* understand.

"Yes, Monsignor, I think I do."

Lonsdale nodded with a vigor that belied his condition. "Of course you do!" He hesitated, and then he said, his voice a cultured growl, "You were *me*, Cobb! Me! Everything I might have been thirty years ago, you threatened to become. And you had the one thing I lacked. Integrity."

He paused, and neither man said anything. Then Lonsdale, his voice weaker than ever, said simply, "Now clear out. And if you find it in you, mutter the odd prayer for me. . . ."

His voice faded, the words slurred into silence. Cobb leaned forward, hoping to catch them.

Then, suddenly, as if reinvigorated, the old man said, in a voice once more strong and forceful:

"Cobb, get out of Rome. Go wherever it is you can again be a priest of God and not some grandly titled clerk. Get out before you become *me*!"

45

Two days later, returning joyously to Rome from his triumphant mission to Warsaw, Pope Gregory's 707 slammed into a mountain in the Tyrolean Alps, killing the Pontiff and everyone else in his party.

As his remains were gathered up into a banal Italian army body-bag, the world mourned.

Even the Communists, even Moscow, mourned. The initial suspicion, shouted out in a hundred tabloid newspaper headlines, was of a RED PLOT! There had been no plot, no deadly bomb planted at Warsaw's airport. There was only an early autumn storm, an erring pilot, an unfortunately sited Alp. None of this was clear during the first few days and Moscow and Poland both writhed in embarrassment. Ten thousand political detainees were released by Warsaw as a gesture of sympathy toward the Church. Archbishop Josef Kronk was permitted to eulogize his Pope on national television. And in St. John's Square, a million Poles knelt, and wept, where they had knelt with Gregory only a few days earlier.

In Rome, there was mingled grief and relief. Traditionalists shook their heads and remarked, irrationally, that this was the sort of thing that happened when you elected Popes who were not Italian. The Jesuits prayed for Gregory's soul and some of them actually forgave him his iniquities. The maneuvering began in the College of Cardinals with men like Amadeo Cardinal Grassi again bending themselves to the task of electing yet another Pontiff. Vatican bureaucrats hoped that this time they would choose someone with a decent respect for routine. Liberals piously offered up fervent wishes for a Pope who would relax the papal reins. Conservatives were already lobbying for a man who would resist change, would turn back clocks, would say no. The Italian government hoped the man would be manageable, even as it declared official mourning for his predecessor. Ordinary Romans wept or shrugged or lifted a glass to his memory, depending on their own concerns.

Peter Cobb did not weep. He had seen death too often, too closely. But there was deep in his soul a sense of personal loss he had not felt since that last time he had seen Pedro Figueroa, toying with a bit of string on the urine-soaked floor of the municipal asylum in the city of Mirador. He was an articulate man but he could not put into words what he felt about Gregory. Jane called him from Milan, Marella Massai called. Somehow, they felt it was to Peter that they should offer their condolences. He thanked them both, understanding the generosity of their motives, but without saying more.

He had lost a Pope, he had lost a friend, he had lost a father. In Rome they draped purple and black and rang muted bells that tolled in Peter's heart. He put on a black suit and went with the thousands of others into the Piazza San Pietro to shuffle by the closed casket, a plain wooden box chosen for its symbolic simplicity. It took four hours to pass the body. At the end of those four hours Peter knew the only real service he could yet pay, the one true tribute he could render, would be to carry out Gregory's wishes, to function as the ailing Falcone would have done as the overseer and, he gritted his teeth at the word, the "reformer" of his Order, the vast, turbulent, troubled Society of Jesus.

He would call on Falcone at the hospital, then meet again with Malachy Hanlon, perhaps with some of the other senior Jesuits, to determine where and how a start might be made. He owed this to Gregory. He would carry out his program.

When he got back to his apartment that afternoon the letter was waiting, grimy, smudged and bearing a Mexican postmark. It had been forwarded, several times. It was from Mirador. From Flor Duarte.

"Dear Peter," it began.

I hope you are well and that this reaches you. Once more, it is like notes in bottles tossed on the sea. But I feel an urgent need to communicate. With someone who used to understand who we are and what we are trying to accomplish—someone who perhaps still loves us.

Joaquin has been taken. Our spies tell us he is still alive and we are reasonably sure of them. The government has huge internment camps now near the capital. Thousands of our people are behind the wire. We hope he is in one of those and not in prison. But given his rank in the revolution and his celebrity, that may be too much to expect. Our only optimism is that they may feel they can use him as barter for some of their officers and civilian officials we have taken. I hope they treat Joaquin better than we treat our prisoners.

The war swings this way and that. It was the Cubans' fault,

343

I believe, that Joaquin was captured. You know how he is! He sensed the Cubans were turning *our* revolution into *their* war. This he could not support. So he led some harebrained raid into the suburbs of Cathuelpho—where we had never ventured before—and was ambushed. Eighty men died or were taken.

The cruelty and the hate grow worse. There are summary executions by both sides. Crucifixion has become a favorite method. Torture, beatings, burnings. How—after all this—can Mirador ever be one again?

I am well—but tired. Oh, I am pregnant. Four months. I want the baby desperately. For its own sake, for mine, for Joaquin's. I know you have far more significant work to do, but if only you were here, not to lay mortars or teach farmboys the machine gun, but to baptize my child when it comes, and to minister to our souls—what is left of them.

Weariness, not cynicism, flowed through her words. Carefully, as if handling the sacramental bread, Peter Cobb folded her letter and put it aside while he knelt and prayed.

Popes died. The Church went on. Gregory had not been dead a week and Rome was already bustling with preparations for a new consistory. Cardinals flew in from six continents. The press flocked. Cab drivers and politicians, movie producers and aging aristocrats, pasta cooks and bank tellers, all had their pet theories as to who Gregory's successor might be. A hard liner—a pastoral figure—an interim Pope of a certain age—a Third Worlder—a traditional Italian bureaucrat.

Everything was as it had always been. Some, Cobb among them, found this difficult to accept. It was as if Gregory had never even lived, had made no impact, had initiated no meaningful changes. His dramatic triumph in Poland, the stunning shock of his death, were yesterday's headlines. Peter could not accept this. It was impossible for him to shrug off Gregory's life as meaningless, his death as a historic inevitability. Others might view it that way. Cobb could not.

Falcone was a dead man. Or very nearly. At the hospital Peter spoke with his physician.

"Father, the man is eighty. He's had another stroke, this one massive. He'll never speak again, never move. With tubes and luck we can keep him alive for a week, a fortnight, a month. But recover . . . ?" He rolled expressive eyes toward the ceiling.

So there was to be no help from that quarter. Preposterously, it was up to Cobb now, Cobb alone, to reform the Jesuits. And he had to start with Malachy Hanlon. Peter called on him at the Trastevere school that next morning.

"Well, Cobb?" Hanlon asked.

Hanlon remained seated. Peter Cobb swallowed once and then began to speak. "Father, I have been to see Father Falcone. The prognosis is not good. The doctors do not think he will ever recover the use of his faculties. But with your help and cooperation, I think we can carry through with the program the late Pope intended for our Order. A program that for none of us promises to be pleasant, but which Gregory believed necessary and constructive. And which will eventually, we all hope, result in a stronger and *better* Society of Jesus."

"Cobb?"

Hanlon, big, solid, confident, lounged now almost languorously in an overstuffed chair.

"Yes, Father?"

"I know of no such program, Cobb. No idea what you're talking about."

"The reform! The letter Gregory wrote you. That day when I came to you and delivered it myself!"

Hanlon looked at him in mock innocence. "My boy, is it possible that grief for your Pope, understandable, laudable grief, has caused you to imagine things?"

"Imagine, hell!" Cobb said bitterly. He saw no sympathy in his eyes. None.

Hanlon got up now. "My dear Cobb, when you came to me that day you seemed a deeply concerned man. Your own personal problems appeared quite to overwhelm you. If we discussed the Pope at all it was in the most general terms. The entire time was spent in wrestling with your own concerns."

"*My* concerns? What are you talking about?"

Hanlon smiled, a terrible smile, that of a man who knows he holds cards. "Your misguided flirtation with the infamous Italo DeBragga that had so involved you with an Italian criminal investigation."

"Lonsdale told you that. Poor, pitiful Lonsdale. And you believed it?"

"Oh, yes. Monsignor Lonsdale is very highly considered in Vatican circles. When Edmund Lonsdale tells you something, you can bank on it."

Cobb shook his head. "Father, I don't know what to say. How can I defend myself against charges that have no basis? Where is a rational starting point for discussion? There isn't any. Because there was no trafficking

345

with DeBragga or anyone else. It's a phony. And you"—he stared at Hanlon—"you know it."

"Father Cobb, you're upset. Young men have been taken in before in such schemes. It isn't held against you personally. These things happen. They can be forgiven."

Peter determined to try once more. Deliberately, he said:

"Father, Pope Gregory assigned me on an interim basis to replace Father Falcone as the overseer of the Order. He had delivered to me certain documents, histories, dossiers, and papers, sheafs of papers, which I still have in my possession. I was to study those and, on his return from Warsaw, to sit down with senior members of the Order to begin the task of cleaning house."

The noise the old man made in the back of his throat was decidedly unfriendly. Cobb didn't care. He pushed ahead now, speaking fast.

"I have those papers. Gregory gave them to me. He sent you a note ordering you to help organize the task. You were angered, resentful, but you said you would. Falcone knows all about this. So do you. So do I."

Then, quite smoothly, reining in resentment, Hanlon said, "Gregory is dead. Falcone is dying. I deny the truth of what you say. It is you alone, Cobb, you against the Society."

Cobb said, almost pleading, "Come to my apartment, then, come and see the paperwork, the draft papers I've already written, the files, the documents . . ."

Hanlon was barely listening.

". . . the dossiers," Hanlon said sarcastically.

"Yes," Peter said doggedly, "the dossiers."

"And," Hanlon asked, his hands folded before him, "is there a dossier on this poor, neurotic widow . . . the Contessa Massai . . . ?"

Peter knew then that he was beaten.

46

"So they've screwed you, eh, Peter?"

Charles Cobb, somehow, had learned of his son's betrayal by the Jesuits. He had no details, he knew nothing of Gregory's seminal role in the aborted affair, he had never heard of Malachy Hanlon, he hadn't witnessed Peter's impotent fury, but he knew something had gone bad, very bad, and being Charles Cobb—and despite his infatuation with the Church—he intended to do something about it.

It was midnight in Rome. Peter, groggy with sleep and the usual September heat wave, tucked the phone under his left ear and groped for a cigarette. C.C. went on.

"Mind you, Peter, there are always going to be injustices in great organizations, be they public corporations or armies or churches. Can't be helped. The sheer size and complexity make them inevitable. Good men get passed over. The wrong men advance and prosper. It happens. Damn shame, but it does."

"Yes, Father, I'm sure you're right."

"Now don't patronize me, Peter. I know your tactics—agree with everything and hope to shut me up that way."

"Father, I'm half asleep. It's . . ." He looked at the clock.

"I know what time it is. Not seven yet."

"How's the Duchess?"

"Don't change the subject. She's fine, thank God."

"Good."

"A miracle," C.C. murmured, almost to himself.

"Yes," Peter said, still unsure of whether he believed.

"Well," C.C. said, forcing the conversation back to his son, "this big job you were getting. I take it they've reneged."

"Oh, you know, Father."

Then, with the shrewd instinct that made Charles Cobb so feared on the Street, the old man, guessing, said:

"It was Gregory himself who appointed you, wasn't it?"

"Yes, it was Gregory." Peter knew he could not lie when his father was like this.

"Hmmmm," C.C. said, sounding impressed, "he thought that much of you?"

"Well, I guess he did. Silly, I suppose. I must have provided novelty value."

"No, I don't think so." He paused. "That Pope of yours didn't seem the sort who promoted court jesters."

Peter inhaled.

"Well, all academic now."

"You think so?"

"Of course. Gregory's dead. The new Pope will have his own concerns, his theories, his own set of priorities. Pet projects."

"The Church goes on. That it?"

"Yes, Father."

"Peter, for years I've been at war with God, with the Church. Over your mother's death, over you, over many things. Sicily changed all that. I don't pretend to understand everything, to believe all that tommyrot as you do, certainly not with your fervor. But I've stopped fighting. Stopped criticizing. I accept your priesthood, Peter. Now, I'd like to help."

His son did not understand. "Help? What do you mean?"

"Help you, of course. Help your career within the Church. You've made your choice. Religion is your life. What can I do for you? Just tell me. If it's do-able, I'll do it."

Sitting on his bed in Rome, lighting one cigarette from another, Peter Cobb shook his head.

"It's not that simple, Father."

"Of course it is. Cardinals and bishops are only men. Saintly men, I'm sure, many of them. But men. Even Popes are men. Open to persuasion. They listen to reason. They know a fair offer when they hear one."

". . . and they'll take a bribe. Is that it?"

"Peter, cynicism doesn't become you."

"Sorry, Father."

There was a pause in the torrent of C.C.'s words. Peter could hear the faint crackle of the transatlantic cable. He drew on a cigarette, preferring to let his father do the running.

"Now listen, Peter. I don't know just what's going on. But I know that

Gregory promised you some sort of big job. And now that he's gone the bastards are ganging up on you. Maybe they've got their reasons. You aren't the most malleable young man, you know. But I'm damned if I'll let them cheat you out of an appointment you deserve."

"Father," Cobb said, and the fatigue in his voice was a symptom of neither the hour nor the lack of sleep, "let it go. It doesn't matter. It's just not meant to be."

"Gregory wanted it for you," the old man said shrewdly. "Gregory couldn't have been wrong, could he? Infallibility. One of those tenets of your faith, isn't it?"

"Not in a case like this. No. Besides, it was a job I'd never have been able to pull off without Gregory's being there, backing me. It was a real long shot. Even if he'd lived, the odds were against me. Without Gregory . . . no chance. None at all."

"You quitting?"

Peter said icily, "You know me better than that, Father."

"All right, then," C.C. said quickly, "let me help. Tell me what you'd like to do. Your next assignment. There in Rome? Back home in the States? A university presidency? What?"

"No tidy little archdiocese with a financial surplus and a weekly television show?"

"Don't be nasty, Peter."

"Sorry. It's just your attitude. That even in the Church, if you've got the money and the connections, you can buy anything."

"Can't you?" Charles Cobb asked.

In the end Peter told his father he was thinking of going back to the missions. He did not mention Mirador. But that didn't fool the old man.

"You'll die there, you know. They'll kill you. For what you did before. Because of your book."

"Well, I don't think so. I hope not. Who knows?"

Tom Hathaway's apartment, typically, was the sort of place *Architectural Digest* might feature as the ideal bachelor pad for a young diplomat whose current assignment in Rome was but the curtain-raiser to an even more brilliant future in Foggy Bottom. Peter Cobb stood by the floor-to-ceiling windows and looked out on a Tiber silvered by the crescent moon.

"You do it right, Tom," he said admiringly. "You always did."

Hathaway, lounging with one leg hooked over the arm of his chair, nodded.

"First class all the way, Pete."

"Yeah."

Cobb was there to say goodbye. And to say other things. They'd had dinner, served by Hathaway's "man," a pansified little Genoese with a genius for the kitchen. Now, over *amaretto* and dragging luxuriously on a couple of Hathaway's panatellas, they talked about the things avoided over the meal.

"Mirador," Tom said. "You're crazy, you know. Fucking nuts."

"That's what everyone says. But I'm the only one's ever been there."

"Hell, I read the cables. Your pals are losing. Getting shit beat out of them. This year the *junta* wins the pennant."

"That's how these civil wars go—in cycles. The government wins one, the rebs win one. Probably by the time I get there the balance of power will have shifted again."

"I'm surprised the goddamned Jesuits are letting you go."

Peter laughed. "They can't wait. Convenient way of getting rid of me."

"Bastards."

Peter shook his head. "Look at it from their point of view. I've turned out to be a pain in the ass. I've asked their permission to go back into mission work. They're short of priests in Mirador. I know the language, the country, the job. Perfect setup for the Order. If I get bumped off, fine. If I don't, then they get some constructive work out of my hide."

"Pretty fatalistic, aren't you?"

Cobb turned from the window, throwing up his hands. "Tom, if I started worrying about all the bad things that could happen, I'd go nuts. Who the hell could have predicted everything that's happened to me since I got to Rome? Getting to know Gregory. Jane's husband damned near burning himself to death. The Duchess's recovery. My old man's conversion. Getting dragged into the *Brigate Rosse* business just because we happened to be having dinner in a *trattoria* some kid decided to blow up. Listen, compared to Rome, Mirador's going to be a long weekend."

Hathaway puffed at his cigar. Cobb walked across the room and threw himself down on a chesterfield couch.

"One thing I feel rotten about, Tom. You and Pia. I wasn't much help on that."

"You tried."

"What are you going to do, Tom? Still seeing her?"

"Nope, hurts too much. Can't keep my hands off the girl. Rather stay away."

"So you'll stick it out, keep trying for the annulment?"

"What choice have I? I love her. She's not going to walk away from her damned Church. She's got a lot of guts, you know. What sort of character would I be if I didn't play it her way? If I didn't wait for her?"

Peter looked at his old friend.

"You've got some guts yourself, Tom."

Hathaway nodded.

"You know, you're right. Never realized it before. Always took the smooth and easy road. First time in my life I've hung tough on anything. But Pia's hanging tough and so am I. Kind of a pact we have. She's worth waiting for. So I'll wait."

"Good man, Tom."

Hathaway shook his head.

"*Not* a good man. But willing, this once, to give it a try . . ."

That night, tidying up his life as men do who are about to start long journeys, Peter burned the manuscript of *Holy Wars*, feeding it a few pages at a time into the fireplace in his living room, watching the smoke rise like murmured prayers toward heaven.

47

Marella had never looked more beautiful. Or more determined.

It was her dinner. The Piazza del Popolo, one of those small and lovely restaurants where fashion designers and *principessas* and foreign correspondents ate and where no ordinary Roman would think of going. Peter got there first, just before ten. The table was in her name. The name seemed to mean something to the maitre d'hotel. Certainly Cobb's face didn't. Across the room a middle-aged man waved. Peter thought he might be from *Newsweek*. He wasn't sure. What did it matter? He was no longer news. Let *Newsweek* snoop, let *Time* theorize. Gregory was gone. And with him all the great plans, the grandiose projects, noble reforms, all bundled away like forgotten dreams.

And if Marella seemed determined, positive, with a new or renewed sureness about what she thought, what she wanted, and how she would get it, Peter had rarely been as uneasy, as unsure of just what he would say, what he *should* say to her.

He began by telling her of his return to Mirador.

"You're sure about this?" she said.

"Yes."

"You don't feel you have responsibilities closer to home? Jane, your father, yourself?"

"Jane's fine. She's pulled out of it. She has a job now. Gigi. My father . . . well, he's got the Duchess. He has his work. His wealth. His power. And now this flirtation with religion."

"And you, Peter?"

"To paraphrase Descartes . . . I am where I work."

She shook her head.

"When you came to Val for the skiing, I was still in shock. My husband was there one instant, the next he was bloody meat. Jane took me in. I didn't

352

cry so much as fantasize. I had these romantic visions of a seemly, middle-aged virginity, sustained by my work, my art. I would sublimate loss, sublimate sex. All would be well. Just as in the catechism, you know. The questions there, they all have answers. There are no blank spaces."

"I know. We're all so damned sure we know everything. And we know bloody little."

"Little? We know bloody *nothing*."

She sipped at her drink. Then, "I was still having my nervous breakdowns. I was unable to work. But by the time I met you in the chalet I was having them quietly. No more screaming. No more weeping. A little Valium and a decorous madness. Very un-Italian."

"You looked fine to me. Normal, admirably so."

"That was shyness. I didn't mind cracking up in private or in front of Jane. She was a pal. She had her own stinking hell to go through. You were something new . . . and very strange.

"Very strange," she repeated, "very strange and very . . . appealing. As if you'd been sent in my hour of need. As if prayers had finally been answered."

"Hardly. Screwed-up Jesuits aren't the answers to anyone's prayers. If anyone needed help then, I was the one. Someone with as much going for her as you had, and have, you didn't need anything but time."

Quite calmly now she continued, her voice soft but sure:

"And then I fell in love with you."

"Marella . . ."

"No, don't stop me. This must be said. I was getting better. The pain was easing. You were here and loneliness was going, too. Oh, I knew it had no future. You weren't that sort of man . . . that sort of priest. And there are plenty of them. You were, well, Peter Cobb. You were important. An intelligent man with a book to write, a role to play, a Pope to advise . . ."

"Hardly," he said again. She ignored the interruption.

"I was willing to accept your unavailability. The impossibility that anything could come of it. It ached, but I understood. I was in love with someone I couldn't have. Not precisely a unique situation. It happens all the time. Others survive it. I would. . . ."

"You have," he said quietly.

"No, Peter, you're wrong. Because now everything is changed. What was impossible a few months ago . . ."

". . . is still impossible."

She shook her head, the dark curls tossing. "I don't think so. Not anymore."

He said nothing, but waited for her to go on, to make her case.

"Peter, the Church is changed. The Pope you served is dead. There'll be a new Pope, a new order. Who knows who or what he'll be. Your own Society betrayed you."

He sat up straighter. "Marella, who told you that?"

"Peter, I told you a long time ago, Rome is a village. Who can keep a secret in this town? The Jesuits, they turned on you once Gregory was gone and broke every promise they'd made."

"They'd made no promises," he said.

"All right, I don't know everything. All I know is that something bad happened to you. And that now they're sending you to Mirador to die. What in the name of God do you owe any of them anymore? Haven't you paid your dues, fulfilled your vows, satisfied your Church? What about you, Peter? You! Don't you owe yourself something? Must you go on paying and paying and paying? Don't *you* get something in return?"

"We sign on for life, you know. And it *isn't* all paying."

She put her head down. The waiter came and Cobb waved him away. Her hand, delicate and strong at the same time, moved to her hair. She was fighting for control.

"I'm all right," she said. She didn't sound it.

"I know you are."

She resumed. "You call going back to Mirador not paying? Where they'll shoot you down on sight?"

"Marella, you don't understand."

"I do, I do, Peter. And you've got to understand me. I want to be your lover. I want to be your wife. I want your children. Is it fair that two people like us *have* no children? I want you. To be your life, to be your love. And you're throwing everything away for an irrational, romantic martyrdom of the sort that went out of fashion centuries ago, even in this crazy country. Can't you see that? Don't you realize what you're giving up?"

She was crying now and, abruptly, she got up to go to the ladies' room. Cobb waved the waiter over and ordered another drink.

There was faith and there was doubt. And they were at war, as always. He had never denied having doubts. And for twenty years he had declared his faith. He knew you could not banish doubt simply by reiterating faith. Everything was too complicated, life itself had become too complex for primitive, emotional, anguished cries of *Credo*! The "I believe" could become the "I doubt . . . I am not sure."

With the canny instinct of an artist confronting the clay, Marella had understood this, had pressed in on him. On his confusion and his hurt.

What she did not reckon on, could not understand, was the passionate depth of his love, not for her, but for God.

She came back to the table.

"There," she said, "that's better." She smiled and the hovering waiter, nervously waiting, now came and took their order.

They settled down and had their meal. Marella was sweet and charming and just slightly wicked with her references to various people in the place, their pomposities, their poses. She was fun to be with. Intelligent, instinctive, warm. Then, over coffee, it all changed again. Accidentally, reaching out for the sugar, he'd touched her hand.

"Don't," she said. "Don't touch me, Peter. I can't stand having you touch me and knowing I'm losing you . . ."

"Marella, stop hurting yourself. Please." He wanted to say, "Stop hurting me." To tell her there were limits beyond which a man was not to be tried.

"I'll never see you again. Never hear you play the piano again."

"Never is a long time," he said, knowing how banal it sounded.

"Oh, don't I know it," she said bitterly. "Haven't I learned all about 'never' and just how long it is . . . ?"

She started crying again, silently and without tears, her shoulders shaken by the sobs.

"Marella," he said softly, "I'm a priest . . ."

She recoiled. "Oh, yes," she said, "how good of you to remind me."

Peter finished packing that night. He'd picked up the newspaper on the way back to the apartment and when the packing was through he sat down to read it.

"DeBragga Killed!" screamed the headlines.

Italo DeBragga was dead. In a police ambush. The dialectician and the soul of the *Brigate Rosse*. The man who'd sat in this room and drunk coffee and argued his case. Who'd confessed to Cobb in a restaurant kitchen.

Not a man to be mourned. Hardly that. A killer. A terrorist. Funny, Cobb realized, that was how the papers in Mirador would have described him if he'd been killed in any one of a hundred bloody fire fights with the regime. It all depends on your point of view, doesn't it?

It was midnight. He knew that if he went to bed now he wouldn't sleep. Perhaps he should just sit here in one of the big old chairs and read and smoke until it became light. He could always sleep on the plane. Then, on an impulse, he jumped up and grabbed his jacket and went downstairs and outside and went quickly up to the corner where he could hail a cab.

"Piazza San Pietro," he said, and sank back against the cushion.

Except that it wasn't cold, it was as it was that first night. It was January then. He'd stood here in this same spot with the old beggar cadging cigarettes and peddling folklore. The beggar had been right about the one thing—that *was* Gregory's window up there. It was lighted then. It was dark now. The square was not as empty. Some policemen, a priest or two, a few functionaries, getting ready for the dawn when the pilgrims would come again to line up and mourn their Pope.

Gregory!

The same Church that had spawned Malachy Hanlon, had spawned Lonsdale, had thrown up a man like Stefan Holstowski. A man like Peter Cobb. All of them wearing the same uniform, praying to the same God. All different.

He wanted Marella so fiercely that it frightened him. Never before in more than twenty years as a seminarian, as a priest had he felt such an overwhelming hunger. This wasn't the momentary lust of a tropic night, the cinema-like visions of a woman's face, a body, a breast. This was real and here and now. She was his if he wanted her. And, oh, but he wanted her.

There was Marella here. And Flor Duarte back on the Rio Negro with Joaquin's child in her belly and her man shackled in some *junta* dungeon. There was duty and there was need. There were vows and there was love. From the time that he was a boy Peter had always known what to do, choices had always come easily, even the hard ones. Now . . .

If only Gregory were alive. If only . . .

Some workmen, using lamps, were repairing and strengthening the wooden hoarding around the little obelisk in the center of the piazza. The crowds of mourners must have knocked some of the boards loose. The sound of the hammering echoed in the great square. If only he could hammer straight and tight and solid the boards and planks and two-by-fours of his own life.

He shrugged and began to walk back toward the exit from the square. And when he had reached the outer perimeter he turned for one final glance back at the piazza and the complex of buildings that had been, for the past year, so much a part of his life. The lamps had been turned down. The hammering ended. Somewhere in the gloom a workman laughed. They mourned a Pope but still, there was laughter. A policeman called to another. A routine remark. Life went on. The great mystery, life.

And then, without explanation, high on the facade of the Vatican, a light. In *his* room. Gregory's room. A workman, or a nun, tidying it up, he supposed, a secretary securing some of Gregory's papers, opening a drawer, locking a desk. Who knew? And he remembered that room and the man who had lived there. Dead. But neither gone nor forgotten. Not by Cobb. Not *ever*. He was with Peter now. He would be always with him.

Cobb was *not* alone.

The light in the papal apartment blinked off. He stood there for another moment, staring upward. To the Vatican and beyond it. And then he turned from it for the last time, no longer unsure, no longer doubting.

Tomorrow he was going to Mirador. He was going . . . home.

BOOK VII

HOME

48

The Church, one, holy, Catholic and apostolic, as it called itself and believed it *was*, now came to Rome. A Pope had died, a new Pope was to be
elected. Absent the suddenness of Gregory's death, the shock, there was
about the tragic affair the consolation of routine. The Church, like the tides
and the phases of the moon, was predictable, measured, consistent. Man was
meant to die. Popes were men. Gregory was gone. A successor would be
chosen. And it was to Rome the great Church had come to make its choice.

A cab took Peter Cobb to Leonardo da Vinci airport. Austerity—and airline buses—would come later. He watched through the windshield as Italy,
green and bustling, so well remembered, flashed by, perhaps for the last
time. His driver, young and reckless, with black hair that curled over his
collar, jabbered on about Gregory.

"I am an anarchist, naturally," the boy said.

"Of course."

"But this Pope was a man. Not an Italian—which was clearly a mistake
and will not be repeated—but nonetheless a man. Not one of these old
women in black skirts."

Cobb had worn a black suit, a collar. It seemed appropriate. The driver
sensed he had been rude.

"I meant no offense."

"None was taken."

"Good. You are Polish yourself? You speak Italian quite well."

"No, American."

It was all the same to the driver. Poles, Americans. Italy was permanent.
These other peoples came, they went. He philosophized about it. Peter
half-listened. He was still thinking about Marella. About how she looked,
the things she said, their final meeting.

She would find someone, someone would find her. Peter was sure of it.

361

She was too good, too healthy, too *wise* to waste a life. He would never forget her. She would always be part of him. A sense of loss mingled with triumph.

Leonardo da Vinci airport was its usual chaotic self. Cobb declined the services of a porter and walked down the long corridors toward the ticket counter. Past him bustled the incoming members of the consistory, great and noble men with their entourages, their robes, their air of proximity to power, their saintliness. He was pushed aside, a lone young man in a plain black suit with a single bag.

The whole Church was coming to Rome. Jesuits, Franciscans, Dominicans, Benedictines, Passionists, jabbering Africans, inscrutable Asians, red-faced Irishmen from Chicago, ascetics from Ireland, mystic Indians, ponderous Germans. The Church was gathering. A Roman Church coming home to Rome.

Nearly a year had passed since Cobb's summons. How far he had come from Harvard. How far from Mirador. He had arrived in Rome a minor celebrity, a best-selling author flushed with success and certain his next book would be even more important, more influential, the distillation of everything he thought he knew and was sure he would learn. Those were, he supposed now, the salad days. Yet there had also been fear, a nervous dread of what Rome would say, just why he had been called. And those first days *had* been intimidating. Monsignor Lonsdale. Lonsdale, dead now, a brief obit in this morning's *Corriere*, a longer article in *Osservatore Romano*. Poor man. Unfulfilled, joyless, and knowing it. In some ways, like his father. Unfair to C.C., perhaps, who always believed in himself, in his works and pomps, in ways Edmund Lonsdale never did. How far had Peter come to see a Pope. Like the cat who came to London to look at a Queen. Or was it a King? No matter.

A hot afternoon and the loudspeakers droned on. Arriving flights, departing flights. The glass and steel and marble and plastic of da Vinci echoed to their sound, above the voices, the laughter, the sobbing, the normal day's commerce of a world on the move. Cobb pushed through the crowds to a counter where a young girl with a sweaty face and damp ringlets of hair served him a lemon drink, and a smile, through her fatigue. The Italians work hard. Cobb wondered where it began that they were an indolent people.

Rome, then, had been a failure. His, of course, not its. His book had been burned, his thesis of the holy war unproved. He had failed poor Tom and his lovely Pia. Cobb had seemed to promise so much and to deliver

. . . nothing. Marella, Marella! Gregory had wanted him to reform the Jesuits and in that too, he would fail. Gregory was dead, the epic death of a great man. Lonsdale, too, dead. Horribly, ignominiously. DeBragga, dead. Shot to pieces. Casualties, all. Losses.

There *had* been victories. Jane's. Helen's. C.C.'s. Not his, *theirs.*

He sipped his lemon drink and watched the surge of travelers ebbing and flowing through the *Star Trek* corridors and waiting rooms and gates of the airport, noisy, smelly, bustling, impatient, loving, weeping, hurrying, alive. He loved Italy. Its savagery and its civilization, its elegance and its squalor. Ruined churches, ruined pagan temples. Despite his defeats, he would not have missed Italy.

When he came here in January his concerns were ego-centered. *His* book, *his* thesis, *his* priesthood, *his* rebellion, *his* fears, *his* dreams and aspirations. Italy had knocked that out of him. Gregory had knocked it out of him. Italy had given back some of what he feared Mirador had taken away forever.

"*Ancora?*" the counter girl asked.

"*No, grazie.*"

His flight had been called. New York. Then Mexico City. Then—well, from there on to Mirador the loudspeakers were silent. From there on it would be a fishing smack at night on a hostile beach or an old truck running contraband along a rutted dirt track. A long hike over mountains. A damp slog through swamp.

Back to the wars. The holy wars.

Only Gregory, himself the old soldier, the guerrilla, the killer, knew there *were* no holy wars. At last, Peter Cobb knew that, too. He was going to Mirador not to fight, but to heal.

In Mirador again he would be a priest of God. He knew he was right to go; in the end *he* knew it, Marella knew it.

Again the loudspeakers called to him.

He shoved through the crowd, his battered typewriter in hand, the suitcase checked through, the old trenchcoat tossed casually over the shoulder. Once he was forced back, forced to step aside when a flying wedge of *carabinieri* shoved Cobb and the rest of the crowd back against the wall to make way for yet another red-robed cardinal arriving importantly to attend the consistory.

"*Attenzione,*" a young cop told Cobb with a knowing grin, "little priest, there are bigger fishes than you in the ocean."

The cardinal and his entourage swept past, all the grandeur and glory of the Church in full panoply.

363

"They got to find another Pope," the young cop said, apologetically.

Peter Cobb smiled. "Yes," he said, "they must find another Gregory." He did not say this ironically or cynically but with infinite hope.

Then the cop let him pass, the way clear to his plane.

49

The small rubber raft nudged against sand and Peter Cobb lowered himself over its side into the warm surf of Mirador.

"*Vaya con Dios,*" came a hoarse whisper from the raft and Cobb murmured thanks and waded up toward the beach, two rucksacks of cotton clothes and medicines and writing materials and a chalice and other liturgical vessels slung heavily across his back. The raft was already gone. Cobb was alone on a distant shore. Distant, but not strange.

It was night. They only made such landings at night. There was cloud across the moon. But he knew the place. The smell was the same, the heat the same, already drying his trousers, the swish of the low surf, the hum and crackle of night's insects. Peter had been away for nearly two years and nothing had changed. Only he had changed.

Then the lantern showed and he crossed the spit of sand toward it, toward where his guide was. Water still sloshed in his sneakers. He hurried across the open place into the darker night of the bush. The man with the hooded lantern stepped forward, smiling. I know you, Cobb thought, your face. Not the name, but what they called him, "*alcalde* . . . the mayor,*" an argumentative sort given to spouting Marxist theories.

Aloud, in Spanish, Peter said, "*Alcalde,* I'm back. After so long. And to stay this time."

There was no remorse in his words, no irony, only happiness and the serenity of having done right.

"Good, *Padre Pedro,*" and he reached out a hand.

"We go?" said Peter.

"Yes, *Padre.*" But the *alcalde* hesitated.

Peter waited.

"There are government patrols, *Padre.*"

Peter gave a short laugh.

"*Alcalde,* there are *always* government patrols."

The man nodded solemnly. And then he knelt.

"Perhaps first, a blessing on our travels?"

"Yes," said Peter Cobb, "first a blessing."

When he had been blessed the *alcalde* reached out to take one of the rucksacks and the two men, moving lightly and with speed, were soon lost in the forest under the clouded moon.